IMMATERIAL DEFENSE

ONCE AND FOREVER BOOK 4

LAUREN STEWART

ALSO BY LAUREN STEWART

The Hyde series

Hyde, an urban fantasy

Jekyll

Strange Case

The Heights

Unseen

Unearthed

Into the Light

Once and Forever

Darker Water

Virtually Impossible

Deeper Water

Immaterial Defense

No Experience Required

Second Bite

Go to Lauren's website to find out how to sign up for her mailing list and get exclusive extras from the *Once and Forever* series.

www.LaurenStewartAuthor.com

For anyone who's ever been afraid to speak, or felt unheard, or not been believed.

In other words: All of us.

Once Upon a Time...

there was a woman whose life had been blessed from the moment of her birth. She wore beautiful gowns and went to fancy balls and danced with handsome princes.

And hated every second of it.

For though none but the woman knew it, these things of beauty were not real but imagined. And the reason she understood this was because she wasn't real either, having been unmade in a single moment in time...by an enemy she had once trusted...in a way that left her body wounded and her soul scarred.

And so, while the fancy balls and dances went on, the woman did not. For she had finally learned the truth of the world—no one was safe and no one cared, and all the happy times before had been naught but fantastical lies.

Sadly, she feared that no one would ever believe her, and she felt alone beyond imagining. Even sadder than that was the day she gave up trying to make people hear her, when she gave up on people altogether. And even sadder still was the day she gave up on herself.

Thus, the woman began a new life apart from all others. Though outwardly, people still believed her to be beautiful and blessed, inwardly, she knew it wasn't true. Even while surrounded by admirers, she was alone, for she knew they were admiring someone who wasn't real, whose truth could not be seen by their eyes. And though her appearance and wealth continued to bring compliments and accolades, she saw what none other could—that for the rest of her nonexistence she would be invisible to all.

1

SARA

*O*h crap. This was bad. Not like bad-sex bad. In fact, what we had just done was *nothing* like bad sex. Which made it bad in the *too*-good-sex way. And everyone knew that too-good sex with a guy you barely knew was bad. Because if the sex was that good the first time, you'd want to see what it would be like the second time and the third...and the twenty-third. And then, even if he turned out to be the world's most horrible person, you were already attached. So you couldn't just forget about him.

Because, well, yeah, he was an asshole, but he had so much *potential,* and you believed him when he told you that he couldn't call because he'd lost his phone and that you should ignore the tan line in the shape of a wedding ring on his finger. Because, sure, obviously, meeting you had made him realize that he was finally ready to move on from his wife's sudden and tragic death that you'll find out later never happened.

Riiiight.

Just because the guy knew how to give you multiple orgasms.

Yep, at some unfortunate point in our biological development, women decided that if a man cared enough to figure out what they needed to get off, he cared about the person attached to the vagina.

All of last night and this morning until a few minutes ago, I'd been really close to forgetting that. It was easy to tell myself that each orgasm was unique and having more than one was fine as long as different...*tools* were used each time.

Honestly, it had never really been an issue before. Let's be real, all men were not equal when it came to being good with his hands, or his mouth, or his cock. It was completely normal for men to have different areas of expertise.

So, the biggest problem with the man passed out next to me, with his long eyelashes and a body too perfectly formed for even a long-dead, gay Italian to have sculpted, was that *this* man was really good with *all* of his tools.

And he had a remarkably large tool belt.

Thankfully, the second I'd felt another orgasm gearing up while he was using the same tool that had given me my *last* orgasm, I shoved his face away, closed my legs, and I ran into the bathroom, yelling "intermission" before slamming the door shut. After a couple of minutes of forcing myself to think of baseball and oatmeal raisin cookies, I came out, we switched positions, and I made sure his mouth didn't go lower than my belly button again.

Damn, he had a fantastic mouth. And lips. And...

I needed to leave.

In a second.

It would've been so much easier if he wasn't so warm, and his chest wasn't so comfortable.

The jerk.

Crap. I hadn't been tempted to sleep over at a guy's house in over a year, never even closed my eyes or cuddled after all the tools had been put away. But as this guy pulled me into his side and sleepily brushed his lips across my forehead, using his chest as a pillow and letting the beat of his heart lull me to sleep seemed so natural. So desirable. So perfect.

I should've known this time would be different. I'd spent an incredible night with a beautiful man whose name I didn't know. If anyone ever found out, I'd be *almost* as embarrassed as I was all night being too chicken-shit to ask him if it was Dylan or Declan. What can I say? The bar where we'd met had been so loud all I heard was that it started with a *D,* ended with a *N,* and had two syllables.

We'd started talking, and before I knew what was happening we were on our way to his place. Then we were kissing, hands were rubbing, and hips were moving. Once the hips started moving, I was pretty sure the acceptable time to ask someone to repeat their name had come and gone.

All the more reason I needed to leave. Yep, if I stayed any longer, I'd be in serious trouble. Plus, regardless of what his name was, he was dangerous in an emotional way.

Emotional danger was the worst. Because physical injuries heal a lot quicker than emotional ones do.

So as soon as I caught my breath, I slid out of his bed and went foraging for my clothes.

"What are you doing?" he asked, sitting up.

"I'm going home. It's past my bedtime."

Damn, he was gorgeous. His spiky, light brown hair looked even better than it had before the last few hours of full-body wrestling we'd done. A small dimple dented each of his cheeks, even when he wasn't smiling. I could feel a purr of longing start in my stomach. Okay, fine, it might have started a little lower than that.

I slipped on my undies and then my pants. I wanted to go over and kiss him one more time, but that would risk him pulling me back in for another round.

"Huh. So, what'd you use me for?"

"I—" I didn't look up. And I didn't answer his question.

Then he was in front of me, his hands on my waist. "Is this the first time you've done it?"

I laughed. "Wow. Was I that bad?"

"The sex? No, the sex was fantastic. Phenomenal. Every time. I meant, is this the first time you've buttoned up your pants?"

"I don't get it."

"Look at me."

Ugh. If someone could reproduce the low grumble of his voice and put it on a ten-minute loop, women wouldn't need vibrators anymore.

"Sara, look at me," he repeated when I hesitated, then smiled when I raised my chin and made eye contact. I'd forgotten how tall he was. And oddly, how far from tall *I* was.

"Well, there has to be a reason you would be so focused on your jeans that you couldn't even bother to look at me. So, buttoning your pants... It's pretty easy once you get the hang of it. I'll show you." He brushed my hands out of the way and buttoned my jeans, holding my eyes and feeling his way through the process. I tried not to visibly shiver every time he brushed my bare skin.

"Don't worry. You'll get it eventually. And then you won't even have to look." He pulled me toward him. "Now, kiss me."

I shook my head and ran my lip through my teeth. "I probably have terrible morning breath."

"This is a continuation of last night. You have to sleep to have morning breath. So, kiss me already."

I did, lightly, until his lips demanded more. My arms stayed by my sides, stuck there immobile—the only thing with any control whatsoever it seemed because the rest of my body responded to his every touch. His tongue slipped inside my mouth, and his arms wrapped tightly around me, lifting me up onto my tiptoes.

He pulled away slightly and lowered me to the ground. "You're right. You have terrible morning breath." His smile was wicked. "That was such a horrible experience I'd like to do it again. Right now and then intermittently throughout the rest of the day."

Oh no, that couldn't happen. "Actually, I need to go."

He released me, sighing. "If I asked you for your number so we could see each other again, would you give me a fake one?"

I shook my head. "I'd just say no."

"Fuck, that's harsh," he said, running his hand through his hair. "A guy could take that personally, you know."

"You shouldn't. You were great, and you seem like..." a smart, sweet, and generous guy who I connected with almost immediately. Not to mention a few other adjectives that proved how easy it would be to get attached if we spent any more time together.

"Is there an end to that sentence?" he asked, already cringing as if I actually could say anything bad about him. "I seem like a...?"

"Like a really great guy." Wow, that was one of the most inadequate descriptions I'd ever used. "It's nothing personal, I swear. I don't give my number to anyone."

"Huh. So, either you're already involved with someone, or you have serious issues. Which is it?"

"I'm not already involved with someone."

He grimaced and then went to his dresser. "Well, if you ever want to be, give me a call." He took a business card out of his wallet, wrote something down on it, and handed it to me. "It's not my card, but my number's on the back. Call me."

"Me and my issues?"

"We all have issues, Sara. And we all have ways to cope."

I wondered what his were. All I knew was that they were *nothing* like mine. Guaranteed. "How do you cope?"

"Self-destructively. I'm really good at it. Last night, for example, I went to a bar looking for an amazing woman who would want nothing to do with me in the morning. All so I could spend the next few days pounding my head against the wall, wondering what happened, and where I went wrong. Totally successful endeavor, by the way. In fact, it's probably better you don't give me your number because I'm going to be busy telling myself what a fuck-up I am until...at least Thursday or Friday."

I curled my fingers around his card instead of giving it back like I'd planned. "I don't do the relationship thing."

"Obviously." He held up his hands and motioned to himself. "'Cause if you did, how could you possibly pass this mess up?"

"Maybe we could just..." I shrugged. Damn it. He was ten times as gorgeous as anyone I'd ever been with, had an incredible body he knew exactly how to use, and a sense of humor I could definitely get used to. Shit, for the first time in forever, I'd actually enjoyed our conversations between bouts of sex more than the bouts of sex themselves. At a couple of points, I'd caught myself thinking about getting to know him better, maybe even letting him know more about me. All of which added up to more complications than I could carry.

Another hookup would be dangerous, regardless of how much I wanted to.

"Okay, I think I got your hint," he said, nodding. "Well, Sara. It was nice to meet you, it was great to fuck you, and I wish you, your issues, and your coping mechanisms long and happy lives."

"Same to you. I'm gonna...I mean, I could..." Situations like these were exactly why I liked rules. Rules limited my options. Sometimes they even got rid of them altogether. I don't give out my number. I don't share too much about myself. I don't—

"Look," he said. "If you want to leave, leave. If you want to stay, then great! Because I'd love you to stay. Shit, if you need a coin to toss, I'll give you one. But I'm feeling slightly insecure right now, so I would appreciate it if you could make a decision without any more of the mixed signals."

He was right—my actions *defined* mixed signals. It seemed like that was all my mind could manage right now. What needed to happen was a decision. The same one I always made. In the past year, at least.

"Bye."

I ran. But I didn't close the doors behind me. If that was my subconscious' way of hinting that I didn't want those doors to close, it could go to hell. I knew what I wanted, and it wasn't him.

Not really...I didn't think.

No. It wasn't him. It wasn't any of them. The only person I could count on was myself. I was the only one who could keep me safe. I was the only person I could trust.

When I got to the sidewalk, I took out the card he'd given me and smoothed it on my leg. Some guy who was a music executive of some kind. But on the other side, there was a name and a number—Declan. Declan. It was a nice name. Nice guy. A nice guy with a nice name who I would never see again.

Besides, Declan was wrong—one-nighters weren't coping mechanisms. They were distractions, something to relieve the pressure and blow off steam. Two people getting what they wanted without the inevitable hurt that trusting someone led to.

Did my friends think I had trust issues? Hell, yes. Trust, intimacy, you name it. But I saw myself as a realist. No one should trust anyone. That was a fact.

No one saw pain coming, or it wouldn't hurt so much when it happened. You wouldn't feel humiliated and spend weeks in shock, living in a blurred reality. That wouldn't happen if you were prepared, stayed vigilant, didn't look for things that weren't real. The only thing you could trust was that people were liars and did whatever the hell they wanted to do without concern for anyone else.

I hadn't been prepared once, and it had almost killed me. A mistake I'd never repeat. Ever.

2

DECLAN

"*W*ell, that could've gone better," I mumbled as I flopped back onto the bed. What the hell had just happened?

My mind ran through it all again as if it were a movie. A movie I'd been waiting to see for years and knew I wanted to see again before it was even over. But then, in the last few minutes, the whole fucking thing had turned to complete shit, and all I could do was lie here—*alone*—and wonder how everything had gone from perfect to nothing in the blink of eye.

I knew how messed up I was, but it usually took until at least lunchtime for a woman to figure it out. I'd never had a one-night stand that only lasted one night. Leave it to me to want someone who couldn't even wait for one night to be over before she ran for it.

Yeah, that hurt.

I needed unconditional love. Stat.

"Kitty."

Unfortunately, the guy I was subletting the place from didn't even allow pocket dogs, let alone eighty-pound fuzzy monsters like mine. But thankfully, the couple who lived next door owned their own place, and *he* was constantly going out of town for work. So, since Rebecca was a dog lover who wasn't comfortable being alone at night, I ended up with a perfect babysitter.

I kept Kitty at my place during the day, but not having to fight her for the covers all night was nice, too. And it had definitely come in handy *last* night because, as much as I loved my dog, seeing her spread out on my bed didn't even compare to seeing Sara spread out there.

I threw on some pants and a hoodie and went to the apartment next to mine.

As soon as Rebecca opened the door, Kitty pushed past her, jumped up, and gave me a sloppy, open-mouthed kiss as if she hadn't seen me in months.

"Thanks for watching her," I said, using my sleeve to wipe drool off my face.

Rebecca smiled sleepily. "You don't have to thank me all the time. I'm getting more out of it than you are."

"Actually, I think Kitty's getting the best deal. Aren't you, you big golden pile of fluff?" I shoved her paws off my chest. "You should get one of your own, Rebecca, so you don't get lonely after we move to LA." That was the plan, anyway. One I couldn't see a way out of. Go on tour for another couple of months and then end up back in Los Angeles, hopefully to sign a recording contract with one of the big labels.

Unfortunately, I'd grown up in Southern California and had no desire to live there again. I think Kitty hated it, too. She didn't want to hang out with all those prissy little purse dogs in their fancy sweaters. She needed a place where she could have lots of friends—dogs that she didn't have to lie down to be low enough to smell the asses of.

Plus, while the band was doing well, it wasn't as if Self Defense was a household name or anything. And any money we made had to be split four ways, so the chance of me being able to rent an apartment in Los Angeles with a Kitty-sized yard was slim. We'd only been living in San Francisco for a couple of weeks, and she was already running out of interesting corners to sniff.

"I wish," Rebecca said. "I think I'd get a poodle mix like Kitty. I love that she doesn't shed all over, and whenever Blake is home, he doesn't complain about his allergies." She went into her living room to grab Kitty's newest favorite toy off the ground. "Sadly, he's a...cat person"—she whispered, smiling—"so I can't get a dog until after we break up."

I grimaced. "Things are that bad?"

"Things are great...when he's here." She tossed the squeaky toy down the hall for Kitty to attack. "I just feel like he's holding something back, you know?"

I'd been living here for a couple of weeks and had met Blake once, so I only knew what Rebecca had told me about him. But Rebecca was really great and Blake seemed like an ass, so I nodded.

"Dang, I think she's gotta go." I whistled for Kitty as I walked back to my apartment. "Thanks again, Rebecca. See you later."

I should've taken her out for a walk, but I was still barefoot, so I let her out on my balcony. A four-foot square of fake grass was nowhere for a self-respecting dog to do their business, but Kitty forgave me. That's unconditional love for you.

I went into my bedroom to give her some privacy and sighed when I saw the mess of sheets on my bed. It had been a *really* great night. I hadn't had that good of a night in a long, long time. Or ever.

Fuck, I wished I'd gotten her number.

I lay back down and took a deep breath, hoping to capture Sara's scent again. Kind of flowery but not too much. Very womanly, the kind of smell that made a cock go from zero to sixty in three seconds. I breathed it in until Kitty jumped onto the bed and blew dog breath right in my face.

"Now *that* is morning breath."

She shoved her nose into my cheek and then nudged me until I got up again.

"Alright, alright. What will it be today, girl? Kibble or kibble?" I followed her wagging tail into the kitchenette of my temporary home. "Think Sara would have stayed if I'd fed her, too?"

Typically, Sunday was the band's day of rest and recovery. So, I had no plans with the guys or to spend any time at the basketball court with my best friend pretending the NBA was still a possibility.

Great, I had all day long to obsess about last night and wonder where I'd gone wrong. It had been a long time since I'd brought a woman home. Who knew what had changed in that time. How many orgasms did they expect nowadays?

As soon as Kitty dug into her breakfast, I went back into the bedroom, stripped down, and grabbed a towel. With so many memories of last night still fresh on my mind, I did a lot of disappointed sighing. The longest and most regretful sounding one slipped out as soon as I stepped into the shower.

Four hours ago, I'd been in this exact spot, standing behind her and watching the water rain down over her shoulder onto her breasts...

3

DECLAN

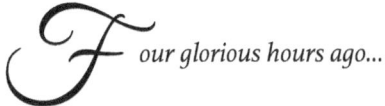 *our glorious hours ago...*

Shit. I really liked this girl. More than should be possible at this point. It was hard to believe I'd only met her a couple of hours ago. But as soon as I'd seen her onstage with her friend, doing a truly regrettable karaoke rendition of Aretha Franklin's "Respect", I was smitten. It probably had to do with the way she seemed both confident and embarrassed at the same time. Or her commitment to every wrong note she'd sung. Or maybe it was the way her expression completely shifted when she saw me leaning against the bar and our eyes locked until she seemed to realize she was singing the "Sock it to me" part of the song directly to me and burst out laughing. Whatever the initial reason, things had only gotten better since then.

"Are you sure it's okay?" I asked.

"Mmm..." Sara moaned happily. "There's no such thing as too hot."

Normally, I would've agreed — when it came to both women *and* water. But we'd taken a break from the bedroom to come take a shower that would cool us off. Unfortunately, I already knew there was little I could refuse her. If she didn't want us to cool off, I'd happily keep things hot.

I leaned down to kiss her neck, my hands reaching around to cup her breasts.

Absolutely perfect breasts, by the way. The woman had breasts I wanted to be holding when I took my last breath. Full but not too big, in perfect proportion to the curve of her waist and her round little ass. Nipples that had stiffened with the first light brush of my finger and had stayed that way ever since, as if not a second went by when she wasn't as turned on as I was.

I was far from a virgin. In my twenty-four years of life—nine of those having been after losing my virginity—I'd had my fair share of one-night stands. But besides already hoping this would turn into more than that, I'd never experienced anything like this before. Feeling like I understood someone so quickly. It was as if we'd jumped ahead to when two people really knew each other's bodies without having lost any of the excitement of being with someone new. Knowing someone would take care of you and give you what you needed, but not being able to predict when or how they'd do it.

The feeling went beyond the physical. When I'd walked into that bar, I hadn't been looking for someone to bring home. But as soon as I saw her, I knew I was supposed to be there, looking in her direction at exactly that moment. And she was supposed to be looking in mine.

So far, she seemed as close to perfect as people ever got. Sexually, she was everything I could ask for, plus a little extra that I never would've dared request. We hadn't had hours and hours of conversations, but it didn't take long to figure out she was smart, honest, funny, and open-minded.

Yep. Tonight was filled with firsts. For instance, I'd never had to think about physics when I was with a woman before. But since Sara was so much shorter than I was, physics demanded that I pick her up to get inside her. It would've been easier if we were facing each other, but then I wouldn't get to see her ass move every time I thrust. I put one hand on her waist and slid the other down to her thigh, preparing to lift her up.

"Whoa!" She laughed, stretching her toes out to reach the tile.

Of course, that's when I realized the impossibility of doing what I so desperately wanted to do. The temptation alone had me holding the majority of her body weight—not that there was much of it.

I blew out a breath, knowing I should put her down. Because, unfortunately, I wasn't smart enough to keep a condom within reach of the shower. Granted, it had never been necessary before, but a guy should be prepared for all of his sexual fantasies to come true at any moment. Lesson learned. I'd never make that mistake again, even if I had to wallpaper the whole place with them.

Fuck. My cock slipped between her cheeks and slid lower as if it were a heat-seeking missile. Nope. Not going to happen. Because life was unfair.

"Hello?" Her voice had a tinge of frustration in it, which was pretty much the last thing I wanted her to feel tonight. "You still back there?"

"Huh? Oh yeah. Sorry." I was also sorry I had to set her down. I'd been so busy enjoying her curves and her softness pressing up against my very hard cock, I hadn't heard what she said the first time. "Although, in all honesty, I think you should be apologizing to *me*."

"Oh, do you now?" She turned her head to the side so I could see one half of her smile. "And what should I be apologizing for exactly?"

"For having such a remarkably distracting ass." I used both of my hands to squeeze it. You know, just in case she forgot where it was. "Yep, this ass is almost as interesting as the rest of you."

"Isn't *interesting* usually a bad thing? Like when you have nothing nicer to say?"

"Not for me. In fact, I just came up with a whole list of nice things to say about you. A long list. If you need an ego boost, I can write it down for you."

"I'm good, thanks. Are you a list person?"

"Not normally, but I made an exception for you," I said, right before I decided my lips would be better used on her neck rather than forming words. Actually, a list of all the different ways I wanted to take her was a great idea. Then I wouldn't forget any of them and have to cry myself to sleep every night until we got together again.

"So, what's this, then?"

I blinked to regain control of my eyes and keep them open long enough to figure out what she was talking about.

Damn it. She was pointing up to a small, waterproof slate stuck to the wall with a pencil clipped to it.

"Um... That thing? It's..." I reached past her and slammed my hand over the lyrics for a new song I'd written there earlier. "Well...it's nothing really."

To anyone other than me, my random, brain-dumped ideas for new songs would read like the emo scribblings of an angsty teen carving his latest poem into his desk in home-room. So I really, really didn't want Sara to read it. Hopefully, I could rub away the pencil marks with my thumb without her noticing.

"Nothing, huh? Weird. They looked more like words to me,

but for all I know, they're hieroglyphics. I guess being abnormally tall is useful sometimes, huh?"

"You think six two is abnormally tall?" I grabbed her waist and started tickling her with all ten fingers until she begged me to stop.

"I surrender," she said, still giggling. "You win." She paused.

"Now you have to take it back."

"I just did. It's not my fault if you're too abnormally tall to hear me." She cringed before I'd even touched her. So, I decided to try another tactic, raking my fingers up the nape of her neck and pushing her wet hair out of my way.

"I do some of my best thinking in the shower." From then on, every word I said was whispered into the shell of her ear or the warmth of her neck. "Not right now, obviously, but when I'm alone. I use the slate to jot down notes or ideas before I forget them."

"You have terrible handwriting," she said breathlessly. "What does it say?"

Even as she tilted her head to give me more room, I knew she was only pretending to hand herself over to me. Instead of leaning into my body, she held herself upright, as if she were afraid to give up too much control. So I curled my hand into a fist and used her hair to slowly dip her backwards far enough to take her lips with mine. Eventually, I let go of her so we both could replenish our oxygen levels.

"By not telling me, you're making my need to know go ballistic. So, thanks for that."

"Fine, I'll tell you." Moving my eyes back and forth as if I were actually reading the text, I leaned forward, pushing her up against the wall. "It says, 'Someday, I want to meet an intelligent, beautiful, sexy-as-fuck woman who enjoys karaoke.'" I grabbed the pencil from its clip and wrote DONE in all caps right across it.

"For the sake of my pride, I'm going to assume that refers to me."

"Your pride is correct." I hadn't brought a woman home in a long time, and I'd never had one in this apartment.

"In that case, *enjoy* might be too strong a word for how I feel about karaoke. I've just always been a sucker for that song."

"How does that last part go again?" I hummed the "sock it to me" section until she elbowed me.

"Shut up! Believe me, it's a lot harder than it looks. I didn't see you up there in front of that...medium-sized crowd singing, did I?"

Little did she know. "You're right. You couldn't pay me to have gone up there." But not for the reason she thought.

"Good. Then no making fun of me or my taste in music." She took the pencil away from me and stood on her tiptoes to write something. She could barely reach the bottom of the slate. "Take pity on me, tall man?"

I lifted her up by the waist and held her so she was high enough to see. She stood on the thin edge of the bathtub and leaned back against my chest to stay up. If my erection weren't getting in the way, I wouldn't have needed any help holding her. But while my cock was definitely rock-hard, I couldn't exactly set her down on it without getting into trouble.

"Oh shit!" she said melodramatically. "This thing is magical!"

"Really?" I wasn't about to admit that, for a second there, I'd thought she was talking about my cock. Luckily, I realized she had actually been talking about the slate before I said anything truly stupid.

I waited until she slid down and was standing solely on her own before reading aloud. Her handwriting was a lot better than mine. "Someday, a gorgeous, sexy-as-fuck man will take me back to his bed and torture me with his tongue."

"See? It's magical." She dropped the pencil and turned

around to face me. "Whatever's written on it will come true, right?"

"I hope not. That one's mine, and I'm not into men." I reached behind her to turn off the water, swept her up into my arms, and slid the shower door open with my elbow. "You need to get your own."

As we passed the door, she grabbed a towel off the hook, threw it over both of our heads, and tried to get some of the water out of our hair. Luckily, the room was clean enough that I didn't trip and drop her until we reached the bed. Once I'd set her down, I watched her giggle as I dried myself off a little more.

"Oh my God," she said, smoothing her hair back and cupping the end in her hands. "I'm soaking wet!"

"Damn, woman. I don't think I've ever heard anything hotter than that."

She tilted her head and smiled. "I was talking about the water in my hair."

"No, you weren't." I shrugged. "Well, maybe you were, but I'm choosing to believe you meant it in exactly the way I took it, so you might as well just go along with it."

"Shut up and give me that towel." Laughing, she caught the end that I flicked at her and tugged, pulling me up onto the bed at the same time.

"Damn, you're strong...and greedy." I pulled the towel away from her. I started with her toes, then her feet and ankles, rubbing piece by piece before using my lips to make sure each bit of her was dry.

She propped herself up on her elbows and watched me with wide eyes, occasionally giggling and jerking when I hit a ticklish spot.

By the time I'd worked my way up to her knees, I'd stopped bothering with the towel. "Tortured by my tongue, huh?"

She swallowed and nodded almost nervously. When I

lowered my head between her thighs and brushed my lips over her center, she moaned and flopped back onto the pillows. Oh yeah. She was definitely soaking wet. My lower lip dragged behind, my mouth opening as I started to explore her with my tongue.

R-E-S-P-E-C-T

Nothing like having a great song in your head while you're doing one of your favorite things.

I ran my tongue up her slit a few times, silently laughing to myself every time she let out a disappointed sigh as I moved back to where I'd started. When I decided she'd had enough teasing, I used my tongue and a couple fingers to focus on what I could do so that she'd never be disappointed again. With my other hand, I held her down, making sure none of her squirming let her get away from me.

Any guy who didn't offer to get a woman off this way was a moron. Oral sex was the best way to really learn what a woman needed to get off.

And with the *right* woman, it was the only time a man could ever truly control her.

She'd been pulling my hair and speaking incoherently for a while before I got her hint and looked up at her.

"You're so good at that," she said breathlessly. "But you need to come up here now."

"Why? Am I boring you?"

She laughed. "Hardly. It feels incredible. But I'm a few orgasms ahead of you, so I think it's my turn."

"Nope." I kissed her again before shaking my head. "I'm not done down here yet. You're not done down here yet either."

"But—"

"I'm going to get back to what I was doing now. If you need me for anything, or if you want me to stop for a better reason than feeling guilty about letting me make you feel good, let me know."

Sara said a lot of things about God, cursed like a sailor, and did a hell of a lot of moaning, but she definitely didn't try to stop me again.

4

SARA

Stop dreaming about the guy you'll never see again, and get your ass out of bed. If I screwed up this job and couldn't find another, I'd have to live in my stepfather's house forever. I'd already been here eight months longer than I'd wanted to. I could still feel the sticky humiliation of having to let go of my apartment and crawl back to my mom and Timothy to keep a roof over my head. Still, better *they* witness my humiliation than my two best and oldest friends.

Emilia and Andi both had guest rooms they'd have let me use for as long as I needed, but there had to be a limit as to how much of my patheticness they'd put up with. And, even though they'd never said anything, I was fairly sure I'd used up all my allowance already. Not to mention they had actual lives with the men they loved. Basically, they were happy, and that fact alone made them extraordinarily unpleasant to be around sometimes.

Plus, I already owed them so much. Emilia had been right to demote me from virtual assistant to chick who answers the phone and emails contracts to new clients. Occasionally, she still tossed the overflow work to me, but times were tough and we'd lost a lot of our small business clients. Fewer clients meant less overflow to give me and fewer opportunities I had to make up for what I'd done.

All hell had broken loose after my ex-client's wife—who he'd forgotten to mention—called Emilia to scream about the *harlot* who'd seduced her husband. And, yes, she'd used the word *harlot*, and yes, she either didn't know or pretended not to know that *this* harlot was probably one of a hundred that her poor, too-weak-to-keep-his-dick-in-his-pants husband had seduced.

I didn't know if the asshole—who should've been a much better lay considering all the time he spent lying, in all meanings of the word—was ever punished, but it didn't matter. I'd broken Emilia's number-one rule: Don't get laid where you get paid.

And more importantly, my mistake could've cost the company a lot of business. Luckily, I'd been able to explain to the asshole how to tell his wife that the "corruption" of her practically-virginal, thirty-seven-year-old husband wasn't the kind people got arrested for. At least he'd felt bad enough to agree that he and his wife were better off working on their marriage instead of wasting time on a frivolous lawsuit against the harlot —aka me—or Emilia's company. Only a lawyer who was crazy would've taken the case anyway, especially once they found out Emilia's husband, Rob, had just made partner at his firm. But sadly, crazier things happened every day.

Accepting the new job title and a seriously hefty pay cut was the least I could do. Unfortunately, the lower salary left me unable to pay for my overpriced apartment in San Francisco's South of Market district, so I'd had to move back into my mom and stepdad's place. Not that Emilia knew that, of course. Knowing the real reason I'd moved back in with my parents would just make her feel bad, and *she* wasn't the one who'd screwed up. Silly me, I'd thought I was smart enough not to let my terrible judgment and overactive hormones affect my work life and an incredible friend's business.

It had been tough to keep her and Andi from figuring out why I'd moved back into a place I so desperately hated, but I'd done it. Unfortunately, putting up the front of not having a care in the world was taking a toll on our friendship, and I wasn't sure how much longer I'd be able to keep up the lie.

What kept me going was knowing how lucky I was. If I'd been working for anyone other than Emilia, I wouldn't have a paycheck at *all* right now. I'd probably be spending all day calling my stepdad at work and asking if he could lend me money for all the aspirin it took to deal with my mother.

Aside from having passed down some evil DNA to his son, Cal, my stepdad was a flawed-but-mostly-decent man. Although, even *imagining* him introducing himself to prospective business partners as "Timothy" made me cringe a little. Not as much as I'd be cringing if I had to beg him for a job, but close.

Timothy played by so many of the traditional rules I sometimes wondered if he was actually a very well-preserved eighty-year-old. If my mom and their occasional screaming matches were accurate, he was even sleeping with his secretary. But every other day, he'd come home, have a martini with my mom, and then change out of his suit into a much more comfortable pair of slacks, button-down shirt, and casual blazer.

Since he'd started out with nothing and had earned everything he had now, he didn't believe in handouts. So, if I asked him for a job, I knew he'd give me the shittiest job for the shittiest pay in the shittiest closet of his real estate development company. Then I'd have to take the bus back to his house every day at six thirty-two because, obviously, I would never learn my lesson if he gave me a ride in his town car.

I didn't expect any special treatment and could handle a crappy job. But no matter how small my cubicle was, the idea of working in the same office as Cal was a non-starter. Living in the house he still had a key to was bad enough.

Unfortunately, Timothy's guilt for not having a relationship with his kid for the first sixteen years of his life meant Cal could get away with pretty much anything he wanted to, including pretending to work at Timothy's company all day. No way did he know what his son did after clocking out, though. Being married to an alcoholic was one thing. Being the father of a drug dealer was another. Selling cocaine, ecstasy, and who knew what else in the alleys behind local nightclubs was way too blue collar of a crime for Timothy to ever believe his heir would do.

That disbelief went double for what, if anything, my mom had told him about what Cal had done to me. Anyway, I couldn't expect Timothy to believe something my own mother thought I'd made up.

Honestly, without the possibility of running into my stepbrother in the office lobby every morning, if it got me out of this house, I'd happily bring fresh coffee to Timothy's office every morning and put a flowery *Thank You* note on his desk before leaving every night at six thirty-two.

That wasn't a commitment I could make on an empty stomach, though, so I needed to move my ass, grab something to eat on the go, and get to my current no-stepbrother-in-sight job. Stat.

The one and only perk of living in a house as big as this one was the ease of avoiding anyone you didn't want to see. Timothy would already be at work by now, and my mom was probably in the library finishing off her second Bloody Mary before starting to get ready to meet her friends for her third and fourth. Every day was the same—she pretended to use the library for reading, and everyone else pretended not to hear the clink of her glass every time we passed by the door. Co-dependency could be tough, but I'd earned my PhD in it.

I threw on some clothes and carefully crept down the stairs and to the front door. Timothy had once bragged the latch was imported from an eighteenth-century building in France. He hadn't even cracked a smile when I'd asked if he'd bought it at the prison swap meet when they'd updated all the doors to the cells his ancestors had called home.

"Saaaarrrraaaa!"

Ugh. I liked my name, except at whatever decibel my mother screeched it. It actually took effort to ignore her, but it was energy well spent.

We'd never been as close as I wished we were, but our relationship had taken a nosedive into the abyss last year. It was funny how people react to tragedy. Some went into emotional hiding. Others got stronger. And then there were always a few who just didn't care. Or, at least, chose not to believe there ever *was* a tragedy, even after you broke down and told them about it.

My mom fell into the latter group and still seemed confused as to why we didn't talk like we used to.

"Saaaarrrraaaa! I know it's you. Come here."

"Can't! Gotta go to work!" So I can keep my job and not end up buzzed and miserable every day, wondering how my life had ended up like this. If she'd ever asked, I could've told her why. But, of course, she'd never ask, and I doubt she'd believe me if she ever did.

The only thing my mom cared about was what other people thought of her. She'd forgotten all about the person underneath the makeup, polite smile, and *couture* clothing. So, when that stuff came off and no one was around to tell her who she was, everything left felt incomplete or lacking, like something she needed to hide. Or cover up with a few Bloody Mary's.

"See you later!"

Hopefully, she'd have forgotten whatever she wanted to talk to me about by then. I jogged down the imported, prison-gray-colored stone stairs and down the driveway until I reached the sidewalk.

I checked the app on my phone to make sure the Honda stopped in the no-parking zone in front of the house was actually the car I'd ordered. No reason to make life too easy for serial killers, right?

"Hi. What's your name?" I asked the driver through the open passenger window.

"John. You coming?" Without waiting for an answer, he pressed the button to raise the window.

"Nice to meet you, too, John." And you're lucky I didn't leave online reviews or had enough money to potentially leave you a tip.

At least he didn't look like a serial killer, but then again, from the outside, no one could tell what an emotional mess I was. As if I needed more proof that first impressions were absolutely worthless.

Although...

As I slid into the back of John's car I thought of Declan. My first impression of him had been amazing. And, not that I wanted it to happen, but if I *did* see him again, I bet his second impression would be great, too. In fact, I couldn't imagine him having a flaw bad enough to change that. The only negative I'd seen in him was how hard he'd made it to leave his place Sunday morning. And if I thought about it too much, I might start seeing that less as a negative and more of something to respect him for.

Crap. That made me wonder if there was a way to *accidentally* find out what kind of second impression he gave.

On the bright side, no one was that good all the time, especially not any man *I'd* ever known, so it would only be a matter of time before I got to know and be disappointed by the *real* him.

I shook off all thoughts of Declan and focused on the traffic as John drove toward downtown.

Having a friend with a car, almost the same class schedule, and enough money to park it made my school life a lot easier. But getting to and from work was different. The car-share service wasn't super expensive, but two rides a day, five half-days of work a week, kept my credit card company very, very happy.

Obviously, since I needed to be alive when I got to the office, biking wasn't possible.

I could've figured out which, and at what times, buses ran between my parents' house and work. But doing that would be proof that I'd accepted my unfortunate living arrangements long enough to commit to learning bus numbers and routes. And commitment was to be avoided at all cost, including knowing how many times I'd have to switch modes of transport to go five miles in the city.

Basically, I was screwed either way—I spent more money because I didn't want to admit that I wouldn't be able to move out anytime soon, but that meant I couldn't save enough money to escape. Having a job was expensive. Having a massively screwed-up family was even more expensive.

At least cover charges at the clubs were always waived for the young and fuckable portion of the population, and drinks were always free for those with vaginas. It might not have seemed right to my feminist side, but since women were paid less and harassed more than men, it seemed only fair to use the few perks we had.

Plus, if a guy was stupid enough to believe that one drink was all he had to put out to get *me* to put out, that was *his* problem. Like my stepfather always said, "How someone chooses to spend his money is up to him." I doubt that's what Timothy was referring to, but he was right.

Although, it almost always cost the guy a minimum of one

drink for me, and five more for my closest female friends—at least in proximity—before I let anyone into my pants.

I flinched when I heard my ringtone—a man's voice saying, "This is not a text. I repeat, this is not a text. We interrupt your regularly scheduled day to tell you to pick up your damn phone!" and dug my phone out of my bag. But evidently, John shared my inability to accept that people actually still used phones to speak to each other because he cursed at the same moment I saw that no one was calling me.

He glanced into his rearview mirror at me, mumbled an apology, and held his phone up to his ear. "Can't talk now. I'm driving." Pause. "Because it's illegal to hold my phone in my hand while I drive in California." Another pause, but he used this one to curse under his breath. "Because that's what I *do*, Lin. People give me money to drive them around. Good thing they do, too, because obviously *someone* has to pay for your new shoes." Probably a woman. Possibly an angry one. "If I put you on speaker, the lady in the back seat could hear you, and I'd guess she—" He jerked the phone away from his ear when the yelling started and held the phone out to me. "Could you please tell my sister you don't want to hear us fight?"

"I...um..." I hesitantly leaned closer to the phone. "John's right—I'd prefer not to listen to anyone fighting." I only leaned back a few inches before stopping myself. "Sorry." Unfortunately, that's when I heard her start to cry.

"Like I told you before, Lin," John called out, "I gotta go."

"You can't!" Grabbing his arm so he couldn't pull it away, I covered the phone with my other hand. "She's crying, John. You can't just hang up on her when she's crying."

Thankfully, we were at a light, so no one was in danger when he shifted around to look at me. Or *stare* at me, actually. Eventually he spoke. "Last weekend, she went on a two-thousand-dollar shopping spree. With *my* credit card."

"Oh. That's not good." I let go of him and leaned back on the seat. "Didn't mean to intrude."

"Two grand," he repeated. "So, I think I'm allowed to hang up on her if I want to."

"I agree." Neither of us moved or looked away from the phone. "Why aren't you hanging up then?"

As soon as the light changed, he tapped the screen with his thumb and tossed the phone onto the seat next to him. My heart broke a little when he turned frontward again. Because that's when I looked in the rearview mirror and saw how watery his eyes were.

"Have you figured out what you're going to do about it?" I asked before I thought about it. "I'm sorry. I don't know what I'm talking about. Just ignore me."

"There's nothing I can do." Well, at least he got the *ignore me* part right. "Other than work myself into the ground to pay it off. *She's* never going to do it." If I hadn't known why he was upset, his dry, dark chuckle would've set off every "Stranger Danger" alarm in a five-block radius. "I'm barely keeping my head above water for me and my kids as it is. Lin *knew* that, and she still went and pulled this shit."

"It's none of my business...." I straightened up in the seat and looked at the street outside to figure out how far we were from my office. Yep, I had enough time. "But as someone who's witnessed many, *many* shopping sprees and a close-to-equal amount of the subsequent fights, I can tell you what I'd do." Which happened to be the exact opposite of how I'd seen it happen between Timothy and my mother.

"At this point, I'm open to anything that ends without me going to jail." He kept his eyes on the road, but no way could he hide the emotion in his voice. "And even then, I'd probably do it."

I felt my chest tighten. "Nothing illegal, John. You have kids. And other options."

"Yeah, like what?" he asked skeptically.

"First thing you do is call your credit card company and tell them to shut off your card so she can't order anything else. But don't tell them the card was stolen unless you're okay with your sister potentially being tracked down and arrested."

He paused long enough to let me know he'd need more time to contemplate it.

"Regardless..." I continued. "The card company will contact the retailers and stop any orders that haven't shipped out already. Then you should bring a list of everything else Lin bought over to her house and help her repack and return everything returnable. Because the last thing you want her to learn is that she can do something really awful, apologize, and then still get to keep the good shit."

"You can return that stuff?" Obviously, John didn't shop online. And since he'd probably never done too much retail therapy and regretted it afterwards, I had to explain how online returns worked.

"Oh, and when you get your new card? Don't give it to anyone with a shopping addiction, okay?"

"Got it." My new friend John pulled up to the curb in front of the building where Emilia had set up the company's main-and-only office.

"Good luck with everything," I said, sliding out of the car.

He rolled his window down. "Thanks, Sara. You really helped me out."

"Great. Then can we consider it your tip?" I grimaced. "I'm trying to save enough to move out of the house where you picked me up."

"Why? That place was gorgeous."

"From the outside, sure. But believe me, it's an emotional hellhole inside."

"Shouldn't judge a book, right?" He smiled. "Take care of yourself, Sara. And thanks again."

He grabbed his phone, speed-dialed someone, and gave me a quick wave. As he drove off, I heard a woman answer and John say, "Look, Lin, this is what's going to happen…"

Considering that Emilia's employees—other than me—didn't need to be babysat and could work remotely from home, plus very, very few clients actually came into the office, the two-room space on the sixth floor did the job. Very professional, very well decorated, and deceptively small.

I sighed with relief when I tested the office door. It was still locked. That meant I'd gotten here before Emilia and could get a little extra work done. She was probably out jogging with Andi, my other best friend who didn't know how to mind her own business.

That wasn't fair. Both Emilia and Andi were great women and better friends than I deserved, especially lately. It wasn't that I didn't appreciate that they cared about me—I really did—but they wanted an explanation for everything I did, while I was trying hard to make sure that what I did defied explanation.

I was going to disappoint them regardless, so it was just easier to do it this way. Plus, it wasn't as if I could tell them the truth. Even if they believed me, it would just create more questions and discussions about a word I could barely form inside my own head.

The only four-letter word I'd never been able to say, at least not since it happened to me.

5

SARA

"You wouldn't *believe* the morning I had," Emilia said as she walked through the front door, tossed her purse toward her office, and headed for the office's tiny break room that originally had been a closet.

"I still don't understand why you and Andi think jogging is healthy." I teased her about it almost every time we saw each other, but it never failed to make me laugh. "All jogging does is dehydrate you, make you stink, and put you in a rancid mood."

She finished adding artificial sweetener to her coffee before turning toward me and tilting her head in what looked like annoyance. "First of all, I didn't go running with Andi this morning, so my rancid mood is"—she switched to a bad French accent—"as you say, *au naturale.*"

"Well...your mood can't possibly be worse than that accent, so at least there's that."

I was just about to apologize for my rancid bitchiness and badly timed joke when a smile slowly developed on her face. "And my *stink* is a personalized blend of organic lavender, cypress, and grapefruit essential oils that the homeopath said would open up my fifth chakra."

"Which one is fifth? Is that the moodiness one? I don't think mine has been opened in years."

"The fifth one is the mouth. When it's not open"—she opened her mouth as widely as she could, so everything she said afterwards was nearly impossible to understand—"we have a hard time communicating. I also have it in tea form, too, and yours could use some serious balancing. Want some?"

Hint understood and rejected. "Not unless it tastes like strong coffee with fat-free creamer."

"I wish." She laughed.

We each fixed up our own beverages side by side, dramatically shoving each other to grab a stir stick or one of the mini muffins she'd brought in yesterday. They tasted like sugary chalk, had enough preservatives in them to outlast a cockroach, and were addictive enough for her to keep buying them and for both of us to keep eating them.

"How's school?" she asked.

I shrugged. "Okay. How's Andi?" Unfortunately, the girls and I hadn't hung out very often over the last year, and I hadn't seen Andi since her and Hayden's wedding in the Maldives. The pressure of them caring about me had just gotten to be too much. I could bitterly laugh at the stupidity of it all I wanted, but it didn't change the feeling. They needed me to talk about something I couldn't talk about, and they confused my lack of conversation with a lack of trust. So, it was just easier to keep my distance instead of rubbing their noses in their misunderstanding. Since then, our text conversations had been shallow, and when Emilia and I were both in the office, I deliberately kept our talk small.

"Good. But get this—the other day, Hayden brought up having a baby."

"Wow, that's big." And yet another sign my friends were moving forward with their lives. I doubted I'd ever be able to catch up, even if I *wanted* to get married or have kids. "How'd she react?"

"Just like you'd imagine she would," she said, smiling. "I wish I'd been there to see her face."

I laughed at the image that popped into my mind. "She'd be a great mom, though. And if they ever ran out of money, they could make serious bank by selling pictures of Hayden holding the baby. You should mention it to her."

"Why don't you? We're way overdue for a get-together."

"That would be fun." I'd been coming up with excuses not to see them for so long, I didn't even have to pause to think of one. "But between school and work, I'm swamped."

"Sure." She nodded slowly, seeing my excuse for exactly what it was. "Maybe once school is over."

"Yeah," I agreed too quickly. "How's Rob?"

"He's tired of house shopping, but good." Usually, any mention of her husband was enough to distract her. They adored each other so much she couldn't say his name without beaming. Since she wasn't smiling as much as normal, I could tell that she had something serious on her mind.

I wasn't the type to ask because I wasn't the type to answer, but Emilia and I had been friends way too long enough for any silence to be awkward. Besides, Emilia had never been shy—when she was ready to tell me, she would.

For the next two hours, I did my nails, answered a few calls, opened the mail, and did some filing. The kind of vital work this company couldn't legally hire a monkey to do. I'm not stupid or inept. I just have underdeveloped good-decision-making skills. Thus the reason Emilia had taken away all my clients and decided I was better off where she could see me. Or at least hear me from the next room.

I peeked into her office. She was squinting at her computer monitor and frowning. I wondered how long it had been since she'd moved.

"That look usually means it's break time," I said, leaning against the doorjamb.

"I can't." Her eyes never moved from the screen. "I'm trying to understand this new contract Rob drew up for me."

"Can't you just ask him to explain the legalese to you?"

She shook her head and blinked. "Do you know how much it sucks to be married to a lawyer?"

"I'd imagine it sucks as much as being married to anyone else." Seriously, there had to be a reason they called it the *institution* of marriage. If I ever ended up institutionalized, it wouldn't be in marriage.

She let out a long sigh. "I'm all for trading free legal work for blowjobs—"

"Didn't need to know that."

"—but no matter how hard Rob tries, when he explains it to me, he sounds so condescending. Honestly, it's his fault he married me instead of someone who could understand this shit. It's just better if I keep my mouth shut—after I finish the blowjob, of course—"

"Did you not hear me when I said I didn't need to know about that?"

"—and pretend I know what the hell it means. It's my way of keeping our marriage intact." She pinched the bridge of her nose and sat back.

"Very admirable," I mumbled. "Want me to take a look?"

"Would you?" Her face lit up as I walked around her desk to squint at her monitor.

"As long as you promise not to mention any other methods of payment your husband takes."

"It's on a *sliding* scale, Sara." She burst out laughing at her unpleasantly visual joke, even without the open-mouthed sliding she pantomimed.

I stuck out my hip and crossed my arms. "Are you trying to get me to throw up or help?"

"Help! I want your help! Please!" She pushed her chair back a little, giving me room to get closer to the monitor. "No more payment jokes. Promise."

"If I can figure this out and explain it in a way that doesn't make you feel inferior, you owe me lunch."

"And a raise," she said, nodding. "I completely forgot you studied this crap."

Sometimes, so did I. My goal of being an attorney had evaporated faster than nail polish remover, but all that preparation hadn't gone away. All throughout high school and my first two years of college, I'd studied torts and laws, determined to enter law school way ahead of everybody else. My plan was to intern every summer at one of the top three firms in the city—I couldn't decide which, but having it be the same firm every year would be preferable—graduate summa cum laude, become an associate, and work my way to partner before I was thirty.

Of course, I'd also thought that somewhere in there I would find time to fall in love, get married, take a three-month honeymoon to see the world, and end up in Africa, where we'd start the process of adopting a few orphans. Shockingly, not a single thing in that meticulously planned-out timeline had actually happened.

Equally shocking was that my perfect life track had started to derail the day I found out that, before she'd married Timothy, my mother had burned through every cent my dad had left me —including the college fund that would've paid for my last two years as an undergrad and all of law school.

After that, the goal started to seem more like a dream. A dream filled with images of me working myself to death to repay student loans instead of traveling the world, adopting orphans, and taking cases *pro bono* for causes I believed in.

Now, even that depressing dream had faded away. It was all I could do to get through each day, one misstep at a time.

"Which part is confusing?" I asked after I'd skimmed the section on the screen.

"From here"—she pointed to a blank area between the company's letterhead and where the contract actually started —"to"—she used the mouse to scroll through the rest of the nine-page document and then pointed to the period after the last clause—"about here."

Oh, boy. "Well, at least you understood the signature lines."

"Those are signature lines?"

I stopped breathing until I heard her half-hearted chuckle. All was not lost.

Emilia sighed loudly and then cursed even more loudly. "Why does this stuff have to be incomprehensible to anyone but lawyers?"

"Job security. Would you really pay someone a couple hundred dollars an hour to come up with a contract that anyone could just jot down on a napkin and have notarized?"

"Wow. And to think Rob did it for a blowjob." She leaned back in her chair and slipped her hands behind her head. "I've never felt like an expensive hooker before." She smirked. "I kind of like it."

"Go with your strengths, not your weaknesses, right?" Speaking of... I straightened up, stretched out my neck a little, and then snuck the mouse out from under her hand so I could print the whole doc out. "I'm going to need a highlighter, a blue pen, a cup of coffee, and a fifty-cent-an-hour raise."

"Done, done, done, and absolutely." She happily scrambled to get the pens out of her desk drawer and then got up to get me another cup of coffee.

I cleared some random stuff off a chair and pulled it up to the desk. While I grabbed the contract from the printer, Emilia set down two cups of coffee and wheeled her chair around to my side so we could both look at the document right-side up.

It took us about thirty minutes to go through each section. Emilia was a smart woman, so it wasn't the actual content that was giving her trouble, but how each provision could directly affect her business and employees. So, my job was less translation and more turning the words into tangible potential issues.

After I'd answered the last of her four thousand what-if questions, I held my pen over the pages like a microphone and dropped it. "Boom."

Emilia leaned back in her chair. "You are amazing, Sara. Truly. I can't thank you enough."

I shrugged. "You're paying me, remember?" Working with a friend always made things more complicated. If I did something to help, was I doing a friend a favor or just doing my job?

"True. And as of an hour ago, I'm paying you *more*."

"I was just kidding about that." But I could sure use the money.

"I wasn't. You deserve it. Almost as much as you deserve a long lunch." She glanced at her watch. "Oh shit! I completely forgot." She stood, grabbed her bag, and started fishing around in it. "I'm so sorry. I would totally take you out for a thank-you lunch, but I'm supposed to meet Rob and our realtor to check out a few houses." She looked at me guiltily.

"Don't worry about it. Just think how impressed he'll be when you slip *due diligence* into your house hunting conversation."

She laughed as she pulled her wallet out of her bag. She took out two twenties and handed them to me.

"You don't have to do that." It took all my willpower not to snatch the cash out of the air and call it *precious*. Being poor seriously sucked.

"I know I don't have to. I *want* to. And that means you have to take it." She shoved the bills toward me again, and my pride slipped.

"Thank you." Hopefully, she wouldn't change her mind because there was no chance she'd be able to get them out of my hand now.

Emilia shook her head. "Thank *you*. You're a fantastic coach. I didn't feel stupid or patronized once. And my jaw isn't even sore."

"Eww. You need to leave now."

"Seriously, Sara. Thanks. I don't know why you're wasting that big brain of yours working here."

I opened my mouth before I remembered that I didn't have a good answer. Explaining how guilty I felt about almost ruining her business would just make her scoff and make light of the whole depressing episode. So, I went with the same lie I'd been telling her all year.

"I like working here. My boss gives me free coffee and disgusting muffins. Plus, she doesn't care if I do my homework whenever I don't have any actual work to do."

"And a lot less money than you'd be making if you let me give you your old virtual assistant job back."

With the potential of screwing up again? Maybe even worse next time? Nah, I still had to figure out a way to pay her back for all that she'd had to put up with from me.

I shook my head and grimaced. "It would be too stressful to do that and get my homework done. Maybe once I graduate."

"You know, I haven't given up on the idea that you'll find something you love doing in the next five months."

"What happens in five months?"

She stopped and stared at me, confused.

"Expressions like that will give you wrinkles, Em." Her exaggerated-anger face was even worse, but I didn't say anything.

"You graduate in five months, you idiot."

"That can't be right. I mean, I would know." I started counting on my fingers. After I'd found out about my mom using up my college fund, I'd stopped packing as many classes into my schedule as I possibly could. Since then, I'd taken one class per semester, maybe two if I was feeling ambitious. Then last year, I'd gone back to taking three at a time, so I could live at Timothy's place. So...

"Oh shit."

"Who's going to get wrinkles now?" she asked, laughing.

"Me! Because I'm graduating from college in only five fucking months!"

"Told you." As she ran out of the office, she said, "Take however long a lunch you want. Lock up for me?"

At exactly that moment, my stomach growled, and I realized I hadn't eaten anything but a mini muffin all day. So, damn it, I was going to have to spend some of my newly earned cash to buy lunch. Easy come, easier go.

6

DECLAN

*A*t a quarter to noon sharp, Kitty and I took the elevator down to the second floor and waited for Trevor outside his door. Luckily, we'd found the only place in the city that had two one-bedroom apartments open for sublet at the same time and weren't obscenely expensive. Pete and Sam, the guys who made up the rest of Self Defense, shared an over-priced, tiny flat closer to downtown. Trev had wanted us to share a place, too, but that had been the easiest 'fuck no' ever. If I didn't have somewhere to hide out in—just me, my guitar, and my dog—I would lose what was left of my sanity.

The hotels our manager had booked for Self Defense's first big West Coast tour didn't allow eighty-pound dogs, and saying 'fuck no' to leaving Kitty behind in a kennel for two months was even easier than saying it to Trevor. So, she and I had been sharing a thin, lumpy mattress in a converted bus every night until the tour had ended two weeks ago. As uncomfortable as it had been, the bus was still a step up from sharing a room with a bandmate who rarely came home before dawn. And I knew that if *Kitty* ever got drunk and brought a woman home to hump her leg, she'd have been subtler about it than Trevor would be.

Once Trev came out of his apartment, still wiping sleep from his eyes but already smiling, we took the stairs down to the lobby and then walked the ten blocks to the public basketball courts.

As the band's bassist, Trev had decided that basketball would increase our endurance for shows. As my best friend since before puberty, he'd decided playing at a public court might get us women. Not surprisingly, he ignored me when I pointed out that women who hung out at a park in the middle of the day were either moms pushing strollers or addicts waiting for their drug pusher.

Trev didn't care who they were, as long as they had breasts and recognized us from a gig or the band's YouTube channel.

Me? I cared. I cared a lot. Especially when, every once in a while, a woman I didn't know, and who definitely didn't know me, would follow me on the street or show up at my door. Trevor thought it was something to envy, no matter how many times I told him it freaked me the fuck out. I didn't even want to think about what would happen if the band ever got really big.

Even though Trevor joked that the occasional stares we got while walking down the street were directed at *me* and not us, he loved it. If it were up to me, we'd never have posted anything on the internet, strangers wouldn't know who the hell I was, and life would be about the music, not the fame.

But it wasn't up to me anymore. Thinking I was doing the right thing, I'd gone along with all of it, never imagining any of this actually happening. And who the fuck knew what the future might look like? All I knew was that there was no going back to the beginning when things were simple. When fame was so intangible I had no idea how much I would hate it.

But Trevor wouldn't have understood, even if I'd laid it all out for him. The band and the attention it brought him were all he wanted in life, everything he could've wished for.

Unfortunately, I fucking loved the guy—when he wasn't drinking. Since, at least lately, he started drinking immediately after our daily endurance training, I tried to stretch out our games for as long as possible. I swear it had nothing to do with me actually enjoying myself or even that Trevor's current endurance needs consisted of standing absolutely still and plucking strings while I jumped, sang, and ran around the stage to get the crowd going.

We scored an open court at the back of the park, far away from the groups of guys who really knew what they were doing. I tied Kitty's leash to a pole so she could wander around a ten-foot radius while we played. When she finished exploring, she usually watched us make fools of ourselves, scratched the occasional itch, and napped.

As soon as Trevor got winded and needed a break, he stopped to admire the other, better players. "Think we'll ever be that good?"

"No. But if you really want to try, we'll have to give up on music and devote all our time to the game."

"That's never going to happen. The only reason I get laid occasionally is because of the band. Self Defense is my golden ticket. Someday, I'll write a tell-all autobiography and call it *Trevor Finley and the Pussy Factory*."

"The only thing keeping my breakfast down right now is that I know you're kidding."

We both grabbed our towels to wipe off some sweat.

"You should've seen what my golden ticket almost landed Saturday night."

"Almost?" I tossed my towel on top of my bag.

"Almost," he grumbled. "I change my mind. 'Almost' is a much better title for my autobiography." He shook it off—literally and figuratively. "But enough with the jealousy, loser. It just makes you seem more pathetic." He didn't even try to hide his sarcasm. "I posted a pic of Almost-girl on Instagram. If you knew what Instagram was, you could check her out and be suitably impressed. Or if you'd, say, actually still been at the club when I needed you, things could've turned out differently, and I would've invited you to have Sunday brunch with us. You're a shitty wingman, you know that?"

"Sure, because me just being there would've guaranteed she went home with you."

"Fuck, you're probably right. If you'd been there, she definitely would've wanted to go home with someone. Except that someone would've been *you*, not me." He finally put down his towel so we could start playing again. "Must suck being so damn good-looking. I can't imagine how tough it must be to have to pick out which of your fangirls to take home. How do you do it? Oh, right—you don't."

I let him laugh. We'd been in these roles since we were teenagers. He made fun of my looks. I made fun of his intelligence. He was one of the brainiest people I knew—he just preferred to not let it show. At some point his brain had turned off just long enough for him to have the backwards realization that being seen as fun was better than people finding out he was smart.

"Where'd you disappear to that night anyway?" he asked.

"I grabbed a drink on the way home." With an amazing woman who liked me so much she didn't give me her number.

Trevor and the boys had stayed at the club after our set was done, enjoying the low-hanging fruit that came with being what the *San Francisco Examiner* had called "a promising new sound on the Bay Area music scene." Bizarre, since we were actually from Southern California and had never officially lived in this area until two weeks ago. If anyone doubted that, they could read the apartment subletting contracts we'd signed for only three months because we weren't sure how long we'd be here. Staying in the city had been our new manager's idea. Booking gigs was easier for him because this was his home. Plus, San Francisco had enough live-music venues to give us exposure while not being as jam packed of up-and-coming indie bands as cities like New York and LA were. Or at least that's how he sold the idea to Trevor and the guys.

Since landing the new manager, Self Defense was now touted as "a mashup of Green Day and The Kinks." The praise was both bullshit and nerve-wracking. No way were we that good, and no way would we ever be as huge as those bands. Honestly, being internationally known was pretty much my worst nightmare. I was already uncomfortable with people recognizing my face or my music. I never thought it would get this far, let alone far enough to be compared to two amazing bands that'd broken records, relationships, and lives.

"Heads up."

He was staring at his phone when I tossed him the ball, so it bounced right by him. I took the opportunity to disentangle Kitty from the pole I'd tied her leash to and let her explore more of the terrain.

"Seriously, did you take someone home or not?" Trevor asked, eyes still stuck on his phone. "Because if you bailed on us to go home and cuddle with your mutt I'm going to be unhappy."

"If that's what determines your level of happiness these days then you should be very, *very* happy right now." I wasn't trying to gloat, but I had a lot of confusing thoughts floating around my head, and it might help to hear what he thought I should do. And then do the opposite.

Kitty and I jogged over to get the ball, and I lobbed it back to him one-handed. Again, he didn't even reach for it.

"Nice." From the way he drew out the word and the slightly lecherous expression on his face, I knew he was referring to me getting laid, not my NBA-quality pass. "From the club we played?"

I shook my head. "I stopped by a little place just to check it out, you know, on my way home to cuddle with my *mutt*." I glanced down at Kitty and grimaced, so she knew I wouldn't have chosen that word if I weren't quoting him. "I met her there."

"First off, I've decided that from now on, 'cuddling your mutt' is my new expression for jerking off." He slowly wandered over to the basketball and picked it up. "Second, since I got nothing but blue balls after you left me wingman-less, I deserve to hear everything that happened with the girl who pity-fucked you."

"Pity fuck, huh? If that was her version of a pity fuck, I don't think I could handle her respect."

"Seriously? You're such a fucking tease. Tell me everything."

"I'm not telling you shit if you keep looking at me like that."

"Like what?"

"Like you're going to be fantasizing about whatever I tell you the next time you cuddle your mutt." Knowing he was jerking off to it would ruin all my memories of the best night I could remember having with the most amazing woman I could remember having.

He stood at the free-throw line and took a shot. It wasn't even close. "Trust me, you've never, ever made an appearance in my head when my *mutt* was in my hand, bro."

"That's reassuring," I muttered. As if I were going to thank him for mentioning a possibility that had never entered my mind before now. I released Kitty's leash and let her go push the ball around the court a little. "Fine. I'll tell you. But only because it's the only way to shut you up about your puny, little mutt."

"It's incredible how well you know me. Start at the beginning and then skip to the good part."

He'd better be satisfied with the PG-13 version. "When I want to pretend like none of this is happening and my life is still a little normal, I go somewhere no one will ever recognize me. So, obviously, it has to be a place that plays different kinds of music —country, blues, jazz, even show tunes. But not rock or alternative because...you know."

"Because someone might know who Declan Hollis is? Oh no!" He opened his mouth up wide and slapped both sides of his face. "You're such a freak, man."

"Thank you, my friend. Means a lot."

"Just keeping you humble. Okay, besides still not understanding why you'd ever *not* want to be recognized, I guess it makes sense." Trevor called Kitty over, knowing she'd bring the ball with her. "Although, you could try wearing a big, furry mustache sometime."

I got the hint when he took the ball away from Kitty, grimaced at the amount of drool she'd left on it, and shoved it into his bag. Game over. "If you quit this early, you'll never get better."

"True. But more importantly, if I quit this early we can get to the donut place before all the good ones are gone."

I shrugged. "At least your priorities are sound."

7

DECLAN

*W*e took a different route back to our building so we'd pass our favorite donut shop. Luckily, the decision about what kind and how many to get distracted Trev from our conversation about Saturday night. Maybe he'd forget about it, and I wouldn't have to tell him anything.

By the time we got there, he'd narrowed it down to a Boston cream-filled or a bacon-topped maple bar.

"Think I'll do one of each. You want something?" he asked, knowing I had to wait outside with Kitty.

I nodded. "Big and black."

"You're talking about coffee or cocks?"

"Ha." I took a breath. "Ha."

"No judgment, Dec. I don't care who gets your rocks off." Walking backwards toward the door, he held up his hands and shrugged. "But until you mentioned this chick, it had been so long since you took a woman home I figured you didn't like them anymore."

"Wow," I said dryly. "It's as if you can see right into my soul."

"Must've rubbed off from all those sessions I had with your dad." At least *he* could laugh at that.

I found it nearly impossible to laugh at anything having to do with my father. The only good thing the man had ever done for me was to accidentally introduce me to my best friend. And sometimes, knowing Trev as well as I did, I wondered if that was actually a good thing.

I couldn't remember why I'd been at my dad's office that day, but I do remember his look of annoyance and then-ten-year-old Trevor's look of surprise when they saw me sitting in the waiting room. They'd just finished a therapy session, and my dad wanted to speak to Trevor's mother alone. So for the next five minutes the kid and I stared at each other. It was Trev who'd broken the awkwardness, in the way I'd soon learn he dealt with any uncomfortable situation—with a joke. It had actually been an impression of my father and was just rude enough to make me burst out laughing. He kept me giggling until his mom dragged him out, and my dad started his lecture about appropriate office behavior.

A year later, on the first day of middle school, Trev and I met again. From then on, we were inseparable, despite my dad's disapproval of me befriending one of his patients. I never found out why Trevor had been seeing my dad, or which of his issues had made his mom decide it was worth paying one of the most prominent shrinks in Los Angeles to fix. Eventually, our parents had realized nothing they said or did could stop us from being friends, so Trev had switched to another shrink. Or at least that's the story my dad guilted me with. Not for the loss of his client, though. Nope, Dr. Andrew Hollis tried to make me feel bad for forcing my best friend to go to a lower-class doctor. Because, obviously, every doctor was lower class than dear old Dad.

"Knock it off," I said as Kitty shoved her nose into my ass cheek, right where I kept her treats. "You ate them all at the park." She sat down and pouted until she saw a line of ants on the sidewalk that needed some intense scrutiny.

"Hey, Trev?" I called. "Grab one of those doggie donuts they have while you're in there."

"You spoil that drooly mutt, dude."

"Stop bitching—I spoil you, too."

"Truth. Speaking of...my belly needs rubbing. But I think I'd rather have a tall blonde do it." Laughing, the idiot patted his stomach and went into the shop.

Sara's hair was blond, more pale than golden. Long enough to spread out beautifully across a pillow or fall like a curtain around both of us while she was on top, and we were kissing. But tall? Nope. Far from it. She had to be at least a foot shorter than my six foot two, maybe more. And every part of her was tiny. I loved being able to hold both of her hands in one of mine and use my other to tickle her and then make her moan.

Shit. I needed to stop torturing myself.

Maybe I should've claimed Kitty was an emotional support dog—something she'd been since I took her in two years ago—and gone inside with Trev. Because as soon as the door closed behind him, I had nothing more important to think about than that night. And that led directly to the fact that I didn't get Sara's number, had no way of contacting her, and would probably never see her again.

That's why I wrote songs—to do something with all the shit floating around in my head that I couldn't do anything about. It's also why I considered Kitty an emotional support animal. She always seemed to know when I went too far down a bad road, and she knew how to bring me back to the real world, back to the here and now.

I ruffled the fur on top of her head. "You would've liked her, girl."

Hopefully, I had some good karma left, and they would have a chance to meet. Right before I took Sara out for dinner and got to know everything about her. Especially how she could leave so fast after what was probably the most amazing night of my life. No way could it have meant nothing to her.

Trevor came out a few minutes later with a greasy bag tucked in the crook of his arm, his finger through the hole of Kitty's treat, and a gigantic cup of steaming coffee in each hand. He dropped Kitty's donut in front of her and handed my cup to me. About three seconds later, once all signs of the dog treat had disappeared, we started walking again.

"So, Saturday night…" he said with half a donut in his mouth. "While I was in dire need of a wingman, you met this girl at a…"

"Karaoke bar." And, unfortunately, she'd told me that night would be her first and last time there. Leaving me with zero ways to contact her.

"Karaoke bar?" He cringed. "Those things still exist?"

"Look around you—everything exists in San Francisco. Even things you wish didn't." Ironically, we were passing through a section of the city that offered everything from male burlesque shows to *tobacco* pipes. Two streets away from some of the most exclusive and expensive mansions in the country, brick walls and shop windows were covered with ad posters for escorts, the revolution, and local music events, including an upcoming one of ours.

See Self Defense Live Onstage. As opposed to seeing us dead onstage, I guess. Actually, that would probably draw a much bigger crowd. Maybe I should float the idea past the band, our new manager, and whoever the fuck else controlled my every move.

"So, you met this chick at a bar that shouldn't exist and—can she sing?"

"She *can,* but I'm not sure she should. By the way, calling women *chicks* stopped being cool at least a decade ago. I think they actually prefer to be called by their names now." I feigned lack of understanding. "Weird, right?"

"Damn. What'll they want next? Respect?" Trevor had the incredibly rare ability of being able to say something *way* over-the-top sarcastic without his face giving anything away. Neither of us had figured out a situation where the skill would be beneficial, but we agreed that, as soon we could think of one, he'd be ready to take full advantage of it.

"So, what's this woman's name, then?" he asked. "The one with horrible taste in forms of entertainment and even worse taste in men she goes home with?"

"Thanks, and her name is Sara."

"Sara." He paused, taking a moment to absorb all four letters, I guess. "And this *Sara*...she didn't recognize you at all?"

"Not everyone knows who I am, Trev. In fact, most of the time people call me 'the guy who stands next to Trevor Finley.'"

His face lit up. "Really?"

"Yeah. I think we should change the name of the band: *Trevor and a Couple Other Guys*. Nice ring, right?"

"Fuck. I'd take anything." He pointed at the poster-sized ad for an upcoming gig that had been stapled to the building's stucco. The club's logo was at the top, the pint glass of beer tipped over so the liquid poured onto an obnoxiously large graphic of our album cover. "You see that little guy behind the huge pic of your ugly mug? He's way in back with all the other little guys. It helps if you squint."

No amount of squinting made it any less obnoxious. Unfortunately, I'd been out-voted by our manager and his minions, as if not even my face belonged to me anymore.

"Meh." I stared at the brooding, miserable-looking version of myself. It might have been one of the first shots the photographer took, or one of the last. Hard to tell since I'd actually been brooding and miserable the entire day. Ironically, most people got a bad boy vibe from my expression, or at least that's what I've been told.

I shook off the memories of the whole unpleasant experience. "That's just because I have better hair."

"Wrong. It's because you have better everything that counts on an album cover."

Trevor wasn't an unattractive guy. Neither was Pete. Sam was...not the best-looking guy I'd ever seen, but he *was* the best drummer I'd ever known. And I'd rather be good than good-looking any day of the week. Supposedly, I was both. Lucky me. Unfortunately, a band's popularity was more about presentation than performance nowadays. So, my looks were abused at every opportunity, and my skills were rarely noticed, let alone mentioned. Most of our fans didn't even know I wrote all our songs. Or, more likely, they didn't care.

"It's not complicated." I tugged Kitty's leash so we could walk away faster. "Haircut, couple tats, and more outdoor exercise. That's the difference between you and me."

"Yeah, okay," he grumbled. "Sure. Let's go back to talking about your failures with this chick. I was enjoying that."

"Sara," I reminded him. "And it was a colossal failure. Seriously, like the biggest fail to-date—including that girl in sixth grade who kicked me in the balls and then ran off with her friends after I told her I was in love with her. What was her name again?"

"Lisa Burton. God bless that girl and her aim." He put his hand over his heart. "That's one of my most cherished memories. I wonder if she's still cute."

"She's all yours, Trev. Neither my ego nor my balls could take another hit like that one. Plus, I'm not looking for anything serious." I paused to wonder if that was true. Serious was different than *real*, and I could really use something real right about now. Someone real. Sara had felt real—literally and figuratively.

Fuck, she'd felt incredible, and we'd clicked so perfectly, and so quickly. As if we knew what the other was thinking.

Right up until she walked out. I definitely hadn't seen that coming.

"I swear, as soon as I realized she was gone, and I had no way to contact or find her, it was as if my brain turned on a neon sign with the word *commitment* on it." A neon sign that hadn't been turned on in a really, really long time. If ever.

"Seriously?"

"Maybe. I don't know," I grumbled, shaking my head. A serious commitment was on the long list of shit I couldn't deal with right now. "Would I like to see her again? Hell, yes. Regularly? Yeah. But we only had one incredibly hot night to get to know each other, so *forever* seems a little premature."

Although, the more well-known the band got, the closer forever felt.

"Nothing is forever," Trevor said. "Not fame, not women, not even your pretty face—so don't worry about it. If you really want to get her, maybe you should send her something romantic yet practical. Like a therapist with a bow on his chest and a big bottle of anti-psychotic meds."

I slugged him. "Maybe. If I knew where to send him. Except why would it work on her when it didn't work on you?"

"Fuck you. I'm the healthiest mental patient you know."

"Considering the people we know, that's saying a shitload."

"Forget her, man. You'll find another soon, maybe even a normal one."

"Yeah, maybe." I hadn't met a sane woman in years, so what was the chance that Sara wasn't crazy, too? Obviously, she had issues. So, maybe it was better this way, after all. Between mine, Trevor's, and the other guys' I already had more than I could manage.

8

DECLAN

I'd been joking when I told Sara I'd be spending the rest of the week telling myself what a fuck-up I was. It wasn't as funny on Tuesday. Or Wednesday. And by Thursday it was just sad.

I couldn't stop thinking about her and wondering what I'd done to make her run away so fast. I considered myself a decent guy, but I'd be lying if I said I'd never slept with someone and regretted it the next day. But it had never been because the chemistry was too strong, or because I was too interested in getting to know the woman better. So, no matter what issues she had, I couldn't avoid taking her frantic escape personally. I'd thought our connection was deep enough to at least warrant meeting up for coffee...that would lead to another amazing night of getting naked and sweaty with each other...that would lead to a quickie in the shower and then maybe a full week of getting dirty with each other again.

Of course, there was a strong possibility all my woeful pining was because she'd managed to bruise my pride. Since I didn't bruise easily, maybe my ego was making me remember things that hadn't actually been there or weren't as good as I remembered. And the things I remembered were really, really good.

All to mask that what we'd really had was just a really good night together, one she'd been able to easily brush off, one I'd hoped could be more.

Shit, I sounded more and more like my father every day. Next thing I knew, I'd be charging myself four hundred bucks an hour to talk to myself.

Trev, Pete, Sam, and I spent most of the morning with our agent, Doug Blackstone. "The man who's going to make Self Defense a household name," as he'd first introduced himself. My response had been to suggest we just change the band's name to Tide or Sony and save him the trouble.

Today's meeting involved a lot of hype and promises of six-figure contracts with a big label. The guys ate it up while I just sat there, wondering where on the six-figure scale we were talking. There were a lot of numbers between 100,000 and 999,999. I wasn't greedy, but a hundred grand after taxes, equipment, and travel expenses the label wouldn't cover, minus Doug's cut, and then split between the band's four members meant we'd all be better off getting jobs at Starbucks. At least then we'd get free coffee.

But music had been the dream ever since Trev got me and two of our friends together in his parents' garage back in high school. He'd promised an all-you-can-eat buffet of women, pointing to posters of our favorite bands and saying, "Do you think those guys ever have to work to get girls? No way. Music is like crack to women. Something in their DNA."

Ten years later, he was still spouting the same shit. To be honest, I'd never had to work very hard to get a woman's attention, and I didn't think it had much to do with the music. If anything, being the lead singer of a rock band with a decent-sized following made relationships harder. A woman's naked body was a thing of beauty I'd never tire of, and I had absolutely nothing against two people using each other for sex. But nothing turned me off faster than knowing a woman was fucking me just to be able to say that she'd banged the lead singer of a band. Was it wrong to want someone who hadn't decided to go home with me until *after* she'd actually met me? Or even seen me in person?

But Trevor was my best friend, and I knew how much he wanted this. So, I'd stuck by him through a series of other guys joining up, fighting, and walking out before we finally found a group that worked. I'd listened to hours and hours of wrong notes and screeching amps until Trev had learned how to play the guitar. The guy dealt with some serious issues, but once he decided what he wanted, he worked his ass off until he got it.

"I need to call my mom." Pete shifted in his chair to get his cell phone from his back pocket. "She's going to fly off the rails."

"You can't tell her over the phone, man." Sam snatched the phone out of Pete's hand. "It's gotta be in person. With the rest of us there."

I guessed Trevor and Sam were doing the same thing I was—imagining the dance Pete's mom did every time the band got good news. Doug was the only one who didn't laugh. He'd been our manager for about five months, but he hadn't yet had the pleasure of meeting Ms. Lopez.

"Tell her we're coming to Sunday dinner this weekend," Trevor said. "We can rent a car and drive down there."

"I fucking hate you guys," Pete growled, grabbing Sam's arm and taking his phone back.

"Why?" Trevor asked innocently. "She's an awesome cook. Plus, it's not our fault—"

"Shut your mouth right now!"

"That your mom is such a—"

"Don't say it!"

I jumped out of my chair and got between the two of them before the inevitable happened.

"MILF," Trev finished loudly.

"Oooh, boy." Sam covered his face with his hands but didn't stop laughing. "He said it."

"Oh, Mama Lopez," Trevor mimicked. "Guess what happened!"

Pete reached around me, trying to get ahold of Trevor. "You motherfucker."

"Not yet, but if we go to Sunday dinner..." *And*, like always, Trevor had to keep poking the bear. "Does that mean I have your permission, Petey? I didn't want to say anything, but I think your *mama* wants me to be her dirty little boy."

"Knock it off, Trev." I grabbed Pete by the shoulders, trying my best not to laugh because it would only encourage Trevor and piss off Pete more. But I couldn't deny the truth—besides being the band's biggest cheerleader and an amazing cook, Pete's forty-five-year-old single mom was also smoking hot. And no man—other than her blood relations—wouldn't have enjoyed watching her celebratory dance routine.

"Are you guys done?" The seriousness of Doug's tone shut us all up.

"Come on, Doug," I said, gently pushing Pete back into his seat. "You just told us a couple labels are interested in us. That's news worth celebrating, right?"

"Definitely good news." The insincerity of his smile was blinding. "You guys have a funny way of celebrating, is all."

Not sure what he expected. So, the guys were a little happy drunk. Big deal. They'd just come back to reality after spending the last two months acting out all their teenage fantasies. Being on tour was hard work, especially since Self Defense didn't have a label to pay roadies to carry our shit around and set it up for us at each venue.

The bright side of having to do everything ourselves was being able to control what we did in our free time. After our equipment was where it needed to be, sound checks were good, and we'd finished doing any local promotion spots Doug had set up, we had about fifteen minutes to do whatever the hell we wanted.

Of course, the second a show ended until we woke up the next day we were truly on our own. That meant a lot of nights involved getting drunk, being surrounded by women who were willing and able, and having no one to rely on except ourselves and each other.

Now, after two weeks of reality in a city we didn't know, Doug shared his impossibly good news and expected the guys not to get a little slap-happy. While I was the only one who seemed to be wondering just how full of shit our manager was, I couldn't help but pick up on their great moods.

"So, what now?" Trevor asked impatiently.

"Now, you keep doing what you've been doing." Doug stood up from his high-backed leather chair and went to his "Wall of Fame," which consisted of large black and white photos of him with other bands he'd managed and some big record producers he'd met. He straightened the picture of him at the Grammys, standing in a small group of other managers and a couple of producers, including Jay Z. "Perform well, give those beautiful fangirls something to talk about on social media and leave comments on YouTube, and start writing a lot more songs to show whoever we end up signing with. Show up"—he turned around to glance at each of us in turn—"on time to the gigs, interviews, and photo shoots I have lined up for you, and stay out of trouble." His gaze stopped on me. "And get Declan to start posting some damn selfies on your social sites already, would you?"

"What's a selfie?" I asked innocently.

When his eyes narrowed, I leaned down and slowly retied my Converse.

"If you guys can do that," he continued, "my team will take care of everything else. My girl has already given a schedule of your upcoming shows to all the interested labels. So, hopefully they'll all have a chance to see you in person over the next few weeks, maybe months."

I was the only one who didn't groan. Probably because I'd been silently groaning since he started talking.

"Months?" Sam whined.

"What can I say?" Doug shrugged. "That's how it goes. They don't need you as much as you need them, so we take what we can get. And believe me, you'll be thankful for that time once the ball starts rolling. As soon as the ink dries on the contract, don't expect to see your families for a while."

We all looked at each other. Besides Pete's mom, we were pretty much all the family each of us had.

"What's the worst-case scenario?" I asked, knowing the look I'd get from the guys. And I got it.

"Damn, Dec," Trevor said, rolling his eyes with far more drama than necessary. "Way to be optimistic."

Doug responded before I could. "Declan's right to wonder. Even though my gut is telling me that I'll have a contract in my hand soon, nothing is for sure. Which is why I've already told my team to start working on Plan B."

"Which is?"

"In a couple of months, you go back on tour—more cities, bigger venues, larger crowds, more media, and another round of waiting."

Pete and Sam shrugged.

"That's Plan B?" Trevor asked, smiling. "Shit. When I heard 'worst-case scenario,' I imagined sore knees and my mouth being stuck in this position"—he made a large O with his lips and pantomimed giving a blowjob—"so I'm good."

The guys cracked up. They were riding high right now, even after hearing Doug's timeline. They couldn't imagine a possibility that didn't end with a contract, while I was *hoping* for one.

"That's Plan C." It was the first time any of us had heard Doug make a joke, so it took a second for us all to realize it *was* one.

"Let me know if you need to practice, Trev." Bouncing his eyebrows in parodied seduction, Pete grabbed his junk.

"Okay, that's all I have for now. Just do what I tell you to do, and we should be good." Doug opened the door, stepped back, and motioned for us to leave. "Oh, and keep your noses clean. The last thing we need right now is any press that makes you look like you're hard to work with. Got it?"

The guys answered with a mixture of "Yessir," "Aye-aye, Captain," bad salutes, and excited smiles as they walked out.

When Doug flicked his head and held up his index finger to me, my shoulders tightened. Somehow, he'd completely missed the fact that I detested him. The last thing I wanted to do was spend one more minute with him, especially without the other guys around me to act as buffers.

"You coming?" Trevor asked.

Doug shooed him away. "I need Dec for another couple of minutes. He'll catch up." The asshole just left it like that—no explanation. So, the look of suspicion on Trev's face didn't surprise me at all. What *did* surprise me was that it was directed more at me than Doug. *I* wasn't the shifty one here.

I didn't know what Doug wanted, but I felt the need to make up an excuse and lie to my friend. "Let me guess, it's about my wardrobe again. Dude, I'm not going to stuff my junk into leather pants just because some guy you hired thinks it'll make me look like trouble." Yep, the stylist Doug had hired to 'define our image' had actually said that. Well, his exact words to describe me in leather were *hot* and *sexy as sin*, but I wasn't going to repeat that shit out loud. The guys had laughed hard enough the first time.

I kept bitching about leather pants and chafing until Doug closed the door on Trevor's face.

Then I was done pretending. I cared about my friend's feelings—not the asshole's. "What the fuck do you want from me now? I'm writing what you want me to write, playing what you want me to play, doing everything your way." To the point where nothing of me was left. Yep, I'd sold out down to the penny.

"I need to know if you're ready to leave those idiots behind."

I shut my eyes, wondering why he'd "forgotten" to mention any of this while we were talking about worst-case scenarios earlier.

For months, I'd followed his fucking advice for the good of the band. Saying okay to everything Doug claimed would give us a better chance of making it big. Not for Doug, and definitely not for myself. I'd done it for the guys he'd just called idiots. Hell, maybe they *were* idiots sometimes. But at least they were going after what they'd always dreamed of. That's more than Doug or I were doing. I doubted Doug's lifelong goal was to be surrounded by ugly-ass office furniture, smoothing his greasy hair, and pretending he knew anything about music. Or even *liked* music. Unless when he was a little kid, he dreamt of growing up and becoming a shallow, narcissistic asshole.

As for me? Well, it's hard to go after a dream knowing it will ruin three other people's attempts to get theirs. Plus, I still hadn't figured out exactly what I wanted, anyway. "Not this" wasn't specific enough to fuck over my friends for.

So, until I had a plan, helping the guys reach their goals

didn't seem like a bad way to spend a year or two. I just wished it didn't make me so miserable.

"Tick tock." Doug tapped the expensive watch on his wrist. "Just say the word, and I'll have a producer and a recording studio booked in ten minutes. Ten minutes after that, I'll have the album cover done, and you'll be opening up for Fall Out Boy."

Even if he weren't lying through his teeth, it would be impossible.

"How exactly would I write a full album of songs in ten minutes, Doug?"

"You wouldn't have to. We'd change up Self Defense's songs a little and use those."

I nodded slowly. "Leaving the guys with nothing to play."

"Oh, come on, Dec." He shook his head with all the conde-scension he could manage. "You know they're not what I'm sell-ing. Let's do this right, man. Who knows how big you'll get. Fuck, someday, Fall Out Boy could be opening for *you*."

I'd let him talk too long. He was actually starting to believe I might say yes.

"No matter how many times we discuss this, or what bullshit you promise me, I'm not leaving the other guys behind." The only reason I was in this to begin with was because of them. I sure as hell wasn't in it for myself. So, going solo would never happen, even if it *wouldn't* crush Trevor.

"You don't seem to understand what I'm offering you, Declan."

"Believe me, I understand. Which is why it's never going to happen. So stop asking."

"There's a limit to how much of their shit I'm willing to put up with. You wait too long, and I might just give up on all of you. Then, when you come crying to me, begging for another shot, guess what I'll say."

"Um…" I squinted, pretending to give it some thought. "Exactly the same thing I'm saying now: No."

He shook his head, his lips smashed together. A single sad chuckle jerked his chest. "Then you'd better make sure none of those idiots pisses me off too badly. Or it's over. For good this time."

He said it as if I'd be sad to see it all end. Hell, maybe that was my best way of getting out of this cleanly—make it someone else's fault that everything fell apart. Nah, it wasn't worth the risk. Not after what had happened after our last big shot had gone bust. Nothing was worth living through that again.

"Is that all?" I asked. "Or do you want to tell me how tight my pants should be for the next show?"

"That's it. Until you smarten up, at least."

Asshole. "Why don't you go ahead and start calling me an idiot, too? So you get into the habit." I slammed the door on my way out. It didn't make me feel any better. Not a lot did these days.

Trevor was the only one waiting for me. "What was that about?"

I considered telling him the truth, but it would do more harm than good. Trevor wanted this. No, Trevor *needed* this. I couldn't be the one to ruin it for him. If I were the one to kill his dream, it would be my fault if he shoved a bottle of pills down his throat again. Fortunately, I'd been there in time to get help last time. Unfortunately, I'd been partially responsible. I'd been his best friend and had missed all the clues that seemed so clear in hindsight.

I'd had no idea how bad he was hurting back then. But I swear he hadn't stopped smiling since the band started getting more popular. Ironic, since that's the same thing that made most of my smiles disappear. The difference between us was I knew I'd come out the other side okay.

Until then, I could put up with a lot. As long as I had something to love and something to hope for, I could live through almost anything.

9

DECLAN

*W*e grabbed a couple of burritos in the Mission District—cheap, delicious, and as gigantic as Pete claimed his dick was. A fun fact that ruined everybody's appetite and no one believed. No one was willing to verify Pete's claim either.

Somehow, our conversation maneuvered to the sad state of my love life. I'm fairly sure Trevor had guided us here, if for no other reason than to give me shit about how pathetic it was.

I sighed and pushed my food away, almost untouched. "If five years ago anyone had said, 'Hey, Dec. How would you like it if every woman you met wanted to sleep with you, just so she could tell her friends she'd banged the lead singer of a band?' My response would've been: 'Did you say something after 'every woman I met wanted to sleep with me?' And I wouldn't have cared what the answer was. Now, knowing women are using me is just depressing."

"Fuck that," Trevor said. "I swear to the gods of music, if a woman wants to use me for sex, you sure as hell won't hear me complaining about it."

"That's the difference between you and Declan," Pete said,

already smiling. "You said, '*if* a woman wants to use you.' And that's a pretty good-sized 'if'."

Everyone other than Trevor laughed. It made sense—he couldn't see his own expression.

"Shit," Pete continued. "No shame in it—none of us sees the amount of action Declan could."

"If he weren't such a pussy, you mean."

"Obviously."

"Hey!" I said it loud enough to know they'd all heard me. So they were just *pretending* not to.

There was no way to explain it so they'd understand. Or not think I was insane. I'd guess that would be the natural reaction to a guy talking about how he feels like he's two separate people —the one he's always been and the one everyone expects him to be. It's even sadder when the guy realizes that almost everyone he meets nowadays likes the fake him more than the real one. Shit like that can really mess with a guy's head.

Trevor would've gone cross-eyed if I told him that until Sara, sex just wasn't as good as it had been before anyone knew who we were. It was a conclusion I didn't come to without a lot of rigorous testing, by the way. My folks didn't raise a quitter. But it became a little unpleasant when every time I fucked someone I couldn't get over the idea that it wasn't really me who was getting laid. It was the guy I played onstage.

We might have looked the same, but every day he seemed more and more foreign to me. We didn't wear the same clothes, use the same words, share the same values. I felt more like an actor now than a musician. Slipping into a role as I slipped into a costume that had been picked out and prepped by someone who'd barely ever spoken to me.

That was what made my one night with Sara stick with me. Not only was it physically amazing, Sara hadn't met Declan Hollis, the lead singer of Self Defense who someone else had designed. She'd met Declan Hollis, the man who just wanted to be normal, get a house somewhere quiet where my dog didn't have to run on concrete and shit on a four-by-four square of fake grass.

And she'd liked that Declan. She'd reminded me that he was enough, that he was attractive and could make someone laugh.

"Wait a sec. Does that shit really bother you?" Trevor asked. "Seriously? Fuck, that's the only reason I'm here. If women didn't want to use me to say they'd fucked a rock star I'd be sitting in front of a bonfire on the beach somewhere, drinking beer, and playing somebody else's tunes."

"First of all, you're not a rock star."

"Not yet. And luckily, these girls don't think that far ahead."

I grumbled but couldn't disagree. "Secondly, you'd be playing someone else's tunes? What the fuck is wrong with *our* tunes?"

He laughed. "Don't worry, bro. The writing is flawless. It's just not really my style."

Again, I couldn't disagree, at least with the second part. It wasn't my style either. I'd stopped writing what I wanted to a while ago. Now I wrote to market—shit that crowds loved and that gave us the best shot at being picked up by a good label.

After dinner, we headed to our new favorite club in the city— Blurred. Trevor had made it to every live-music night since we moved here. He came for the drinks and stayed to criticize whichever band was playing. But tonight, we were here for a cause—to celebrate all the empty promises Doug had spouted earlier. It's an odd situation to be in—I wanted big things to happen for these guys because they were good people who fucking deserved it. But if that happened, I'd be even farther from finding a way out. And I was already so damn tired of faking it.

I had a couple of beers, trying to keep my head low just in case any Self Defense fans were here. Since we'd come off the tour there were a lot more of them. It just made me feel worse. Every time I stepped onstage or signed a napkin and pretended to be the guy they wanted, I was just spreading the lies.

Trevor had been a different person since we'd left Doug's office. Normally, at this point of the night he'd be calling his blood-alcohol "PLL"—post legal limit—and actively looking for a woman with low standards who recognized us. But not tonight. Nope, he was too busy giving me shit. Instead of working my ass off to keep him from getting wasted, all I had to do tonight was stand here and be humiliated. Hell of a trade-off.

In the brief moments he stopped making fun of me, he would tell the other guy more about the woman who'd dumped me. During the brief moments Sam and Pete weren't hearing about Sara, they argued about visiting Pete's mom.

Eventually, I'd had enough—to drink and of my friends—and told them I was leaving.

"It's early, man," Trevor yelled way louder than necessary. Live-music night was loud, but whoever had designed this place was a genius. The side of the club that held the stage and the dance floor could get deafeningly loud, but the bar area was insulated enough that you could talk without screaming, and the bartenders could hear your order.

"Stick around, Dec! At least until this set is over."

"Nah." I waved him off. "I'm tired. I'll see you tomorrow. Don't get so wasted you can't wake up for basketball."

"*Daaaad*," he whined, "you're so damn old."

I nodded because I felt old. Twenty-four going on eighty. "That reminds me—after basketball tomorrow I'm going to start shopping for a house with a lawn, so I can scream at kids to stay off it."

As soon as I stood up from the bar stool someone slid onto it.

"Buy me a drink!" She was as direct as she was attractive. Her hair was long and dark except above and around her right ear, where it had been shaved short and dyed pink. "I'm Carissa."

She looked familiar, but I couldn't place the name or the face. Then again, I'd been introduced to hundreds of people in the last year and had sung in front of thousands of faces. So, I'd pretty much given up on remembering any of them.

"Hi, Carissa," I said, sticking out my hand. "I'm—"

"You're Declan Hollis. Born and bred just outside of Los Angeles. Dad's a shrink. Mom's a school guidance counselor."

Well, that settled it—I was out of here.

"You started playing guitar when you were thirteen and created Self Defense with your bestie, Trevor Finley, when you were both fifteen. Pete Lopez and Sam Hawthorn were added a few years later. Except the band wasn't called Self Defense back then—"

"Carissa, I say this with the utmost respect, but that was really fucking creepy."

I guessed she wasn't offended when she leaned back and burst out laughing. "I swear I'm not a stalker or crazy or anything. I just love your music and the way you sing it."

Nope, this never got any easier. Or as humbling. "Thanks." No matter how much I hated the music industry's bullshit, I don't think hearing someone compliment my music would ever stop feeling fucking incredible.

She leaned closer as if she wanted to tell me a secret. "Plus, I'm not sure if you know this, but you're kind of nice to look at."

I pulled backwards as soon as her comment made it through the noise of the crowd and into my ears.

"Only in clubs with bad lighting, I swear." In another time

and place, I might've wanted to keep talking to her. But at *this* time and place she wasn't the woman I wanted to talk to. And until I could stop thinking about Sara I'd just be faking it with anyone else.

"Carissa, it was a pleasure to meet you. Unfortunately, I'm actually taking off—"

"No, you can't!" She grabbed my arm and paused for a second. As if she were having trouble thinking of a reason to make me stay. "Not until we make the friend I came here with insanely jealous. I can pretty much guarantee she has no idea who Self Defense is, but you're so her type. Or, like, her type on steroids. She even texted me a picture of you last week. Damn, I keep forgetting to give her shit about that. She's around here somewhere."

"Carissa..."

"Damn it!" She held on to my shoulder to raise onto her toes and look around the club, pointing toward the bathrooms. "She was right over there, like, a second ago."

"Maybe another time." After all the letting women down easy I'd been doing lately, you'd think I'd be more comfortable with it.

"Don't go," she pouted. "Do you really have to?"

"Yeah." In fact, it was quickly becoming a life or death situation.

Luckily, that's when Trevor accidentally saved the day by backing up right onto my foot.

"Speaking of friends"—I grabbed Trevor's shoulder and turned him around—"this guy would *love* to get you a drink. If you can do that creepy thing you did before, but with Trevor's life instead of mine, I bet he'd buy you more than one. Right, buddy?"

"Should I be following this?" he asked, glancing back and

forth between us skeptically. Thankfully, Carissa didn't see him wink at me and mouth, 'Best wingman ever.'

"I wish you didn't have to leave." She was really good at pouting. "Fine. Before you go, can I at least get a picture of us together?"

I couldn't think of an excuse why not to, so…"Sure."

Carissa handed her phone to me, raising her arm to silently show me the angle I should take the selfie at. I reached my other arm around her and pulled Trevor closer until all three of us were in the frame. When Carissa threw both arms around my neck, I bent my knees so she wouldn't strangle me. Trevor stood slightly behind her, peeking his head around her to be seen.

"Say—"

At the last second, Carissa forced my head to turn and kissed me. If I hadn't been so surprised and jerked away as far as her grip allowed, the kiss would've been head-on and involved my shocked-open mouth.

What the fuck? "Nope." In one motion, I peeled her arms off me and stepped back. "That wasn't cool."

It wasn't an *actual* kiss, and she'd only done it as a stupid joke or to have something scandalous to show her friend. And maybe I was feeling too sensitive after my talk with Doug, but I had the sudden desire to chuck her phone into the nearest wall. Objectification aside, what if I had a girlfriend and she saw the picture?

"I'm sorry, Declan." At least she looked sincere. "Are you mad at me?"

Mad? "No." But I'd never felt less like a person than I did in that moment. Unfortunately, I'd only make things worse if I tried to explain it to her. So, with a clenched jaw, I handed her phone back.

"Did you take the picture?" she asked.

Instead of answering, I wiped the side of my mouth where

her lips had landed. "Good night, you two. Be safe and stay out of trouble." For some reason, it seemed apropos to say it to both of them.

As I turned to walk away, I heard Carissa ask Trevor if he was sure that I wasn't angry.

"Nah, he's fine. Dec's just a little grumpy because the girl he likes dumped him."

I couldn't have explained it better myself. Although, I might've added a couple more details. None of them would've been flattering.

10

DECLAN

*B*rushing everything off before my emotions ended up blowing shit even further out of proportion, I made my way through the crowd. It was so thick in here, I opted to use the side door that led out to the side alley versus battling my way to the front of the club.

As soon as I shoved the push bar, cold, fresh air filled my lungs.

"Sweet, sweet relief." The mad chaos of the club muted as the door closed behind me. Then I heard the sharp shout of a woman from farther up the alley, closer to the street.

"Leave me alone, Cal!" she yelled.

They were far enough away that I could only see shapes—a tiny woman with her back against the wall, and a much larger guy trapping her there. It could've just been a lover's quarrel, but the guy should've known better than to use his bulk to intimidate her.

Already walking toward them, I called out, "You alright, miss?"

They turned toward me, their faces still in the shadow.

"Mind your own business," the guy yelled back. "She's fine."

"I'm going to need to hear that from her, actually." My steps sped up the closer I got. "Miss?"

As soon as I could make out her face, I stopped. What were the chances I would run into her again, a week after she'd fled my apartment?

"Hey. Are you okay?" I asked more softly.

Sara didn't nod, and she didn't shake her head—it was kind of a mix of the two, which meant I wasn't leaving.

"Do you need help?"

"Back off, idiot," the guy said. "We know each other."

"Cool." I kept my eyes locked on Sara's. "Except knowing someone and wanting to be cornered in a dark alley by someone are two very different things."

"Back the fuck off."

I hadn't even realized my feet were still moving—my entire body tense and ready for anything.

"You need to follow your own suggestion, Cal," she finally said. "It's the first intelligent thing you've said in weeks."

"Jesus, Sara. I just want to talk to you," he whined. "Alone."

"Hey, man," I said. "I think there's something wrong with your ears."

"Thanks for your help, idiot, but we're fine."

"No, I don't think you are." I was within swinging distance now and waiting. "The lady just told you in a straight-forward and fairly amusing way that she wasn't interested in talking to you anymore. But you didn't seem to hear her."

"How 'bout you mind your own business and let us finish our conversation?" Sure, it might've sounded like a question, but I didn't think he'd like my answer.

"Now I'm really starting to worry about your ears, Cal. You should get them checked. Do you get headaches? Ever hear ringing?"

"Are you a fucking optometrist?"

I would've laughed if the guy weren't being such an asshole. Okay, I laughed anyway. I mean, come on—an optometrist? For ears?

"My ears are fine. *We* are fine. Now, go away."

"Cal—"

He pushed her against the brick wall and then shoved me in the chest.

I swung, my fist connecting with the guy's jaw, sending him barreling back into a dumpster. "How about now, Cal? Headache? Ringing in your ears? You feeling better or worse?"

"Motherfucker!" he cried. "I think you broke my nose!"

"Shoot. You should probably get an optometrist to look at that."

Blood dripped out from between his fingers and onto the pavement. Right next to about six small baggies filled with white powder that Cal snatched up and slipped into his pocket with a blood-covered hand.

"Serves you right, asshole," Sara shouted at him, her foot lifting as if she wanted to kick him.

I glanced at her, wondering if I'd just stepped into a lot more than I bargained for. Was this creep her dealer? Fuck it. Even if he were, I didn't regret helping her.

While Cal was busy blinking, stumbling, and cursing, I grabbed Sara's hand and led her to the sidewalk in front of the club, ducking under the covered awning. I could tell she didn't want to stay anywhere near the ass in the alley, but when she yanked her hand out of mine, I got the feeling she didn't want to stay anywhere near my ass either.

"Are you okay?"

She nodded at the ground, then took a deep breath and smoothed down her shirt. When she looked back up at me, she was smiling.

"What just happened?" I asked.

Good thing I didn't expect an answer because she didn't really give me one.

"That was a case of an asshole acting like an asshole. And a good guy acting like a good guy." She reached out and took my hand gently. "Does it hurt?"

"Oddly, no." I looked at my knuckles, expecting to see a lot of blood and finding nothing. "Cal must have soft bones."

I opened and closed my fist a few times to check for damage, then sighed in relief. I'd never hit anyone in my life. And not to be prissy, but my hands were important to me. I couldn't play guitar without them.

"I don't mean this to sound ungrateful," she said, "but are you stalking me?"

I laughed. "Nope. Purely coincidence." Not sure why her comment seemed so funny. Maybe because, in the split second between seeing her face and realizing why I recognized her, I'd wondered the same thing about her. Even in my relatively short time as the front man of the band, I'd already had to deal with potential stalkers. Fans who were just a little too attached or a lot too unstable.

"Not a stalker, I swear." I held up both of my hands, hoping Sara understood that the last thing I'd ever do was hurt her. "Honestly, I didn't even recognize you at first." Shit, that sounded cold—like I'd slept with her and, a week later, had already forgotten her face. "I mean, it was too dark to see you until I got close enough." What was it about her that made me feel like I had to over-explain everything?

"So, I shouldn't call the cops?" she asked.

"On me? Definitely not. On him?" I flicked my head back toward the alley. "Absolutely."

"I think he learned his lesson." She shrugged. "Besides, if the police were involved, you might get in trouble, too." She had a point but not a good enough one. "I doubt he'd tell them very many nice things about you."

"I never claimed to be nice."

She laughed. "You're totally nice."

Doug would've flipped if he heard that. After everything he and his team had done to make me seem one hundred percent bad boy.

I held my stomach as if she'd slugged me. "Again with the painful jabs—first you tell me you're not going to give me your number, and now you say I'm nice."

"You *are* nice. A lot nicer than that asshole is."

"That's not exactly a high bar. Please tell me you didn't give Cal your number either."

"Unfortunately, I've known him since I was in high school, so he already had my old one. Back in the days before I was smart enough to never give it out." She didn't offer more.

But I had to know. "Is he your dealer?"

Her face squished up in disgust. "Are you kidding? I wouldn't buy *Nutella* from that prick, even if he had the last jar on earth. Besides, I don't do drugs."

I let out a sigh of relief. If I had a real problem with people doing drugs my best friend wouldn't be my best friend, and I'd never speak to my bandmates or almost anyone in the music and club industries ever again. But I'd tried dating an addict once. It'd worked for a day and a half. A day and a half of constantly thinking that there was nothing worse than having to stop what we were doing because her buzz was wearing off and she needed a top-off.

Of course, that was before I'd experienced something worse. Specifically, not knowing if the woman was with me because she was attracted to me, or if she'd just popped some Ecstasy and would've jumped on a seventy-year-old politician if she'd seen him first. Yep, that was actually the worst...that I'd encountered so far anyway.

"What about you?" she asked, her eyes narrowing in suspicion. "Do *you* do drugs?"

"Never really saw the point of taking something illegal to make me stupider. That's what booze is for. Just as effective, and legal in more places."

"Amen," she said, laughing. "Speaking of... Something about Cal always makes me need a drink. Can I buy you one as a thank-you for"—she flicked her head in the direction of the alley—"saving me from that highly unpleasant situation?"

"Absolutely not. But I'll buy *you* one. As a you're-welcome for doing my civic duty."

She studied my face for a moment. "It's just a drink, you know? Nothing else."

"Thanks for the clarification, but I actually know what a drink is," I said. "And I also know that, unless it's clearly stated on the menu, it doesn't automatically come with sex. You're welcome to add that on as a side at any time if you'd like, though. It'd be on the house."

She smiled. "Thanks, but I'm not hungry tonight."

"That's too bad. Because I'm famished."

I didn't touch her as I followed her back into the bar, even though my hand twitched, longing to feel her, hold on to her a little while. But I kept my hands to myself and my face tilted down as we made our way through the crowd, hoping no one would recognize me, including Trevor. Being recognized was never fun, but being spotted with a woman meant people would talk, rumors would get started, and something casual could turn into a problem.

Plus, this woman was different. I wasn't sure casual would be enough. No, that's not right. I *knew* casual wasn't enough. I wanted to get to know her, figure her out, understand why I couldn't get her out of my head.

I've been lucky in my life—not too many rejections from women, jobs, venues, fans. Maybe that was it. Maybe I liked her because she'd rejected me. Because she rejected me for who I *was*, not who people *thought* I was. How's that for fucked up? I was actively looking for a chance to fail and rub my own face in it. Shit.

Since the barstools were all taken, I used my body to make some room for her, then waved the bartender over. He wasn't the same guy who'd served me earlier. His eyes widened briefly when he saw me—either gay or a music lover. Or both. Whatever got us our drinks faster worked for me.

He slid a napkin in front of me, frowning and adding another when he nodded toward Sara. Definitely gay. No straight man would frown when he saw her face—beautiful, pure, but with a little wickedness in it somehow. Smooth skin. Long, blond hair spilling down her back, messy as if she'd just come from the beach...or had an argument with an ex-boyfriend in the alley.

"What are you drinking?" I asked her.

"Vodka tonic."

Would've thought she'd go for something sweeter, something with more mix than booze since she was so small. But I let it go. Stupid to assume I knew anything about her.

I ordered her drink and a ginger ale for myself.

"You don't drink?"

"Not tonight. For some reason, when I'm around you, it feels like a good idea to keep my wits about me."

She laughed lightly, a lock of hair falling over her eyes. Before she could brush it back, I did. I had to touch her, any way

I could. When she flicked her head, I wasn't sure if it was to avoid my touch or to move her hair.

When someone pounded my back, I spun around, expecting it to be the asshole from the alley again. Nope, different asshole.

"Hey, Trev," I grumbled.

Damn it. That had happened fast. Between when I'd said goodbye and now, Trevor had found the time to empty one too many glasses—I could see it in the gloss of his eyes and the way he leaned on me for support. Along with the way he leered at Sara.

"You look familiar," he said to her. "Who are you?"

With a look of doubt, she answered, "Who are you?"

"Declan's best friend, ally, and wingman."

Her brow lifted when she glanced at me. "You need a wingman?"

I shook my head slowly. "This is Trevor, who won't be my friend much longer if he keeps embarrassing me in front of beautiful women."

"Why not?" She smiled. "You look cute when you're embarrassed. I think you should keep him around just for that." She held out her hand out to Trevor. "Nice to meet you. I'm Sara."

Trevor gasped and turned to me. "*The* Sara?"

I shut my eyes. "How cute do I look now?"

"Yep," she said. "*The* Sara. I'm surprised you didn't recognize me, considering what a rare name I have." She'd meant it as a joke, but I couldn't even fake a laugh. It just reminded me that since my name was pretty rare in the States, people *did* recognize me by my name, at least people who followed music. And they thought they knew me—the real me, not just the guy they saw onstage. The person I pretended to be.

"Wow, Dec, you weren't kidding. She's gorgeous. She's got a really great body, too."

"Dude!" I smacked him in the arm. "Apologize."

"You know what else she has?" she said. "A brain. And a severe dislike of people who talk about her like she's a horse at auction."

"You're right," he said. "Sorry. That was me getting a little too excited and forgetting to use my brain." Leaning toward her, Trev cupped his hand and put it on one side of his mouth. The *wrong* side of his mouth if he'd actually been trying not to let me hear what he was about to say. "This is the first time in *years* that Declan has introduced me to a woman he likes."

"I heard that," I grumbled.

She mirrored his position exactly. "Maybe he was worried they'd all be overwhelmed by your excellent manners and intense sexuality."

I shifted uncomfortably. "Heard that, too."

"I was thinking the same thing. Poor guy. So, *the* Sara, are you overwhelmed yet?"

She tilted her head side to side. "I'm about fifty percent there."

"Let me know when you hit seventy-five percent, so I know when to leave."

"*Now*, Trev." I grabbed him by his shoulder and pulled him away from her a step. "How 'bout you and your intense sexuality leave now?"

"I like this one." Trevor caught his mistake. "I like you, *the* Sara. I like you a lot. And I don't want you to hate me. So, can we start over?"

After a brief pause, she nodded. "What do you have in mind?"

"Hi." He stuck out his hand again. "I'm Trevor, Declan's friend. He's told me a lot about you—but nothing too graphic. And all of it was good stuff."

Not sure that was any better, I pushed him into the crowd. "Go somewhere else, Trev. I'll see you later."

With a nod, he turned and left me to do damage control.

"Sorry," I said once he was absorbed by the crowd. "He's not normally like that."

"An idiot?" At least she was smiling.

"No, he's always an idiot. But he's usually less of an asshole. When he celebrates something, he really celebrates."

"No worries. The friend I came here with tonight is a sociology major and would find him fascinating." She took a quick look around the place, probably looking for her friend. "Wherever she is." Hearing that pronoun was a relief.

"We may have to get our friends together sometime then. Trevor loves anyone who thinks he's fascinating."

"What's he celebrating, anyway?"

I didn't want to tell her about the promised contract, or being done with the tour, or anything else about the band. If I brought her into that side of my life, she wouldn't be *mine* anymore. Not that she was actually mine now. But I liked having a little normalcy in my life, someone who wasn't trying to use me for something.

"Trevor and I work together. We just got some good news about a potential new project."

"Congrats. So, why aren't you celebrating with him?"

"Because I'd rather celebrate with you."

"That's sweet. Thanks." She held up her drink for a toast. "And congratulations on your good news, whatever it is."

Anyone else would've probed for more information, but not her. Like she didn't want to know or didn't care. Or maybe she still wanted to keep her distance. After everything we'd done to each other.

I couldn't really fault her for it—I was doing the same thing. Could I have it both ways? Could I keep her away from the music and share everything else? Was that even possible?

11

DECLAN

"So, you told your wingman about me?" Sara said, taking a sip of her drink.

"I may have mentioned you. In passing."

"In passing?"

"You can't blame me—no one can meet *the* Sara and not mention it."

She laughed. "We definitely met, didn't we?"

"I was trying not to think about it too much, but yeah. That was a fantastic...meeting. Maybe we could meet again some-time." I tried to keep it light, especially after her earlier run-in with her ex or whoever Cal was, but she'd started it.

"I don't know. I mean, usually, subsequent *meetings* aren't as...mutually beneficial as the first."

We edged forward, toward each other under the guise of needing to hear one another over the noise of the place.

"Normally, I'd agree with you. But in our case, I really think any future meetings we have would be highly beneficial to both of us."

She hid her smile by taking a long sip of her drink. "Are you really confident you can provide me with any and all goods and services I need, Declan?"

"I would be more than happy to service you in any way I can, Sara."

I also needed to change the subject because this one was literally becoming painful. The harder my cock got, the more I regretted trusting the saleswoman who'd talked me into these jeans. Regardless of how good she thought my ass looked in them, I really should've gone with my gut and bought the ones with a roomier fit.

More importantly, all I really knew about Sara was external —she was amazing in bed and had a body I'd happily explore for the next couple of weeks—so I'd be stupid not to use this time to get to know the rest of her. But I had to move slowly so I didn't scare her off again.

The night we met, she'd told me she grew up in the city and worked in an office downtown. Work seemed like a bland enough place to start.

"Do you meet a lot of people at work?" I asked.

She gasped.

"Oh shit! I didn't mean it that way. I meant the 'Hi, my name is' kind of meet...in real life, at your job. It just sounded like you might..." I don't think I'd ever failed at anything so epically before. "You're good with people. I just thought you probably worked with...people," I muttered. "Sorry, that came out totally wrong."

Smiling, she put her hand on my arm. "It's okay. It only took me about ten seconds of seeing your expression to figure out you weren't calling me a hooker. You must be a shitty poker player."

"Hurtful but true." I pantomimed wiping sweat off my brow. "I need to clarify something you just said, though. You're right— I would never call a woman a hooker. 'Escort' is a lot classier."

Turning my embarrassment into a joke had been a risk, but better she be laughing than walking away. And thankfully, she got it.

A minute later, she stopped laughing but kept smiling as she took a deep breath.

"I've been called a lot of things, but you're the first man who's ever told me if I were a sex worker I'd be the classy kind. I mean, wow. Am I blushing?" She waved her hand as if it were a fan.

"You're amazing," I said.

"Anyway…" She rolled her eyes and pretended to shove me away. "To answer your horribly worded question…no, I don't meet a lot of people at work. In fact, it's only me and my boss in the office. I answer phones and do general office crap for my friend's virtual assistant company."

"Huh," I said as gratefully as possible. "Interesting."

"It's not. It's actually really boring. I used to be one of the virtual assistants. *That* was interesting. Kind of fun, even. But…" She tilted her head side to side as if to weigh her wording. "I had a run-in with a client, and not in a good way. So, until I prove I won't make that mistake again I get to sit in an office and be bored. But whatever pays the rent, you know?"

I'd been nodding along the whole time. I'd also been studying her face and how she held herself. She'd told me more in the last two minutes than in the entire night we'd been together.

"That was a long and confusing answer, wasn't it? So, Declan, what pays *your* rent?"

I swallowed. The question wasn't unexpected—after all, I'd asked her. But I didn't want to tell her about my job. In the past few years, I'd gotten one of two reactions from women. Either they wanted to be with me because I was famous enough for them to already know what I did, or as soon as they found out, they assumed I had no interests other than partying, womanizing, and anything else that fit into the stereotype of a musician.

I didn't want Sara to judge me for what I did. I wanted her to judge me for who I *was*. If she hated me then, fine. I just wanted the chance to get to know one another slowly, naturally, and in a real way.

Granted, our relationship had started, literally speaking, *below the belt*, which might not be the best way two people who could actually like each other should meet. But who could say for sure how it would turn out? Hell, even if it didn't work out like I hoped it would, it was refreshing to talk to someone who didn't want to talk about the band. Especially someone I was interested in.

I couldn't stomach one more question about what it was like to tour, how much money we made, or if I ever got nervous before a show. I liked not having to lie or watch a woman's smile disappear when I told her the truth about my life: I'd rather be at home with my dog. Or that most of the time the band made just enough to cover expenses and bar tabs. And the reason I didn't get nervous before a show was because it wasn't really me who walked onto the stage—it was a guy who'd been manufactured by agents and stylists to appeal to a wide audience.

So, what should I tell Sara? "What pays my rent?" I repeated. "You may need another drink before you hear the bad news." When I caught the bartender's eye, I motioned to her empty glass and then to mine.

"Actually..." she said, shaking her head at the bartender. Then she pointed to my glass and put up two fingers. "It's hard enough to behave myself around you sober. Who knows what would happen after a few more drinks?"

I pressed my lips together before I said something like 'Let's find out' and ordered her a few more drinks.

There was nothing sexy about a woman deciding to sleep

with you only after she got a good buzz going. Just like there was something *incredibly* sexy about a woman switching to a non-alcoholic drink because she wasn't sure she could trust herself around you.

"I'm a writer."

"In the music industry?" she asked.

Fuck. So, she already knew. "How did you—?"

"The card you gave me. It was an agent or manager or something, right? Doug somebody?"

Oh, right. "I wrote my number on Doug's business card, didn't I? Doug's a..." So many different words I could use to describe him, none of which she needed to know. She'd never be within forty feet of him if I could help it. "Doug manages up-and-coming bands. He's always terrified he'll be caught without a fancy business card when he wants to impress a woman. So, the way I figure it, deliberately making him run out of them helps him overcome his fear."

"Sounds like you're helping all the women he meets, too."

Smiling, I nodded. "It's my small way of apologizing on behalf of my entire gender."

"Apology accepted, but only for you. Unless you're about to tell me that when not protecting women from managers or assholes in dark alleys, you write magazine articles about why women should be seen and not heard, or how old white guys should be allowed to define what equality means."

"I thought about the magazine thing. But then I found out that women were only getting an average of 19.5 cent less per dollar than men. For the same job. It seemed so unfair to the men, you know?" I couldn't believe I was able to get that all out with a straight face. "I don't know how those old white guys can look us poor bastards in the eyes after letting us down like that."

"Wow. Only 19.5 cents less a dollar? That's crazy." She slid her empty glass away from her. "By the way, remind me to never make fun of your poker face again."

It almost slipped. "My face and I would be happy to do that. Thanks." With perfect timing, the bartender brought our drinks over.

She thanked him and then thanked me as I handed him some cash.

Since I hoped this conversation would be continuing for a while, I picked up both of our glasses. "I'm tired of yelling over all the noise. Can we go somewhere a little quieter?"

She paused and stared at me for a moment.

"Come on. I haven't finished telling you what I do for a living yet. I'd hate for you to walk out of here thinking I'm the unclassy kind of sex worker or something."

She looked at me silently before eventually nodding. "But just for minute. Then I should find my friend."

"If a minute is all you'll give me, a minute is what I'll take."

I shouldn't have picked up our drinks, then I would've had a free hand to grab hers as I made a path through the crowd. I suppressed a shudder when I felt her finger hook through one of the belt loops of my jeans. That connection made me smile and let me know she was following close behind, her smaller steps creating tiny, bouncing tugs on my pants.

My first thought was to go outside, where the air was fresh and quiet, but I didn't want her to be thinking about Cal while she was with me. What I'd really like to have done is to set our drinks down and invite her back to my place. But I already knew what her answer would've been.

So, I led her toward the only other place I could think of—a hallway just around the corner from a room I'd spotted when the band had played here. Supposedly, they opened up the room to use as a coat check-in closet in the winter. The rest of the time, it was used for storage. Unfortunately, the room itself would be locked, but just beyond it was the hallway to the owner's office and, from what I'd seen, no one but the staff ever got close. Not sure what that said about the friendliness of the owner, but having a little privacy with Sara was worth the risk of getting shit for being here.

I stopped and turned to hand her drink to her, regretting the move as soon as she let go of my jeans.

"Wow, it's so romantic," she joked, peering down the hallway.

I opened my mouth to tell her how happy I'd be to take her somewhere romantic, but nothing made it out. It was bizarre not knowing what a woman wanted from me. The ones I'd met over the last year or so had made it pretty clear—in one way or another, it was always about the band. Another reason why this woman was so different.

Sara took a sip of ginger ale. "Alright, I let you bring me someplace a bit quieter. So, now I think I deserve the truth, don't you?"

"Yeah," I mumbled.

"So, Declan, tell me: Are you really a writer? Or did I get a freebie from a very talented male prostitute last weekend?" She held up her finger before I could answer. "That last part was payback for the ten seconds you made me think you were calling me a whore."

"I'm really a writer." Technically, that was true. It just wasn't everything. In a perfect world, I'd spend every day with nothing but my guitar, a notepad, and my dog, knowing I was in control of my own music. And I wouldn't have to do it knowing my songs were going to be completely redesigned into Self Defense's current goal of mass market appeal.

"The 'freebie' you got last weekend was me doing my best to convince you to come back for more. Except now you have to pay for it with conversations and the occasional dinner out." Then I quickly added, "My treat, of course."

She dropped her head forward a little to hide her face and let me worry about what she was thinking.

"What do you write?" she asked casually, as if she hadn't heard my last comment. "Anything I might know?"

"I would be shocked stupid if you did." At least in the form I'd originally written them. Besides me, very few people ever heard my songs before they were redesigned for the band—Self Defense's drummer, Sam, our guitarist, Pete, Trevor, and Ed, a DJ friend who'd lent us his home studio to record before we could afford to rent a professional setup.

"I bet you make shocked stupid look good."

"I'd take that bet." I leaned against the wall, thinking about what to tell her. "Sadly, I spend more time in clubs, listening to music and meeting people than I do writing these days." Not a single lie had come out of my mouth.

Unless you considered leaving the most important bits out lying. Like I did.

12

SARA

I wasn't sure how it had happened or when my brain took a break, but at some point in the evening, I started laughing. Then I started flirting, touching Declan's arm or his chest every chance I could. Like a damn teenager. I'd become a master at using every tiny excuse to get closer to him —he made a joke or bad innuendo. I even held on to him when I put my empty glass on the floor. Right. Because a five-foot-tall, stone-cold sober woman really needed help reaching the ground.

If I hadn't been so busy enjoying the moment, I would've had time to be disgusted with myself. Maybe later.

The next thing I knew, I was standing on my tiptoes, yanking Declan into me. I gave up wondering what I was doing as soon as our lips touched. Even his kiss was different, better, more delicious.

He brushed his lips across mine and pulled away, forcing me to reach for him again. As if he knew exactly how to draw me out and drive me absolutely crazy. I tugged on his T-shirt, undoubtedly ruining it, and my mind flashed onto how he'd look to anyone who walked by—perfect ass, his shirt stretched tightly across his back, showing the definition of every muscle.

He held himself away from me with one hand on the wall behind me and ran the fingertips of his other down my cheek and then behind my neck.

"Are you sure you want me to kiss you?" he asked, coming closer *way* too slowly.

I couldn't move my head, but I think I squeaked approvingly. Ugh. Yep. That would definitely be called a squeak. He caught himself right before we touched and pulled back to where he'd started. My squeak was whiney that time.

"I like you a lot, Sara."

"That's good to hear," I whispered.

"I like everything about you. And believe me, the last thing I want you thinking about right now is another guy, but earlier..." He swallowed and looked at the wall where his hand rested.

Were women allowed to blame slow brain function on the redistribution of blood like men could? There was definitely a powerful reason it took me so damn long to figure out what he was referring to.

"Oh! You mean with Cal?" I shook my head. "God, no. Nothing like this was happening, or would ever happen, with Cal."

"That's good to hear." He laughed. "It's not exactly what I meant, though."

"Then be more direct. I'm a big girl—I can handle it."

"Okay." His smile disappeared so fast, I almost doubted it had ever been there. "There's nothing I would rather do right now than to push you up against this wall, get under your skirt, and make you come so hard your scream would cover up the sound of that crappy music out there. For starters. *But*"—he dragged out the word—"I don't want to pressure you into doing something you're uncomfortable with."

Was he kidding? "The only thing I'm uncomfortable with is that your mouth is about three inches too far away."

He smiled, his gaze locked onto mine. "You'll let me know if you change your mind?"

"I'm not going to—"

The rest of my thought—and all of them after that—were lost in his kiss.

It didn't take much for his tongue to coax my mouth open. We both moaned when his hand moved up my thigh and under my skirt. He squeezed my ass and lifted me up one-handed. When I moved to wrap both legs around him, he stopped me by slipping his other hand between us and running his fingertips along the edge of my panties. Thank God he was strong enough to support my body while the leg he wasn't holding kicked and tried to find purchase somewhere. I probably looked like a dog kicking her leg out when her owner started scratching that perfect spot. Come to think of it, aside from the bitch part, that was pretty accurate.

He chuckled when he realized I was struggling and bent lower so my foot could touch the ground. But he didn't let go of my other leg, holding it to his hip with his forearm and stroking my core with his thumb. When his mouth moved to my neck, I pressed my lips tightly together to stifle my moan. If someone heard me in the next two minutes, they might interrupt the absolute best and only public orgasm I'd ever had.

For the next minute and a half, I prayed to every deity there was. Thanking all of them together when Declan moved back to my lips again, just in time for me to scream my orgasm into his mouth.

I slumped into him as all the strength left my body and mumbled, "That was…"

"Something I'd like to do regularly," he finished for me.

While I recovered, I had no idea how many times he very

sweetly asked me to go back to his place with him. All I knew was that while my brain was smart enough to refuse each request, it couldn't stop the rest of me from aching for everything he promised we'd do.

Shit! I wished he weren't so damn sexy. I wished he hadn't seen me with Cal. I wished Cal wasn't such an asshole. In fact, if I'd gotten those three wishes, I'd be a completely different person right now. And if the last one wasn't so true, I'd be able to enjoy this moment with Declan without feeling as if I were making a huge mistake.

But facts are facts—Cal *was* an asshole. I'd known that from the second we met seven years ago when his dad started dating my mom.

Unfortunately, it had taken me another six years to figure out that he also didn't understand the word *no*.

"Wait." I think I said that out loud, but honestly, I wasn't the best judge of reality at this particular moment.

"We should stop," I said in the brief time it took for our mouths to separate, reposition, and dive right back into each other. "Declan, we need to stop."

"Are you sure about that?"

God no. "Yeah." I squeezed my eyes shut tight, trying to break out of the hold he had on me. "Declan? I need an intermission."

"Okay." He pulled back. A little. "But do I have to let go of you entirely? I'd really prefer not to."

"And yet, it would be a lot easier for me to think if you did."

"You scare me a little when you think." He let out a big sigh, then inhaled deeply. "Especially because I have this awful feeling you're about to say that it's nothing personal, but this isn't going to work out."

"Wow," I said, unhappy he was right. "You're good."

"No. Good is what I think *we* could be. Together." He paused, studying my face, his gaze moving from the eyes I'd just opened to the lips his had just released. "You're serious. Fuck, of course, you're serious."

"Sorry." I was trying to be smart and not get hurt, and the universe dropped *him* into my path. A test of strength I wasn't sure I was up to.

"Don't be sorry. Be..." He briefly dropped his head forward and then looked up again. "Before you tell me to go away, can I have a minute to make my case?"

"It's not going to change anything." Ugh. I'd never heard anything said with as much regret.

"Come on... I deserve one measly minute, don't I?" He looked so sincere...and kind of needy. A big, beautiful man needed me. Not that I'd never seen need on a man's face before, but everything about Declan was different. Not only did he want to sleep with me, he wanted to *talk* to me, too. Part of me actually thought he might still want to talk to me even if he were one hundred percent sure he'd never get to sleep with me again.

"One minute. And only if you step back at least a foot."

"A foot?" Even in the dark, his eyes shone with life and a little humor. "Is that at all negotiable?"

I grumbled under my breath. "Fine. Stay...six inches away."

"If you really don't want any part of me to touch you, there needs to be more than six inches between us," he said, adjusting the erection stretching the front of his jeans.

I raised an eyebrow and put my hands on his chest. "Well, aren't you cocky."

"Yep. And, for the record? I'm a good inch, inch-and-a-half cockier than six inches."

"Huh. Are you sure about that?" I teased. He didn't need to know I thought he was selling himself short at seven and a half inches.

"Damn, woman." Running a hand through his hair, he chuckled. "Are you this hard on everyone's ego?"

"Just yours." I pressed my lips together to stop myself from laughing. "I guess that means you're lucky."

"Not unless you let me kiss you again, I'm not."

I'd always been proud of not being the type of woman who led men on. I was always upfront and honest. Declan showed me why it had been so easy with other men. Because now, with him, all my rules seemed impossible to follow. It wasn't supposed to be this hard not to care, not to want to find out what would happen next.

It made me feel weak, and nothing was worse than feeling weak.

He must have read the seriousness of my expression, the solemnity or the disappointment. "Fine," he said, holding up his hands, "but you should know that I'm silently protesting." He rested one palm against the wall next to my shoulder. Deliberately allowing me room to breathe or run. Nothing trapping me here, other than the look in his dark blue-gray eyes and my desire to stare into them. They sparkled like the reflection off of the ocean when, just for a second, the sun peeked out from behind the clouds.

"I don't want to tell you how to live your life," he said.

I laughed. "But...?"

"But I want to be a part of it. We click, and I'm not talking physically."

"You don't think we click physically?"

"Nope. Physically, I see us like more of a slam than a click. Like charged magnets." He looked down between us to prove he was right.

I'd said six inches apart, but I'd have been shocked if there was an inch separating us. I wasn't exactly sure whose fault that was or whose hips were reaching for whose. Okay, fine. It was completely my fault. I tucked my traitorous reproductive organs back in line and straightened my skirt.

"Doesn't it feel like we've already known each other a long time?" he asked. "Even though we've only spent a handful of hours together." During most of which, we'd been a little too out of breath to talk.

I forced myself not to nod, not to admit that it felt as if we'd slid past any of the awkwardness that always came with something new. Everything was easy with him. Beyond both of us having *been* easy the night we met, I'd never felt so comfortable with anyone so quickly before—man or woman.

But comfortable and good for me wasn't how I picked out shoes, and picking out a man was no different. Plus, I couldn't afford either right now.

"Look, Declan, I think you're great—"

"Don't." He pushed off the wall. "Don't give me the I-think-you're-great-*but* line. That's bullshit, and you know it. Want to know what I think? I think you feel exactly the same way I do, *but* you can't admit it. What I can't understand is why you refuse to even try."

"I told you I had issues." I held out my arms to the sides. "So, I'm not sure why you're suddenly surprised."

"I'm surprised you want to walk away from something this good. Something I think could be amazing if given half a chance."

"It's not about what I want. It's about what I have to do."

"*Have* to? Why? You're not seeing someone else, right?"

I shook my head.

"So, what is it then? Did some asshole get inside your head and fuck with it so badly that every guy after him doesn't even get a chance to prove he's not the same?"

I didn't think I reacted, but when he blew out his breath and his eyes softened I knew I had. I'd told him more in one facial expression than I'd told my friends in hours and hours of brunches and girls' nights in.

"That's what happened, isn't it?" he asked sadly. "I'm sorry he did that. I'm sorry he made you too afraid to trust any of us. But I hate that you're letting that douchebag's actions form every single decision you make."

Even if that were true...

Shit, maybe it was. I'd lived the last year giving men what they wanted before they could take it from me. It had made me feel strong that the choice was mine, not theirs. *I* was the one in control. I decided who, when, and what. And then I decided when to walk away. Before they could hurt me in the way only someone you trust could.

"You know you're letting him win, right? By not allowing yourself to be happy for more than one night at a time, you're still letting him and that experience control you."

"Are you done psychoanalyzing me or is there more? No? Cool, because I think it's time for me to go." I ducked under his arm and started to walk away, tugging down my skirt.

"Tell me I'm wrong, Sara," he called out. "Tell me you were lying. That you don't think I'm great, *but* you wanted to spare my feelings. Tell me you aren't attracted to me or that you don't feel a connection between us, and that's why you won't even give me a chance. Fuck, tell me there's someone else you'd rather be with if that's the reason. But don't walk away if you want me...if you're afraid we could have something real."

I couldn't move another step. I knew how unfair this was to him. I didn't want to hurt anyone, especially not someone who'd done nothing to deserve it. Someone who'd actually been amazingly good to me in every way. Someone who thought we could have all the things I was afraid of.

"All I want is the truth, Sara. I'm not going to give up if it's just because you're afraid I'm like the guy who hurt you. Because

I can prove I'm not. Let me prove I'm not him. Just...I just want a chance."

I turned around to look at him. "You're right...about a lot of things. But I can't be who you want me to be. So, if you really want to be part of my life, I need you to respect my limits. And they don't include negotiation or therapy sessions." I smiled, hoping this would work, and we'd both be happy. "Like you said, we're like magnets, and I still owe you an orgasm. So, what if we stick with that—just the physical? Maybe the occasional conversation because I really do think you're great." I sighed. "But I'm not interested in talking about my issues." With him or with anyone else. "So, let's keep it casual—nothing official and nothing emotional. From either of us."

He took a deep breath and ran a hand through his hair, coming toward me slowly. "That's the only way?"

"Yep."

"Just physical, no emotion. At all."

He leaned in and kissed me softly. I melted into it, grabbing his shirt and pulling him tighter to me.

"I can't believe I'm going to say this." He peeled my fingers off him. "It's too late. I can't go back to not feeling anything for you."

I wished I could lie to him. But I couldn't. And I couldn't explain why it had to be like this, that I was still hurting and needed to protect myself. I was still screwed up, and until I stopped being screwed up I was no good to anyone.

"I hope you have a great life, Sara. A happy one. I really, really do." He kissed me lightly one last time, and then he walked away.

I almost stopped him. I *wanted* to stop him. Desperately.

But I let him go anyway.

13

DECLAN

"Wake up," Trevor said, shaking the entire bed. "We were supposed to be at the studio an hour ago."

I never should've given him a key to my place. "Who decided that?"

He shrugged. "Somebody."

"Not us, that's for sure." We'd handed over our lives and had no more need to make decisions about anything. *Anything.* Clothes appeared out of nowhere from a magical being called a *stylist.* The music I wrote was stripped of every bit of *me* in it and turned into things I didn't recognize anymore but would appeal to promoters and prospective labels.

What we'd done with our time during the tour had been decided by Doug. And since that so-called free time was scheduled weeks in advance and was almost too short to even be *called* time, I usually spent my *free* time holed up in bed with my dog, trying to remember when I had control over my life.

"Quit bitching, you little bitch." Trevor climbed up onto the bed and started jumping up and down like a kid whose mom wasn't around.

Kitty grumbled at him and hopped off the bed. I grumbled at

him, too, and curled up so my slightly hefty best friend wouldn't land on one of my legs and break it.

"Go away, Trev! I'm in a shitty mood."

"No shit." He bounced again. "Come on, man! You have what we've always wanted. What *everyone's* always wanted."

What I had *never* wanted.

"I have never hated you more than at this exact moment." But I would go to the studio and write what the music people expected me to write and act the way people expected me to act and hope for only three things:

That my best friend wouldn't try to off himself again.

That I could find a way out of a life I never wanted without hurting all the people counting on the band's success.

And that Sara would call and give me a fucking chance. Hell, at this point, I'd be happy with another night like the last.

Except this time, *I'd* been the one to walk away from her. Any other man would've jumped at a beautiful woman's offer of no strings or emotion sex. Hell, before I'd met her, *I* probably would've jumped at the offer, too.

But she was just screwed up enough to make her irresistible to *my* screwed-up side. She wore her pain so transparently, as if she were screaming for help but could never, ever bring herself to ask for it. How could I sleep with her and pretend it wasn't there? Pretend I didn't care she was hurting?

I climbed out of bed just in time. Trevor's foot got caught in the sheet, and he face-planted right where I'd just been, letting out a wail that startled Kitty. She jumped on top of him, barking.

"Shit." If anyone heard her bark, they might tell my landlord. "Tell her you're okay, Trev. Come on, lie."

He rolled over onto his back and reached out to ruffle the fur on her head. "It's okay, baby. I'm fine. But your dad is so mean." He raised the pitch of his voice until Kitty was almost the only one who could hear it. "Isn't he? Isn't he?"

I stepped backwards when her tail started wagging violently. She could knock over a grown man with that thing when it really got going. I wandered into the bathroom and turned on the shower.

"I'm not a bad guy, am I?" I called into the bedroom. "I'm a good guy, right?"

"Yeah, you're great, aside from your poor taste in women." Then he raised the pitch of his voice again. "Except you, of course. You're a good girl. Aren't you? Yes, you are."

I stepped under the stream of hot water and closed my eyes, pushing my hair back so the drops fell directly on my face.

I heard Trevor come into the bathroom. "Why are you feeling so existential this morning? Usually, you don't start questioning your ethical decision-making until after lunch."

"Our mornings *are* after lunch."

"May it always remain so," he said with fake solemnity. "Mornings are for farmers and boring people."

"Too bad your brain doesn't kick in until mid-afternoon."

"At the earliest." He laughed.

The cold hit me as soon as he opened the glass door.

"Hurry up! We gotta get going."

"Geez, man! Get the fuck out of my shower!"

"Just making sure you weren't thinking of that girl and cuddling with your mutt in here. We don't have time for that." Thankfully, he kept his eyes on my face.

We'd been friends forever, so I was well aware that he lacked a proper understanding of privacy or the limits of friendship.

"I'd be out quicker if you'd quit perving on me!" I shoved him back and slid the door shut.

"Seriously, man. Hurry. It's Friday. We gotta finish at the studio by two thirty, or I'll be late for an appointment with my shrink. Speaking of shrinks and shrinkage..." He opened the shower door just enough to stick his hand through and make a big show of pointing down. "I think your boys would be happy in warmer water."

"Appreciate the concern, but my balls are just fine. Thanks." Even though he was obviously joking, I covered my junk with one hand as I slid the door shut with the other.

Trev squealed when the metal frame smashed into his fingers, even though there was no way it had hit that hard.

I gasped. "Oh shit! Did I just break the hand you make love to?"

"No, thank God," he said seriously. "Although, you bring up a scary point—what would I do if my fingers were really damaged? Provided I don't mention masturbation and just focus on not being able to play guitar without my hand, I wonder if an insurance company will insure her."

"Worth a try, I guess." I wiped the water from my eyes and opened them. "Wait, did you just call your hand *her*?"

"Duh. I'm not gay, Dec."

"How much would I regret asking what you called your other hand?"

"Probably a fair amount." His voice came from over by the vanity. "Especially because, after I told you, I'd probably make a sad joke about the only threesome I've ever had."

"Glad I didn't ask, then. You know actual threesomes are overrated, though, right?"

"It all has to do with expectations, my friend. I've always tried to set my expectations and my standards equally low. That way I'm rarely disappointed."

"That's something you may want to bring up at your appointment today." I felt my cheek, wondering if I should bother shaving. Nah, we were already running late. "If you want to help me get ready faster, go feed my dog."

"Should I pack up a lunch for you, too?" he said, slamming the bathroom door behind him as he finally left. Then I heard his muffled, "Come on, dawg. What's your dad got to eat around here?"

I finished rinsing off, stood under the hot water for one more minute, and shut it off. Then, grabbing a towel to dry off with as I walked, I headed towards the small walk-in closet.

"Yes," he said from the bedroom. "Yes, you're a good guy. Always have been. So, why are you suddenly worried you're not?"

I did up my jeans and slipped a T-shirt over my head. "That girl. Sara. She's making me think about shit and re-evaluate how I treat people."

"Better dump her quick, then. If she can't tell what a catch you are she's not worth the trouble. Honestly, if you didn't have a dick, I'd take you like that." He snapped his fingers.

I laughed at the irony as I came out of the closet. "Damn that whole penis thing. Even knowing how low your standards are, I appreciate you saying that, my friend. Makes me feel a lot better about getting rejected again the other night."

He whistled through his teeth. "A woman rejects Declan Hollis, lead singer of the Self Defense, not once but twice? Never thought I'd see the day. I'm sorry, buddy." He put his hand on my shoulder.

"Thanks?" I said, knowing how insincere that was.

"But I'm liking this chick more and more," he said, his smile already up and running. "She may be shit for your self-esteem, but she's making me feel a lot better about myself."

"Dude!" I smacked his hand off and stood. "It's not a joke. I really like her. It's been a long time since I liked someone this much."

"You're right. I shouldn't have said that." This time, he actually looked like he meant it. "I'm just not used to being the one of us who has to comfort the other after a rejection. It's awkward as hell, isn't it?"

"Oh yeah." After slipping on my shoes, I went into the kitchen to find something to eat and to make sure Trevor fed Kitty her expensive dog food instead of Cheerios. Again.

"Next time I get shot down," he said, following me, "you have my permission to sic my miserable ass on Pete or Sam."

I tried to keep my tone serious but lost it before I even started speaking. "What about all the times *after* the next one?"

When Trevor shoved me in the back of my shoulder, knocking me a step forward, all Kitty did was look up from her bowl with a brief glare of annoyance. "The fact that lame joke actually made sense is why I can't miss the one-and-possibly-only opportunity I may ever get to tease you about a woman."

The difference was that Trev never actually cared about any of the women he tried to pick up. So, five minutes after they brushed him off, he'd already moved on. And the truth was, even though we both kidded about his horrible luck, his dry spells never actually lasted very long.

"Fine," I said, grabbing a protein bar out of the cupboard and heading to the bathroom to brush my teeth. "You can be as big a tease as you want to. I can take it."

No matter how many bad jokes he made at my expense, they didn't make me feel any worse than I did walking away from Sara.

"Seriously, though." He leaned up against the doorjamb and watched me brush for a second. "Was she really *that* good of a lay?"

"*Oh yeah.*" Not sure how much he could understand while I was foaming at the mouth, but he seemed to catch my meaning. "But that's not why I want to..." What *did* I want to from her? *For* her?

"Why are you letting some screwed-up girl get into your head like this? If you want something long-term, there are plenty of women who'd *love* to love Declan Hollis forever and ever and ever." He did a terrible impression of a girlie wiggle. "Besides—and this may come as a surprise to you—you're not your dad. You don't get paid three hundred bucks an hour to deal with other people's shit."

I waited until I'd rinsed before speaking. "Four hundred."

"Jesus, four hundred an hour? I still hate thinking about the hundred and twenty my quack gets for listening to me bitch. What does your dad do for that extra"—he looked up and squinted to figure out the math—"two hundred and eighty bucks? Shit, that's one forty per ear! He must have incredible hearing."

"Only if you're paying him." When it came to family, my father was practically deaf. He'd missed eighteen years of clues that I had no interest in following in his footprints. Then, for the two minutes between sitting him down and telling him I wanted to be a songwriter, he'd finally heard me. He'd been so ashamed of my decision to go on tour instead of college, you'd have thought I'd confessed to murder.

"You don't always have to be the one to save people, Dec. Even your dad can't help people who don't want to be helped."

But Sara did. I knew it. She wanted it but couldn't ask. And, yeah, I wasn't a shrink to the rich and famous, but I also wasn't the kind of guy who ignored a stray dog or crossed the street to avoid a homeless person. Everyone had shit to deal with, but once I understood how much it was holding them back from living, I couldn't move on. Even if it ended up hurting me, too.

I said a quick goodbye to Kitty, made sure she had a fresh bowl of water, and shooed Trevor out the door so I could lock up.

"Can't you just use the night you two had as good spanking material and let the rest go? You're always talking about self-destructive behavior—mostly mine and with fairly good reason —so why can't you see it in Sara? I mean, you know how I believe the world is a much better place because of the abundance of wonderful women who enjoy one-night stands as much as I do."

"You may have mentioned it a few dozen times, yeah."

"Well, going home with a total stranger who's as creepy as you are kind of screams self-destruction, doesn't it?"

"Thanks for that, and not necessarily. She took a picture of me and my license and sent it to a friend of hers, so someone would know who I was if anything happened."

"Then she's intelligently and safely self-destructive."

"You're probably right."

"Not probably," Trev said, following me toward the elevator. "I'm right. How long do you think it would last with someone like that anyway? A week? Two? As soon as the sex gets boring, she's gone."

"Do you really have boring sex after two weeks, Trevor? You've gotta be doing something wrong. Wanna go over the basics? In the spring, a bird—"

"Why the fuck do they call it the birds and the bees? Birds and bees do not get together. Ever. Unless the bird is eating the bee. Huh. Do you think it's actually about oral sex?"

I laughed. "You're completely nuts, you know that?"

"Totally. My parents gave me the you're-completely-nuts talk long before the oral sex one."

"They royally fucked you up, too."

"Yeah," he said, his laugh superficial. "They sure did." He ran his hands over his face, and when he lowered them, it was as if all traces of unhappiness had disappeared. "So, you really like this chick then?"

I nodded. "A lot more than she likes me."

I wasn't sure if his eye roll was due to my comment or the fact that I'd just opened the door to the stairwell instead of heading toward the elevator.

"No way I believe that. She's probably just intimidated by your studliness or something. Or she just doesn't know you well enough yet."

"There is no *yet*, Trev. She made it very clear she wasn't interested in the same thing I am."

"Have you learned nothing from me, Dec? No matter what it is, until you quit trying, every moment you have is a moment you can make something incredible happen."

As we went down the stairs, I thought about what he'd said. But there was too much to unpack in a few flights. Too many connections to how he lived his life, and the ways my life had changed because of him.

Trev had quit once. I remembered that night as if it were yesterday. I just tried not to.

Coming home from a date with a woman I'd never see again and finding my best friend on the floor in a puddle of tequila. I'd laughed when I saw him. I'd laughed and called him a shithead and nudged him with my foot. When he hadn't responded, I'd kicked him again. That's when I saw the pill bottle. *My* pill bottle—oxycodone I'd never used from when I had shoulder surgery. When I'd left that night, there'd been ten pills in the bottle. When I got back and found him on the floor of our apartment, there was only an empty bottle, and my best friend was barely breathing.

The paramedics got him to the hospital in time, and we'd barely spoken about it since. Not even his parents knew. Just me, him, the medical heroes, and my father, who'd ended up paying for the mess because Trev was still insured by his parents and refused to tell them what had happened. The only sign he even remembered it happening at all was that he'd kept his promise —talk to a shrink once a week until he paid my father back. Something that was probably going to take forever unless this contract with the record label actually went through.

Trevor smacked me on the arm to get me to pay attention. "We're gonna find this chick for you, man. I won't rest until we've hit every club and drinking establishment in the city."

"Gee, the sacrifices you make for me..."

"Fuck off, man. This isn't about having fun. This is work. So, because I love you as much as a man can love another man without breaking some countries' laws, I'm going to stay stone-cold sober until we find her. Or until next week, whichever happens first."

"Seriously?"

"That it's illegal to fuck another guy in some countries? Yeah. Can you believe that shit?"

"You're not going to drink? Even if it takes all weekend?"

"It won't. I know I've seen her before, which means she must hang at one of the places I do. So, if you get your ass moving and we finish the track for the new song in time, we can begin the search at 3:02, as soon as I'm done spilling my guts to my shrink. You're welcome, my friend."

"Thanks, Trevor. Thanks a lot."

We spent the next three days searching for Sara. We didn't find her. But Trevor was true to his word—not drinking anything stronger than soda all weekend. I could tell it hurt, saw the pained expression on his face when he didn't know I was looking. So, as disappointed as I was that we didn't find Sara, at least my friend had shown me I was worth caring about.

14

___

SARA

I hadn't stayed home for an entire weekend in a while, but if I'd gone out I would've had to talk to people, and after my last run-in with Declan, I just wasn't up to it. So, I caught up on some homework I'd been putting off and tried to put the whole Declan thing behind me.

The next week was equally useless—wake up, go to work, go home, and hang out there until Carissa picked me up for class. By Friday, I was going a little stir-crazy and had decided the hermit lifestyle wasn't for me, after all.

On the bright side, having nothing interesting to think about for five days meant I'd had time to go through all of the company's old contracts, make a stack of the horribly outdated ones and any that needed serious reframing, and write up a detailed index of all of them.

I dropped the whole pile onto Emilia's desk. I recognized her expression—shock and dread.

"The recycling bucket is next to your desk," she joked. "Did you forget again?"

"That new contract from last week made me wonder how

many others should be updated." I patted the pile. "This is the first batch."

"You're fired."

"No, I'm not. I'm earning my fifty-cent raise. Tell Rob to start with the index I put together. It has all my notes about what I think should be changed for our current clients. I also wrote down everything that should probably go into our future contracts."

"You want me to get a divorce, is that it?"

I laughed. "It's just a lot of paper, Em. But I swear, you must have written every single contract from scratch because they're all different. Once Rob goes through them and tells me what I got right and wrong in my notes, I'll write up exactly what we need going forward and contact the clients who need to sign new ones. Did you know there's this thing called a computer that can store things digitally now? Our clients don't even have to print anything out."

"That's just crazy." She flipped through the pages. "When did you do all this?"

I shrugged. "Lately, I've had a lot of stuff on my mind that I don't want in there. Lucky for you, that means I have to use my brain for something else."

"For good instead of evil, huh?" She didn't wait for a response—she knew me well enough to know how right she was. "Thanks, Sara. This is great. But once you've made up the new contracts, I'll reach out to our clients—gotta earn my keep around here, you know?"

"Perfect," I said, relieved. Emilia might not be great with paper and contracts, but she was fantastic with people. Her business did well because she knew how people worked and could convey her desire to see others succeed and that she could help them do it.

"Thanks, Sara. This is huge. Rob will be as impressed as I am."

"No problem." As soon as I felt the heat on my cheeks I spun around and went back to my desk. I hated blushing almost as much as I hated being complimented. Both were things I had little experience with, and I was fine with that. Most of the time.

At around noon, hefting a paper box full of the contracts I'd given her, Emilia left for a Women in Business luncheon followed by more house hunting. So, I spent the rest of the day alone.

Aside from my nails, I did the filing, some homework, and, unfortunately, some thinking. To keep my brain from replaying and critiquing everything I'd said and done with Declan, I started thinking about a topic only slightly less painful—what I wanted to do after graduation.

Basically, I spent about an hour silently and uselessly panicking about the future without coming to any conclusions.

Carissa had signed us up for an extra-credit seminar that started at four o'clock, so at three, I locked the office door behind me and took the elevator downstairs. The tenants of this building ran the gamut—small businesses like Emilia's, insurance sales-people, a few high-end acupuncturists, and a deli on the ground floor.

But the fourth floor was special. And whenever the elevator stopped there, I came very close to stepping out of it. But I never did. In fact, I *never-did* so hard, the opposite happened—I decided to judge all the people braver than me.

Okay, so I'm not perfect. In fact, occasionally, I can be slightly...horrible. The fourth floor consisted of nothing but therapists. Every time someone got on the elevator on the fourth floor, I always said, "I see crazy people." But never out loud—

that would've been cruel. I just said it to myself and then giggled internally.

Huh. I say things and then respond, all inside my own head. What was that expression about not throwing stones?

Everyone should be in therapy these days, and almost everyone I knew was. Oddly, it was always the people who needed it most who didn't go. My mother, my stepfather, my stepbrother.

Me.

At least they always seemed like well-functioning and nice crazy people. If I were completely honest with myself and had much bigger balls than I did, one of these days I'd get off on the fourth floor and beg one of the therapists for an emergency appointment. But since I wasn't always honest with myself and didn't have any balls, I made myself feel better by judging people who were braver and probably saner than me. Yeah, that was really horrible.

When the doors opened, my jaw dropped in surprise. What were the chances? In a city as populated as this one?

The second to the last person I expected to see leaving the fourth floor smiled and yelled, "Holy shit! It's *the* Sara!"

"What are you—?"

"This is why you looked so familiar!" Trevor didn't stop, bounding into the elevator while I desperately pressed the lobby button over and over. "And to think I spent an entire weekend sober because I was so sure I'd seen you somewhere before."

"Excuse me?"

"Do you work in this building?"

"Yep." I stopped his hug by putting both palms on his chest and holding my ground. "Hi, Trevor."

"Aww," he said, backing up a step, his grin never wavering. "You remembered me."

"You're pretty hard to forget, but I think you know that."

"You flatter me, darlin'," he said, feigning shyness. "Keep it coming."

Trevor reminded me of the chubby and charming sidekick in a rom-com whose job it was to crack distasteful jokes and make sure the film deserved its *R* rating. No one could be near him and not smile. As if he had laugh-inducing pheromones or used nitrous oxide-spiked breath mints.

"How are you?" I asked tentatively. I didn't want to embarrass him into admitting why he was here. Even though I was dying to know.

"Not too bad. Not too bad. Just got the stamp of approval from my shrink, so I'm cleared from the looney bin for another week."

I had no idea if he was kidding or not. His smile never faltered, but he'd definitely be the type to cover his pain with humor. So, I kept my mouth shut and smiled back at him.

"Well, well, well. *The* Sara..." The wall was a step too far away from him, so when he tried to lean back against it, he did a dramatic air-flail before catching himself at the last minute. I got the feeling he planned out his comedy routines in advance. "Wanna get something to eat and talk about how great Declan is?"

"Um..."

"Or we could talk about how great I am, if you'd prefer."

That, I could laugh about. But it didn't change my mind. "I can't. I have to get to a meeting. Work, work, work. Know what I mean?"

"Nope, never had a nine-to-five job, but you know what they say, 'Lunch is the most important meal of the day.'"

"I think they say that about breakfast, actually. Plus, it's three o'clock." And a little late for lunch.

"Breakfast? At three o'clock. That doesn't sound right." He

shrugged. "Maybe we should call Declan—he knows normal people stuff."

"That's not what I meant, but..." I couldn't exactly tell him that the last thing I wanted to do was talk about, or to, Declan. The last time we'd spoken, he'd told me to have a nice life. So, knowing more good things about him would only depress me more and ruin the decent and boring day I was currently having.

"Thanks for the offer, Trevor, but I really can't." Just then, the elevator stopped, and the doors opened. Perfect timing...if it had been the ground floor.

Trevor nodded as two middle-aged men got on. "I get it. The last time we met, I spooked you, didn't I?" He put his hand over his heart. "I'm all talk, I swear. Obnoxious, inappropriate talk that sometimes gets me in trouble. That's why I keep Dec around. He keeps me in line, and I keep him from being boring." His eyes widened momentarily. "Hey, that reminds me..." He reached into his back pocket, took out a flyer, and smoothed it on the wall. "Dec and I are going to be at Tunnel Vision tomorrow night. You know it?"

"Of course. Who doesn't?" I took the flyer he pushed at me and read it. Apparently, some band called Self Defense was playing there tomorrow at eight. "Is the band any good?"

"The best!" he shouted, raising his hands to shoulder height and shaking them. "You should come. I know Declan would love it if you were there."

I raised an eyebrow. "You might have read him wrong about that."

"Impossible. I know that guy better than I know myself. I've known him so long that when we met, his voice was about three octaves higher than it is now and he'd literally never held a guitar." He leaned in a bit and waited expectantly. "He's pretty fucking good, too. Have you ever heard him play?"

With my arms folded tightly across my chest, I just nodded. I hoped the silence would force Trevor into saying something —*anything*—that would take my mind of Declan and his damn guitar.

And, of course, at that exact moment, an image of the last guitar I'd seen popped into my head. On the night Declan and I met, when we'd stumbled into his apartment, I'd briefly let go of him to get my shirt off and had noticed a guitar hanging on the wall.

Once we'd started kissing again, I forgot all about it and pretty much everything else I'd ever noticed before. Until later.

When he'd showed me how good he was with his hands, I discovered that his fingers were not only the perfect length for foreplay, they were also very, very dexterous. So, when I came out of the bathroom that night and saw him playing his guitar while he waited for me, it all clicked together. Including where his creativity came from.

I hadn't realized it at the time, but the way his fingers moved on that guitar had practically hypnotized me. One hand shifted from perfect position to perfect position without him even having to look where they were, and the other plucking each string separately or strumming them all together? Ugh. Who knew all that skill could be transferred to a woman's body so flawlessly?

It had taken me twenty-three years to figure out why everyone thought guitarists were so sexy. And it made me want to cry to know that some women might go their entire lives without ever realizing it.

So, had I heard him play? Of course—that night and in a few of my more...*detailed* fantasies. Did I know he was amazing at it? Yep. Playing guitar and lots and lots of other things.

Did I know Declan had ruined every string instrument for me because I could no longer look at them without remembering the orgasm he'd given me shortly afterwards? Oh, good

God, yes. Yep, for the rest of my life, I would never be able to look at a guitar without having a hot flash. At twenty-three.

"So, will you come?" Trevor asked, holding the elevator door open for me on the ground floor.

"I don't think I can make it." Not if just the memory of Declan and his guitar made certain parts of me clench and start tingling. No way could I trust myself to be around him before that stopped happening.

"Come on, *the* Sara. He'd want you there. Promise."

"Um..." I couldn't agree to go, but I also couldn't deny that I'd kind of enjoy seeing Declan again. I could handle going home with lady blue balls for one night. Besides, I'd just bought new batteries. "I'll try. Maybe stay for one drink or something."

"Nah, you gotta stay for the band's whole set. Seriously, you'll love it."

"No promises, but I'll think about it," I lied. I knew he meant well and obviously cared about his friend but had no idea where his friend and I had left things the other night.

"Sweet! See you there." He bounded off, the crowd of people in the lobby seeming to step out of his way at exactly the right moment so his gait never changed. Once I couldn't see him anymore, I made my way much less gracefully through the crowd, wondering if Carissa would be waiting for me out front when I finally got there. What I wasn't going to wonder about was what I would wear to the club tomorrow if I were to go. Because I wasn't going to the club tomorrow.

When we first met, I remembered Declan mentioning that his favorite color was the same as my Electric Lemonade. Strangely, I just happened to have a really cute top with that exact shade of blue in it.

Damn it. I was planning out what to wear to the club tomorrow, wasn't I?

15

SARA

$\mathcal{I}$ tried not to eat out very often. The way I saw it, every meal I ate at a restaurant equaled one more day I couldn't afford to get my own apartment. But after a week of doing nothing, I guess I was especially vulnerable to peer pressure when Carissa invited me to dinner after the seminar. Or maybe I was just looking for a distraction, anything that would stop my mind from replaying the best parts of my night with Declan over and over.

There were a lot of *best* parts to replay. It was annoying as hell. A week since he'd rejected me, and I still couldn't get him out of my head.

I'd been with gorgeous men before. Six-pack abs, tight asses, and big cocks weren't completely new to me. And I'd even had some great sex. Not a *lot* of great sex, but more than many women have in a lifetime.

So, why was it so hard to stop thinking about this particular night of great sex with this particular six pack, tight ass, and incredible amount of endurance? And worse, why was I thinking about how much I wanted to ignore all that stuff and just *talk* to him again?

Okay, sure. Realistically, finding all of those attributes in one person wasn't something I'd run into before, but those things were superficial. Remembering him should've just made me horny. I should be feeling my crotch tighten with the memories, not my chest. And my stomach definitely shouldn't be the organ that fluttered.

Maybe I was coming down with something.

When Carissa looked across the table at me I had my hand on my forehead. "Are you getting sick?"

"No," I said, dropping my hand. "I just feel a little off, I guess." I had to be the only person on earth hoping they had a tapeworm.

Maybe it was E. coli. I dropped my fork and pushed my salad toward the middle of the table.

"Well, I'm glad you felt up to joining me for tonight's excursion."

Since Carissa had only lived in San Francisco for about a year and a half, she was on a mission to try out as many different bars and restaurants as she could. I'd lived in the city my entire life, but since I'd only gotten a fake ID four years ago and had only been able to drink *legally* for two years, almost everywhere we'd gone was new to me, too.

Thankfully, she stuck to the cheaper spots on her list when she was with me since I didn't have the liquid assets she did and hated feeling like a mooch. Weekends didn't matter because everything was free for women in the big nightclubs. Except for gay clubs, obviously. Gay men didn't give a shit about how hot we looked.

She leaned back in her chair and sipped her drink through two thin straws. "This place is cute, right?" The pub was a lot smaller and quieter than the other places she'd dragged me to.

I nodded. "I feel a little like I'm inside a coffin, but yeah, it's cute." We were encased in wood—the chairs, bar, walls, ceiling, everything.

She laughed. "I was thinking more of a hunting lodge, but I see your point."

"Is that why you ordered the steak? Because it reminded you of hunting trips back home?"

"Not everyone from my hometown hunts, Sara." She poked her fork into the giant chunk of meat on her plate. "But we wouldn't be able to call ourselves Texans if we ordered salad at a restaurant either. At least not in my family."

Carissa and I had met on her first day at SF State. She'd chosen to spend her last two years of undergrad at the school that was as far as politically possible away from her very conservative parents back home. And I'd chosen to finally, someday, maybe finish my degree at the school where my very annoying parents were forcing me to take more than one class at a time. According to my stepfather, taking three classes was the absolute minimum if I wanted to live under his roof. Ironically, the *last* thing I wanted was to live under his roof. Unfortunately, I didn't have a choice in that either.

But it was my own fault that I'd had to give up my apartment and move back in with my mom and Timothy, so I tried not to bitch about it too much. I had way more important stuff to bitch about anyway.

Plus, when I was being particularly honest with myself, I'd admit that I actually really liked school. In fact, up until the dream started to die, I thought my life would include four years of college at Berkeley or Stanford and then three years of law school at UCSF.

Now, my life included doing monkey work at Emilia's virtual assistant company during the day and taking three night classes at SF State. I spent my weekends going to clubs, partying, going home with the occasional man, and then recovering before Monday rolled around again. Except last weekend. Going out just didn't appeal as much since I'd met Declan.

"Oh shit," Carissa said, looking up from her phone. "I can't believe I haven't given you shit for this yet."

"Shit for what?"

"For making me almost pee my pants at that karaoke bar a couple weeks ago."

"I don't remember you peeing your pants. Was it after I left?" I'd grudgingly agreed to go to the karaoke bar with her. Carissa had never been to one, and I'd never wanted to *go* to one. Of course, that's where I'd met Declan, and considering the way the night ended, I should probably thank her. Or never forgive her.

"Duh." She started scrolling through our texts. "You realize the whole point of sending me a picture of a guy's driver's license is so I know who he is in case you disappear, right?"

"Duh back at you." Of course, I did—I'd been the one to tell her about it. Safe casual sex wasn't just about condoms these days. Safe casual sex meant a friend knew the name of the guy you were going home with and could give his license number to the police if you didn't check in the next day.

"So...?"

"So..." she repeated, holding up the picture I'd sent her right before I'd left with Declan that night. "I swear, I almost peed my pants when I got your text."

Oh shit. I'd had his stupid name in my phone the whole time. I'd spent one of the most glorious nights of my life with him, being too embarrassed to admit I hadn't heard his name when he'd told me. Thankfully, he'd kept me so distracted that I'd forgotten my *own* name for most of the night, but still...

I don't slut-shame anyone—including myself—but not knowing if the guy's name was Declan or Dylan until *after* you left his place wasn't good. I really should've just sucked it up and asked him. Or looked for a piece of mail. Or, you know, remembered I'd sent a picture of his license to a friend.

"Damn, he looks good." I grabbed her phone to take a closer look. His address wasn't right, though. According to his ID, he lived in Los Angeles. "He's even hotter in person. And naked." And with his head between my legs.

"You wish." She tore the phone away from me. "You wouldn't believe how many times I've googled images of him. So, yeah, believe me, if a picture existed of him naked, I'd have found it by now." She flicked the screen, probably swiping through pictures.

I'd always assumed everyone from Texas spoke slowly and with a drawl. But not Carissa. She had a drawl but spoke so quickly, it sometimes took my brain a minute to translate what she said into something I could understand.

"I didn't even tell you I met the *real* him last week, did I? After you left with your stepbrother. I can't believe how much I embarrassed myself. He makes me turn into a tween, I swear. I will murder you if you tell anyone that, by the way."

She groaned as she swiped through some more pictures. "Where did you even get a picture of Declan's driver's license anyway?"

"I took it before we went back to his place," I said, confused.

"Wait. *This* is the guy you were talking to that night?" Staring at me with huge eyes, she slowly raised up her phone again. "The one you went home with?" The seriousness of her expression was actually starting to freak me out. "No fucking way."

"What?" I asked. "What's wrong with him? He seemed so nice." ...*said the neighbor of every serial killer ever.*

"You slept with Declan Hollis, Sara. Declan-fucking-Hollis."

Calm down. I wasn't dead. I still had all the body parts I'd started out the evening with. We'd used condoms, a bunch of condoms, actually, because Declan's version of "foreplay" was more like "fore, during, then back to fore, then even more fore, during again, in another room, during, during, even more during, and then after-play".

Oh, my God. Had he learned how to do some of those things in prison?

I grabbed her arm. "Tell me what he did!"

People's heads spun toward us when she squealed.

"Owww!" She swatted at my hand. "Stop squeezing me so hard, and I'll tell you."

I let go of her and pretended I didn't massively regret texting her the picture of his license. If I hadn't, we wouldn't be having this conversation, and all the fantasies I'd had about Declan ever since that night would still be making me feel the *good* kind of dirty instead of the disgusted kind.

She glared at me and rubbed her arm.

"Oh, come on, Carissa. I don't have enough upper body strength to have hurt you that badly." I sighed. "I'm sorry. Now, can you please tell me if the guy I slept with is a fugitive or something?"

"You really don't know who he is?" After another century of making me wait, she burst out laughing. "You slept with Declan Hollis, and you didn't know who he was!"

"Sure, enjoy your laughter. I'll just be over here having a heart attack trying to figure out what kind of psycho he is."

"He's a singer."

"A what?"

"Singer—a person who sings. In a band." She waited. "How can someone so smart be so clueless? Sara Antonopoulos meet"—she held up her phone again and turned it over, showing me a picture of—"Declan Hollis."

"Oh, my God, is that him?" I snatched her phone back.

The background was dark, colored overhead lighting creating splotches of color everywhere. But right in the middle, holding a microphone, his hair wet and falling forward into his eyes was a guy who looked a lot like the man I'd been obsessing about for the past few weeks.

"It's hard to see him." I used the phone's zoom feature to see his face better.

"I have better pictures. Swipe right."

I glanced up at her in shock. She had pictures of Declan saved on her phone.

"Don't judge me," she said, blushing. "Besides, I'm not the one who went home with a celebrity without knowing it."

"He's not a celebrity!" Oh shit. "Is he?"

She shrugged. "Depends on what you think celebrity means. Does everyone our age who has decent taste in music know who he is? Yeah. Does everyone he takes home and bangs the shit out of? Obviously not." She laughed so loudly the people next to us started staring.

I shushed her and then looked down at the phone again. "This is why I never tell you about my sex life, by the way."

In the next picture, Declan was standing with three other guys, one of whom was Trevor. Declan looked pissed or bored, maybe. I swiped past a few of Carissa's selfies at school and clubs, some screenshots and memes, then a picture of the two of us with our faces squished together.

My finger froze and I let out a long sigh when I got to another one of Declan. He looked just as amazing as the last time I'd seen him, except this one was in black and white, and he was sitting on a stool with his guitar. But his expression was the same—sad and a little hurt. I couldn't help but wonder who he'd been thinking about when the picture had been taken.

Luckily, that thought reminded me of how stupid I was, and that I really needed to stop obsessing about him.

"Go be as tweeny as you want." I shoved the phone back at Carissa. "Doesn't matter to me. Because I'm not going to ever see him again."

"Really?" She raised an eyebrow. "So, he has nothing to do with why you've been so out of it lately? And by *lately*, I mean ever since that night."

"Nope." I dropped my head forward and focused on my salad. "He's all yours. And whoever else wants him."

"Great," she said mockingly. "His band is playing tomorrow night. I was going to invite you to go with."

"I was already invited," I grumbled, stabbing a crouton to death. "And I'm not going."

"That's too bad. But just so we're clear, you'd be one hundred percent okay if I went home with Declan after the show, right?"

"Yep," I said tightly.

"What if I asked you to watch the door, so we could fuck in the bathroom?"

Good thing I hadn't eaten much because I would've thrown up all over the table.

"Damn, Carissa. That was way too graphic."

"And you'd be fine if, say...I had a picture of us kissing."

"I wouldn't want a copy to put on my wall or anything, but yeah, I'd be totally okay with that."

"You mean this?" She slipped her phone between my eyes and my salad.

It was a mistake to sit back in my chair because it gave my eyes a chance to focus on the screen of her phone. I turned away as fast as I could, but the image had already burned a hole in my retinas.

Great. I would spend the rest of my life seeing their lips pressed together. As if he wasn't already on my mind twenty-four seven.

"Relax, girl," she said, laughing wickedly. "I practically had to tackle him to do it, and he wasn't pleased with me afterwards. But I'll have the picture to fantasize over forever."

Oh, thank God. I'd been the one to give the ultimatum, and

Declan was exactly what I *didn't* need in my life. But telling myself that and *knowing* that were two very different things.

"Plus, you don't care anyway, right?"

My smile hurt. "Right."

"Perfect." She stared at me another minute. "You *sure* you don't want to go with me tomorrow?"

"Well..." I swallowed. "Maybe I'll go, after all. Just to see if their music is any good."

Her smile held nothing back. "Thought you might."

16

DECLAN

*R*ight after our set, I made my way through the small group of women waiting for us offstage and headed out the back door of the club.

"You better come back, Dec!" Trevor yelled after me. "You promised. Remember?"

"Yeah, yeah." I jogged around the building to grab a cab back to my place to drop off my guitar and let Kitty take care of business. Unfortunately, I'd let the adrenaline of the show and my need for a strong drink make me agree to hang out with my bandmates as soon as I was done, so I had to come back.

Normally, after a gig we'd all help carry our equipment out to our volunteer roadie's van. Then I'd say good night to the guys before they went back into the venue and I went home. Tonight, in exchange for my promise to come back, Trevor told me they'd take care of loading up our stuff, so I could make a quick trip home and still get back before everyone was wasted.

So, after telling Kitty I'd rather hang out with her and would be home as soon as I could, I went back to the club. I got there just in time to see to our one-and-only roadie, Ed, packing up the last of our equipment into the passenger side of his van.

Ed—or as he was known by his small following of fans, DJ REC'Ed, and pronounced like 'wrecked'—jumped about a foot off the ground when I smacked him on his back. Thankfully, the piece of sound equipment was only about two inches above the seat when he let go of it.

"Holy shit, man! You just knocked two years off my life."

I shrugged. "They'll come off the end, so I wouldn't be too busted up about it."

"Are you kidding? That's two years less of being a dirty old man who can get away with anything."

"I see your point," I said, "and I apologize for making you scream like a little girl. Now, please tell me that the guys didn't make you load everything up by yourself."

"They did fine. The last couple things are mine, and no one else is allowed to touch them. You need to stop treating them like they're your kids, Dec. They really can manage without you looking over their shoulders." He shook his head before diving halfway into the passenger side and moving shit around.

"At least for the small stuff," he added, chuckling as he came back out.

"You really think I treat them like children?"

He slammed the door and turned to face me. "I get it—sometimes they act like children. But if you keep treating them as if they can't take care of themselves, don't be surprised when you're right. 'Cause you'll have been the one who taught them they can't manage on their own."

Legally, Ed wasn't even old enough to get into the clubs we played. Thankfully, nobody ever carded the twenty-year-old musical prodigy who helped carry in our stuff and set up his gerry-rigged sound equipment alongside the venues' that made us sound even better.

"Are all DJs so wise or just the ones who are going to be household names someday?"

Just referring to him as a DJ made the volume of his smile turn up all the way. He spent all his free time staring at his computer with his headphones on, sampling different pieces of music and magically turning them into something totally different. That part of the industry made no sense to me, and I had to respect the talent and work he put into it.

He'd gotten work DJ'ing a few small events but was still waiting for his big break. Until then, he was happy to learn about the music business by helping us out, and we were ecstatic to let him.

"You want to sneak inside for a few minutes and have a drink? My treat."

"Can't." Ed shook his head and pointed at the van. "Loading zone only. Besides, I do my best mixing at night."

"Yeah, probably should make the most of the time you have left. Since I accidently stole two years of it." I stuck out my hand to shake his. "Thanks, Ed. See you later."

I watched him jump into the driver's side and drive off before going through the back door of the club and kicking away the cement block he'd used to prop it open.

I went around the side of the stage and out into the crowd. The whole area was packed so tightly, I had to look at the ceiling just to suck in a somewhat clear breath of air. Still stank like booze and sweat, though. And yet, these were members of the privileged class who dropped two hundred bucks for cologne and had free all-you-can-waste access to clean water.

As I pushed my way through, I thanked the people who told me they'd enjoyed the show and absorbed a few overzealous congratulatory smacks on my back. All I wanted to do was to have a drink with the guys and get Trevor home before he passed out somewhere dangerous. Although, at least if he fell unconscious here, his body would be kept fully upright by all these fucking people.

I didn't see him until I was practically on top of him. Still mostly conscious but looking as if he were trying his damnedest to take the "mostly" out of my assessment. How long had I been gone? Damn it. So much for having a drink of my own. He'd probably already emptied out the bar.

"Trev!" I yelled in his ear. "Come on, big fella. I'm taking you home."

We were standing too close to each other for him to push me away. I grabbed his arm and dragged him behind me, forcing bodies apart so both of us could pass. I held back a curse when I felt someone's stiletto dig into my Chucks.

Just keep swimming. Upstream. Like a fucking salmon.

"Wait!" he yelled as if we were actually moving. "Let go of me!" He continued to yell at me while yanking his arm from my grip. If he'd had more control over his motor skills, he might've had a chance of getting away. The one perk of his drinking problem.

I let go of him as soon as we cleared the mob and could breathe again, shaking out my sore foot and checking to see if the heel had left a bloody hole in my shoe.

"Hey, Dec!" Trevor said, surprised. Damn it, he'd just realized it was me.

"Somebody drags your sorry ass out of that pit, and you didn't know it was me? What if it had been—?" Who? Who would be stupid enough to drag a drunk out of the middle of a mosh pit? "A cop!"

"You're not a cop."

I nodded slowly, wiping a sweaty lock of hair off my forehead. "I'm glad you still have a good understanding of the obvious."

We had to yell to hear each other over the music, even

standing a foot away from each other. He wiggled his eyebrows and moved his mouth, but for the life of me, I couldn't decipher what he said.

"Say that again 'cause I'm sure it was important."

He didn't catch my sarcasm. *"Mumble-mumble-here-mumble-*for you."

"Sounds good. Even though I still have no idea what you just said."

He grabbed my collar and pulled me into him. "I said," he yelled into my ear, "I found Sara! She was here looking for you a couple minutes ago. Surprise!"

As I was waving away the flammable fumes of his breath, the words sank in.

"Sara. *My* Sara?" Then I added, "Who isn't mine."

"There are a lot of Sara's who aren't yours, man." He laughed. "But this Sara who isn't yours is about this tall." He held up his hand to his belly, which meant he was either dumb as shit or talking about a small child. Probably both. "Wait. That's not right." He finally moved his hand up to a more reasonable approximation of Sara's height. "And she's blond and hot and has..." He squished up his mouth. "Um...lots of good...parts." For the big finish, he actually pantomimed holding those good parts as if he had two of his own.

"Yes, Trev, she's got amazing breasts. I know this, and obviously, you know this. It's not an international secret."

Trevor nodded. "Considering where they are."

I looked at my friend with serious doubt of whether I wanted to keep considering him one. "You need to stop drinking. Now. And take a cab home."

"Yesssssir," he answered, smiling sloppily. Probably having already forgotten my suggestion.

But I needed to know if he'd really been talking about the Sara I wanted to see. Was she really here? Shit. What if she'd seen us play? I'd told her I was a writer—which was true—so maybe she'd think the band was just a hobby. Lots of normal guys with normal jobs play in bands on the weekend. Not at huge clubs like Tunnel Vision, but maybe that wouldn't occur to her.

Wait. If I actually got a chance to talk to her again, did I really want to have another lie ready? We'd moved past that. In fact, she'd made herself perfectly clear last time we saw each other. She wasn't offering what I wanted and vice versa. So, why keep lying about something I shouldn't have lied about to begin with?

"Focus for one more second, buddy. Then we'll get a cab." I snapped my fingers in front of Trevor's face. "What did she say besides my name?"

"She asked about the band, but mostly she asked about you. I introduced her to Sam and Pete."

Great. Now they'd have more fodder to tease me with.

"She really likes you, Dec. And you like her. That's why I invited her to come tonight. For *you*." He poked me in the chest with his finger. "Because you're too stupid to go after her yourself, and you deserve somebody who makes you happy. You're welcome, my friend."

"Thanks, Trev." Although I wasn't sure how thankful I felt. When had he invited her? What did he tell her about me?

He glanced around the club for who knows what before opening his eyes and mouth widely and pointing toward the bar. "Hey! There's the chick who was with her." There were a dozen different women he could've been pointing at.

"The one in the red dress."

Shockingly, there was only one in a red dress.

As much as I'd have liked to talk to her, especially if Sara were still here somewhere, I had a drunk to take care of. Fuck it.

As long as Trevor didn't drink anything else... Speaking of which...

I took the empty beer bottle out of his fist. "Let's go talk to her, buddy."

"And then I can get another beer."

"No, that's not going to happen. But I do respect your perseverance." I grabbed both of his shoulders, spun him around, and marched him toward the woman in the red dress. "Hang out here a second, Trev. Then we'll go."

"M'kay." Trevor got distracted by something only he saw and pulled away from me to go find it. I really wanted to find out if Sara was still here and if she'd seen the set, but I couldn't do that with two hands on my friend. So, I let him go. Right after I slipped his wallet out of his pocket just in case. Since he wasn't female, no money meant no more drinks.

I had to be quick. I walked up to the woman in red, knowing there was a good chance Trevor had gotten her mixed up with someone else. Or that the Sara who'd asked for me wasn't the one I wanted it to be.

I tapped the woman on the shoulder. "Hey, are you a friend of Sara...?" Fuck, I didn't even know her last name. And they were probably fifty thousand women named Sara in San Francisco.

Oh shit. The smile that had appeared when she turned around disappeared faster than it had shown up.

"Oh, my gosh." Her excitement was non-existent, but her sarcasm was completely on point. "If it isn't Declan Hollis." She downed the rest of whatever she'd been drinking. If the glossiness of her eyes was any indication, that glass hadn't been the first she'd emptied tonight.

"Hey, Carissa," I said hesitantly. "Small world. Good to see you again." I was ninety-nine percent sure Trevor had pointed me toward the wrong woman, but I had to check on that last one percent. "Do you know a woman—?

"You guys need to figure out what the fuck is going on between you."

"Me and..." I said slowly, "Trevor?"

"No," she grumbled. "You and Sara. It's annoying."

"Sorry about that." Although, I wasn't exactly sure what *that* was. Did she mean Sara was complaining about me in the same stupid, confusing way as I was with Trevor? "Maybe, if I knew where Sara was, she and I could talk and stop annoying our friends." I looked at her with a pitiful expression until she responded.

She shrugged. "Worth a shot. Although, you know how she is."

No, I didn't. Not really. But I wanted to. "Can you tell me where she is?"

"She tried to find you, but I haven't seen her in a while."

"How long ago?"

"She tried to get close to you right after your set was done, but she couldn't get past those girls who swarmed you." She took a step closer to me and tilted her head. "That's gotta be freaky. Women just coming up, thinking they can have a piece of you."

"It's pretty freaky alright."

"Seriously, Declan..."

Almost as freaky as hearing my name slurred like that.

"You look so fucking hot when you sing. If things don't work out between you and Sara, I'd be happy to take your mind of it."

"Thanks, Carissa," I said. "That's...nice of you."

If she could actually remember this moment in the morning, she would probably regret coming on to the guy her friend kept annoying her about.

"Did she say where she was going?"

"Can you believe she didn't know who you were? Not a clue. I'm mean, not that you're world-famous...yet. But you're California-famous. And West Coast-famous. And a lot of other places-famous."

So Sara knew. She must have found out before Trevor had invited her to see us play. But when? Before or after she'd listened to my idiotic attempt to keep her from finding out?

"Seriously, Declan, you should've seen her face when I told her..." She turned back to the bar and waved at the bartender's back. "Hey, Micky!"

"When did you tell her? Carissa?" Damn, I was losing her. "Hey." I patted her shoulder, knowing my time to find out anything else was almost up. "When did you tell Sara about me?"

"Micky!" When the bartender turned our way, she looked down to get her glass.

Luckily, I was a head taller than her, so he could see me, too. I shook my head and signaled that he should cut her off.

"Bastard," she yelled when he pretended he hadn't heard her and went to get someone else's order. "I was with her at the karaoke bar that night, you know that? It was my idea to go there to begin with. If I hadn't begged her to come with me it could've been you and me that night."

I thought about repeating my question a third time, but it wasn't worth it. "I'm gonna find you a ride home, okay? Right after you tell me where Sara went."

She looked up, trying to access a memory that couldn't have been more than fifteen minutes old. Then she shrugged. "To your guy's house, I guess."

My breath stopped. "What guy?"

"Your drum guy." She pantomimed playing. "Um...Sam!"

"Wait a sec. She went home with Sam?" I felt my body tighten, my hand curl into a fist. Sam knew I was interested in her. He'd had just as much fun teasing me about it as Trevor had. *Almost* as much, anyway.

If she'd been asking about me, how the fuck did both of them decide it was a good idea to go home together?

Carissa leaned toward me to whisper, but it came out just as loud as every other word she'd said. "Every girl should sleep with someone in a band at least once in her life. I told her that." The more she said, the more I wished this noise would drown her out. "Not a shitty nothing band, a *good* one. Like yours." She laughed. "I still can't believe she didn't know who you even were. Isn't that crazy?"

"Yep. Pretty crazy." It was impossible to laugh with all my brainpower being used up by the idea that Sam had taken Sara home. Was everyone going crazy? Including me?

"She thought you were just a regular guy."

"I am just a regular guy," I mumbled.

I grew up with an alcoholic as a best friend, and my office consisted of whichever nightclub or special event venue we booked that week. So, I'd had more than my fair share of conversations with drunks. That's why, when Carissa's lips turned into a pout, I knew she had already derailed from her previous thought and was about to switch to a completely different topic.

"Declan," she whined, leaning on me. "Will you take me to the Grammys? Your drummer guy said he'd take Sara, but I want to go, too."

What came out of my mouth didn't qualify as a laugh. "First off, the *drummer guy* isn't going to the Grammys. Second—" Why bother explaining anything to someone who didn't care? Fuck it. I was beginning to wonder if anyone cared about *anything* anymore. "Carissa, are you here with someone?"

When she bit her lower lip, I added, "Someone who can make sure you get home."

"Sara, but she left," she said, shaking her head. "Didn't I just tell you that?"

"Come with me." I offered her my arm, which she happily took, and went outside. I put her in the first cab I saw, handing the driver forty bucks and repeating the address Carissa had given me. Hopefully not because she assumed I was going with her.

"Good night, Carissa. Make sure you take an aspirin and drink some water as soon as you get home." I slammed the door on her confused expression, wanting to scream, break something, throw a huge temper tantrum in the middle of the road.

And the most fucked-up part is that no one would be surprised. Because guys in bands get loaded and fuck whoever's the closest. Right? Guys in bands didn't want to get to know a woman because he thought there was something special about her, something he wanted to figure out. Guys in bands shared the spoils of being guys in bands and didn't care when one of them took home a woman his friend was confused about.

I stormed back into the club to find Trevor, cursing him, everyone else in this hellhole, and the two people I'd thought I knew who had left earlier...together.

Fuck it. Sam hadn't forced her. The more I thought about it, the more I realized that the joke was on me for thinking she was different. Different than anybody else who wanted nothing from me but a good fuck and to say she'd screwed a musician. I'd met enough of them—you'd think I'd be able to recognize the signs.

But no. I'd thought Sara was real. I'd thought she actually liked me. I'd even considered the possibility that we could last—because she hadn't known who I was. Didn't see me as *that guy in the band*. Actually saw me as a man. As me.

But she'd already known who I was, probably from the very first night we were together. Carissa must have recognized me at the karaoke bar and filled Sara in when they'd gone to the bathroom or something. So, while I'd thought everything was real, it had been just as phony as everything else. And the fact that she was the most amazing woman I'd ever been with made me feel even worse.

More used.

More used up.

"I want out of this life!" Even though I screamed it, the music was too loud for anyone to hear me.

Or maybe they had, and they just didn't care. Because it didn't matter what that guy in the band wanted anyway, did it?

17

SARA

I *swear, if Declan saves me from this man within the next two minutes I'll give up chocolate and start going to church every Sunday with my mom.*

I took it back as soon as I thought it. Nothing was worth that sacrifice. And I didn't really need saving from Sam. He was a million times nicer than Cal and couldn't hurt a fly. But damn, could he talk.

I'd been standing there, nodding and agreeing with him for over—I glanced at my phone—twenty minutes, and I hadn't even tried to end the one-sided conversation. Probably because the music was so loud, I could only make out half of what he was saying.

When the band's drummer had told me he knew where Declan was I'd thought he would take me right to him. But Sam had somehow decided that by choosing to following him, I'd also agreed to listen to him complain about how hard his life was. I mean, yeah, it wasn't all Nobel Peace prizes and parades, but what did he expect? He had great rhythm and got paid to hit some drums with two sticks of wood in front of shockingly impressed fans. It wasn't as if he were flipping burgers for minimum wage.

At least he recognized the irony—slipping in occasional comments about how this had been his dream for as long as he could remember and that, despite his complaints, he knew how lucky he was.

Made me wonder if anyone thought about all the potential downsides of their dream before they were actually living it.

Thankfully, Sam hadn't said anything I'd consider a come-on. No bad pickup lines or hints he was interested in doing anything other than talk my ear off.

"Declan will be back soon, right?" I shouted to make sure he could hear me above the music.

My interruption didn't even faze him. "Yep. He promised. Dec always keeps his promises."

Oh, how I hoped that were true. For countless reasons. Of course, I had to fault Declan a little on his truthfulness. Or lack thereof. Granted, we hadn't spent that much time together...*talking*, but why did he tell me he was a writer and leave out everything else?

Now I knew he was the lead singer of a really popular band. Oddly, the lie that might've angered someone else actually made me *more* interested in him. I knew my reasons for hiding parts of my life, but I didn't know his. And that created a sad little bond I didn't have with anyone else.

Why would anyone hide that? The crowd adored him. And damn, he was a fantastic singer. I loved the gritty, sex-oozing quality of his speaking voice, and his singing voice was even better. I could still hear it when I closed my eyes. Something I'd been doing a lot while Sam explained in great detail how drummers never get the girls.

I could still picture Declan gripping the microphone during the only slow song they'd played, closing his eyes and holding the mic to his mouth. There was actually something incredibly sexual about it—a gorgeous man brushing his lips across something shaped an awful lot like my vibrator. I'd never imagined that would be hot, but it was. So very, *very* hot.

I'd never been into popular music much. I was someone who loved to groove out to whatever was on the radio, but I didn't care about the names or personalities of the musicians, let alone who they were dating. Until now, anyway.

Now, I cared very deeply about who one particular musician was dating. And even though I had absolutely no right to feel that way, I really hoped he wasn't dating or sleeping with anyone. Anyone...else. How ironic that I'd been the one to tell him he wasn't allowed to care about me and then, once I'd effectively pushed him away, I prayed he *did* care.

I didn't believe in fate. Declan rescuing me from Cal in that alley a week after we'd spent the night together was totally random. So was my office being in the same building as Trevor's shrink, and that I happened to be on that elevator at the exact moment Trevor stepped onto it. And that he'd handed me a flyer to a club where unbeknownst to me, he and Declan's band was playing.

Totally circumstantial. Not that I'd want to have to prove it to a jury of my peers or anything.

"Maybe we should go to the entrance," I said, mostly to stop thinking. "Then we'll see him come in."

Sam shrugged. "Okay." He led me through the crowd with his arm over my shoulder to shield me from the occasional flailing appendage of a few overexcited clubgoers.

"You really don't have to wait with me, Sam." I felt a little guilty, as if I were using this perfectly nice guy to get to Declan. But that's not how it had started and certainly wasn't my intent. Sam didn't seem to mind or be surprised, though. I guess it happened a lot.

"I want to. It's nice to have someone to talk to. Girls tend to notice the guy in front more than the guy in back hiding behind the drum set."

My guilt disappeared, and my insecurity flooded in as I imagined countless women throwing themselves at Declan. He was the lead singer of a band, gorgeous, and sexy as hell.

Since the end of my awkward teen years, I'd never doubted my attractiveness, never had any problems getting whomever I wanted, but then again, I'd never competed with an entire city of other women before.

No, this wasn't a competition. And even if it were, I was fairly sure I'd be among the top contenders. I mean, how many other women did Declan have time to actively pursue? How many other women did he admit to caring about...right before he walked away?

So, tonight wasn't about proving anything. Tonight was just about congratulating him on a great performance and wishing him the best for the future. Right?

It took my brain a minute to snap out of my insecurity and focus on the message my eyes were sending. Maybe it was because a single person was standing still in this flood of people pouring through the entrance.

"Declan." I smiled at him and lifted my hand to wave.

He stared at me, his eyes tight and intense, occasionally glancing at Sam before shooting back to me.

I never got around to actually waving, my hand just hanging in the air. Again, there was a short delay between what I was seeing and what my mind actually took in, but it got there eventually.

He looked pissed. Even more so when he shoved his way through the crowd toward us. If I'd been able to, I would've backed up, but the space had already been filled, and I had nowhere left to go.

"Hey, Dec!" Sam yelled. "I was—"

"I know what you were doing, Sam. And we'll discuss it tomorrow." He didn't even look at his friend, his glare solely for me. For a reason I didn't understand. "But I'd like to have a quick chat with your date, if that's okay with you."

When Sam's arm flew off my shoulder and he stepped back, I understood what Declan might have misunderstood.

"Sam's not my date."

"Right," he snapped. "Because you don't date. Can't believe I forgot that. Well, then I'd like to have a quick word before you go fuck my friend. That better?"

My jaw tightened. I suddenly wished this part of the club were as loud as the farther inside, so I wouldn't have heard him say that. "No, actually. That's worse. Not to mention incredibly rude, judgmental, and an all-around shitty thing to say. Aside from it not being true, of course."

"Of course, it's not. I'm sure fucking me had nothing to do with the band either." He leaned closer to me. "You know, it would've been a lot easier on both of us if you'd just asked me for an autograph."

"Oh, wow. Am I supposed to be impressed? Too bad I didn't even know you were in a stupid band until last night. Partly because you somehow left that out when you told me about your job."

He briefly shut his eyes and took a breath. "You're right—I shouldn't have lied. It was wrong." Then he nodded. "And no matter what your reasons for being here, I shouldn't have said that. I'm sorry. My mind's been having a tough time sorting things out tonight."

I could tell he meant the apology, but the rest didn't make sense. "My reasons for being here? What does that mean?"

"Your friend—Carissa. She told me you knew who I was. I guess I was hoping a little too desperately that wasn't the case."

"I find it a little hard to believe you're desperate, Declan. And I seriously doubt you need to lie to get in a girl's pants." I clenched my eyes shut, hoping at least some of this would start making sense. "Guys lie about *being* in bands to get women to sleep with them." I knew this because a few of them had tried. It hadn't done anything for me, but when I thought about it, it had definitely worked on Carissa. "I've never heard of someone lying about *not* being in one."

"If it's any consolation, I only partially lied to you." One side of his mouth curled into a guilty grin, deepening the dimple on his cheek and giving me a peek into what he'd looked like as a little boy. I bet he got away with everything. "I really *am* a writer. But instead of books or articles, I write songs."

"You also sing and play the guitar in front of big crowds of cheering people."

"Sometimes." He nodded. "I'm a songwriter who's really sorry for assuming the worst and being an asshole."

"Don't worry about it, dude," Sam cut in. "I was just talking to her while we waited for you to get back, anyway."

"Were you really waiting for me?" he asked me hopefully.

I wasn't ready to let him off the hook. "Don't worry, it'll never happen again. Now that I know better."

"I'm really sorry, Sara." He ran his hand through his hair, but it flopped right back into place. "I did exactly what I asked you not to do the last time we saw each other. I shouldn't have assumed you were anything like other women. Can we start over, go back to before I turned into a jealous asshole?"

He was jealous. That shouldn't have made me so happy to hear. Jealousy was a terrible emotion—always.

"Please," Declan said. "Can we find somewhere to talk? Just for a minute?"

I wasn't sure anymore. I hadn't expected this reaction and, frankly, it hurt. I slowly blew out a breath, giving myself a chance to figure out what I wanted from him. Unfortunately, it wasn't something I could decide in a single exhalation. All I knew was that I didn't want to be here anymore.

"I'm leaving. If you really want to talk, you'll have to do it while I'm waiting for a cab."

He nodded quickly. "I'll take it." Then he turned to Sam. "Sorry, man."

Sam slapped him on the shoulder. "No prob. But you owe me one. You wouldn't believe how many assholes were gawking at her, even though it was so obvious how into me she was." He winked at me. "If I'd have turned away for a second, they all would've pounced. Women are right—men are fucking pigs."

"Speaking of pigs..." Declan said with a half-grin that was more a showcase of his dimple than a smile. "Somebody needs to make sure Trevor gets home—the sooner, the better." Then he turned to Sam, peeled a twenty-dollar bill from his billfold, and gave it to the drummer. After shoving the rest of his cash into his back pocket, he reached into the other one and pulled out a worn canvas wallet. "This is Trevor's. Do you mind helping—?"

"Our little piggy go wee-wee-wee all the way home? Sure, no prob. I was going to take off soon, anyway." Sam grabbed the wallet and peeked inside.

Declan laughed at his look of disappointment. "Damn, you shitheads are expensive." He reached for his cash again and handed over another bill. "Thanks, man. I owe you two now."

"Nah, I was just kidding about that. After all, your tardiness let me get in some quality time with a very beautiful, very sweet listener." Winking, Sam put his arms out to me as if he expected me to run in for a bear hug.

I grabbed his face and gave him two kisses, one on each cheek. I really did appreciate him keeping me company.

Although, at this exact moment, I wasn't sure how smart it had been for me to stay.

Thankfully, Sam seemed to understand, motioning me in with his pointer finger as soon as I let him go. Maybe he hadn't understood. I leaned in warily.

"I've never seen Declan freak out about a girl before," he said. "He must really like you. Give him another shot. Dec's one of the good guys, and there aren't enough of them anymore."

Everyone's definition of *good guy* was different. Mine didn't include men who yell at me. But I'd hear him out because, even though he and I would never have a future together, I didn't want to walk away feeling the way I was right now. Plus, Sam was right—there weren't enough good guys left.

"Take care of yourself, Sam. Thanks for your help." Then I turned around and headed toward the front door without checking to see if Declan followed. If he really wanted to talk, it was up to him to keep up.

18

SARA

*T*he first breath of night air made up for all the shallow, dirty ones inside the club. Normally, by this time of the evening, I'd be so drunk I wouldn't have even noticed. But I'd been so enthralled watching Declan perform, I'd forgotten all about my drink, so I was too damn sober.

I stood on the sidewalk and looked down the street, expecting to hear his voice any second. I heard lots of other voices, but not his. But I didn't want to turn around. I was still pissed at the way he'd spoken to me and didn't want to take the chance he'd be standing right behind me, silently looking at my ass. Because then I might start laughing, and then he'd think everything was okay.

This not-dating thing was a killer. If it had been any other guy on any other day, I'd have just left and chalked it up to him being an asshole and me not caring. But unfortunately, while I wasn't paying attention, Declan and I had moved past that point.

I was hoping. I wanted him to be following me, staring at my ass. I wanted him to apologize and go back to being the guy I thought he was. But I also *didn't* want that. I also wanted this whole thing to stop, and for me not to care if he was objectifying me.

Unfortunately, what happened was much, much worse than anything I'd imagined.

I heard him whisper my name, felt his heat as he stepped closer to me, his breath sending ripples of goose bumps down my back. No part of him actually made contact with my body, but I could feel him in every cell.

"I'm sorry."

"I'm not that kind of person." I turned around, jerking backwards when I realized how close he actually was. "I don't deliberately fuck with people. I would never go after one of your friends, knowing that you…" What was the right word? One that meant something without meaning too much. "That you think you want more from me."

"I don't think that."

"Oh." I squeezed my eyes shut in humiliation.

"I *know* that. Which is why I was an idiot. A jealous idiot who assumed the worst because I was afraid—"

"Of me?"

He laughed. "No. As intimidating as you are, I'm not afraid of you. I was afraid I'd never get to *talk* to you again. When I found out you were here, I thought, 'This is my chance.' But when I heard you'd left with Sam, I flipped. I thought…" He shook his head.

"What?"

"I'm in a band that's doing pretty well. It's hard for people to understand exactly what that means. But one thing that's different now is the way women…" He cocked his head, probably weighing his words. "Women treat me differently now." He chuckled. "At least I hope they don't treat everyone the way they treat me."

Sam's complaints came back to me—drummers don't get the

girls. Which meant lead singers probably did. And for some reason, Declan didn't seem happy about it.

"How do they treat you?"

"As if they think all I want to do is party and fuck. As if I don't have feelings or want more than that."

Was that why he didn't tell me what he really did for a living?

"When I heard you'd left with Sam, I figured that I was just something to cross off your to-do list—sleep with a guy in case his band gets famous."

"I didn't leave with Sam. I waited for you with Sam. And I didn't know about the band."

"I spoke to Carissa, Sara. I know she told you about me."

"Yeah. Yesterday. Right after she made me think you were a serial killer. She thought it was hysterical."

He paused to study my face, maybe judging my expression. I hoped he could recognize honesty because that's all that would be there. Along with a little bit of hurt, I guess.

"You really didn't know about me or the band before yesterday."

"I really didn't. And honestly, I don't understand why you think it would be a big deal to me."

"Because it's a big deal to everyone else. Big enough to make me shamefully paranoid that every woman I meet cares more about the band than about me. Then, when I finally meet someone I think I really like that paranoia makes me believe things that aren't true and act like an asshole."

"Not sure if this will make you feel better or not, but it definitely should prove I didn't know who you were." I couldn't believe I was about to tell him this. "Until I looked at the card with your name on it that morning...I wasn't even sure if your name was Declan or Dylan." I pretended not to notice how huge his eyes got, but inside, the humiliation was complete. "That karaoke bar was really loud and, once we left...I was too embarrassed to ask."

"Seriously, Sara?" He ducked his head down and laughed.

"Yes, *Dylan*, seriously."

That only made him laugh harder. "You were right—that definitely proves it."

"The reason I went home with you was because you're insanely hot and have a fantastically honest-looking smile. And there aren't enough of those in the world."

He looked at me and proved my point. "Then why'd you run away so fast?"

"You wouldn't understand if I told you."

"I hate that answer. You won't give me a chance because I don't understand, but there's no way I *could* understand because you're not giving me a chance. So, who *do* you let in, Sara? Carissa? Assholes like Cal?"

"Are you kidding? Carissa thinks I'm insane for not having already tattooed a flag with my name on it across your chest to claim you. And Cal?" Even his name left a bad taste in my mouth. "Cal has never understood a single thing about me."

"Can I at least know what the deal is with you two?" He caught my arm before I could get away, but his grip was light, as if he knew that being trapped was how I'd felt with Cal. "Is it his fault? Is he the one who fucked you over?"

"I don't want to talk about him."

"Then what do you want to talk about?"

I shrugged. "Nothing."

"Yes, you do," he said, "or you wouldn't have come here tonight. One conversation. Sitting down in a quiet, public place. No fucking around. Just talking. Honestly. No judgment, no hiding, no shame."

"You mean, tell each other our deepest, darkest secrets?"

He nodded slowly. "If you want, we can even do each other's

nails and talk about who we're crushing on. But spoiler—I'm probably going to say you."

I would definitely say him. "Sounds like a blast, but I don't think so."

"Come on, Sara. Don't you want to get out all the shit you're pretending not to feel? If we both confess our"—he used air quotes—"'deepest, darkest secrets,' both of us have something to lose if someone blabs. Ladies first, except this time. I'll start if it'll make you more comfortable."

I looked away, not wanting him to know how tempted I was to say yes. To stop dancing around the truth and finally just admit it to someone.

"Maybe the fact that we can't affect each other's lives right now is exactly the reason we could understand each other. We barely know each other, and nobody's life will fall apart if we never see each other again, so why not at least try? What do we have to lose?"

"Why do you want to know me so badly?"

"Because I'm ninety-nine percent sure we're both trying to hide in plain sight. So, we might be able to understand each other better than someone else ever could."

"What do you mean—hiding in plain sight?"

"My guess is that you stick to one-night-onlys because you don't care enough to have to pretend to be someone else. I think you're afraid of giving me a chance because if I get to know you, you'll have to start being that other person with me, too. So you stick to strangers because it's the only time you don't have to convince anyone that you're the person they think you are."

He took a deep breath before continuing. "And even though our reasons aren't the same, I feel exactly the same way. All I do is pretend. I work my ass off to convince other people that I'm someone I'm not, someone happy, someone who's in control, someone who's not scared shitless that he'll spend the rest of his life pretending to be who everyone needs him to be."

He was right—he felt exactly the same way I did. He was just better at it, I guess.

"I don't have anyone to talk to, Sara. If I came clean, the lives of everyone around me would change. And that's a shitload of pressure I don't want."

"One conversation." My voice was small, scared.

"I'll take it." He took my hand and started walking.

"Where are we going?"

"Far enough away that we can talk without being interrupted."

19
_____

SARA

*T*he quiet, public place we went to talk turned out to be a complete dive that had probably never seen anyone under fifty...who'd taken a shower in the last two weeks.

"Think we'll see any of your friends in here?" Declan asked, holding the door open for me.

"Doubt it." When it came to men, Carissa's standards were pretty low, but her credit card maximum expectations were high. "You?"

"Nah. The place is too clean for my boys."

I groaned. "I just kissed one of your boys' cheeks, so I hope you're kidding."

At least the pub was quieter and the floor less sticky than the club we'd just left. Most of the patrons sat on stools around the bar. They all must have felt the sweep of colder air from outside at the exact same moment. Everyone turned to look at us in unison as if all of their necks were on the same track. Twenty seconds later, they all turned back to their drinks.

No one spoke and, aside from the twenty seconds of interest they showed Declan and me, no one looked at anybody else. Maybe they were too busy staring into their drinks, almost all of which were pint glasses of beer at varying degrees of empty. Or full, I guess.

"Go get us a table before they're all gone," Declan joked, nudging me forward with the hand on my lower back. It had felt so normal I hadn't noticed it was there until it wasn't. Shit. Everything about Declan confused me. Over the past year, I'd been hyperaware of every touch instigated by a man, accidental or deliberate. But somehow, my subconscious knew Declan could be trusted.

A small group of men were playing pool in the back of the bar, near a dark hallway only slightly lit by the restroom sign hanging from the ceiling above it. These guys were nothing like those of my generation who yelled and danced around as if they'd just hit the final home run in the World Series versus managing to sink a two-inch ball into a pocket.

These men were serious players with serious drinking problems who probably didn't have much to celebrate. And now they were all staring at me. There was nothing that could stop a girl from needing to pee faster than the realization a trip to the bathroom would entail going into a dark hallway, right after walking past a group of depressed-looking, middle-aged alcoholics.

I glanced toward the bar, trying to decide how long it would take Declan to run back after I yelled, "Help."

Declan ordered drinks while I grabbed a booth. I slid into one side and used an old napkin to wipe away the condensation circles left by whomever had been here last. Tons of empty tables, and someone else had chosen the same spot I did. I wonder if they were this uncomfortable, too.

As soon as Declan turned around, a bottle in each hand and a grin on his face, my shoulders came down. How could someone who looked so much like a stereotypical bad boy onstage make me feel so safe? More often than not, men who looked that good were jerks because they could get away with it.

And I doubt musicians even had to look that good to get away with being assholes. Declan was both damn good-looking *and* a musician, but I'd never seen kinder eyes or understated confidence.

"Good choice," he said, motioning to the booth. He set one of the bottles down in front of me and slid into the other bench seat. "I wasn't sure you were a beer drinker, but it was the safest way to go. If you'd seen the glasses anything else would've come in, you'd be kissing me for getting you beer in a bottle."

I climbed onto my knees and leaned over the table to give him the kiss he'd mentioned, melting into him despite the atmosphere and the sounds around us. Every time we kissed, things got explosive really quickly, and neither of us could keep our hands to ourselves.

But not this time. At some point, we'd silently agreed he was in control tonight. He gently pushed me away, the look on his face still screaming for more.

"You promised me a conversation, and you're not allowed to kiss your way out of it." He paused, his gaze dropping from my eyes to my mouth. "You have the most amazing lips, did you know that? I'm pretty partial to your tongue, too." He blinked. "Damn. I haven't been this distracted by a woman since I was fifteen."

"Who was she?" No one in the place could've missed my full-body cringe. Why the hell did I ask that? As if I could be jealous of someone he'd known almost a decade ago. "Can we pretend I didn't say that?"

"Are you wondering if I have a type?" He smiled. "I can honestly say that you have next to nothing in common with her, or any woman I've dated. That's a good thing, by the way."

"Man, did you blow that one," I teased. "Now you *have* to tell me about her, so I know what you don't think I'm like."

"In the spirit of open and honest conversation—"

"Wait, let me guess. She was the head cheerleader." I raised my hand to stop him. "No, she was the mother of one of your friends. Am I close?"

"To explaining the plot to every teenage movie from the 80s?" He shook his head and took a sip of his beer. "You forgot the tomboyish best friend who's been right in front of him the whole time but still invisible. Then there's the science experiment that gets out of hand, or the love potion gone wrong."

"Darn it! How could I have forgotten the best one?" I dropped the volume of my voice as soon as I realized everyone had heard me. "I *loved* the tomboy best friend. In fact, I *was* the tomboy best friend."

"No way." He grimaced. "That can't possibly be true."

"What?" I asked, mildly offended. "There's nothing wrong with being a tomboy."

"I completely agree. But the premise of those films is that the guy knows how great his best friend is, but it takes the whole movie for him to see how incredible inside *and* out. And I have a hard time believing anyone who's ever known you could miss that for more than a day. Two max."

"Nobody wanted me back then. I was a late bloomer." I took a sip of my beer, hoping it would cool the blush off my cheeks. "But enough about me."

"I can't imagine ever getting enough of you."

"Stop doing that!"

"What?" he asked innocently.

"Being...so nice."

"Huh." He cocked his head to the side. "I guess you really *were* the best friend. Because if you'd always been the way you are now, you'd be better at taking a compliment."

"Thank you," I muttered. "Now you have to tell me about this woman you found so distracting. She wasn't a cheerleader or your best friend, so she was...?"

"Señora Martinez, obviously."

"Your teacher! Of course. Damn, I wasn't even close."

"I'm a sucker for the traditional clichés, I guess. Fifteen-year-old guy enamored with his thirty-something-year-old teacher who was very cute, very married, and very not interested in him in the slightest."

"Poor Declan," I teased. "How long did it take to get over the rejection?"

"I'm not sure I'll ever get over it." His dimples became deeper as he fought to hold in his smile. "I had to take Spanish II a second time...in summer school. I gave up an entire summer vacation for that woman, and I *still* barely passed. I was too busy imagining her talking dirty to me in Spanish to pay attention. I don't think I—"

"*Dices algo provocativo para me, mi estudiante caliente.*"

He groaned. "If we can get through an honest conversation without either of us walking out, I would love to play teacher with you sometime. If you're interested."

Very. But... "*Un paso a la vez.*"

"You're right—one step at a time. So, let's start stepping." He nodded and took a drink. "Okay, completely honest conversation." He sat up straighter. "I said I would start, didn't I? Unfortunately, I can't think of a single thing that's ever been wrong in my life. Other than my failed relationship with Señora Martinez, of course." He laughed. "Okay. Here goes."

I loved the length of his pause. It let me know that this wasn't something easy for him either. It also showed me how much he was willing to go through to hear what I would say. *If* I could say it.

"I've never told anyone this because...I don't know if I've ever had anyone to tell. Anyone I *could* tell without creating bad feelings or messing up someone else's life. So...um..." He set the bottle onto the table and leaned in. "The band. Self Defense has ruined every relationship I've ever had—my father, Trevor, every woman I've liked. I lied to you about it because I didn't want it to ruin the one I hoped we could have. Sorry. I know you don't want to hear me say stuff like that, but—"

"It doesn't matter." I motioned for him to continue, not wanting him to censor himself. That was what the point of this was, right? "Keep going."

He nodded. "I *hate* it. Every time a music producer or promoter comes to see a show, I pray they stop us in the middle of a song and tell us we should give up right now because we'll never go anywhere. Or that the crowd will turn on us, and we'll have to run away from a screaming mob."

"Why don't you just stop doing it, then?"

"Because this is what the guys have always dreamed of, and I don't want to be the reason their dream dies. Our piece-of-shit manager took us on because of me and made it clear that, if I ever quit he'll drop Self Defense, and they'd never stand a chance of getting a contract without me."

"How does he know? Maybe he's wrong."

"Fuck." He looked up at the ceiling for a moment. "I would love to see them prove that asshole wrong. To be clear—it isn't *me* specifically. They could do it with *any* jackass up front. I'm just not sure any other jackass would be able to keep them from self-destructing."

"What do you mean, self-destruct?"

"It's happened before. When we were just starting out, we landed another manager, a bigger one actually. He found a great label that wanted to sign us. Except it turned out the label only wanted to sign *me*. They wanted to take me out of Self Defense and shove me and my songs into one of their other bands who'd just lost their lead singer. When I said no, the contract, the label, and the manager all disappeared. And Trevor, he..."

He wiped a hand over his mouth and stared at the table for a minute. I didn't know what he was thinking, but it obviously wasn't a good memory. Just as I was trying to come up with something to say to distract him, pull him out of wherever he was, he sighed and looked up at me.

"Trevor had a hard time dealing with it," he said finally. "Then about six months ago, I talked a new manager into taking all of us...on one condition."

"That you didn't quit."

He nodded. "That I didn't quit. Unfortunately, he never gets tired of telling me how easy it would be to get me a solo contract, no matter how many times I've said no."

"You said no," I muttered without thinking. Or maybe I was thinking too much, but not about him or his manager.

"I said no," he said, thankfully not knowing what was happening inside my mind, "multiple times."

Three ordinary words, and the fear of having to share my secret had tossed me right back into that moment. I winced at the pain just the memory caused me. The memory and everything that had happened afterwards.

"Sara? Is everything okay?"

"Huh? Oh yeah." I hadn't planned on taking such a long swig of my beer, but I needed a chance to recover. "So...um...what does the rest of the band think?"

He studied me for a minute, unsure he should continue after my silent freak-out probably.

"The other guys..." I prompted. "What's their take on all of it?"

"I can't tell them. What could they do about it besides be hurt?"

"Even if you're miserable? That's not fair. And don't you dare say 'Life's not fair.'"

"I hadn't planned on it," he said, shrugging. "Yeah, it's not fair, but it's still life. A life my best friend has been dreaming about since we were in sixth grade. At first, I did it because it was fun. Then I did it because girls liked the bad boy musician thing."

I laughed. "That's true. We do like the bad boy thing, and you're really good at it onstage."

He wiped his hands over his face. "It was fun at first, and I never imagined we'd stay together past sophomore year. Then shit started snowballing, and I got caught in the middle of it. Now, I can't leave without hurting the one guy who's more like a brother than a friend. At least not until I know he and the other guys will be okay.

"And unfortunately, things keep getting derailed before that happens. So, whenever we have a show or do an interview, I can't stop feeling like I'm in a cage. Even sometimes when we're just sitting around playing guitar. That's what sucks the most, you know? I used to fucking love hanging out with Trevor and playing him something new I came up with. Now, I kind of dread it."

He paused, taking another swig of his beer. "This must be how Catholics feel after confession. I actually feel really great, lighter or something. You should try it sometime. Like, say, *now*." He smiled.

"It's my turn already?"

"If you're ready to talk, I'm ready to listen."

I stared at him, knowing I should speak. I owed him, and I'd said I would. Plus, I wanted to tell someone. No, not someone. *Him*. I wanted to tell Declan because I knew he would believe me. So, why couldn't I get my mouth to work?

He waited patiently. Gave me a little time and space by leaning back against the bench seat. He was on his third lift-sip-and-glance by the time I was ready.

"When...um...When someone you love tells you that something bad happened to her, you should believe her." I wasn't exactly sure how much I'd end up saying but, for only the second time, I let the words come in whatever order they wanted to. "You shouldn't tell her to stop being dramatic or lying. And you shouldn't pretend she never said anything just because you like your life the way it is, and you know that if you *did* believe her, everything would change. And whatever you do, please, please, please"—I looked up at the ceiling to make sure no tears would fall—"don't force her to sit across from the person who—"

That was the moment the words ran out. Right before the one I was still too afraid to say, even to myself. But I'd already said more than I'd thought I would be able to. Even though I hadn't really said anything at all.

My eyes never lifting, I apologized.

"Come here." He scooted farther into the bench, patting the spot next to him.

I hesitated until I realized how much I wanted to be close to him. I trusted him not to hurt me. And when he touched me, it didn't sting, it didn't feel like a punishment. I didn't cry and close my eyes and beg him to stop.

He didn't try to touch me or say anything inadequate. Somehow, he knew I wasn't ready yet. And that I'd tell him when I was.

"You were the first," I said quietly.

"The first what?"

"The first guy I'd been with in the last year who didn't make me feel used." I hadn't cried at all on my way home from Declan's place, not one single tear. Of course, now was a totally different story, but my tears weren't his fault. "I didn't realize it until I got home, but..." I shrugged, unable to keep talking, not knowing what he was thinking or how pathetic I looked. I laughed nervously. "I promised you a conversation, and I don't think I've said a complete sentence yet."

"That one was," he said, his smile reassuring. "I think you were doing pretty good before that one, too."

"You were honest with me, and I want to be honest with you, but I can't seem to..." I'd said it out loud once, to my mother, and maybe my words had been broken, but all the important ones had been there. Unfortunately, none of them had meant enough for her to care.

"Do you want to get out of here?" he said after another minute of my awkward silence. "We don't have to go back to my place. Maybe we just walk around for a while."

"That sounds good."

"But just to warn you, I may try to hold your hand." He scooted out of the booth after me. "And at some point, I might want to put my arm around your shoulder. But in a badass way."

"That sounds good, too."

He held out his hand as soon as he stood. "Don't get any weird ideas about what this means, though."

I slipped my fingers through his gratefully and let him lead me outside. "I wasn't going to, but now that you said that..."

20

SARA

*N*ormally, I never had a problem wearing heels, but we'd walked for so long my feet gave up before the rest of me was ready to.

"Damn," he said, pretending he had to bend over just to keep hold of my hand once my heels were off and I carried them. "I forgot how short you are."

"Is memory loss a side effect of being abnormally tall? Not getting enough blood all the way up to your brain or something?"

He laughed. "Not that I know of. I think it's more of an issue for those of us with big cocks."

I groaned. "Not enough blood to go around, right?" I swung my shoes at him, smacking him in the belly.

"Ouch. You're strong for a tiny, little person."

"Knock it off before I remember what very sensitive area of your body someone as short and strong as I am happens to be closest to."

His eyes widened at my threat. "Teasing over. Promise. But you shouldn't walk barefoot around here."

Before I had a chance to react, he slid his arm under my butt and scooped me up into his arms.

"Is this so I don't step on glass or just an excuse to kiss me?" From this position, all either of us had to do was lean in an inch or two.

He scoffed. "Actually, it was to impress you with how strong and manly I am. But I suppose you could show me how impressed you are by kissing me...if you really want to." He bounced me a little higher so he could adjust his grip. "On second thought, keep your lips to yourself. We're supposed to talk, not kiss."

"Good, because I wasn't that impressed with your strength or manliness, anyway," I lied.

"You're incredibly heavy for a short person, too," he joked. "Wrap your legs around me to help out."

After a quick check to make sure my skirt was covering my ass, I did as he asked.

As soon as my legs were wrapped around his waist, his laugh cut off, and he swallowed.

"This was a bad idea."

"Why?" Knowing exactly why, I squeezed my legs until he groaned, feeling his growing erection press against my core. The temperature suddenly rising everywhere our bodies touched.

"Stop it." His gaze darted between my eyes and my lips as our hips ground together the tiniest bit.

"You put me here."

"Yeah, and then immediately admitted it was a bad idea." He shifted my weight to have a hand free to brush the hair out of my eyes. "So, would you rather I give you a proper piggyback ride or carry you over my shoulder? Or get a cab to take you home before you make me lose all semblance of control?"

"Or...we could get a cab to take both of us to your house so we can lose all semblance of control together."

"Or that." He groaned again, his eyes slid shut, and his grip tightened. "But...are you sure? We don't have to. Don't get me wrong, I definitely want to, but only if you're absolutely sure. Because nothing's changed. I can't take the deal—sex without caring. Not with you."

I shut him up with a kiss. It wasn't soft or hesitant. Nope, as soon as my lips landed on his, I silently begged him to let me in. After a moment of doubt, he gave in, kissing me back with a force that matched mine.

I open my mouth for his tongue, knowing it was wrong. Knowing but not caring enough to stop. My shoes clunked onto the ground behind him. I needed my hands to feel his hair between my fingers and holding him tighter.

Kneading my ass, he pulled me closer every time his hips rocked into mine, and staggered around the closest building. I grunted when my back hit something hard and smooth—the glass window of a shop, maybe? Didn't know. Didn't care. Not even if a crowd of people were gathering inside to stare at my ass.

Declan held himself away enough to slide his hand up under my shirt, his strong, talented fingers pushing the fabric of my bra down for better access. He cupped my breast in his palm and swiped his thumb across my nipple.

"You're fucking perfect," he mumbled into my neck, between kisses and drags of his tongue and teeth.

The heat between my legs was almost unbearable. I needed more, needed him to relieve the burn. As if he'd read my mind, his hips grew more insistent, pushing his erection against me, spreading my legs apart until I couldn't keep my legs wrapped around him.

"Declan," I moaned. I'd never wanted to be part of someone this much, to have them be part of me.

He'd already become so much more than just a great lay. I

liked him too much, wanted him too much. I didn't know what we were doing or where it would go. All I knew was that I wanted more. I tried not to think about the fact that I didn't know *how* to be more to someone.

"Sara," he said breathlessly. "This is—"

I kissed him again, not wanting to hear him tell me this was wrong or a mistake. Eventually, we'd have to decide what it was, but all I wanted to think about now was how right he felt. Maybe that's why I blurted out the question that wouldn't stop swirling in my mind.

"Have you ever made love to anyone before?" Ugh. As soon as the words left my mouth, I regretted them. No matter how much I wanted to know his answer, how much I wanted him to have been thinking something similar, I shouldn't have said the words.

He didn't even flinch, or ask for clarification, or look horrified as he set me down. "I'm not sure." His kiss was light, a reminder of how gentle he could be. "Is *making love* the slow, gentle, deep kind with lots of kissing and moaning and long strokes? When you know without words that there's no one else the other person has wanted to be with more than you? Or that the physical connection isn't nearly as powerful as the emotional one?"

I nodded without breathing, afraid everything I felt was just a trick of the mind. A cruel lie my heart was leading me toward. "Have you ever done that before?"

"Well, I've done slow and deep. I think that's the *making* part of it." A smile barely touched his lips.

"Have you ever done the other parts?" I wasn't even sure what I wished his response would be. That he'd never felt like this either, or that he *had* and could tell me it wasn't as terrifying as it seemed.

"No," he said after a moment, his eyes never leaving mine. "What about you?"

"I don't..." I shook my head. "I don't think I'm ready for that."

"But you could be? With the right person and the right timing."

I wouldn't have thought so, but... "Yeah. I think so."

"Good to know." He kissed me again, a little longer than before. "Definitely good to know."

"But..." I ran my lips between my teeth. "For now, I think I need someone to practice with."

He cocked a brow. "I've been looking for a good opportunity to volunteer somewhere. This one might work."

I sighed when I felt the warmth of his breath on my neck, then again when his mouth touched my skin.

"It's going to be hard."

"Believe me, I already am," he said, chuckling.

After unsuccessfully trying to push him away, I left my hands on his abs, closing my eyes as my fingertips traced each muscle. "I meant difficult."

"Only if you keep me waiting much longer."

I couldn't stop myself from smiling. "It'll take a lot more patience than that, Declan."

"Will I be inside you when this patience is required?"

"Partially." I tilted my head to give him more room as he reached a spot just under my ear. "The patience will be required, not you. You're required to be all the way inside."

He let out a heavy breath when my hand ran the length of his erection. The rough fabric of his jeans kept me from stroking him the way we both needed me to.

"Jesus, woman. You're killing me."

"I want you inside me, Declan," I moaned in his ear. "Now."

He looked around us, cursing under his breath before dragging me into the late-night coffee shop across the street.

He set me down long enough to take ten bucks out of his pocket and drop it onto the counter. "We'll have two cups of coffee and the keys to the bathroom."

"Oh, my God." I ducked my face into his side and laughed.

The cashier must have given him a look or said something I didn't hear, so Declan reached back into his pocket for more cash.

"I better not have to clean up after you," the cashier said.

"Gross. You won't—I give you my word." After picking up the key and then me, Declan headed to the back of the practically empty café, not stopping until we were inside the bathroom.

As soon as the door was closed, he pressed my back against it and took my mouth before I could finish gasping. His hands were up my skirt, in my panties, and at my core three seconds later. I tore at his belt and pants, impatience making my movements clumsy

"Here." He reached into his back pocket with the hand that wasn't caressing me and shoved his wallet at me. "Condom. Get it out. Fast. I can't do it with one hand, and I really need to be inside you now."

I pulled the condom out just as he made my whole body arch and my hand lose grip of his wallet. "I'm sor—"

"Don't care. I'm losing my mind here, Sara. Hurry the fuck up."

The second I'd slid the condom onto his cock, he picked me up. He was already pressing against me when both of us realized I still had my panties on.

"Sorry."

"For what?" I hadn't finished speaking when he yanked the stretchy fabric to the side so hard it ripped. "Oww!"

"You okay?" He pulled back to look at me, his eyes a mixture of outright need and concern.

"You're forgiven." I watched his concern slip away, leaving

only lust. "Or you will be, just as soon as you— Oh shit!" I would give up every pair of underwear I had to feel him slide into me like that.

I leaned back and rested my head against the door. My back scraped the wood every time he thrust into me, but I couldn't ask him to stop.

Wrapped around his waist, my legs fought to pull him deeper inside, even knowing it was impossible to be any closer than we already were. When I felt the intensity build, I clutched his shoulders and neck tighter.

"Fuck," he groaned, his lips at the base of my throat. "I don't even think this is *making*. I can't do slow making right now, Sara. I'm sorry."

Sorry? He was sorry for making me forget where we were or that anything else existed?

"Declan? Shut up and fuck me. We can practice making later."

"God, I think I love you." He jerked his head back to look at me. "I..."

The expression on the poor guy's face cracked me up. Attempting to wipe his shock and horrified look away, I put my hand across his open lips.

"Fuck me. Now."

He nodded quickly and flicked his tongue at two of my fingers when they dipped inside his mouth.

"Then, afterwards, we can do the awkward discussion about saying things you don't mean during sex. Okay?"

"Um..."

"Make me come, Declan. That's all you need to think about right now."

"You're amazing." He smiled. "And I'm not just saying that."

"I think you have something you need to do now," I said sternly. "So, shut up and do it."

"Yes, ma'am," he said, laughing.

It didn't take me long—the man had perfect rhythm and his hands were practically magical.

In the middle of one of the best orgasms of my life, my mind momentarily flashed to the barista who could probably hear me screaming. The thought wasn't enough to diminish any of the pleasure rippling through my body, though. I doubt anything could've.

But as I melted, collapsing in Declan's arms, I did decide to leave some more money in the tip jar on the way out.

21

SARA

*E*ventually, we made it back to his house and talked until the sky started to lighten up outside. Declan told me about his bandmates and what being on tour was like, but he listened more than he spoke. He nodded along as I complained about school and how I didn't know what I was going to do after graduation. He laughed as I recounted stupid stories about my parents and growing up in the city. And when I finally shut up and yawned, he pulled the covers up to my chin and made sure I was tucked in properly before starting to hum something.

With my head on his shoulder and his lips on my forehead, I closed my eyes, the vibration of his voice lulling me to sleep.

I woke up wrapped in his arms, his breath warming my neck. I needed to pee but didn't want to move. When the horror of peeing in his bed became a distinct possibility, I hurriedly tiptoed into his bathroom, hoping I could sneak back into bed before he woke up.

Once I was done, had washed my hands, and splashed some water on my face, I opened the door to one of the world's most beautiful sights. Declan was standing right there, in the middle of a full-body, heart-stopping stretch.

"Good morning, stranger." Before I could respond, he grabbed me around the waist, dragged me against his naked body, and kissed me. A couple of minutes later, he pulled back and grimaced. "That's some morning breath you've got there, babe."

I smacked him. "You're not supposed to say that!"

"I didn't say it was bad—just that it was morning. But don't worry, I'm man enough to handle it."

"Gee, thanks." When he leaned down to kiss me again, I pushed him away, keeping my face tucked down so he wouldn't be subjected to my breath again.

"I told you I'm man enough to handle it. But I guess you're not." After blowing into his hand to check his own breath, he went to the bathroom vanity, opening the mirrored cabinet. Then he paused. "Promise not to get weird about this."

"About my awful breath?"

"I said morning, not awful." He shook his head and pulled out a new toothbrush. "Red's your favorite color, right?"

How did he—?

"That wasn't me being creepy, by the way." He must have been responding to my expression. "You mentioned it the night we met."

"You remembered an off-hand comment I made about my favorite color?"

"And you didn't remember my name, yeah." At least *he* could laugh about it.

"Gee, thanks a lot, *Dylan*." I yanked the toothbrush away from him. "Did you really buy this for me?"

He shrugged, his cheeks almost the same color as the tooth-brush. "The day after you forgot my name. Yeah. Wishful think-ing, I guess." He closed the cabinet and leaned against the counter. "You could take it home if you want—think of me whenever you put it in your mouth."

I would've caught the innuendo even if he hadn't added the not-at-all-subtle bounce of his eyebrows.

"*Or*...I could leave it here for the next girl you bring home."

"Gross, no. It'd have been in your mouth."

"My entire body has been in your mouth."

"Mmm...yeah." He smiled and smacked his lips together, reaching for me. "And yet, I'm still hungry."

I pushed him away and ripped open the toothbrush packaging. "Down, boy."

"Oh shit." He stood up straight, his eyes wide. "I can't believe I forgot about her. She's going to kill me."

She?

"Hurry up." He brushed past me and threw on some jeans and a T-shirt. "We gotta go do something."

With a mouth full of paste, I mumbled, "Where are we going?" But he was already gone. So, I finished brushing and got dressed as fast as I could. He whizzed past me again to brush his own teeth. As soon as he was done, he grabbed my hand and pulled me out of the apartment. But we didn't head for the elevator—we turned left, went twenty feet down the hallway and stopped in front of the apartment next door.

He faced me and spoke seriously. "Before this goes any further, I need you to meet someone."

"Okay," I said slowly, skeptically.

"She's the most important thing in my life, and her opinion means everything."

I suddenly got nervous. It was a little early to be meeting his parents. "What if she doesn't like me?"

"She will. Unless you like cats. You don't, do you?"

"Um...they're okay."

"But you don't have one."

"Nope. I've never had a pet."

"Wow. That's the saddest thing I've ever heard. Not even when you were a kid?"

I shook my head. "My mother wouldn't allow them. She values her furniture too much. Anything that sheds or might pee on the rug isn't welcome in her home."

"Then she'd hate Trevor," he said, laughing. "At least when he's drunk."

"Actually, she loves everyone when she's drunk." Mostly. "So, who am I meeting now?"

"Kitty."

Before I could ask who Kitty was, a long-haired brunette about our age opened the door with a smile. She was pretty and really tall. Great. So this was—

"Rebecca, this is Sara, my...someone I'm not dating." Thankfully, he was looking over the woman's shoulder and didn't see the confusion all over my face. "I want to introduce her to my little girl. Where is she?"

His *what*? It sounded as if he'd said his "little girl," but that was impossible.

"Nice to meet you, Sara," Rebecca said, rolling her eyes at Declan. "Kitty got a little grumpy when I tried to move her food, so she's in timeout in my bedroom."

"Timeout?" I knew my eyes were enormous with confusion. Not mentioning he was a musician was one thing, but not mentioning that he had a kid? That was...something I'd panic over soon, but not in front of Rebecca or a kid. "How old is she?"

"We're not exactly sure," Rebecca said as we passed through her living room.

I may have complimented her on the apartment, but I wasn't sure. Everything had suddenly become foggy. I'd been in shock before, and it was never pleasant. Time moved differently, and my body struggled to stay upright. The worst part was that it also made it impossible to think clearly—thoughts zipping around by the hundreds yet none of them sticking around long enough to grasp on to.

A kid.

Declan turned to me. "I found her living on the streets in LA about two years ago, all matted and hungry. But nearest I can figure, she's about four now."

"Oh, my God, that's...horrible," I managed with a lot of effort. Every word took focus. "How could someone do that to a child?"

Both of them stared at me for a second before busting out laughing.

"Kitty isn't a kid, Sara. She's my very hairy, very opinionated Goldendoodle." He waited for me to acknowledge I knew what the fuck a Goldendoodle was. I wasn't quite there yet. "My dog. Kitty's my dog."

"Oh," I said, covering my eyes in embarrassment. Thankfully, it also gave me a chance to clear my head. I felt the adrenaline drop. "I actually know what those are."

"Are you okay?" Rebecca asked.

"Sara?" Declan grabbed a chair and slipped it behind me, easing me down into it. "Are you allergic to them?"

"I don't think so." *Recover, damn it. And do it quickly.* I pasted on a smile and looked up at their worried faces. "I've never dated anyone who had a dog."

"We're dating?" Declan smirked. "You sure about that?"

I shrugged. "Maybe we should let Kitty decide." When I moved to stand, he put his hand on my shoulder to keep me seated.

"Actually, it might be better to stay sitting down. Kitty's a lot more Golden than Doodle, and you don't weigh that much. When you add her momentum to the equation..." He grimaced. "At least you'll know she's coming and can brace yourself for the eighty-pound pounce."

I gripped the chair when Rebecca opened her bedroom door. A huge, caramel-colored beast came barreling out of the room, heading straight for me. At the last minute, she swerved toward Declan. As she said hello to her...dad, I guess, her tail hammered me in the shin.

"Calm down, girl. I want you to meet someone." He knelt on one knee and put his hand on my thigh, patting it gently. "This is Sara. She finally just admitted that we're dating." He glanced up at me, smirking.

I let Kitty sniff my hand and waited for a four-year-old shaggy dog to pass judgment. It wasn't as if I'd never touched a dog before. It was just that I'd never cared if one liked me before.

When he ruffled the hair on her head, his smile unending, it hit me—this dog was Declan's family. My desperate need of her approval meant that Declan wasn't someone I could walk away from without looking back. There was nothing casual about we were doing.

This was real.

And the scariest part was how good it felt.

22

SARA

"I knew she would like you," Declan said as he handed me Kitty's leash. "But the last test is to see if she accepts you into our pack."

"You mean I have to prove I'm worthy by going on a walk?" I took the lead warily. As soon as Kitty saw it, she went wild, running around the apartment like her tail was on fire.

"I'm more worried she'll take *you* for a walk, so you have to show her who's boss."

Great.

"Kitty," I called. She ignored me. If I couldn't even clip the leash onto her collar, I'd fail the test. I tried again. "Kitty, come *here*." For some reason I stamped my foot, as if that had actually worked for anyone.

Declan just stood there, smiling, watching me make a fool of myself.

"You're not going to help me at all, are you?"

He shook his head.

"I had no idea you had such a mean streak in you, Declan," Rebecca said, "You're doing fine, Sara. You should've seen the way Kitty blew off my fiancé when they met. She's not shy about telling someone how she really feels about them."

"Was that supposed to be encouraging?" I asked as the dog happily ignored me.

"You have to *make* her listen to you. Try it again. More firmly this time."

"Kitty," I said in the lowest pitch I could manage, willing her to listen.

Declan chuckled. Luckily, Rebecca told him to shut up so I didn't have to.

"Come here. Now, Kitty," I repeated in my phony baritone. It sounded ridiculous, even to me. But at least it got her attention. She stopped running and sat down near Rebecca.

I couldn't tell for sure, but there was a good chance Kitty was laughing at me, too. I raised an eyebrow and held the leash out to her. We stared at each other silently.

"What are you doing?" Declan asked quietly.

"Not sure. I think we're having a battle of wills."

"Ah. Who's winning?"

"Whoever blinks first. Wait. Do dogs have eyelids?"

When he and Rebecca both busted out laughing, Kitty's tail reacted, wagging so hard, her whole body swayed with it.

I swatted him. "Shut up and let me prove my dominance."

"As long as you try it with me next time we're naked."

"Wow," Rebecca mumbled. "I really wish I hadn't heard that."

I pressed my lips together so I wouldn't smile. Dominant females never smiled. Every dominant female I'd ever known had perfected their resting bitch face. And not to be arrogant or anything, mine was pretty damn good.

My eyes stung from holding them open for so long. If this dog didn't give in soon, I'd lose.

"Kitty, focus." I said it softly but firmly as if I were speaking to a toddler who didn't want to go to bed. "Do you want to go for a walk." No inflection at the end of the question because dominant females didn't ask questions. They just *knew*. "Come here, so I can put on your leash."

She hesitated for one more second and then took a step toward me. Then another. And another. I didn't react because dominant females expected results and didn't give prizes for participation. Only success.

Rebecca cheered silently, shaking her hands as if she were holding pompoms.

"I think you're winning," Declan whispered.

"Shut up, or I'll put you on a leash, too."

His laugh was broken as he tried unsuccessfully to hold it in.

"*Now*, Kitty." I pointed at the floor just in front of me. She glanced at Declan for permission. Before he could ruin my moment, I threw a glare at him. A very dominant glare.

Kitty trotted over to me and stood at my feet.

When I told her to sit, she did.

"Whoa. Sorry, Dec, but I think there's a new alpha in town," Rebecca said as I rubbed Kitty's head and clipped the leash onto her collar. "Congrats."

I felt like I'd just won an Olympic medal in dogging. If that was actually a thing. "So, where are we going?"

Declan shrugged. "I just got demoted. Alpha's choice."

After saying goodbye to Rebecca, I led Kitty to the elevator. Declan followed.

"Press the button, underling."

"Underling?" He gave me a quick kiss before following my order. "Is that a hint that you want to be on top later?"

"It wasn't, but that's a good idea. Kitty, can I borrow your collar when we get back?"

"Don't answer that, girl," he said as we stepped into the elevator. "I should've known you two would gang up on me."

"Yeah, you really should have."

As soon as we reached the street, Kitty lunged forward, practically yanking my arm out of its socket. I used my entire body weight to hold her back until she gave in and walked at my side.

"Why'd you name her Kitty?"

"I didn't," Declan said. "When I found her, she wasn't wearing a collar. I was living with Trevor at the time, and he didn't want to keep her. So, I spent three weeks posting flyers and calling animal control and shelters to see if anyone was looking for her. I didn't want to take her into one of them, though. She was pretty rough looking back then—super skinny with bald patches where the vet had to shave when he fixed her up. I knew that unless someone could see what I saw in her, she wouldn't have been adopted. I couldn't take the chance they'd put her down. So, when I finally talked Trev into keeping her, I told him he could pick her name."

"Trevor picked Kitty?"

He shook his head. "Have you ever seen the old *Annie* movie? The one where she calls the dog a bunch of names, and he eventually answers to Sandy?"

"You've seen *Annie*?"

"Hey, I thought we said no judgments."

"That was before you admitted to being a little girl."

He elbowed me gently. "Have you seen the movie or not?"

"Probably, when *I* was a little girl, too." I laughed.

"Trust me, I'll remember that later when we're in a place where I can punish you."

"Hey!" I jumped when he swatted my ass. "Alright, alright. Continue with your story."

After a moment, he said, "So, just like in the movie I enjoyed so much *as a little girl*, Trev started saying names. Fluffy, Killer, Fido, etc."

"And she answered to Kitty?"

He nodded. "My guess is that she could bare to listen to any more terrible options. But Kitty fits her—she's independent, smart, sleeps a lot, and thinks she's small enough to sit in my lap." He stopped and looked at me. "Maybe I should start calling you Kitten— you're all those things and *are* small enough to sit in my lap."

"You want to give me a pet name that is literally your pet's name. I don't think so."

My teasing stopped when I saw my mom coming out of the tiny market across the street. I ducked my head, but it was too late.

"Sara!" she called, raising her hand before realizing it was holding a small paper bag and then lifting the other one to wave.

Oh shit. Why was she here? This neighborhood was halfway across the city from hers. The market's sign and window ads were all in Chinese, and my mom never cooked *anything*, let alone Chinese food.

"Sara!" She quickly glanced both ways before crossing the street. I was almost a mean enough person to wish she'd get hit by a car. Almost. But if she, say...got a little bumped—just a very distracting scare, nothing broken or damaged—I'd have been okay with that.

"I think that lady knows you," Declan said as she dodged a car.

"Not very well." I looked up to see her standing in front of us, glancing from me, to Declan, to Kitty. A triangle of confusion.

"What a nice surprise," she said, smiling. "I was just telling Timothy that I barely see you anymore." As if that were a bad thing. I wasn't proud of moving back in with my parents, but this was downright humiliating.

"What are you doing here?" I asked. "How do you even know this neighborhood exists?"

"A yoga friend told me about it." She held up her bag. "That shop is the only place in the whole city that carries this particular brand of Royal Jelly."

I grimaced. "The stuff that comes out of bee butts?"

"*Queen* bees, Sara. Royal Jelly only comes out of—" She glanced at Declan. "It's only *secreted* by the queen." She reached her hand out, palm-side down, to Declan. Oh God. Did she expect him to kiss her ring? "I'm Elaine, Sara's mother. And you are...?"

"Wow, it's so nice to meet you." Declan glanced at me before gently taking her hand, looking as if he were about to laugh. "I'm Declan, Sara's friend." Thankfully, he didn't pause before *friend*. Even more thankfully, he hadn't used a word like *date* or *lover*.

"Okay. Great to see you, Mom," I mumbled. "Enjoy your Queen Bee butt stuff. We need to go."

"Go where?" she asked pointedly. "In this neighborhood? Nonsense. You're not allowed to run off before I've gotten to know Declan a little."

I scrambled for an excuse. Kitty—God bless her—chose that moment to get pushy and yank at her leash. "Kitty needs to... relieve herself. So, we should get going."

My mom looked disdainfully down at the dog. "Oh. Well, Declan, you should come over for dinner sometime."

"I'd enjoy that. Thank you."

"How about tonight?" she suggested before I could set a date three years from now.

I cringed. "Declan's busy tonight. He's very busy. Always."

"Oh? What do you do, Declan?"

Dying. I was dying inside. And I had to stop this in the only way I knew how. By making her disapprove. There was no shame in what he did, but I knew my mother's interest would evaporate as soon as she knew he wasn't a banker, a lawyer, or a real estate investor.

"Declan is in a band." I couldn't look at him, didn't want him to think I didn't respect what he did.

My mom hesitated. "How nice for you. Following your dream, I imagine?"

"I suppose so." The disappointment in his tone trumped my mom's, and I felt awful.

"Well, if you're not busy with *band things* on Sunday, you should come over for dinner."

My groan was silenced by his reply.

"That's really nice of you. Luckily, Sundays are pretty slow when it comes to *band things*. What time should I come over?"

This time, my groan was audible to everyone.

My mom laughed. "Sara's being selfish, wanting to keep you all to herself. How does seven o'clock sound?"

"Seven would be great," Declan said.

Sure, seven o'clock sounded doable. All I had to do was make sure I got hit by a bus by 6:45. "Okay...I guess."

"Wonderful!" She awkwardly reached out as if to pat Kitty on the head. About a foot before her hand would've made contact, she changed her mind and pulled back. "Until Sunday, then. Sara, make sure he has the correct address." Damn it, there went that plan.

"I will." I smiled tightly and said a quick goodbye before prodding Kitty to start walking. Declan said goodbye more politely and caught up to us.

His hand grazed mine until I pulled it away. "Not where she might see."

"Do I embarrass you?"

"Not at all." I looked behind us to make sure she wasn't

watching. "*She* embarrasses me. I was trying to save you the horror of spending an hour in her company."

"I have a lot of experience with parents who think what I do is a disgrace, mainly my parents. So, I think I can handle one more."

Two more—my stepdad would probably be there, too.

23

DECLAN

*W*hen we got to the dog park, Sara let Kitty off her leash.

"Go play, girl." I waved to a few other people in the park who were all standing around, watching the group of dogs Kitty bolted toward.

We found an empty bench and sat down. Not a cloud in the sky, the air scented of freshly mowed grass, and a light breeze taking the edge off the sometimes brutal California heat. I could get used to this.

"I think my dog likes you almost as much as I do."

Sara didn't even react, obviously lost in whatever she'd been thinking about since we left her mother. Meeting Elaine had definitely thrown Sara for a loop. Too much, too soon, probably. She'd had a hard enough time barely admitting that we were dating, and a half hour later, I'd promised her mom I'd come over for a family dinner. I think that pretty much defined too much, too soon. For *her*, at least. Any opportunity to get to know more about her, I'd take happily.

"I didn't mean to rush things," I said. "If you think—"

"Your parents don't like what you do?" *That's* what she'd

been thinking about?

"When my mom doesn't have a strong opinion about something, she defers to my father. Since he thinks I'm wasting my potential, so does she."

"What's your potential?"

"I'm going to pretend I'm not hurt that you haven't realized it yet."

"The potential your parents see is a lot different than the kind of potential I see in you. At least I hope it is because that would be gross." Her head was lowered as she focused on dragging her toe back and forth through the dirt, but I could tell she was smiling.

"My father wants me to follow in his footsteps, become a shrink to the elite, listen to rich people bitch about their problems all day, write a couple books, and have a big house with a kid."

"He's a shrink? Now I know why you're so good at psychoanalyzing people in alleys."

"And why I'm so screwed up." I leaned forward and rested my forearms on my thighs. "What's that expression about a cobbler's kids not having shoes?"

"You're one of the least screwed-up people I know, so he must be pretty good at his job."

"Oh, he's a really good shrink...and also a really shitty father."

"Hey! I have one of those, too," she said, feigning excitement. What a great thing to bond over. "But mine left when I was a toddler and died a few years later. From the little my mom has told me about him he could probably have used your dad's help."

"I'm sorry. Even as much of a disappointment as mine enjoys telling me I am, I still know I'm lucky to have had one around. If nothing else, it's easier to understand all the flaws a parent has when you spend a lot of time with them. When you don't, you can only guess. That must make it a lot harder."

She thought about it a second before nodding. "I've never heard it put that way, but yeah. I can tell myself a million times that it wasn't my fault he left, but I can't get rid of that little piece of doubt that's always there. I wish I could've gotten to know him well enough to be sure he left because he was a selfish asshole who would've walked out on anybody."

We fell into a comfortable silence, watching Kitty play with a dog half her size, taking turns chasing each other.

Leave it to animals who lacked the ability to speak to have figured out what humans couldn't: There doesn't always have to be a winner and a loser.

Something doesn't have to be wrong to know something else is right.

"Oh shit," she muttered.

"What?"

When she leaned over to me, I thought it was for a kiss, which I gladly gave her. Only afterwards did I realize she'd actually been pulling her cell phone out of her back pocket. Cell phones, right. There'd never been a moment those things couldn't ruin.

I watched her thumbs fly from letter to letter. Since I didn't want her to think I was reading over her shoulder, I switched my focus to her face. Sadly, that didn't help—she was mouthing each word as she texted. I didn't catch too many. Just "do it tomorrow" and "I'll make it up to you."

"Everything okay?" I asked while she stared at her phone waiting for a reply.

"My boss...friend..." She shook her head as if to straighten stuff out in it. "My friend who's also my boss. I'm trying to get all her client contracts set up right but needed her husband's advice. He's an attorney. Not a contract attorney, but he knows them well enough." Her smile grew. "*Aaaand* I'm going to stop explaining before I bore you to death. Never mind."

"Nothing about you would bore me. Although, to be honest, the word 'contract' does make me a little sleepy."

"Contracts themselves are pretty dry. But when you really study them to see what both sides are fighting for, it's fascinating."

"I'll have to take your word on that."

She nudged me, laughing. "It is. Knowing what someone is willing to give up is just as important as knowing what they want, maybe more so. Like..." She paused to look at me. "You signed a contract with your manager, right? So, getting a set percentage of whatever deal he can get you motivates him to make the best deal possible, and that benefits you and the guys, too."

"I guess so."

"But from what you've told me, he'd rather get a deal for just you, right? Not for the band. His percentage isn't affected by how many people are involved, just the amount of money he can get. And if he thinks he can get more from a solo contract than for the band, that's what he'll do."

"If you're trying to make him seem like less of an asshole, you'll have to work harder."

"Just because someone's an asshole doesn't mean they can't do simple math."

I shook my head. "Doug gives me the same number whether he's talking about the band or a solo act. And then keeps repeating that if I went out on my own, I wouldn't have to split it four ways."

"Hmm... He wouldn't fight to get you to leave the band if he weren't hoping to get something more out of it. So, there's something he's not telling you, and that something would show up on a contract."

"I've never thought of it like that before," I said, sitting up. What the fuck was that dirtbag up to?

Thankfully, when I saw her smile, I stopped thinking about Doug, promised contracts, and all the shit with the band. I couldn't believe that kind of stuff made her happy, but it obviously did.

"Not that I think it's weird or anything," I said without cracking a smile, "but where does one learn to love contracts so much?"

She swatted at me. "I don't *love* them, but they're important. Ever since I was a kid, I thought I was going to be an attorney. I used to negotiate toy exchanges or come up with shared stuffed animal custody schedules between my friends. Plus, when my mom and Timothy first got hitched, he used to spread paperwork all over the dining room. I'd have to clear off the table without messing up the piles, or he'd freak out. So, I guess, indirectly, that taught me how powerful they were."

"Do you still want to be an attorney?"

She shrugged. "I can barely deal with work and three classes. Even if law school were free, I'm not ready to think about that stuff yet."

"You know, someone once told me that the only way to turn *yet* into *never* is by giving up."

"Wow. That's deep." When her phone buzzed, she looked down at it, reading the text that had just come in. "Everything's fine." Then, with a smile, she tucked it back into her pocket. "Now, where were we?"

"I'm deep, and you were about to tell me"—I scooted a little closer to her—"who I'm going to meet on Sunday. Besides your mother, who seemed nice, by the way."

She cocked an eyebrow at me. "You're joking, right?"

I had so many questions to ask her but didn't know where to start. And how not to sound like a shrink when I did it.

"Speechless." She nodded. "Don't worry. That's exactly how I feel about her, too."

"I'm sure she's just curious about the guy her daughter's with. I'd probably worry about the same thing."

"Do you want to have kids?" The look on her face told me she regretted going there. As if asking me would make things awkward or give me the wrong impression. "I promise that wasn't a test or anything beyond a simple question."

"You mean you haven't already started wondering what kind of soccer coach I'll be? Or if I'll change dirty diapers? What kind of woman are you?" I nudged her in the side and rolled my eyes. "You don't need to worry so much about scaring me off, Sara. First of all, I worked pretty damn hard to be here. Second, I know when a question is just a question and when it's a test. Trust me, growing up with a shrink taught me how to spot when someone's grasping for subtext in every word that comes out of my mouth."

"Good," she said with relief.

"Although, just in case I'm wrong, I've changed a few dirty diapers in my day without even gagging. It helps that I live in the city and have to deal with all the fun stuff that comes with pet ownership." I shook the small container of doggie doo bags clipped onto Kitty's leash. I'm not sure which smelled worse—the crap that went inside them or the crap they scented the bags with.

"But I would make a terrible coach," I continued. "I'm not competitive enough. Plus, while I think kids' sports should definitely be just for fun, in general, I don't believe we should give trophies for participation. Honestly, I don't think trophies are necessary at all—they teach kids to look for validation and acceptance outside themselves."

"That was a super shrinky thing to say."

"Damn it. You caught me."

24

DECLAN

*W*hen Kitty started to slow down, I knew it was time to leave. So, after clipping the leash onto her collar, I slipped my arm around Sara's shoulders and walked home with a beautiful girl on either side.

Then I spent the next hour waiting impatiently in my apartment while Sara went back to her place to change her clothes. Evidently, there was a limit as to how many run-ins I was allowed to have with her mother. I didn't push it—I'd rather spend some time with her mom and stepfather over dinner than not get to know them at all during the quick run-in-run-back-out Sara was doing today.

At least I got in a decent shower while she was gone.

Plus, turned out I was a big fan of how Sara said hello—that first kiss held all kinds of promises for what we'd be doing later. We spent the rest of the day playing with Kitty and then, once Kitty decided to take a nap, Sara and I got into bed and played with each other.

Pushing her hair out of my way as I went, I traced across her shoulder with my fingertips, then down her spine. "Women are so lucky. If men had bodies like this, we'd never make it out of the house. We'd spend all day fondling ourselves."

"As if you don't already."

"Hey, that's not fair—I take breaks. Otherwise I'd never have met you and gotten to fondle your beautiful body."

"Poor Declan. He's gorgeous, and his body is all hard and muscular. I can't imagine what an awful cross to bear that is."

I laughed. "You have no idea." I grabbed her by the hip bone, curling my fingers around it and pulling her tighter to me. "You need to eat more."

"No, I don't."

"You're all bony." When I squeezed her hip bone, she giggled and tried to squirm away. But I held on. "See? Proof you need to eat more."

She turned her head to look at me. "Want me to tell you a secret?"

"Hell, yes. Especially if it involves a fantasy about licking chocolate and whipped cream off me."

"That's no secret." She laughed and moved my hand from her bony hip to the softness of her belly.

"Much better," I said, curling my hand around the feminine curve there.

"You're weird." She seemed to be in a playful mood, not a nervous or embarrassed one like she'd been during our conversation in the dive bar, but I couldn't be sure.

I'd hoped she would eventually be willing to explain what she couldn't then. So, was this it? "Are you going to tell me your secret or not?"

"Yes, but by telling you, I'm breaking an important girl rule, so if you repeat it, I'll deny it."

"I'm good at keeping secrets."

"Good. Okay, here it is: While no woman will ever admit this, ninety-nine percent of us are afraid of letting a guy touch our stomachs when we're lying on our sides."

"I don't get it. That makes no sense."

"It totally does!" She rolled onto her back. "See how nice and flat my stomach looks when I'm on my back? That's hot, right?"

"Extremely."

"Sweet, but watch what happens."

I had no idea where she was going with this but was happy to watch her do anything, especially when she was naked.

"Promise you won't laugh." She flipped onto her side again. Except this time, she faced me.

"I promise laughing is the *last* activity I hope happens next."

"Look!" She grabbed her belly and shook her hand as if there were something there to jiggle.

"Still hot. Still not laughing. And still not understanding what the big secret is."

"It's my pudge! When we lie on our sides, gravity moves whatever is normally on our hips to our bellies and makes them look all poochy."

"You're insane."

"No, I'm not. All women worry about this."

"Okay, then all women are insane. Do you actually think that crosses a man's mind when he sees a naked woman lying on her side? Or any other position?"

She shrugged with one shoulder. "Who knows what men think."

"Then I'm going to let you in on a not-so secret about men." I leaned closer and whispered, "We *don't* think. At least not while we're around women we're attracted to." I shook my head. "Actually, that's not quite true. We think about what we can do to get them naked, what it'd be like to sleep with them, and even though it's never happened to me, I've heard other men worry about how well they'd perform if they ever got the woman naked."

"You've never worried about that?" she asked, an eyebrow raised.

"Nope. You probably want to know why."

"Absolutely."

"Sorry, can't tell you. It's a secret. And like I said, I'm good at keeping secrets."

As soon as I started to laugh, she smacked me on the chest, grumbling something about putting her clothes back on to punish me. And I wasn't about to let her get away with that.

The next morning, I woke up to the best alarm clock in the world. Instead of the blaring screech of a machine, this one made low, mewing sounds, and was hot, and could take most of my cock in her mouth. I flipped the sheet off so I could watch her.

"Morning." My voice was still scratchy from sleep, but obviously, the rest of me was definitely up.

She crawled up my body, still stroking the length of my cock. I wrapped my hand around the nape of her neck and pulled her down to me, our mouths opening as soon as our lips met.

I wanted to be inside her when we came, and I was already a hell of a lot closer than she was.

"Slow down." I put my hand over hers and set a rhythm I could handle without exploding before I wanted to. Unfortunately, my hand on top of hers tightened her grip and increased the friction of every stroke. And it felt too good to tell her to stop.

With my other hand, I blindly reached over to the nightstand for a condom. As soon as I felt the rough edge of plastic, I thanked the heavens and ripped it open. Slipping the condom over my erection was a bittersweet moment—she had to let go of me before I could get it on, but the faster it was on, the sooner I'd be inside her.

She must have been thinking the same thing because before I'd rolled it down all the way, she'd thrown her leg over me and started to sink down my cock.

"Slowly," I begged, knowing she would do whatever the hell she wanted to, and all I could do was pray I didn't come too quickly.

Once she'd taken all of me in, she started moving, a small smile on her lips. I immediately focused my attention on getting her to the finish line as soon as possible, so I wouldn't spend the rest of the day feeling inadequate. But she felt so fucking good.

I held her hips, angling her so that her clit brushed against me every time she rocked forward and backward. Moaning, she spread her hands out on my chest, her fingers digging into the muscle.

Her breathing sped as she slid up and down my cock, ignoring my request that she take pity on me and go slow. I slipped my hand between us and made tiny circles with my thumb to intensify her pleasure, trying different levels of pressure until I found the one that made her lose control.

Unfortunately, the louder her moaning, the harder it was to hold myself back. Once she started cursing and tightening her muscles around my cock, I gave up on the idea of going slow. I clutched her hips and thrust upwards, pushing inside her as deeply as I could.

Her eyes popped open, and she looked down at me, begging me to continue. The pace was punishing, and there was no way I'd be able to keep it up for much longer. But I could see, hear, and feel how close she was.

"Touch yourself," I said breathlessly, wishing I had a third hand and could do it myself.

She nodded silently and brought her hand between us. Ten

seconds later, she couldn't even groan anymore. Instead, she found her full voice and used it. Each thrust pushed out a higher and louder moan.

"Oh fuck." My pleasure receptors had taken over, and I no longer had any control over my body. I was right on the edge and couldn't do a damn thing to stop it from happening.

Pressing my hips up even harder as I came, I heard Sara cry out. When her body clenched, the pressure around my cock was almost painful and moving was impossible. So, I pulled her closer and let her rock against me until she'd finished riding out her orgasm.

She unlocked her elbows and flopped down on top of me, mumbling, "Good morning," into my neck.

"Hell yeah, it is."

Twenty minutes later, she jumped out of bed, too quickly for me to drag her back in. "You're going to get me fired, Declan!"

Huh. Why had it never occurred to me that she had a normal job with normal hours? I unhappily let go of her so she could put her clothes on.

Then I sat up and asked, "You work at a personal assistant company, right?"

"It's a *virtual* assistant company, but close enough." She squished up her face. "The thing is...I did something stupid, and it could've really hurt my friend's business, so I'm in *mea culpa* mode right now. Gotta earn back her trust, which you are not helping with, by the way. She gives me a lot of latitude, and I set my own hours within reason, but I've been pushing it big time since you started annoying me."

"Can I come annoy you at work?"

She stopped and looked directly at me. "Why would you want to do that?"

"You visited me at work. I figure it's only fair."

She paused for a second, her head tilted to the side, her eyes sizing me up.

"Unless I'd embarrass you, of course."

"You're totally embarrassing, but I'm already used to that. Now, I'm just trying to picture how you'd look in a suit."

"And...?"

A smile slowly appeared on her face. "Not too shabby, Mr. Hollis."

"Fuck, that's hot. If I hire you as my assistant, will you call me Mr. Hollis from now on?"

"Sure, but we'd have to stop sleeping together, and we'd only be able to communicate via email, chat, or phone."

"World's biggest deal-breaker right there. It's fine, though—I don't need an assistant."

"What do you need?"

Even before I'd answered, her expression told me she was afraid of what I might say. I could've made a joke and let the moment pass as if it had never happened. But I didn't want this moment to pass. I wanted to use every single second we had together to remind her how right this was. Until there was no way she could pretend otherwise. I just had to find a way to do it without coming off like an obsessed psycho and scaring her away.

So what *did* I need?

Well, I could've gone with the cliché—"you"—or the predictable—"someone incredible"—or maybe the honest—"a hot-as-hell woman who terrifies me a little"—or even the respectable—"a partner." All of them were true, but none of them were quite right.

Fuck it. "I need someone who really sees me for who I am and who cares about me anyway. Who keeps me on my toes, and who isn't afraid to call me on my bullshit."

She was silent, her mouth open a little, her eyes blinking a lot.

"Do you know anybody like that, Sara?" I asked quietly, giving her time.

"You mean someone who wants the exact same things?"

"Uh..." No, that's not what I'd meant. But I could tell that's what *she* meant, what she was admitting she needed. In a way she could expose her vulnerable side without letting her walls come down even an inch.

Whoever messed her up had done a hell of an efficient job with it. If I ever found out who, I'd have to set up a solid alibi and come up with a lie Trevor could remember.

"I'm going to ask you a question right now, but I don't want to scare you off. Ready?"

She grimaced. "Not with an intro like that, I'm not."

"You can answer it, or we can pretend I never said anything. It's totally up to you."

"Okay." She extended the word and swallowed.

"Are you showing me who you really are, Sara? Or are you still afraid?"

"I'm not afraid of you," she said, laughing lightly.

"Not physically, no. But that's just because you know you could take me if you wanted to."

Her laugh grew. "How could I take you?"

"By getting that hungry look in your eyes. Or brushing just one fingertip across my skin. Do that, and four seconds later, I'm flat on my back, exposing all my important bits, incapable of defending myself from you." I showed her what I meant by lying back down, the sheet barely covering anything.

She proved it to both of us by jumping onto the bed and straddling me, then holding my hands and forcing them over my head.

"See what I mean?" Letting her hold most of me still, I lifted my head to try to reach her lips.

She shied away. "Oh man! I can't believe you're such a wuss! I'm not sure I like this submissive side of you."

"No? Well, then..." I slipped my hands out of hers, grabbed her by the waist, and spun us both until I was on top of her. "This better?"

"Much," she said, fighting my grip. Her breath was coming fast—not from exertion but excitement. So, my girl liked to play. This just kept getting better and better.

"You going to answer my question, or are we going to pretend I didn't ask?"

She stopped squirming. "Yes. I'm showing you who I really am." Her eyes softened. "And yes, I'm still afraid. Not that you're going to hurt me, but..."

I waited, relaxing my grip more so she didn't feel trapped— literally or figuratively.

"I'm afraid that once you find out who I really am, you'll be disappointed."

"Hmm..." I rolled off her so I could think with my head instead of my cock. "You shouldn't worry too much about that. Every second we spend together you somehow get better. So, I guess that makes me a little nervous, too, because it's that much harder to believe you're real."

"You mean that?"

"I'm going to pretend you didn't ask that question because it was stupid. Of course, I meant it." I grabbed her hand and pulled her out of bed. "But right now, we need to get going. I'd feel awful if I got you fired, especially since we've already determined that Mr. Hollis doesn't want to hire you."

25

SARA

"This is like the worst walk of shame ever," I said under my breath as Declan and I took the elevator up to my office. I was still wearing yesterday's clothes. But he'd wanted to watch me work so badly, and he was too damn hard to say no to.

I unlocked the door but didn't open it right away. "This is your last chance to run away. I'd hate to have to explain to Trevor that you're quitting the band because you'd found out that your true calling is doing office work."

"Trevor would understand. His favorite fantasy involves a desk, a secretary, and high heels."

"And in this fantasy, is he wearing the high heels?" I joked.

"Come on, already. Stop stalling. We have work to do!" He shoved the door open. "Wow."

"Ta da." I walked inside with my arms out. "Impressive, isn't it?"

"That someone our age runs a successful business and employs a bunch of smart people? Yeah, it's impressive."

"This is my zone. There's the employee lounge." That consisted of a coffee pot, a mini fridge, and a ton of snacks. "Through that door is Emilia's office."

That was pretty much the end of the tour, but he continued to wander around the room, running his hand over each piece of furniture as if he'd never seen anything like it before.

"That's a file cabinet. A chair. My inbox."

"You have your own inbox?" he asked, feigning excitement.

"I told you it was impressive. I even have an entire box of pens."

"This place has everything." He sat down in my chair and spun it around. "Okay, boss, what do we do first?"

"We? You mean you want to be me for the day?"

"Of course," he said, tucking a pencil behind his ear. "But no cross-dressing."

"Okay." It was hard to take this seriously, but if he really wanted to know how boring my days were, who was I not to bore him? "After you check the voice mail, you need to make coffee."

"Brilliant. I need some coffee. How strong do you make it?"

I grabbed his hand and pulled him out of my chair so I could sit down. "As strong as you want to make it. Up to you. If it's too much for me, I'll just add more creamer." I sat back in the chair and put my feet up in an open file drawer.

He stared at me for a second. I stared back.

"Wait. You mean *I'm* supposed to make it?"

I shrugged. "You wanted see what I do all day. That's pretty much all I do. Oh, we can do your nails later, too."

"Can't wait," he muttered.

I booted up my computer while he made coffee. He was watching it brew when the doorknob turned. Oh shit. Maybe I should've checked with Emilia before I brought him here. I didn't think she would be mad about it, but who knew? I'd never brought anyone to work with me before.

"Do you know anyone I can hire to murder my husband for me?" Emilia asked, searching for something in her bag as she came in. "I don't care how much it costs—the man is driving me insane."

"Em?"

She didn't hear me. "We've seen three hundred different houses—give or take a few—"

"Em?"

"And he comes up with a different reason to hate each one of them." She stopped when she finally lifted her head and saw Declan. About six inches in front of her.

"You must be Emilia. I'm Declan."

She glanced back at me, her eyes enormous. She let out a breath as the pieces started to fall together for her.

Then she sucked in another, grabbed his hand, and vomited words all over him. "You're Declan! Oh, my God. You're Declan? Sara's..."

"Yep. I'm Sara's." He shook her hand, smiling. "She just doesn't know it yet."

"I'm so happy to meet you." Without letting go of him, she pulled him into her office, probably because there were more places to sit in there.

I followed slowly, angry at myself for not preparing myself better for this situation.

"Sit down and tell me everything about yourself. Pretend Sara hasn't told me anything." She shot me a look complete with a raised eyebrow. "Because she's mean and hasn't told me anything."

I suddenly knew how Declan must have felt when he'd introduced me to Trevor. He'd dealt with it a lot better than I was.

"I think I'm supposed to get everyone coffee, though," he said as she dragged him.

"He's pretending to be me."

Emilia burst out laughing. "And he thinks that means he's supposed to get me coffee?"

"Shut up," I said. "I've gotten you coffee before."

"You're right. I didn't mean anything by it." The glint in her eye diminished the sincerity of the apology. "In fact, why don't you do it again? Get one for Declan, too."

I did, if only to escape for a minute. And because I really needed some.

"I take mine black," Declan called out helpfully.

"Neither of you should get used to this," I called back.

Thankfully, I could still hear everything they said. By the time I'd filled three cups and doctored mine and Emilia's up the way we liked, they'd stopped loudly making fun of me and had moved on to Emilia's brief description of the company and some of what virtual assistants typically do.

Declan stood up and came to help me with the mugs, whispering, "Thank you," and winking.

For the next half hour, I didn't say much at all. I was content to listen to them chat and watch how fast and how well they got along.

Emilia hadn't met anyone I'd dated since high school, and since we'd gone to the same school, we knew all the same guys, and none of them had been worth getting serious with.

Oh shit. Was *this* serious? Thankfully, neither of them noticed my full-body shiver at the thought. But I couldn't lie, not even to myself—things were amazing. Declan was incredible, in bed and out. If anyone had ever been too good to be true, it was him. And I couldn't help but let his optimism overpower my skepticism and allow myself to bask in the easy, laidback way he lived his life.

I'd never known anyone like him, the way he took everything in stride and altered his view accordingly. No prejudice, no doubts, just peace. It was more addictive than any drug I'd ever tried, and a much more enjoyable ride.

A little while later, I told Declan that if he really wanted to be me, he had work to do.

"You know, Declan," Emilia said, her smile still as bright as it had been the second she'd realized who he was, "you've been working so hard lately. Why don't you take the rest of the day off?" She winked. "And take your lazy assistant with you."

"Okay, boss, but only because you're ordering me to." He grabbed my hand and dragged me out, barely giving me time to thank her. "It was great to meet you, Emilia." He didn't stop until we were on the elevator. "I think my first day at the office went well, don't you?"

"I'd say you have another fan." I couldn't help crossing my fingers that things would go over as smoothly dinner with my parents.

"Why didn't you answer Emilia's question about what you're going to do after you graduate?"

Probably because she'd asked while I was busy overthinking things. "Once it seemed like you two were getting a little too buddy-buddy for my liking, I knew nothing good would come of it, so I stopped listening."

"Makes sense. But if you'd heard her, what would your answer have been?"

My eyebrow shot up. "Um...I don't know."

"What about law school? You said that was your dream when you were younger."

"Emphasis on *when I was younger*."

"Okay, that makes sense. You're too old now, for sure," he said, smiling. "Too old for law school, and definitely too old for dreams."

I opened my mouth to argue, defend my stance against his teasing, but couldn't think of a rebuttal. How ironic. It had been so long since I'd planned anything further than a week in my future, I'd forgotten how. And dreaming? I'd forgotten how to do that, too.

At least until Declan had come along. Now, I couldn't go a day without fantasizing about what might be. It was as annoying as shit.

"Did you say something?" I held my hand up to my ear. "I'm too old to hear you."

I ran for the stairs as soon as I heard the doorbell. Damn it, I'd planned on being ready and waiting for Declan out front so I could go over every last-minute warning I could think of:

Yes, Elaine is my biological mother, and yes, we're both incredibly ashamed of that fact. No, Timothy is not my real dad, and no, neither of us would want it any other way. Yes, they're both elitist assholes and, yes, I grew up thinking most people were beneath me. The only difference was that I was brutally cured of that affliction while in high school, while they're old and still desperately clinging to their bullshit better-than status despite all evidence to the contrary.

Honestly, that I was a total snob hadn't been an easy realization for me. It was humiliating to remember how cluelessly arrogant I'd been. But meeting Andi and Emilia—two of the most down-to-earth, amazing people in the world—had taught me how unimportant wealth is if all you use it for is to buy respect.

Sadly, while my friends had given me life lessons about selfishness, kindness, and integrity, they hadn't managed to hammer in enough honesty to overcome my mother's influence.

I could feel that changing, though. All because of how open Declan was. Hell, I'd almost come clean with him about what had happened to me after only meeting him three times. Emilia, Andi, and I had been friends for years, and they still didn't know. I wanted to tell them, but I couldn't stop wondering if it was too late. That I'd blown my chance by pushing them away for so long.

Over the last year, I'd discovered that there were two different types of friends. The first kind—like Andi and Emilia—believed in you and wanted you to be happy. Sounds horrible, right? Wait for it...

With this kind of friend, making a bad decision made them worry and decide they needed to *fix* you. Even if you couldn't—or didn't want to—be fixed. They wouldn't give up, even if you begged them to, even if you knew you weren't ready to accept their help or their love.

The other kind—like Carissa, for example—was much simpler. We went out to drown our feelings in alcohol, loud music, and one-night stands. You never had to worry if this type of friend would judge you. Mostly because she'd done much worse and was planning to do it *again* just as soon as her hangover was gone. She cared about you but never tried to fix you because that meant you might try to fix *her*.

Unfortunately, by the time I made it downstairs, Declan was standing in the foyer handing Timothy a bottle of wine. His polite smile morphed into surprise when our eyes met and he mouthed, "Wow."

My steps slowed as I made my way to him. Timothy being right there quelled my desire to jump into Declan's arms and kiss him. Instead, he moved the bouquet of white roses he carried into his other arm and kissed me on the cheek.

"Elaine, come out here and meet Declan," my stepdad called before turning to us. "She's been in the kitchen for hours."

"She's cooking?" That was new. My mom never cooked. She ordered in, went out, or when she was on some health kick, ate those prepackaged, gourmet delivery meals out of biodegradable containers. But actual cooking? Like, food in the oven? Nope, not that I could remember.

"Hope you're hungry. Elaine has a tendency to overdo things like this." Timothy led us into the open-concept living room/dining room combo.

"Sounds perfect. Because I'm starved." Declan leaned close to my ear and whispered, "You look good enough to eat."

I cleared my throat to cover my laugh and then gestured to the flowers he still carried. "Are those for me?"

"Nope. Your mother gets these, and you get me." He winked.

"I think I'd rather have the flowers," I joked.

My mom came out of the swinging door between the kitchen and the dining area, folded her apron neatly, and laid it over the back of a chair.

After saying hello to Declan and thanking him for the flowers, she took them to the wet bar to put them into a vase. While she was there, she asked what everyone wanted to drink and refilled the glass I was sure she'd already refilled a few times this evening. Thankfully, my mom could be the perfect hostess in her sleep. Sometimes I wondered how she'd managed to master all the things in life that didn't matter—did she take classes, or did it just come naturally?

The four of us sat down in the living room, and I waited for my first date-interrogation since prom night to begin. When Declan took my hand and squeezed, I silently apologized to him for everything he was about to be put through. Although, it wasn't as if he couldn't have gotten out of it. I'd given him about fifty of my best excuses to pick from, and he'd refused them all.

Timothy got the ball rolling with a really big shove. "Elaine told me you're a musician in a band, Declan. Why don't you tell us more about that?"

I'd never understand why anyone would ask something like that as a question. As if Declan could say, "Because I don't feel like it."

But I'd forgotten that Declan probably got asked about the band constantly, and he was used to being interviewed. So, I sat there being uncomfortable *for* him while he calmly explained how Self Defense got started and what they were doing now.

"And you make money doing that?"

He chuckled at Timothy's question. "Not enough to retire on, but we do pretty well. Much better than I'd ever imagined we would make as an unsigned band. Plus, along with what we make from the shows, we also get a small percentage of the merchandise and from online clicks and interactions with our fans."

"You have fans?" my mom asked, dumbfounded.

"Mom," I whined, feeling defensive. "Of course, they have fans. Tons of them. You have, what?" I asked him. "Two hundred thousand subscribers to your YouTube channel?"

He shifted to face me completely. "Have you been stalking me, Sara?"

"Two hundred thousand?" my mom repeated. "That's incredible, Declan. I had no idea."

"Neither did I," he said, laughing.

"Carissa has followed you guys for almost two years. She showed me all your social media pages and about fifteen Google pages of pictures of you." I turned to my parents. "Part of his job is to give interviews and do photoshoots." Halfway through my brag, I remembered that my plan had been to *stop* my mom from being interested in Declan. But here I was, encouraging the exact opposite, and I didn't even slow down. I told them about the crowd at the show I'd gone to and how big their tour had been.

By the end, even Timothy looked impressed. In fact, the only person who wasn't smiling was Declan.

"Sara's just being nice," he said, squeezing my hand. "It's really not that big a deal. Even with online success, there's a bigger chance of *not* making it onto the big music charts than there is of showing up on one. Besides—" He stopped. "Is something ringing?"

My mom's eyes widened, and she jumped up. "It's the timer!" She ran toward the kitchen.

"Can I help with anything?" Declan was up before I could stop him, so I followed *him* following her, and we all ended up in a kitchen nobody but our housekeeper, Beatrice, ever used. It was expansive, built for entertaining, so the island was a huge slab of granite where caterers could set out their stuff and still have enough room for plates or serving trays to rest until they were ready to go.

My mom came rushing out from the walk-in pantry and started opening and closing each cabinet or drawer one by one.

"What are you looking for, Mom?"

"An oven thingy. To take the chicken out."

Oh great. Her first experiment in cooking, and she picked the meat most likely to kill us all—or at least give us food poisoning. Good thing this house had five bathrooms.

"Damn it," she mumbled. "How am I supposed to get it out of the oven? With a fireplace poker?"

I glanced at Declan to see him biting his lower lip to keep from smiling. "There's a...um..." He pointed at an open cubby under the counter next to the sink, right behind my mom. Matching towels were rolled up in a small basket.

She didn't hear him, so he went around the island, squeezed behind her, and grabbed two of the towels.

"I can take it out for you." He looked at the double oven. "Which one is it?"

"Bless your heart, Declan. Thank you. Chicken is in that one." She pointed to the lower oven. "And the...um...vegetables are in the other."

I got it as soon as she stumbled over the word—Beatrice had done all the prep work and stuck them in the oven before she went home for the day and just in time for my mom to take all the credit. Thank God.

"What kind of veggies did you make, Mom?"

She shot a glare at me before turning back to Declan and directing him to put the chicken down on the counter. "Don't worry, hon. It's one of your favorites."

Well, that solidified things—my mom had no idea what vegetables I did and didn't like. But Beatrice did, so at least it wasn't eggplant—something that had neither the shape, flavor, or color of an egg and tasted like an oily sponge.

Declan and I each carried a dish into the dining room while Mom opened the bottle of wine Declan had brought and poured it into four glasses. Why four? Timothy only drank the hard stuff —never wine.

"Declan, would you mind grabbing the large serving utensils?" my mom asked. "I think I left them on the island. Or they might still be in the drawer next to the stove."

"Of course."

He'd already gone through the door when I counted the place settings.

"Who's the fifth, Mom?" I asked, not holding back on the suspicious tone.

As if on cue, a voice called out from the foyer. "I hope you made enough food for a small army, 'cause I'm starving."

Oh shit. "Please tell me you didn't invite him, Mom."

"This is his home, too, Sara. He has the same right to be here as you do."

"And because tonight isn't stressful enough, you thought you'd turn it into a family reunion?"

"Just think of your stepbrother as another mouth to fill any awkward silences," she said, smiling. "Or to take the pressure off Declan if my interrogation goes on too long, sweetie." *Aaand* if I'd ever doubted my mom had a sense of humor, that was proof I should never doubt myself again.

No amount of bad jokes could cover the awkwardness of sitting at a table with Declan, my parents, and the world's most vile stepbrother. Speak of the devil...

"Hey, sis. Long time, no see."

I could tell Cal had just done a few lines—probably off the dashboard of his car in the driveway. Somehow, my mom had never wondered why Cal's *allergies* were just as bad in the winter as they were when the flowers started blooming and why no allergy medication ever worked for him. If Timothy knew the truth, he'd never mentioned it or even given his son a doubtful look.

"Smells great, Mom."

I hated when he called her *Mom*. He'd started doing it as soon as our parents got married, and it had annoyed me even then. My real father had left before I could speak, but I would never call anyone else *Dad*. From the very beginning, Cal knew how to manipulate her—call her Mom, side with her against his father on the little shit so she'd give him whatever he wanted. Or let him get away with whatever he wanted. Or believe him over her own daughter.

Cal shook his dad's hand and kissed my mom's cheek. Then, for some unknown reason, he started walking toward me.

Thankfully, he froze as soon as he saw Declan step through the kitchen doorway holding a serving fork in one hand and a huge knife in the other.

27

DECLAN

"Wow, sis. Really?" Cal turned his back to his parents, so only Sara and I could see his lips when he mouthed, *"You're supposed to leave garbage on the curb, not invite it in for dinner."*

The serving utensils clanged together as they hit the table. A second later, I was next to Sara, ready to step in front of her if the prick got too close. "Good to see you again."

Cal was her stepbrother. That created a lot of unanswered questions I'd have to ask her about. But not right now. Sara's look of disgust was the same as the one she'd had the first time I met him.

"It's Cal, right?" I asked. "Hey, did you ever get your ears checked?"

"What's wrong with your ears, honey?" Elaine asked.

"Nothing, Mom."

Cal's lips were too tight to form an actual smile as he stared at me. "Keep meaning to. But you know how it is—my boss won't sign my six-figure check if I take time out of the sales day to do errands. I guess you wouldn't know anything about that, would you?"

"Nope. Not a clue." I stuck out my hand politely, for Sara's sake. If it were up to me, I'd have stuck out my fist again. There was something seriously wrong with this guy. "I don't think I could handle working a nine-to-five job. Especially if I had to leave one sales job and go to another one all night. That might be the issue with your hearing, actually—nightclubs are loud places. But I guess you spend more time outside the clubs than inside, don't you?"

Cal glanced at his stepmom, probably to see if she'd picked up on the not-so-subtle hint I shouldn't have made, and quickly shook off my hand.

"Actually," Timothy said, taking his seat at the head of the table, "Cal works with me at my real estate development firm, Declan. He's doing some damn good work there, too."

Made sense. Cal probably considered drug dealing more of a hobby, anyway.

I've always thought myself a polite guy, but since this was a high-stress situation for me, and an even higher one for Sara, I decided to go the extra mile and hold her chair for her. Obviously, Cal was the type who didn't like being outdone, so he stood there for another couple of minutes, impatiently waiting for Elaine to finish arranging the flowers and refill her glass.

After Cal pushed her chair in, he took the seat at the other end of the table.

As soon as I sat down, Sara leaned over and whispered, "I wish you hadn't shaken his hand. Now, you need a decontamination shower before I can touch you again."

"Or you could rub me down with disinfectant," I whispered back.

"What are you smiling about, sis?"

Her grin went from genuine to plastic, and she sighed. "I was just remembering a time when you weren't here. Good times, good times."

"Stop it, you two," my mom snapped. "Do you have siblings, Declan?"

"No, I'm an only child."

Timothy handed the platter of chicken to me after serving himself. "So, it's just you and your parents?"

Easily understanding the subtext, I nodded, suddenly struck by the field day my father would have with this family.

"Declan's parents live in Los Angeles. His mom is a teacher, and his dad is a psychiatrist."

"A psychiatrist?" Elaine perked up. "What's his name?"

I thought she was joking, like someone asking a Brit if they know their roommate from college or something. But she didn't laugh or give any other indication of the joke.

"My mother's hobby is psychiatry." Then Sara added something else under her breath: "Going to them, not being one."

Turned out that Elaine had actually heard of my father and had read one of his articles in a trade magazine. All I could hope was that the topic hadn't been parenting or having an ungrateful son who would never be good enough for anyone's daughter.

Although, thankfully—because my father was well-known and the number of YouTube subscribers I hadn't known I had—she seemed to like me.

Focusing on the food—that even Sara was impressed by—I listened to Timothy brag about his son. After a brief moment of wondering why most of the conversation centered around Cal with only an occasional mention of Sara, I decided to appreciate not having to go through the interrogation I'd expected.

"How do you and Cal know each other?" Elaine asked me as she and Sara cleared the dishes. When I got up to help, she pushed me back into my seat by the shoulder.

"We've only met once." I stared at Cal while I spoke. "But I guess you could say we run in the same alleys, right, Cal?"

"Isn't it *circles?*" she asked, completely misunderstanding my comment.

"You're right, Elaine, of course. Although I never really understood the expression. *Running in the same circles* always makes me think of dogs chasing their tails, or even rats on a wheel. I try not to do too much of that. You, Cal?"

Sara nudged me with her foot as she took my plate from me. I wasn't sure why I was pressing him so much. Maybe it was because of the look in her eyes that night, or the more fearful one now. I wanted to let the prick know he wasn't going to get away with his intimidation anymore.

After another half hour of faking civility, I was exhausted. Watching what I said to Cal and monitoring Sara's reactions had made the time I'd spent here feel more like decades.

My offer to help with the dishes was shot down as well. Apparently, their housekeeper would do it in the morning. Instead, I was told to go into the living room where Timothy and Cal would be having their after-dinner drinks. Sara and I gave each other a look, both of us knowing that, as much as I needed a drink, having one with Cal would be counter-productive.

"Actually, Declan should probably be going." She turned to me. "You have an early morning tomorrow, don't you?"

I could've kissed her. But aside from the inappropriateness of kissing in front of her family, it would've distracted me from coming up with a logical excuse. "Yeah, I have a meeting with my manager."

"I'll walk you out."

After thanking Elaine for the meal and saying goodbye to Timothy, I found myself in front of Cal. Neither of us bothered sticking out a hand.

"I'll keep an eye out for you at the clubs," I said, my tone disguising the underlying warning.

"Sure. See you around, Declan. Take care of my sister, would you?"

"You shouldn't doubt that for a second."

Once we were outside, I took a deep breath of fresh air. "Wow, that was fun. And for some reason, I'm totally cured of that desire to have a brother."

"I'm sorry."

"Don't be." I brushed a lock of hair off her cheek. "Eventually, you might meet my parents. That will give you all sorts of reasons to be sorry—you'll feel sorry for me, sorry you ever met me, sorry you didn't run when you had the chance, and a bunch of others. Although, I do have a couple questions for you." We walked down the driveway to the street. "If Cal hadn't been here tonight, were you ever planning to tell me he was your step-brother?"

"Honestly, I try not to think about him. But, as disgusting as the thought was, initially, letting you think he was an ex seemed like the easiest way to keep some distance between us. Ever since then, it just never felt like the right time to tell you the truth."

"Fair answer. Next question. This one's harder."

She grimaced, expecting the worst.

"What kind of name is 'Cal,' anyway?"

Smiling, she shrugged. "I always figured it was short for 'calorie'—because nobody likes them either."

28

DECLAN

$\mathcal{M}$y apartment felt empty without Sara in it. One night apart was too long.

I woke up to the baby voice Trevor used when he spoke to Kitty.

"Is your daddy awake yet? No? Then he hasn't heard our good news, has he, girl?"

"The good news better not be that I can sleep in this morning."

He came into my bedroom and sat down near my feet. "Dude, I called you, like, ten times last night. Didn't you notice?"

"I noticed. Ironically, times like these remind me why I don't return your calls."

He ignored my dig. "Did you also notice that Doug called, too? Do you know why he called, and then I called?"

"I have a feeling you're going to tell me whether I do or not."

He grabbed my leg and shook it. "Some guy from Moguli Music reached out to Doug about us, Declan!"

I lifted my head. Moguli Music was a sub-label of one of the big three. "Seriously?"

"No, I'm lying. That's why I called you so many times last night—to lie to your voice mail."

I rubbed my eyes as I sat up. "Moguli would be perfect for Self Defense." Signing with them would change everything.

As I got ready for basketball, I found myself getting caught up in Trevor's excitement, imagining all the things we'd do *once* —not if—we signed with Moguli. Until we got to the courts, I didn't even remember that wasn't what I wanted for myself. My plan was to stick with the band until we got a contract, one that wasn't contingent on me being front man forever. Then, once I knew the guys would be okay, I'd help find them someone to replace me, so I could leave.

For the rest of our practice, both of us were grinning like idiots, only our endgames being different.

That afternoon, Sara called and asked if she could come by my place after work. As if I was going to say no. Then she refused my offer to take her out to dinner, saying she preferred the intimacy of it just being the two of us. As if I was going to say no to that either.

I spent the rest of the day wishing I had Emilia's number so I could call and beg her to let Sara go early. Actually, it was probably healthier for everyone that I didn't have her number.

Sara arrived at around five thirty, just as I finished unpacking an extremely large bag of the city's best Japanese takeout.

"Are the guys joining us for dinner?" she said with a hint of disappointment.

"Hell no." I set down chopsticks and forks on the table, not knowing what she used. "I didn't know what you like, so I got a bit of everything."

"Cool. So this is a 'get to know each other' dinner." With wide eyes, she opened the containers one by one, telling me what she liked and what she didn't. The theme continued for the rest of the evening—she'd tell me something about herself, and then I'd follow suit. No topic was off-limits. Neither one of us confessed to anything too traumatic, but we didn't hesitate to answer even the more serious questions.

She packed up the leftovers while I did the dishes and cleaned off the table. Kitty took care of anything that had fallen onto the floor.

Sara rubbed her head. "She's handy to have around, isn't she?

"Kitty's good at a lot of stuff. But mostly she's a great listener. She loves my guitar, too. Every time I take it off the wall, she gets excited. How's that for positive reinforcement?"

"Maybe she just senses that it makes you happy."

"Yeah, maybe." Before meeting Sara, my dog and my guitar were the *only* things that always made me happy. And sometimes, it was as if Kitty knew how I felt before I did. When I was happy, she wagged her tail, and occasionally even sang along. When I was sad, she sat at or on my feet, set her chin on my knee, and looked up at me with her sad puppy-dog eyes.

I fucking adored that dog.

I sat close to Sara on the couch. "Hmm... I don't think this is going to work."

"What isn't?"

Is it wrong I loved the look of disappointment on her face? Like she'd taken my comment as a dismissal of us instead of just that we switch spots?

"I can't play on this side." I tilted the guitar and showed her how the arm hit the side of the couch. "We need to change places. Unless..." I smirked and put my hand on her leg to stop her from standing.

"Unless what?" This time, her expression was wary—still

cute as hell, but definitely not as satisfying as her misplaced disappointment.

I took the strap off my shoulder and set the guitar on her lap. "Unless I teach you how to play."

Her smile was ear-to-ear. "I've never even held one."

"No problem," I said, slipping the strap over her head. "I'm a good teacher."

"You're going to regret this."

"Well, I already know you have a good grip, impeccable rhythm, and know how to play with my equipment." I winked, remembering how she'd proven that to me every time we were horizontal. "This will be easy." I took her hand and placed each of her fingers on a string. Her small fingers could barely reach all of them. "This is E-minor. Give the strings a strum with your other hand."

It was weak, and she didn't hit them all with equal pressure, so it didn't sound great. But even so, she squealed, glancing at me with huge eyes and an even bigger smile before strumming again.

"Better already. I'm an amazing teacher."

She laughed and tried it again. "Incredible."

I'd like to think the compliment was directed at me, but she was staring at the guitar. "Teach me another."

I showed her one more—D—and then had her switch back and forth between the two a few times. She tightened her brow, and the tiniest part of her tongue stuck out of her mouth as she concentrated on switching her fingers from placement to placement.

"E-minor...D...E-minor...D," I said slowly as I helped her get the fingering right.

I think I fell in love a little when I heard her mumble the chorus to the song.

"Break on..."—move fingers—"...through..."—back to E-minor—"to the other..."

She cursed when her finger slipped, and the D went sharp. But she got it right the next time.

"Side," she said, her volume matching the chord's. "Break on...through...to the other...side."

I sat back against the couch, my work done, and watched her go through more of the Doors' song.

When her fingers got confused, she stopped and looked at me. "So, is this *our* song now?"

"It's one of the songs you were singing at the karaoke bar the first time I saw you, and it's the first song you learned how to play, so I guess it could qualify as ours."

"I can't believe there are only two notes in it."

"Well, the vocals are more complicated, but the guitar part is pretty simple."

She took off the strap and handed the guitar to me. "It's tough on the hands, isn't it?" She shook hers out. "Play me something pretty. Something *you* wrote."

I took a breath, wondering if it would be too sappy to play the song I'd written about her. "Well, there is something I've been working on recently. It's just a chorus right now, but..."

"Just play it already, Mr. Defense."

"Okay. It's just something I'm playing around with, so don't expect anything magical." She'd never know it was meant for her anyway.

The intro was quiet but complicated and took a lot of hand dexterity, each note plucked individually. I glanced up at her halfway through, proud I could make her smile like that. Honored that she liked *her* song.

"Reflection... Can't see it. Direction... Turn away from myself..."

I stopped playing and sat back on the couch, letting the

guitar rest on my thighs. "And then I repeat some stuff, and it goes on from there."

"You're a liar."

I looked at her, offended. "What do you mean?"

"That was totally magical," she said, smiling. "I don't understand how you do that—make music and write poetry. I can barely walk and drink a latte without falling over."

Embarrassed, I shrugged. "That might be something you should master. It could come in handy sometime."

She hit me on the shoulder and then laid her head against the spot. "Yeah, well, you should work on how to take a compliment. I think it'll come in handy *a lot*."

"Thank you," I said after kissing the top of her head. "Writing music comes easy for me. *Sharing* it doesn't. Especially the personal stuff. That's why the band doesn't perform many ballads—gotta keep up the appearance of being an uncaring bad boy musician, you know." My favorite songs I'd written solely for myself. It felt wrong to lay my shit on other people. Wrong and fucking depressing. I wasn't Adele—I couldn't pull off that kind of shit.

"You do the bad-boy thing really well onstage, but if you ever want it to work when you're not performing, the uncaring part needs serious help."

"Yeah, I know. I suck. It's terrible."

"Actually, your sucking is amazing." She smacked herself in the face, trying to cover her mouth. I guess she was embarrassed by the comment. I was flattered. And completely falling for her.

"Listen, I've been thinking about something," I said. "I want to get a good recording of this song—nothing formal, just do it on my computer. But I need your help to write it."

"What's in it for me?"

"Well, if you help me finish it, I'll let you come to my next gig and hang out with the other groupies. Who knows? Maybe you'll get really lucky and be invited backstage to meet the band."

"Gee, thanks." This time she smacked *me*.

I set down my guitar and pulled her into my lap. "Actually, I need you to be there." I explained how big a deal it was that Moguli Music had contacted Doug. "If Self Defense signs with them, and I know my leaving won't screw over the guys, I'll be free. I might keep writing music for them, but no touring or promotion."

"So, basically, you'd be able to do what you love doing and not do what you hate? That's incredible!" She threw her arms around me.

"But the real reason I need you there is because I'm going to need all the emotional support I can get. I've been lying to them for years, and I need to tell them the truth. Finally." I hated lying, but it had always seemed preferable to making the guys angry or self-destructive. And nobody could do self-destructive better than Trevor. All it took to remind me was a bottle of tequila or a bottle of pills.

"I'd tell you that you have nothing to worry about, but I know you'd never believe me." Sara squeezed me tighter. "So, I will absolutely, one hundred percent be there."

"Promise?"

"Promise."

29

SARA

I was still high on Declan-pheromones as I got ready for his gig, smiling like an idiot and blissfully happy as I did my hair and picked out just the right outfit. A new hope had appeared in my head, and I felt as if I could see a bright future laid out in front of me instead of a bunch of depressing gray road bumps.

Once Declan told Trevor and the other guys how he felt and that he wanted to leave the band, he and I would date for a while. Depending on their transition plan, I'd follow Declan to Los Angeles or on tour or wherever he went until they found a new lead singer. I'd be on his arm through it all, supporting him and helping him deal with the parts of the music business he disliked. Be his refuge from the bullshit, his safe place.

The irony wasn't lost on me—it had been a long time since I'd felt safe, even in my own home, but if things continued the way they were going, this wouldn't be my home much longer. I could leave, ask Emilia to let me work as a virtual assistant from the road. I wouldn't be dependent on my stepdad or Declan. I'd be free.

I practically bounced down the stairs, so ready to get out of this tomb and into a mass of sweaty strangers. I couldn't wait to be part of a crowd screaming for more Declan and know that I was the only one who'd actually *get* more Declan after the show. After he had the big talk with his bandmates, of course.

When I saw Cal in the kitchen, all those good feelings disappeared. He was standing at the island in the kitchen, shoving cheese into his disgusting face. He'd moved out four years ago but came back unannounced whenever he felt like it. Just like I'd done from the second I turned eighteen until I couldn't afford my apartment anymore and had to move back in.

He didn't visit often, but after what he'd done to me last year, each time I was forced to see him felt like its own never-ending prison sentence.

My gaze suddenly stuck onto the floor, right where it felt like my stomach had dropped. Every muscle contracted. I hated how weak his proximity made me. I'd always been able to stand up for myself and for anyone else who needed standing up for. And in every other scenario, that was still true. But whenever Cal was near me, everything changed. I'd been blindsided, caught completely unaware by how naïve I'd been, thinking nothing like that could ever happen to me. Thinking I'd never be anyone's victim—let alone my own stepbrother's.

"Why are you here, Cal?"

"Mom and Dad went out with some business associates of Dad's. And hello to you, too."

"It's seven o'clock. I figured you'd be weighing baggies and filling your pockets with pills to get ready for your night job."

When he pretended to laugh hysterically, a tiny chunk of cheddar fell out of his mouth and landed on the counter. Gross. I'd never look at cheese the same way again.

"It's a good thing you're so hot," he said, his gaze running up and down my body, "because I don't think the comedy thing is going to pan out, little sis."

"Don't ever call me that again," I snapped, spinning around on my heel and heading back out. I had to change my outfit—his comment made me hate it. Made me hate myself for needing to flee instead of screaming at him.

"Hey," he called after me.

"Go deal your stupid drugs and leave me alone, Cal." I moved faster as I heard his footsteps tap the wood floor. "Don't even talk to me." It was more than not wanting to—I couldn't. I just couldn't handle it. And this time, Declan wasn't there to rescue me.

My stepfather never got home this early, but my mom was usually here. So, I rushed toward the living room, hoping I'd find her or the housekeeper, Beatrice. Damn it. Where was everyone?

He caught up with me in the family room. "What the fuck is wrong with you? I just said hello."

Great. We were in the only room on the first floor of this giant house with only one door. And he was blocking it.

I put up my hand, as if that would keep him from taking a step closer. "Don't touch me." But it had never really been about the touch, had it? The feeling of helplessness was what had lingered, the knowledge that I hadn't been able to stop someone from hurting me, taking something from me by force.

"No, Cal!" The strength of my voice made both of us flinch. "Back the fuck off." I was stronger than this now. Smarter than this. And I knew what he was capable of. No way would I let him hurt me again.

"God, you're so stupid." He rolled his eyes. "Move on already, Sara. It was forever ago." He wiped his hands over his eyes and then all the way down his face. "Fine. You regret it. But can we please be in the same room with each other without you freaking out? Can we just forget it happened and be friends?"

"Friends?" The strength in my voice had morphed into

something with a definite shrieking quality to it. But I couldn't believe he had the nerve to tell me to just move on. "Do you have a lot of friends who've raped you, Cal? Because I don't. And I don't want any."

"Whoooaaa." He jerked back a step, his arms out to his sides.

Rape. I'd finally said it. Shit, I'd never even used the word in my head. But it had always been there, waiting at the edge of my mind until I was brave enough to use it.

"What are you talking about, Sara? That wasn't rape."

"I said no." After it had happened, I made sure I was never alone with him, so we'd definitely never talked about it before. But to claim it wasn't rape? How dare he?

He made a stupid face and snorted. "Yeah, like, once."

"Are you serious?" My body shook with fear and rage. "I said no and tried to push you off and was crying and begging you to stop. How the fuck is that not rape?"

"That's not how I remember it," he said snidely. "Not at all. What I remember is a spoiled little bitch who had way too much to drink and who was looking to get laid. All I did was give you what you were asking for, Sara. Get over it." He sighed. "You want to regret it? Fine. That's your choice. But just because you want to pretend it wasn't your fault doesn't mean you get to claim rape."

"I—" The air left my lungs. I didn't know what to say. I'd dreamt of this moment for so long—finally having the courage to confront him. Fantasizing about every word I'd say had been the only way to stop myself from crying every time I thought of it.

One thousand different scenarios of what would happen, and this wasn't even close to any of them. How could he pretend what had happened didn't? Just like my mother when I told her.

It had happened. I know it did. I hadn't been asking for it, didn't want it. I'd begged him to stop. I know I did. I...

My jaw quivered. When the two people who knew you best tell you something didn't happen, you can't help but doubt yourself. You can't help but question every horrible second of the nightmare.

I'd said no. I'd *screamed* no. At least, I thought I did. But Cal was right—I'd been drinking. I was one hundred percent sure I hadn't wanted it to happen. But what if I'd never said it out loud? What if I'd been so shocked, horrified, and scared that I'd never actually said no?

"I didn't want that." I shook my head violently. "I was crying and trying to get away. I would've *never* asked for that." I rubbed my wrists where he'd held me down when he pushed himself inside me. "You forced yourself on me. It was not my fault." Tears burned streaks down my cheeks. "It was *your* fault."

He stared at me for a minute, but I couldn't tell what he was thinking. Was he trying to decide how to say sorry? How to explain how horrible he felt about what he'd done? Even if he begged for my forgiveness on his knees, he wouldn't get it. It had been too long. I'd been forced to spend too many dinners sitting across the table from him, pretending like we were a family.

So, what now? Should I hit him, walk away with my tail between my legs, say something hurtful before stalking off? Something that I couldn't think of right now. What?

My indecision took away my choice.

"You're so fucked in the head, Sara, and I'm done putting up with all your bullshit. Just stay away from me."

I watched his back as he left, the way he sauntered. Exactly how he'd walked away from me that night. And I'd stayed frozen with hot tears running down my cheeks, unable to speak, breathe, or think. Just like now.

"And believe me," he said over his shoulder, "if you even *think* about saying that word to Mom and Dad, you'll learn the true meaning of regret."

The slam of the front door brought me back to life. At least enough to get a bottle of scotch and bring it up to my room.

The moment I'd been dreading for an entire year was supposed to have made everything better. I was supposed to feel freer now, be ready to finally get closure so I could go back to being the woman I used to be. Maybe even a better version of that woman—a little wiser, a lot tougher.

So, where was she?

"Declan," I whispered as I dragged my feet up the stairs. "You would've loved her." It hadn't occurred to me before, but that was where that brief moment of courage had come from. I'd finally been brave enough to face Cal because my desire to have a future with Declan was more powerful than my fear of confronting my rapist.

I'd wanted to be a woman who was that strong. For myself and for Declan. So, where did that leave me now?

Opening my bedroom door with my left hand felt awkward, but I wasn't sure my right fist would unclench from around the neck of the bottle of scotch.

"Huh," I said as I looked around my room.

I hadn't planned for tonight to have been *the* night, but regardless, I thought I'd know what would happen afterwards. Everything should've looked different, *been* different.

But nothing had changed—all my shit was right where I'd left it. Count on me to put every makeup brush, hair tie, and piece of clothing back right where it was supposed to go.

Count on me to never admit I needed help when I wasn't sure where the rest of my life was going.

I locked the door and went to my bed. When I sat down, I noticed what I was wearing. It had taken me forever to decide on what to wear. Something that Declan would like but didn't look as if I were trying too hard. Something that he might want to show me off in. Be proud of me. For the way I looked and what I wore. Right. Because that's pretty much all I had.

I got under the covers, leaning against the headboard of a little girl's bed. A little girl who'd turned eighteen four years ago and had never felt smaller and less significant than she did at this very moment.

The scotch smelled terrible. Tasted worse. But after a few more lifts of the bottle, it wasn't too bad.

30

DECLAN

I wiped the sweat from my forehead as I stepped off the stage. It had been a spectacular crowd. Their energy fed mine as the set got going, making my nervousness about coming clean with the guys manageable. But now that the show was over, it was coming back with a vengeance.

I just had to get through a bunch of small talk with the people from Moguli Music without having a panic attack. Nothing would be agreed upon or even stated outright tonight, but if they mentioned anything about a pen, where we saw ourselves in five years, or that they would meet us in the next few days, we'd know Self Defense had a good chance of getting a contract.

The guys would be ecstatic. So, they'd take *my* news a shit-load better than if the Moguli folks bailed completely or stayed just to say the "Nice show" or the "You guys have talent" shit we'd heard a bunch of times before this.

Either way, I was coming clean with my friends tonight. If I waited one more day, the anxiety would kill me. Although, a bright side of my death would be that I'd get to do a little more role-playing with Sara before I went. Speaking of that little heart stopper...

Unfortunately, there were too many people and lights to have been able to see her anywhere during the show. I wished she'd have pushed her way to the front, but then, she was tiny and probably would have been trampled if she'd tried.

"Dec!" Trevor called out. "We have to meet the Moguli guys! Where're you going?"

Just looking at him made me feel a little guilty—he had no idea what I was planning to tell him and the other guys. But Sara was right—being a part of something that made me miserable wasn't doing anyone any favors. That shit was bound to hit the fan eventually, and if I came clean before that happened, I might be able to salvage three friendships that meant the world to me.

"Just need to find my girl." Having her next to me would be a perfect reminder of what I could look forward to when the time came to actually say the words. "I'll be back in a sec."

"Hurry the fuck up, man! They're not going to wait around until it's convenient for you."

"I'll be there in two." I waved him off and headed straight toward the bar where Sara and I said we'd meet. I shoved past a few people who tried to get my attention, telling them I needed a second. I took one turn around the bar, then another, peering over shoulders, turning women about Sara's height around to see their faces. But I couldn't find her.

A small hand grabbed my arm, tugging it. I turned around, happily, ready to swoop her up and take her somewhere more private. But it wasn't Sara.

"That was incredible, Declan!" Carissa squealed. "Trevor told me you guys are meeting with a label tonight. Is that true?"

I tried to hold back my disappointment. "If Trevor said it, I guess it's true."

"So cool."

"Where's Sara?" I asked.

She shrugged. "No idea. She never showed up and hasn't been answering my texts."

Fuck. I pulled my phone out of my pocket and called her, covering my other ear to block out some of the noise.

She picked up on the third ring. "Declan?"

"Yeah." I walked toward a moderately empty corner of the club. "Are you okay? What happened?"

"What do you mean?" There was something off about her tone, but I didn't know what.

I switched direction and headed for an exit. "You're going to have to speak up—I can barely hear you." Maybe that was the problem. "Hang on." With one hand holding my phone and the other covering my ear, I pressed the bar on the door with my hip and push it open it with my shoulder. "Where are you? You're supposed to be here. For the show and"—more importantly —"when I talk to the guys."

"Oh, right." Oh, right? Had she actually forgotten something we'd discussed at length for the past week up until a few hours ago? Something she'd known I was nervous as hell to actually do?

"What's going on?" I asked.

"I...um...something came up." Her words were slurred. Her fucking words were slurred.

I stopped moving halfway out the door.

"Something came up?" I snapped, my anxiety level jumping up about three levels. "Something meaning you decided to get drunk somewhere instead of being here for me like you said you would? Like you promised me you would?" I laughed bitterly. "Got it."

So, this was her new and improved barrier. Things were great when we were together, but as soon as we spent any time apart, she overthought and panicked. She must have decided she'd let herself get too close and then balked, shut me down before things got too serious. Then she probably went somewhere to get wasted, so she didn't have to think about it anymore. "Right. I get it. I guess I'm on my own, then. Have...*fun*."

"Wait, Declan. Listen, I..."

"It's—" Fine? Nope. No problem? Nope. Not a big deal? Nope. It was a big deal. Tonight was supposed to be a fresh start for me, the end of something that had been slowly tearing me apart for years. And I'd thought—hoped—Sara would be part of my new beginning. I'd fallen for her. Hard. And between my wishful thinking and hopeful arrogance, I thought she'd fallen for me, too. Hell, maybe she had. But she couldn't let stupid shit like respect and love keep her from believing she didn't deserve it. And I didn't know how to get her to see herself as I saw her.

I couldn't put my life on hold because of someone else's issues anymore. I'd done it with Trevor for years, and ironically, it had been Sara who convinced me to let it go. Stop living for someone else's dreams. Someone else's problems.

From the second I'd met her, I wanted to save her, too. Be a hero. Be *her* hero.

Who the fuck did I think I was to save anyone? Especially when it was practically killing me to do it.

How many times did she need to brush me off before I got it? I guess I'd been counting on her a little too much for anyone's good.

"It's just as hard for me to ask for help as it is for you, Sara. So, when I finally do it and count on you to be here when I need you, and then you bail on me..." I sighed. "Anyway, thanks for the life lesson."

"It's really loud there, Declan. I couldn't hear—"

"Don't worry about it," I said miserably. "All you need to hear is that I want to be with someone who doesn't break their promises. And at least right now, that isn't something you can do."

I wished so much of this were different, but what I wished for most was that she would stop being afraid of something that made both of us happy. Sadly, if my trials with Trevor had taught me nothing else, people don't change just because you wished they would.

"Take care of yourself, Sara."

"Declan! No, wait! Let me explain. Plea—"

I hung up. Drunken excuses only sounded logical to drunks. And I wasn't drunk. And I didn't want to be.

Fuck that. Yes, I did. I wanted to be so wasted I didn't care anymore. Wanted to guzzle down so much poison I couldn't think anymore. It seemed to work for her, and for Trevor, even for my father. So, why not me?

Maybe once I was wasted, all of this would make sense. I'd be able to put all logical thought behind me and figure out what everyone else around me already had.

Life was better when you're numb, when you can stop thinking about the past and the future doesn't matter. When you stop fighting the people you love and let them self-destruct however the fuck they want to.

I slipped my phone into my pocket when I heard Trev call me over, his arms around the two women next to him, a toxic bronze liquid sloshing onto one of the girl's shoulders. She screamed and called Trevor a name. A pretty accurate one.

"Fucking oaf." I took the drink out of his hand before he spilled more and tossed it back until the ice smacked into my teeth. "Come on, let's go talk to Moguli. Make them want Self Defense so badly they're ready to offer up a human sacrifice for the pleasure of signing us."

"Amen, brother!" He took the girls' drinks from them. "It's

for a great cause, ladies. Plus, Declan will get you another." Then he shoved one into my empty hand and held his up to toast. "Here's to Doug!"

My upper lip curled at the mention of his name. "Why Doug?"

"Because he unknowingly volunteered to be the human sacrifice."

I laughed and raised my glass all the way up. "I'll drink to that."

I was still laughing as I headed toward a future that didn't matter and got swallowed up by the crowd.

It might be for all the wrong reasons, but at least *they* wanted me.

31

SARA

*A*fter Declan had hung up on me, I cried, pouted, and berated myself until I heard the front door open. My mom and Timothy were home. Perfect.

I covered my mouth and stared at the door, hoping Mom wouldn't knock. One look at me, and she'd know I'd been crying. She probably wouldn't care about that or that I was drunk, but she'd be pissed as hell if she saw the half-empty bottle of my stepfather's favorite scotch.

I heard the heavy click of her heels on the stairs. As she passed my door, she let out a long list of passive-aggressive comments about how terrible the evening had been. Things she'd never say to her husband's face or even admit to feeling. I'd gotten used to the angry glares she threw at him whenever his back was turned, whenever he mentioned one of his female employees. Didn't take a lot of intelligence to know why. Didn't take a lot of deduction to know that he was banging them whenever he could and that my mom knew it, too.

I took a deep breath when she slammed her bedroom door. At least I wouldn't have to deal with her until tomorrow. I lifted the bottle to my lips again and thought about Declan.

I hadn't been able to tell him what happened over the phone, not when tonight was supposed to be *his* night for facing his fears and doing something brave. Even now, assuming he'd answer my call, I didn't know what to say that would make him any less furious at me for missing his show and, more importantly, for being there when he told the guys he was leaving the band.

Even though the confrontation with Cal hadn't gone anything like I'd imagined or had been prepared for, I knew Declan would've been proud of me for trying, though. Once he actually *knew* I'd tried.

Keeping the image of his face in my mind was the only way I'd been able to say the things I'd never been able to say before. Until everything had gone upside down, I could still imagine him telling me how proud he was of my courage and strength and that he wanted to be with me. And I'd agree because I would finally be free.

But not tonight.

Tonight, he was supposed to be setting up his future, and I was supposed to be next to him.

And some *other* night, I was supposed to tell him every word I'd used to finally tell off Cal, and Declan was supposed to be listening, cheering when I got to a particularly good comeback.

I didn't get any of that right.

I needed to get out of this place, find someone to tell me it would all be okay, that I'd live. I wanted it to be Declan, but that wasn't possible. I was depressed and drunk—two great reasons to chuck my phone across the room so I wouldn't be tempted to call him back. I flipped it over so the screen faced the floor, but I couldn't let go of it. As if this all-knowing piece of plastic and chips was my only lifeline. Wow, wasn't that the saddest realization of life ever?

"Please, someone just tell me I haven't ruined everything."

Evidently, I'd had my finger on the phone's home button because someone answered.

"I'm not sure I understand." Sure, the smartphone feature was an unfeeling voice that didn't give a shit about me—or anything at all. But at least that stupid singsong voice was listening. She had a totally reasonable answer, too.

"Me neither," I mumbled.

"Here is what I found on the web for *ruined everything.*"

I flipped the phone over to see what she'd found, almost expecting it to be a mirror reflecting my own pathetic face back at me. Nope, but it was almost as good. The lyrics to a Jonathan Coulton song - *"I was fine. I pulled myself together. Just in time to throw myself away..."*

I stopped there.

I clicked the home button to get rid of the YouTube link and saw that I'd been crying through four missed calls and a bunch of unread texts. One call was from Emilia, and three were from Andi. Then I read through the missed texts. They were all on one thread—a three-way chat with my two best friends.

Emilia had started the discussion a few hours ago. *'What's up, ladies? Anyone want to do breakfast tomorrow?'*

Andi had replied almost immediately. *'Sure. Hayden can drop me off around 9 on his way to the office. Does that work?'*

'Does he always work on Sundays?'

'Not normally. But he's working on something important and needs a quiet office. I keep telling him he can work from home, but evidently, I'm too distracting.' Then a winky face.

'Told you married life wouldn't kill your sex life.' A laughing face.

'But my sex life may end up killing me.' Lots more laughing faces from both of them.

'Can you meet us, Sara?' from Emilia. Then, about a minute later, she'd written, *'Hello? Anyone there?'*

'She's probably out, living the life neither of us ever had.'

'Hey, I had that life once! For about fifteen minutes. Ha!'

Obviously, they were just teasing and knew I'd be reading their back and forth, but it felt as if I were eavesdropping on a private conversation. Between two women who managed to have it all, who loved their lives and their husbands, and themselves. And made it look so easy.

I typed a response, the shaking of my fingers having nothing to do with the booze.

'I screwed up. And I need help.' I pressed send before I could think too hard about it. About the possible lectures, the I-told-you-so's, the judgments.

Their replies weren't anything like I'd thought they would be.

'Anything. Just tell us how we can help,' from Andi and 'I'm on my way. Where are you?' from Emilia.

I started sobbing—ugly, ugly tears flooding my eyes and dripping onto the screen. 'Mom's house.'

'Be there in two minutes.'

Emilia lived at least ten minutes away, but I understood.

'Thank you.'

'Do not go anywhere, Sara. Got it?'

I nodded. I didn't have anywhere else to go.

'Bring her over here, Emilia.'

'K.'

Then the phone rang, and a picture of Andi and me appeared on the screen. It had been taken about six weeks ago at her wedding. We were both smiling stupidly at the camera, our arms around each other, laughing. I put her on speaker so I could keep looking at the photo. We'd been so damn happy that day. So damn happy, I'd been able to forget everything painful.

"Hey," I said quietly, trying not to blubber all over the phone.

"Emilia will be there soon, but I thought I'd call to shoot the shit, you know?"

"Keep me talking so I won't fall unconscious?"

"Is that a possibility, Sara?" I heard the edge in her tone, the fear.

"No. I'm not that bad off. I'm just..." I'm just what? Losing it. Miserable. Alone. Afraid life will always be like this.

"Can you give me a little context here?" Andi asked. "Because honestly, I've never been so worried in my life. My brain is doing flip-flops with all the possibilities. Are you in danger?"

"No."

"Are you alone?"

"Yeah. I'm so alone."

"No, you're not, Sara. We're here. We'll always be here. Okay?" When I didn't respond audibly, she repeated herself. "Sara, we're here for you. No matter what. But you've gotta let us know what's going on."

I nodded again, knowing all of it was true. They'd be there for me, and I had to let them in. I had to tell them everything, even though I had no idea where to start.

"We had something, you know?" I whimpered. "Declan and I? I finally had something good, and I screwed it up. I thought I was finally doing the right thing and would finally be able to get over it. But then Cal ruined it again, and I didn't know what to do. He made me forget everything good, so I screwed things up with Declan. It wasn't my fault. Well, I mean it was—it was my fault, but I didn't mean it."

I knew I wasn't making sense and that there was no possible way she could understand me, but she didn't ask for clarification. She just kept saying, "It wasn't your fault," and "Everything will be okay." All the things I wanted to hear, whether or not they were true...and whether or not they were possible.

I took the phone away from my ear when I heard the swish sound of a new text.

'I'm here. Should I knock, or do you just want to come out?'

Emilia must have broken every traffic law on her way over because it definitely hadn't been ten minutes.

'I'll come out,' I quickly typed.

My stepfather might still be downstairs, and I didn't want to see him. He'd passed on his DNA and sense of entitlement to the asshole who'd started all of this. I grabbed my biggest purse and tossed in a change of clothes and my phone, then wedged the bottle of scotch in between layers of clothing, slipped on some boots, and ran downstairs.

"You're home early," Timothy said from the living room as I ran past him. "Leaving late, then."

I was surprised he'd ever noticed when I came home or went out. But I didn't care. I slammed the front door behind me and jogged down the steps to Emilia's car.

She was standing next to it, gripping her phone. As soon as she saw me, she slid back into the driver's seat and reached across to open the passenger side for me. I tossed my bag into the back, grimacing when I remembered the crystal bottle that was in there and hoping it wouldn't empty all over my stuff and Emilia's back seat.

"Shit! I forgot there was liquid in there." After I'd closed the door, I reached into the back to move it to the floor and set it upright.

"Don't worry about it," Emilia said. "Are you okay?"

"I will be. But can we leave now?"

Her reply was to shift the car into drive and hit the gas pedal so hard, the tires squealed. I laughed, imagining how furious my stepfather would be when he saw the ugly marks on his fancy stone driveway.

We drove off in silence, Emilia's hands gripping the wheel.

"What's that sound?"

I looked at her, not knowing what she was referring to. Then I heard it. Someone was yelling something that sounded like my name, their voice distant and muffled. The radio was off, so I looked into the side mirror, not expecting to see my mom running down the street yelling my name or anything, but I didn't know where it was coming from.

"Crap!" I turned around and rummaged through my bag until I found my phone and hit the speaker button.

"...swear to God, I'm calling 911 if you don't answer me right now!"

Emilia and I both jerked at the volume of Andi's voice.

"I'm sorry," I said quickly. "I forgot to end the call."

"I have her, Andi. We're on our way to your place."

Her deep breath was audible. "Okay. Okay, good." Then her voice lowered. "They're fine, Hayden." His reply was mumbled. "I'm okay, too...*now*."

"I'm sorry," I repeated.

"It's fine, Sara. Just make sure Em doesn't crash on the way here. I'm going to calm down and make us some tea. Unless you need something stronger."

"I kind of had a bit too much earlier, so tea sounds good."

"Make mine a double," Emilia said, smiling. "See you soon."

When we arrived, Andi was waiting at the door, arms out and ready for me to walk into them. "We're going to fix whatever's going on, okay?" She let me go and smiled. "And if we can't fix it, we'll kill it."

"Pretend I'm not here." Hayden set down a tea pot on the coffee table in the living room just as we walked in. "Unless you need anything else."

"We're fine, hon. Thanks."

"And you'll—"

"We'll let you know if that changes," Andi said, nodding.

Hayden turned around and headed toward his office. I'd

only been to their house a couple of times since they'd remodeled it. The upgrades had been Hayden's wedding gift to Andi, and he'd gone way over the top, turning the outdated house of Andi's childhood into a larger, smarter, beautiful home for the children they planned to have.

"It's chamomile." Andi poured the steaming liquid into a mug and handed one to me before filling the other two. No one said anything until we all had something hot to wrap our hands around. No one said anything after that either—they just stared at me, obviously waiting for me to start.

One step at a time. "Remember when I told you nothing was wrong?"

"Which time?"

"All of them. At least all of them in the last year or so. Well, that wasn't true—something *was* wrong."

Over the next hour, these women proved over and over why I never should've kept this secret from them. They listened to my whole story without saying a word to insinuate any of it was my fault or to hint that they didn't believe me. One or both of them gave me a hug when I need one and gave me space when I needed a break.

I told them everything—about Cal and my mother, why I'd been afraid to tell them the truth, and what had happened a few hours ago. I didn't leave anything out, and it felt amazing. Amazing and horrible. By the time I'd run out of things to say, I was exhausted.

"I should've come clean a long time ago," I said, sitting back against the couch and stretching out legs that had been tucked under me for too long. "I'm sorry I lied to you."

"Apology not accepted." Emilia set down her tea cup. "Because it's not necessary. I wish it had occurred to me that your silence was because it was too hard for you to say. Instead, I took it personally and treated you in exactly the opposite way I should've."

"It's okay."

"No, it's not," Andi said. "But it's in the past, and from this moment on, we can do better. I'm ready to help you in any way you need, and I'd guess the same thing goes for Emilia." She turned to her. "Yes?"

"Absolutely. Name it."

"I can't go back to that house." I couldn't take running into Cal again, or looking at my mom's face, knowing she took his side over her own daughter's. My mom had chosen her walk-in closet over me. She'd decided not to believe her daughter because believing me would've ruined her perfect, imaginary world.

"Damn straight, you can't. You can stay with Rob and me." Emilia cringed guiltily as she remembered something. "As long as you don't mind tripping over boxes."

"No, you should stay here," Andi said, "for as long as you want. We have the room. Plus, it would give us some time to talk about this Declan guy, who Emilia already got to meet."

I sighed. Emilia and Andi were amazing and completely irreplaceable, and so was Declan. I'd been an idiot to fight how I felt about him, to pretend it wasn't real. It *was* real.

"About Declan...He's the other thing I might have messed up tonight."

32

DECLAN

I knew I was awake because my luck was so fucked up that my head wouldn't feel this close to exploding until I was conscious. My mouth tasted like dirt, and I was in a bed that wasn't mine. Mine was bigger and didn't smell like some kind of plastic flower spray.

One eye...open. The other pressed into the pillow because I was facedown and practically being smothered by it.

"Too old for this shit." I sat up slowly to avoid any further damage to my body.

Oh fuck. I was one hundred percent nude. No girl, though. No guy either, thank the heavens.

So, why was I naked in someone else's bed? Too much alcohol, too fast, and with too little food, that's why.

When I looked at the nightstand and saw a picture of Carissa hugging another woman who looked like her clone, I kind of wanted to die. What was worse than waking up with a raging hangover in a stranger's bed? Waking up with a raging hangover in the bed of Sara's slightly odd friend who I'd met whenever I met her. A couple of months ago, maybe? Shit, for all I knew, I'd been passed out for a few years, and this was a parallel universe. One in which women slept with the guy their friend was, or had pretended to be, interested in. And guys who were interested in one girl woke up in another one's bed with no memory of how he got there.

Fuck.

I found my clothes in a pile on the floor and then navigated to the living room, where I found other naked people, including Trevor. Making very sure to keep my eyes away from certain areas of my friend that I never wanted to see, I shook him awake.

"Trev, let's get out of here."

Trevor groaned and turned over to shove me away and mumble, "Three more hours, Mom."

After a few more tries, I left him to sleep it off, remembering just enough of the previous night to know that neither one of us had been really happy after our talk with Moguli Music guys.

But Trevor recovered a lot faster than I did. In a couple more hours, he'd have completely forgotten his disappointment and would have already moved on to bigger and even more implausible fantasies.

While, in a couple more hours, and for the rest of the foreseeable future, I'd still be thinking about Sara and trying to figure out why the fantasy I'd actually been living had to end.

I stepped over the intertwined feet of a couple who might still be physically stuck together under a small fussy blanket and headed toward the scent of fresh brew.

Carissa was sitting at the table, drinking a cup of coffee from one side of her mouth so she could rest her head in her other hand. Her eye makeup had smeared, making her look as if she'd been crying. Even though she looked like hell, I didn't comment because I *felt* like hell and probably looked even worse.

I nodded to her steaming mug. "Any more of that?"

"Help yourself." She nodded slowly as if moving any faster were impossible. "I thought you would've left already."

"Why's that?" I filled a mug to the very rim and took a careful sip before joining her at the table. The coffee was lava hot—exactly what I deserved. Maybe a third-degree burn on my tongue would remind me how stupid I was the next time I decided getting wasted was a good idea.

"Because you and Sara are"—she shrugged with only one shoulder—"doing something that's more complicated than it needs to be."

I took a deep breath, not sure if I should answer because my brain couldn't possibly be working at full capacity yet.

"You know I'm right. You're into her, and she's into *you*."

Sure, she was into me. Enough to fuck, but not enough to let down her guard or keep her promises. But even worse, having a big blank instead of any memories of last night didn't let me off the hook either. If I'd been able to sleep with someone, I'd been coherent enough to know it was wrong.

"Ta-da!" Carissa barely lifted her hands, but I knew she'd meant to. "I've figured it out for you. You're both welcome."

"Thanks," I said unappreciatively. "You're her friend, right?" After she agreed, I continued, "So, why'd you sleep with me?"

"Because it's my bed?" Her painted brows came together. "Wait, you think we had sex?"

"We didn't?" When she shook her head, the sense of relief almost sobered me up. That was the best news I'd heard all year.

"Believe me, hon, if we'd fucked you'd remember. Although, you're a hell of a cuddler." She chuckled to herself. "Last night, Trevor talked you into going skinny-dipping in the community pool, and ten minutes later, you got all depressed and wandered off. I brought you back here before another tenant found you and called the cops. I tucked you into bed, put on my jammies, and slept on top of the covers next to you. I thought about putting your clothes back on, but I was drunk. If you'd turned or I'd slipped and touched something I wasn't supposed to, I wouldn't be able to look Sara in the eyes again. So, I swear—nothing dirty happened."

I remembered snippets of all that. Swimming, not the naked part. Getting depressed, not being put to bed like a toddler. But I was definitely happy that we hadn't had sex because I wouldn't have been able to look Sara in the eyes again either.

Even though Sara was very possibly waking up naked in some guy's bed right now. Actually, no. It was already eight o'clock—she'd be long gone by now.

"Thanks, Carissa, for..." How did you thank someone for babysitting your drunk ass?

"Not fucking my friend's man?"

"Am I her man?" Even I heard the frustration in my voice.

"You're more her man than anyone else has ever been, at least that she's ever told me about."

That was nice to hear. It also peaked my curiosity. Sara and I had never discussed our relationship history beyond my failed affair with Señora Martinez and Sara being a late bloomer.

"Has she always been like this?" I asked.

"Like what?"

"Partying...not wanting to care about anyone..."

She stared into her coffee for a minute. "Sara has a lot of family shit that she tries to stay away from. And forget about. At first it was just going out a lot. The guys started later, and it wasn't like there was a new one every night or anything. Then, obviously, as soon as you came along, that all stopped."

"Obviously?"

"Look, Sara doesn't talk about herself much, especially not when she's sober. But her dad left when she was tiny, and her stepdad seems like kind of a jackass. So, you know, that can kind of screw with a girl's head." She paused, staring into dead space as if there was more she wanted to say. But for some reason I didn't think it would be about Sara. Should I ask? We barely knew each other and only had the barest of reason to trust one another. But I'd listen if she wanted to talk. Turned out, she didn't.

She looked at me and squinted. "How interested in her are you? It's none of my business, but I want to know. I'm hoping you like her enough to last at least a little while. Because she's basically been no fun whatsoever lately, and although that sucks for me, it's really good for her. So...?"

I rubbed my eye and leaned forward onto my elbows. "I think I'm good for her, Carissa. And I'm good *to* her. But I'm way more interested in her than she is in me. And honestly, I'm getting tired of being treated like shit." Like I didn't matter or wasn't there. Like I was a purse she could use one day and toss in the corner the next.

"Give her one more chance, Declan. Everyone deserves a second chance."

I laughed. "I've already given her three. Does everyone deserve a fourth chance?"

When I got home, Kitty eyed me angrily. Great, another couple of X chromosomes hated me.

"I'm sorry, girl. I didn't expect to be out all night." I let her out onto the balcony, so she could take care of business, and went into the kitchen. At some point during the night, Kitty had decided to punish me by making herself dinner, which meant I got to clean up after her. I'd need a new bag of dog food since she'd torn through it and scattered kibble throughout the kitchen. There was no place to stand without hearing the snap of food crumbling under my foot.

I crunched my way to the pantry to get the broom and

dustpan and started sweeping it into a pile. When I dumped the first load of dog food into the trash, I saw the take-out packages from my last dinner with Sara. Not sure why seeing the remnants of a great evening stung so deeply, but it did. Made me wonder what I was doing with my life. You know, like Japanese food does for everyone. It tasted so great at the time, but the enjoyment didn't last. And the next day, that enjoyment turned to shit. Literally, in the case of Japanese food, figuratively for everything else.

Nothing lasted. Not even life. And it sure as shit was too short to spend it doing things or people you don't want to do. These were supposed to be my peak years. I was young, fit, and confident. So, why was I currently cleaning up after the only being on earth who loved me unconditionally?

Sara didn't love me. She might not even like me. It certainly didn't feel like she respected me. So, what was I to her?

Trevor loved me like a brother, but even though we'd never spoken it aloud, we both knew his dependence on me wasn't at a healthy level. I'd stuck with him and the band all this time because it was the only way I'd know he'd be safe from himself. Even if I'd never been able to really stop him from poisoning himself with liquor, drugs, or thoughts, I'd always felt like I'd been helping keep him alive, but had I? Maybe this whole time I'd just been giving him someone to rebel against. Someone he knew would keep him standing so he never had to try doing it for himself.

All I was to them was a prop—something they could count on to be there whenever they screwed up and couldn't stand alone.

When I took my guitar off the wall and sat down on the couch, Kitty rubbed her head on my knee. Somehow, she knew as soon as the guitar came out, I needed comfort. Companion-ship. Love. And she was right.

My song-writing process was always the same—start what I saw as doodling with the strings, strumming or plucking them in random order until something clicked. Then I'd play that riff over and over until it naturally led to another stanza and another. As soon as the momentum kicked in, my fingers understood where they were supposed to go before my brain did.

Once I had a basic chorus laid out, I said the first thing that came to my mind. Like a bad rapper trying to fit phrases to the beat. But since I knew the song's rhythm, phrases came to me automatically. Some were complete shit, but I kept going, kept saying whatever came into my head until something sounded...*right*.

I didn't know anyone else who composed like I did—trusting myself enough to put something together on the fly. The other guys made fun of me for it, but they'd also never refused to play a song I wrote for them.

I never set out to write a complete and stage-worthy song. I wrote to figure out what was going on in my head. When I was depressed, when nothing in there made sense, playing music helped me sort it all out. Music was my version of therapy, and aside from a new set of strings every once in a while, it had never cost me a dime.

As soon as I had enough notes put together for the beginnings of a chorus, I closed my eyes and played it over and over, listening to the tone and rhythm until I understood it. The notes were soft, pensive. The rhythm was way slower than anything Self Defense would ever play. The pauses were longer but felt true. If I let myself get all metaphysical and deep, I'd have said they sounded like emptiness. And I'd have said the notes sounded like goodbye. No bitterness or anger, just regret for what could've been. Maybe even a little apology.

Then I opened my mouth, not knowing what would come out.

"Who left who?" I kept playing the same few bars of music over and over, saying whatever felt right. I'd worry about getting it to sound right later. Maybe.

One side...to every good story
    One line...to end every joke
    One chance...to say that you're sorry
    One shot...to make this thing work

One side...gets the blue ribbon
    One guy...comes in second place
    One time...to catch her not listening
    One last moment...to look at her face

She could stare at her own reflection,
    And never be able to see what I do.
    So, no matter how strong our connection,
    This will never work out like I wanted it to.

It needed some work, but then, who didn't?

33

DECLAN

"*D*eclan!" Trevor yelled through the door. "Let me in! I can hear you playing, so I know you're in there. Open the damn door!" His pounding set Kitty on edge, and I could've sworn she sighed as she walked toward the door. I could tell she didn't want to see what was on the other side any more than I did, but Trevor was just stubborn enough to stay out there all day.

"Relax, girl. I'll get rid of him as soon as I can." I patted her and then grabbed her collar before I opened the door, just in case she decided to run for it. "Shut up, man. You're scaring my dog." I left the door open and pulled her into the living room, hearing Trev close it behind himself.

"I lost my keys at some point last night." Which also meant he'd lost the spare for my apartment. Great. "Can I grab yours?"

I let Kitty go and went over to the TV stand. The key was in a small drawer, mixed in with remotes, pens, and some other random shit no one ever needs and no one ever gets rid of.

Trevor flopped onto the baby-sized couch that came with the place and stretched out. His head rested on one end, and his feet hung off the other. I tossed his spare key to him, but his eyes were already closed, so it landed on his belly. He didn't react.

I sat down in the chair opposite him. Kitty sat on one of my feet, still watching him suspiciously. It was probably the smell—he reeked of booze and sweat.

"Kitty thinks you should take a shower."

"Kitty's favorite scent is *Ass du Jour*, so forgive me if I'm not too worried about her opinion."

"Fine, *I* think you should shower before your stench works its way into that couch. I'd like to get my security deposit back." I reached out with a foot and nudged him in the leg.

"As soon as you get the apartment to stop spinning, I'm gone."

"The *apartment*?" I sighed. "Yeah, sure."

"You got something to kill the pain in my head? Make it ten somethings."

If anyone else had made the comment, I would've let it go. But Trevor wasn't allowed to. How did he not know that? I stared at him, dumbfounded, while he just lay there with his eyes still closed, acting as if he hadn't made a horribly inappropriate joke.

"Don't fucking say shit like that." My hands gripped the arms of the chair, and I kicked him harder. I wanted to do it standing, to have my full leverage. How many times had I wanted to hit him, to hurt him for everything he'd put me through?

He twisted his head to look at me. "Oh, come on, Dec. That was years ago." As if I didn't know that. "Different times, man. Everything's great now."

"Everything's great?" I snapped. "The only difference between then and now is that *I'm* the miserable one, and you're killing yourself slowly instead of in one swift shot."

He sat up, staring at me. "Why are you miserable? Is it Moguli giving us the whole we-love-you-*but* speech?" He scoffed. "Nah, it's that *girl* giving you the love-you-but speech, isn't it?"

That girl hadn't said any of those words, actually. "Kinda." Because, unfortunately, every thought I had was about *that girl* lately. But not this one. "She's part of it."

"What's the other part?"

I laughed, throwing up my hands, afraid to tell him the truth. Pissed that he chose to focus on that instead of his slow and steady death wish.

"What's the other part, Dec?" Suddenly, he sounded sober, all blur of hangover gone.

"Never mind."

"Fuck you. Tell me. Is it me? Am I making you miserable?"

I let out a deep breath.

"Wow." He leaned back on the couch. "Okay, I'm making you miserable, and yet this is the very first time I've heard anything about it. Way to use those big balls of yours, Dec."

"It's not a big deal." I grabbed my guitar and slipped the strap over my head. Not to play, though. My guitar had been a shield for as long as I could remember, some wood and strings I hid behind whenever I didn't know how else to communicate all the shit going through my mind.

"If it weren't a big deal, you would've said *annoyed* or *pissed-off*. But you didn't. You said *miserable*. When someone like you uses a word like *miserable* to describe himself it automatically becomes it a big deal."

"Someone like me?"

He shrugged. "Someone who has his shit together, who sees the bad but doesn't give up looking until he finds the good."

Was that who I was? "I don't think that's true anymore."

"Thank God. Finally, some proof you're human. Okay, then, spill. Or do you think I can't handle it? Do you think I'm too delicate and weak to know? What the fuck do you want, Dec? You want me to read your mind?"

I shook my head. I'd been avoiding this conversation for years, putting up with all kinds of shit I didn't like because I didn't want to cause trouble. But I was sick of that, and Trevor was right—he was a grown man, despite how he acted. He deserved to know the truth, and I deserved to have the life I wanted. If I didn't say something now, I'd be stuck in this for years. And those years would feel like an eternity.

"Fine, you want to know what I want? Or how 'bout what I *don't* want?" I twisted my body to look at him straight-on. "I *don't* want to be in the band. I haven't wanted to for a while now, but I didn't want to disappoint you."

"Motherfucker." His eyes narrowed. "You want to go solo? After everything we've done *together* to get where we are, you want to dump me on my fucking ass and go solo."

"No, you shithead. I don't want to go solo. I don't want any of this." I held on to my guitar as if it were the last life jacket on the Titanic. "I hate performing. I hate being told what to do. I hate being styled. Don't you? Fuck, if one more person tries to tell me I should wear guyliner, I'm going to break a perfectly good guitar over their idiot head."

The longer I ranted, the wider his eyes got. My guess—he probably couldn't fathom why anyone wouldn't want whatever fame we'd garnered. His mind couldn't wrap around the idea that the thing he'd dreamed about for over a decade was the thing I hated most about my life.

I took a deep breath when I ran out of shit to say, shit I'd been holding back for at least the last few years, probably a lot longer.

"So..." he said after a minute. "I'm not sure I understand what you want."

"Didn't you hear anything I ju—?" I tossed up my arms up

instead of strangling him. "Come on, man. Could you please just take something seriously for once?"

He was silent, staring at me and scratching the scruff on his chin. "What I meant was, do you want to quit because you hate the music or because you hate *me*?"

I didn't even pause. "Neither. I love both of you, even though you piss me the fuck off almost constantly. I don't want to quit our friendship, and I don't want to quit music. I just don't want everything to be about Self Defense. Remember when we used to talk about normal shit before the band became our entire lives? I want to keep writing and playing music. I just don't want to do it for *other* people. I want to do it for myself. Does that make sense?"

If I were talking to anyone else, I wouldn't have had to ask that question. But Trevor had been wearing blinders since the day our first agent came backstage and told us we had a real shot at going pro. Ever since then, the only thing Trev had cared about was reaching that goal. Well, that and all the perks that came with it.

He stood and came over to me, motioning for me to stand. When I did, slowly, he smiled. As soon as I set my guitar down next to me, he smacked me in the chest. "Why didn't you say that in the first place?"

I stiffened, suspicious. No way could someone recover that fast after hearing that their best friend wanted to kill their only goal in life. Could they? Had I misjudged him that badly? After all this time?

"Shit, man." He shook my hand, then pulled me into a half hug, smacking my back a lot harder than my chest. "I can't believe you've been holding all that crap in for so long. What's your problem?"

"Too many to count," I said, laughing, relieved and shocked as hell by his reaction but wanting it to be real.

My happiness fell a little as we parted, and I saw how forced his smile looked. His teeth were showing, but his lips were tight, and the smile didn't even make it halfway to his eyes.

"You sure you're okay with this?" I asked. "We could talk about it more. Maybe come up with a plan."

"The plan's already been made, dude. No more Defense. Done. It's that easy. I'm not going to force my bestie to do something he hates doing."

The words coming out of his mouth were great—exactly what I wanted to hear. But I couldn't help wondering if I'd been right the first time. Nothing was this easy. Nothing came true just because somebody said it. That wasn't how life worked. It wasn't how *people* worked.

"Even if I'm not in the band anymore, you don't have to break it up. I mean, you guys could still make it happen. I could still write the songs, and Pete could sing lead."

He laughed. "No offense, Dec, but neither of us is as stupid as we look. Without a pretty face out front, our chances of going prime time get a whole lot worse."

I could've named ten incredible bands off the top of my head whose lead singers weren't easy on anyone's eyes, but unfortunately, things were different now. With the advent of YouTube and constant cruelty of trolls and the media, the industry nowadays was more about celebrity than music. Sure, there were exceptions, but the more idiotic, immaterial boxes you could check off, the better your shot would be.

"Besides, I've been thinking something similar lately."

I jerked back a step. "I thought the band was your everything."

"It was...is. But I'm tired, man. Too much partying, not enough pussy."

"You're a pig, you know that?"

He busted up. "I told you—I'm not as stupid as I look. All

this shit is just a lot more intense than I thought it would be, and I'm not good at moderation."

"So, you're really not pissed at me?"

He pinched both of my cheeks and forced my head side to side. "How could anyone be pissed at a face like this one?"

I swatted him away, but he'd already let go. "Ever the shithead."

"A man's gotta stay true to who he is." He went back to the couch and grabbed his apartment key. "We're still gonna jam, though, right? You come up with the tune and the lyrics, and I pretend like I'm helping?"

"Always, my brother."

"Hey, have you taken that song into the studio already? The one you were playing when I got here."

"It's not even close to being ready." I shook my head, wishing he hadn't heard it through the door. Not only was the song not good enough to share yet, all the emotion I'd put into it was still a big mess in my head. "It needs a lot of work before I let anyone hear it."

"Except me," he said, smiling. "Play it again."

"Now?" I asked, picking up my guitar without thinking. Part of me was proud that he'd liked what he'd heard enough to want to hear it again. The other part was terrified I'd break down halfway through if I actually played it for him.

"No, the next time I'm pounding on your door. Of course, now."

"It's not finished yet."

"Then play what *is* finished."

When I realized he'd never give up, I nodded slowly. "It's still really rough. There are a couple lines I'm not crazy about, and—"

"Shut up and play, Dec."

I sat down and set my guitar on my lap, taking my time and pretending the perfectly tuned strings needed adjusting.

"How 'bout you play the damn song before I go bald and need a hearing aid?"

"Okay, okay. I'll play." I kept my head down because the song and the pain that had inspired it were too fresh to look anyone in the face. I fucked up the second verse a little, and my fingering wasn't as fast as I wanted it to be in the chorus, but I got through the whole fucking thing without bawling like a little kid.

After the last note, neither of us said anything for a minute. When I finally looked up at him, his face reflected the kind of thoughtful calm I hadn't seen since before all this started.

"Told you it wasn't ready yet," I mumbled.

"Are you kidding? That was some good shit, man. Really good shit. I could hear your heart in it. It's been a while since you put your heart into something like that."

"Yeah," I said quietly. "It has."

"Send it to me. I don't care if it's a shit recording. I just want to listen to it again."

"I can do that." I glanced at my computer, thinking about how easy it was to record a track and email it to someone nowadays. "But it's for your ears only."

"Of course." He slapped his hands together and smiled. "Now, I'm going home to catch up on the z's I missed last night. Then I'll talk to the guys and let them know Self Defense is splitting."

"I think I should do it. Don't you?"

He shook his head as he walked to the door. "It'll be better coming from me. Plus, if they need someone to punch, we don't want anything to mess up that pretty face of yours."

I smiled. "I told you—just because I'm not in Self Defense, doesn't mean you guys can't keep it going."

"Oh, dear, sweet little Declan," he said, laughing. "That's never going to happen. We can't write, can't sing, and I don't think I could handle being the only gorgeous one left after you leave."

"Don't make that call yet, Trev. Let's talk to the guys together."

"Fine. Tomorrow night? They'll both take it better if they have a couple beers in them."

"One beer," I said, shaking my head. "Telling them after more than one will only make things harder."

"Good point. Especially with how weepy Sam gets when he drinks hard liquor."

"Then maybe we can come back here after. Get all nostalgic and play some of our old tunes."

"Double shit, no. We gotta go out to raise some hell before our fame disappears. Our last hurrah while we're potentially famous could make us forever infamous!"

Nothing could sound less appealing than that, actually. "I'm still dealing with being dumped, so I might not be any fun."

"All the more reason to go out, get shit-faced, and let a random long-legged beauty in stripper heels take advantage of you."

"I'll let you know." We shook hands and bro-hugged again at the door. "So, we're good?"

"Always, bro."

"Thanks for understanding, Trev."

"Thanks for coming clean. But next time, maybe do it a year or so earlier?"

"Yeah," I mumbled. "I'll do that."

"And send me that song before you forget."

"I'll do that, too."

That had gone ten thousand times better than I'd imagined it would. Almost made me wonder if I was missing something. I knew how much the band meant to him, and knowing that my happiness meant more than that left me speechless.

I watched him walk to the elevator and press the button. It would be too fucking Hallmark or romantic comedy if I stayed in the open doorway, waiting and hoping he'd turn around to see me again and then reading something into it, so I shut the door and grabbed my laptop.

After I recorded the song and emailed the file to Trevor, I went into my bedroom and got under the covers with Kitty. We stayed there for the rest of the day—her snoring peacefully, and me wondering what would happen next. At least it couldn't get any worse, right?

34

SARA

$\mathcal{I}$ stood outside Declan's apartment, staring at his door for a minute. Okay, fine. But it was no more than ten. Plus, I did a little pacing, too. Gotta get in the cardio when you can, right?

"Oh shit." I jerked, looking for a place to hide when I heard the elevator doors open. Unfortunately, the hallway was just that, a hallway, with no plants or corners to hide behind. There was a window at one end, though. Which, in San Francisco, meant there was probably a fire escape right outside. Unfortunately, all that nervous pacing hadn't improved my ninja skills enough to get there in time. So, I pretended to casually look outside—i.e. hide my face— and hoped it wasn't Declan.

"Sara?" a woman's voice asked. "Sara, is that you?"

I slowly turned around, contemplating my response. Declan's neighbor-slash-dog sitter, Rebecca, stood there, smiling at me while rummaging around in her purse, presumably for her keys.

"Hi," I whispered, praying these walls were thick enough that he hadn't heard Rebecca say my name. "How are you?"

"Good. Is Declan out? Dang it. I should've checked with him

earlier. I was hoping I could borrow Kitty tonight. She's great company. I swear I'm going to miss that dog so much when he leaves."

Should I lie? Tell her he was out even though I still had no idea if he was or not? Because I hadn't built up enough courage to knock on his door. "I'm not sure, actually. I just got here myself." I could tell by her expression she was confused by my implausible timeline. So, I did what any sane person would do—I added another lie on top of the first one. "A bird hit the window. I was checking to see if it was okay." If I were lucky, I'd figure a way out of it before I hit the four-lie maximum during one conversation.

"Oh, the poor thing," she said. "I owe you an apology, then."

"For what?"

"Well, when I saw you here, I assumed you were pretending you hadn't been standing outside Declan's door, wondering if you should knock or not." Thankfully, her smile was friendly, not condescending or judgmental. I wasn't sure I could take any more judgment—I'd already done enough of it.

I threw my hands up. "You won't tell him I'm a total coward, will you?"

"Of course not. It's none of my business. But I don't know what you're afraid of. Declan's incredible, and he really likes you."

I must have reacted visually because her expression changed, and she nodded even though I hadn't said a word. Damn my face.

"Are you guys fighting?"

I shrugged. "It was a misunderstanding—he misunderstood one of my issues for another one of my issues, a more hurtful one."

"Sounds complicated." Her keys clinked together as she pulled them out of her bag. "Will a drink give you courage?"

I followed her toward her door, my stomach churning a warning that under no circumstances should I dare pour anything alcoholic into it. "Maybe a glass of water?" So, if I ever did gather up enough courage to knock on his door, at least my throat wouldn't be too dry to speak.

Just as she cracked open her door, I heard another open behind me. Knowing it was Declan's, I almost shoved Rebecca through hers to get out of the hallway. But all I managed to accomplish was to scare her into stopping and turning around to check what the hell was wrong with me.

"Hey." Declan's tone was too flat to know if he was furious, disappointed, or completely over me. His expression didn't give away anything either. Crap, was it possible to go through all the breakup steps and get to indifference in a single day? I didn't have enough experience with relationships to know. I'd seen a lot of people go through it, but they'd all been fairly high-maintenance women. The kind who broke down and cried if Nordstrom's didn't have the pair of shoes they wanted in their size. I was fairly sure a man wouldn't do that.

Declan stood half in and half out of his doorway, his legs wide to block Kitty from escaping.

"Hi," I muttered lamely.

"Hey, Dec. Sara came here to talk to you, but I've decided to kidnap her instead because you haven't shared her at all. And I'm lonely. Plus, I need more friends. Of course, if you *really, really* want to talk to her, I guess I could wait a bit. Up to you. But you'd owe me...a lot, so think about it carefully."

Whoever this woman was, I needed her to be my friend. She'd casually set it up so that both Declan and I could save face without directly offending the other. Of course, I still hoped Declan wanted to talk to me, but it wasn't my choice anymore. I'd blown my shot when I chose to have a pity party for myself rather than thinking of him and the promise I'd made. But I crossed my fingers anyway.

He stared at me silently for a long time, probably long enough for me to have run to the window and thrown myself out of it.

"I guess I'm going to owe you, Rebecca. Sorry. Add whatever you want to my tab."

I let out a breath of air, feeling my shoulders lower even though I hadn't noticed they'd lifted.

I turned to Rebecca. "I think this one should go on my tab, actually. I'll pay his off, too. Over coffee sometime?"

"Declan's is big enough to buy a Starbucks," she joked. "But I'll happily call it even if you get him to stop moping through the hallway."

"I'll do my best."

His smile only lifted one side of his mouth before Rebecca rushed inside her apartment and slammed the door, her "Bye" muffled from inside, but I could still hear her laughter.

I turned to Declan. "You don't have to talk to me. I mean, I'll understa—"

"Want to come in?" he asked, flicking his head. "Or should we go to neutral ground?"

"You pick."

He chuckled. "Oh, so *now* I get to choose?" Then he blew out a breath and ran both hands over his face, finally pushing his hair back and looking at me. "Shit, I didn't mean that. I'm just...I'm..."

"Mad at me?" I asked as I followed him inside and shut the door behind me. At least Kitty wasn't angry—she nuzzled my leg as I walked carefully, each step a struggle to keep from tripping over her. I rubbed her head to thank her for her support.

"Hurt. Confused. Completely out of my element."

"What do you mean?"

He sat on the arm of the couch, and I took the opposite chair. Kitty stood between us for a second like a child being forced to pick which parent they'd live with. I didn't stand a chance—I wasn't even her stepmom. I was more like the thief who brought her a treat to distract her long enough to steal stuff. When she realized that, she plodded over to her dad and shoved her nose into his hand until he petted her.

"I've been pretty spoiled my whole life," he said. "I have very few wants. And when I do want something, I usually get it without too much struggle. Now, what I want has never been clearer"—he smiled sadly—"and I've never been so unsure of how to get it." He lifted his hand from Kitty's head and curled it into a fist. "Every time I think I finally have it within my grasp, it slips through my fingers, and I'm back where I started—empty." He opened his fist and stared at the palm of his hand.

I was too chicken to ask if he meant a relationship or a relationship with *me*.

Obviously, Kitty knew how he was feeling, or maybe she was just another female who lived for his attention, but she pushed at him until he started petting her again. It must be so great to be a dog. So simple. No games or confusion or misunderstandings. Nothing to feel sorry about, no chance of screwing up and hurting the person you loved. Kitty knew what she needed and demanded it without guilt or worry.

"I'm sorry." It came out so quietly, only Kitty would've been able to hear it. So, I tried again. "I'm sorry, Declan. I didn't mean to miss your gig, and I wasn't out partying."

"Where were you?"

I took a deep breath, steadying myself for the truth. Emilia and Andi had spent months trying to get me to explain what had happened with Cal, and then a few hours last night helping me figure out a way to tell Declan. But now that I was here, in front of him, it was like none of that had happened.

"Remember when we were at that bar, and I told you that people should believe the people they loved when they told them something?"

His eyes darkened. "So, I should just believe that you didn't diss me to go out partying? Without any proof, and despite how slurred your voice was?"

"No! That's not what I'm saying. That comment wasn't about you."

"Then who the hell was it about?" Damn, even Kitty glared at me angrily.

"My stepbrother...because he raped me." I doubted either one of us had expected that to come out of my mouth quite like that. Declan's look of shock made sense—this was the first time he'd heard about it. Mine was because I'd never told anyone so bluntly before. I couldn't remember exactly which words I'd used to explain to my mother what Cal had done to me, but it definitely hadn't been that direct. Neither had it been that bold when I'd told Emilia and Andi last night.

I think I just knew Declan wouldn't blame me, no matter how much I might've blame myself.

35

SARA

"He...?" Declan stuttered. "Cal, the guy I met in the alley...and at your house, he...?"

I nodded. "He raped me." I said it for him, the word already sounding stronger, more sure, even though I'd only said it out loud a handful of times.

"Are you serious?" Then he held up his hand. "I didn't mean that to be a question. I know you're serious. I'm just... That motherfucker." His lips tightened and looked like he wanted to come to me but wasn't sure he was allowed. Eventually, he must have realized he was or decided that he didn't care whether he was or not and came over and sank down onto his knees in front of me. "I believe you."

People always go on about the *big* three little words—*I, love,* and *you*—and I'm sure they're great to hear. But there was no way they could be more powerful, more amazing, than *these* three little words. Saying 'I believe you' to someone who's spent over a year not feeling heard or seen or believed in, those three words let me breathe again.

"I'm here for as long as you need me, and I'll listen to

however much you want to share." He smiled. "As long as you don't blame me for wanting to beat him to a pulp. I won't do it—unless you want me to—but *I* want to. All you have to do is say the word. Deal?"

"Deal." I reached out and touched his cheek, tracing the edge of his jaw and losing myself in his warmth. "You make me happy, prouder to be who I am than anyone else ever has. I thought I was strong enough."

"You are strong enough...for anything."

I shook my head, remembering how badly I'd frozen in what was supposed to be my big moment. "I thought I was ready to confront him last night, to tell him how much he'd hurt me, how much what he'd done had affected my life. But I wasn't. And when he blew me off and walked away, I didn't know what to do. Well, that's not exactly true. I wanted to crawl into your lap, but since you weren't there, I grabbed the only other thing I knew would help me feel better." The rest of my explanation of the night and how my friends had helped me came out between blubbering and wiping away tears. I'm not sure how much of it he understood, but he never stopped listening.

"I did the same thing, except there was more than one bottle involved, I think. Fuck, I wish I'd picked up my phone. I'm sorry." He squeezed my hand.

"You didn't do anything wrong."

"Well, that's an argument we can have later, but for now..." He cleared his throat. "I'm going to ask you something, but if you don't want to, don't feel bad. In fact, to make it easier on both of us, how about you say 'Not right now' instead of a flat out 'You've gotta be fucking kidding me?'"

"You're scaring me."

"I think you should bring some stuff over here. I'm not talking about putting your name on the lease or anything...yet."

He smiled. "But I don't think it's a good idea to stay in that house anymore. Not when that asshole can stop by whenever he wants to."

"Wow." Yep, that was all I could manage. I knew he wasn't actually asking me to move in with him, but it was a big step in that direction. "Don't you think it might put unnecessary pressure on both of us to make it official?"

"To make what official? I'm still not even sure we're dating. But we seem to enjoy having sleepovers, have literally been as close as two people can be, and you already feel comfortable enough here to steal my coffee. Plus, I've walked in on you while you were taking a shower and hope to do it a lot more, so we don't have to worry about those parts. Or did you mean that it'll officially mean we're exclusive? Because then, yeah, I think it will. But I've been okay with that since day one. Are you?"

I don't think I'd ever get tired of his smile. "Yeah. I think I'm okay with that."

"Good. Then you should bring some stuff over here and stay until you find your own apartment. I'm hoping to have at least another three weeks before the owner of this one finds out about Kitty being here and we get kicked out. So, maybe we'll end up..."

In the time it took him to kiss my forehead, my mind went to all kinds of ways we could "end up"—living together, sharing a place, shopping for apartments together...

"...being homeless together," he finished.

"Homeless?" Yeah, no one could possibly miss the disappointment in my voice. "That wasn't the way I thought that sentence was going to go."

"Really?" he asked innocently, his eyes giving him away. "Which way were you hoping it went?"

I shrugged. "Maybe we'll end up being neighbors."

"Only if you sunbathe topless and leave all the drapes open on the side facing my place." He sighed. "But let's not worry about the future quite yet. Let's deal with right now. And right now, I would be very happy if you stayed here with me. For as long as you want to."

"Are you sure you don't mind?"

"I would never have mentioned it if I did."

"Thank you, Declan."

"As if I'm not getting anything out of it." He winked. "Oh, one more thing."

"Geez, you don't want much, do you?"

"I want as much of you as you'll give me, for as long as I can." He slipped his hand behind my neck and brought my lips to his.

I kept my eyes closed even after he pulled away.

"But how about we make each other a promise? No matter what or where or whoever we're with, we pick up our damn phones and talk."

"I can do that."

"Could you also forgive me for assuming the worst?"

"Honestly, I would've done the same thing if I were in your shoes. I haven't exactly proven myself to be forthcoming and reliable."

"Then let's start over. Get it right this time. You'll pick up your phone, and I'll pick up mine. Deal?"

"I like your deals."

"Good, because I have one more for you. If you stop crying all over my dog, I'll let you kiss me. But just once, because I'm suddenly very much in the mood to hold you for as long as I can and make sure no one ever hurts you again."

"Deal." I nodded, not sure when the tears would start. And for the first time ever, I didn't feel like I had to hide them. Because somehow, Declan could already see them and knew exactly the right way to make them go away on their own.

For the rest of the day, I lay on the couch between his legs, leaning against his chest. The plan was to watch a movie or two. But we spent so long laughing at all the horrible-sounding movie descriptions and comparing which we'd seen, we both fell asleep before watching anything.

36

DECLAN

I was so damn happy with Sara in my arms. *Pussy whipped* was what Trevor would've called it. Crap. Why'd I have to think of that shithead? Talk about a turn-off. Focus on the tiny, smart, sexy-as-hell beauty who just happened to be tucked into my arm, her head resting on my shoulder. Her hair smelled like vanilla, and misbehaving strands of it tickled my nose.

If someone had asked me how I imagined the evening going, I never would have guessed it would be like this. Maybe I should work on my imagination. I'd spent all day and most of the night with the other most important female in my life. Thank goodness Kitty wasn't the jealous type. And that she was falling in love with Sara as much as I was.

Oh shit. Was I? Was I falling for this woman who drove me nuts with insecurity almost as often as she drove me crazy with need? Yeah, I was pretty sure I was. My life was better with her around, fuller, deeper, happier. Even when we fought, it was passionate. And neither one of us was afraid to admit our mistakes or misjudgments. Somehow, that said more than anything else.

We were still learning how to communicate, but I knew we'd taken a huge step last night. She'd taken a giant leap by trusting me with her pain. I'd taken a massive bound by not going directly over to Cal's house and beating the ever loving shit out of him. Although, much of that was because I didn't know where he lived.

She and I still had a lot to learn about being with someone, trusting someone, but major steps had been taken.

I jerked when my phone rang. Should've left it in the other room, but my charger was in here, and it was the only alarm clock I had for those rare times when I needed one. I quickly scooted my arm out from under Sara and grabbed the phone on my way into the living room. She needed her sleep. The last couple of nights had been emotionally draining for both of us, but *she'd* been the one to confront her demon.

Fuck, I really wanted to kill that guy.

I didn't look to see who was calling until I shut the door behind me. What the hell? Why was Sam calling at two in the morning? I was going to kill him, too.

I hoped to God he wasn't calling because he was too stupid to call a cab. It had happened before—the guys got too drunk to use the Uber app or do anything other than call me to ask what they should do. Or, occasionally, they forgot how much I yelled at them every time they did it, and they would call me just to talk. In the middle of the night. While they were shit-faced, overly emotional, and thought they'd discovered the solution to one of humanity's biggest problems.

The biggest surprise stemmed from the fact that Trevor had said he wasn't going out tonight. I should've made him promise not to say anything. He was supposed to wait, so we could tell them together, maybe figure out how they could find a front man to replace me instead of breaking Self Defense up completely.

But regardless, if he'd broken the news to them, the least I owed them was a conversation. So, I answered the phone.

"Hey, Sam. So, I guess you heard, huh? Look, I—"

"Dec, you gotta come here." His voice was slurred but panicky as if he'd just realized where he was.

I sighed. Yep, this happened a lot, too. "It's late, man. Just call a cab or grab one outside. I'm sure you'll find one. I'll talk to you tomorrow."

"No, man. You gotta come here. Trevor's fucked."

Again, this happened a lot, too. "Ask the bartender to call a cab. He can drop you off first and then bring Trevor here. I'll meet them downstairs and pay the driver. But we really need to—"

"Declan, shut up a sec! We're at the hospital!"

"What—?" I inhaled sharply and then stopped breathing entirely, my mind overwhelmed with possibilities as to why the fuck they'd be at a hospital. I couldn't come up with a single reason I wanted to hear.

"Pete and Trev got into it, bad," Sam said. "Yelling about breaking up the band or some shit."

"Fuck." This was exactly why I wanted to be there when they found out. Not that I'd ever imagine them actually getting into it with each other.

"Then Pete chucked a beer bottle at Trev and took off all pissed..." He kept talking, but nothing he said made sense.

"Wait a sec. Pete hit Trevor with a bottle?"

"I don't know, Dec. I was standing right next to him, but there were so many people. It all happened so fast, and we were all fucked up to begin with, you know?" Yeah, that much was clear. And obviously, nobody had sobered up since.

"But you guys are at the hospital now, so he's being taken care of."

"Yeah, man." He got quieter. "It's bad, dude. They...uh...they can't get him to wake up."

Fuck. How hard did a bottle have to hit someone to knock them out?

As quietly as I could, I went back into my room with Kitty following on my heels so she wouldn't be kicked out again. I grabbed some pants and tugged them on while holding my phone between my shoulder and ear.

I tried asking Sam for more information—how hard Pete had thrown the bottle, had Trevor been bleeding when they brought him in, was there anyone sober I could speak to—but all I could get out of him was a bunch of different ways of saying, "Are you coming?"

"Yeah, yeah, I'm coming. But you have to tell me where to go."

As soon as he said, "Saint Francis Memorial," I hung up on him and put on a T-shirt. The last thing I needed right now was to hear a drunken shithead's explanation of two other drunken shitheads' fight.

Damn it. Why hadn't Trevor waited like we'd planned? And giving the guys bad news when they were drunk? Not smart. If I'd been there, I could've calmed everybody down. Or tried to keep them sober to begin with.

I tried to be quiet as I slipped some socks and shoes on, but when Kitty jumped up and took her spot in the middle of the bed, she woke Sara up.

Sara sat halfway up and blinked at me. "Why is there a dog sitting on me?"

"Sorry about that. I think she was lonely."

"Is it time to get up already?" She rubbed her eye and glanced at the window.

"No, babe. Go back to sleep."

"Then why are you dressed?"

"I need to go check on Trevor and the guys. I'll be back as soon as I can."

"Is everyone okay? What happened?" she asked, suddenly awake.

"I'm not sure yet, but I need to go find out. All I know is that the guys got into a fight." Because of me. Because I'd decided to break up the band. "Trevor got knocked out or something."

"Oh crap. Seriously? Can I help?" Being something beautiful to look at was already helping.

"Yeah, I need you to go back to sleep now and be here when I get back."

"I meant with Trevor and the guys."

"I know you did." I gave her a quick kiss, trying to smile so I wouldn't worry her. "Honestly, it's probably not nearly as bad as Sam thinks it is, but he's wasted. I'll know more when I speak to someone from the hospital—someone sober."

"Are you sure? Maybe I should come with you, just in case."

I couldn't ask her to come with me, even though, yeah, I wanted her to be there. But if Trevor had gotten hurt because of my revelation, it was my responsibility to take care of it. No one else's. No one had forced me to stay in the band this long, and maybe not being honest from the beginning and letting it get this far had actually made things worse.

I should've gone out with them, explained why I couldn't keep doing it to all three of them at the same time. Maybe we could've come up with some way to salvage the band. There were other guys out there who could sing like me, guys who could sing *better*.

But I'd chosen to be with Sara. Sure, I'd like to think she needed me to listen, but there were plenty of guys out there who would've given anything to be there for her, *better* guys who could've been there for her.

But she trusted you, you lucky asshole. She wanted you. Don't go fucking up something this good.

I shook my head. "Stay here and keep Kitty company. Get some more sleep."

"You can call if you change your mind, Declan. If you need *anything*."

"Thanks, that means a lot. And I'll call as soon as I know what's going on. You just make sure you answer your phone."

"That was our deal, right?" She nodded, her eyes still full of concern. "I'll hold up my end."

"And I'll hold up mine." I gave her a kiss and then rubbed Kitty's head. "Take care of my girl."

"I will."

"Actually, I was talking to Kitty." I kissed Sara again, grabbed my keys, and ran out the door.

"So, I'm your girl?" she called out to me.

"Yes, you are." For as long as humanly possible.

Thankfully, a cab was passing by just as I came out of the building. I practically jumped in front of the car to stop him.

"You do that again," the cab driver said as soon as I slid into the back seat, "and you're going to end up getting a ride in an ambulance, man."

"That would've worked, too. I need to get to the Saint Francis Memorial. As fast as you can get me there." I tossed a few bills into the front seat—easily quadrupling the amount the actual fare would be, hoping the amount would encourage him to stop talking and drive.

"You got it."

I was pushed back against the seat when he slammed his foot down on the pedal. I tilted my head back and looked at the cab's dirty, dark gray ceiling. How the fuck did the ceiling of a car get dirty? I tried to care just to distract myself from thinking about Trevor and what had happened to him, or what could still happen. Any of those thoughts would be useless. I couldn't do anything to help anybody until I got to the hospital, and even then, I probably wouldn't be able to do anything.

I hoped to fuck that Sam had just blown everything out of proportion, and all I'd have to do was smack him for making me worry.

Unfortunately, my life for the last few years had been fairly devoid of anything but thinking about Trevor, the band, and how much life sucked. So, my brain wasn't used to anything else. The only positive was Sara, but I didn't even want to think of her right now. I felt like shit, anxious, and afraid. The last thing I wanted was to equate her with those kinds of feelings.

So, I flashed back to the last conversation I'd had with Trevor. He might've gotten the day wrong or purposefully making me think he'd wait until I was there to keep an eye on him. But he'd basically said he was going to go party like it was his last. And I'd been too absorbed in my own shit to realize what that meant.

The cabbie pulled into the ER's loading area. I didn't wait until he stopped—I shoved the door open and jumped out, nearly face-planting from the abrupt change in momentum.

As I ran through the automatic doors, he yelled, "You're gonna get yourself killed, man!"

Nope, not myself.

37

DECLAN

I headed straight for the intake desk and gave the receptionist Trevor's name. She slowly typed letters into the computer while I tried not to jump through the three-inch hole in the bulletproof glass between us.

"Declan!" someone called.

I turned to see Sam coming toward me. He looked like shit—dark rings under his eyes, pale skin, a terrified look on his face.

I met him halfway. "What the fuck's going on, Sam? Where is he?"

"I just left him. Come on." He motioned for me to follow, then asked the guard at the desk to buzz us through the huge metal door that led into the ICU.

I had to show the guard my ID, repeat Trevor's full name, and watch him write my information down in the visitor's log. Was it just me, or was everyone in this goddamned place moving in slow motion? Even the fucking door opened as if a snail were pushing it.

That thought disappeared as soon as we walked through it. Suddenly, everything was moving four times faster than normal

—nurses power-walking, orderlies narrowly missing each other with their carts or freaky-looking machines.

The smell would've made me want to vomit if I didn't already want to for other reasons.

As we walked through the ICU, I tried to keep my eyes forward and not on the curtained rooms on either side of us, some of them closed and some open. It was like I couldn't trust Sam to take me to the right one, and there was a chance I'd miss Trevor completely. Sam stopped in front of a room with a name-plate that said *13B* next to it. I swear to God, I'd never been as scared as Sam slid open that divider. Like we were on the wrong side of the shower curtain in the movie *Psycho* or something.

Norman Bates wasn't there, nor were any other scary creatures. In fact, the body in the bed, kept running by all the beeping machines around it, looked incredibly fragile. As if the stiff white sheets neatly tucked under both sides of him were all that kept him from falling apart.

"Shit, Trev," I whispered to him. Anything louder was too dangerous—I'd either shatter him or start sobbing. "What the fuck did you do?"

Sam was close enough to hear me. "I thought he was just drunk, but then he collapsed and smacked his head against the floor. It was the scariest fucking thing I've ever seen, Dec. I couldn't catch him." He lifted up his sweater, exposing a sling on his left arm that had been under it. I'd been too overwhelmed to notice his empty sleeve.

"What happened?"

"I tried to keep his head from hitting the floor. Broke a couple bones in my wrist." His eyes glossed over. "Once the swelling goes down, they might have to fuse it together, man. What if I can never...play again?"

"Don't think about that now, Sam. Okay? One step at a time. Did they give you anything for the pain?"

He nodded, his eyes never lifting back to mine. "The good stuff." Well, that explained why nothing he'd said on the phone made any sense.

"Listen, Sam, worrying won't help anyone, okay?" Of course, in the history of man, *saying* that had never helped anyone either.

I glanced at the hard metal chair next to Trevor's hospital bed. I swear, whoever was in charge of buying those things had a masochistic streak. Why else would they buy something to make a paranoid, sad, and anxious person even *more* uncomfortable?

"Sit down," I said to Sam. "I can stand."

He shook his head. "I don't know, Dec. I...I feel like I'm going to lose it any minute. The smell..."

I knew exactly what he meant. The air itself smelled ill, a mixture of too many conflicting scents—antiseptic, medication, sweat, and something like rancid baby powder. The heat only strengthened the nausea factor.

"Do what you gotta do, man. You took care of him, got him here. I can take over." Doing nothing productive. "Go take care of yourself for a while."

"You sure?"

"Totally. Go. Get some rest. I'll call you if—" I caught my slip a second too late—"*when* he wakes up. Come back this afternoon, if you want. We're not going anywhere."

"Thanks. Call me if anything happens, okay?"

After I promised him that I would, he thanked me again for a reason I couldn't fathom, shook my hand with his good one, and then left.

I paced back and forth from Trevor's side to the main hallway, hoping someone would be here soon to answer all the questions I needed to ask. How much they thought he'd had to drink, did they have to pump his stomach, when did they think he would wake up. I even considered looking up concussions online but knew it would only drive me into more of a panic.

After a few minutes, I sat down, staring at the crooked line of Trevor's heartbeat. I ignored the numbers next to it—I'd never been able to remember which one was important and what a normal blood pressure was.

The heart rate line was hypnotic, something my eyes could follow even if they couldn't understand what it meant. Something predictable and human that proved my friend was still alive. It was the only positive thing in the room, the only thing that gave me any hope at all, so I clung to it. An excuse to avoid looking at Trevor's chalky complexion, the dark rings under his closed eyes, and the tube coming out of his nose.

This whole fucking thing was like a bad flashback. Back when I'd been in a similar ER for a similar reason—because my best friend had given up. But the worst was the feeling of resentment I felt just looking at him. The anger...the hurt...the guilt. Was this my fault? Did my selfishness put him in here?

My father—a great shrink who could empathize with everyone except his own son—would've told me that these kinds of feelings were totally natural and normal, but wouldn't release me until I dealt with the underlying issues. Namely, that I took responsibility for other people's problems and wanted to control everything around me. Then he'd also unhelpfully toss in the idea that I had a victim complex and really needed to work on it. But these things take time and work, so instead of being a loser musician, I should spend my time doing more self-contemplation and working on my id and superego or some shit like that.

Things only got worse when the nurse showed up to check Trevor out.

"When is he going to wake up?" I asked, moving out of her way.

She looked at me warily as if I didn't have a right to know. So,

I took Trevor's hand in mine, then looked at her again, my eyes pleading with her. A perk of living in San Francisco—people were used to gay couples. Hopefully, the nurse would assume that Trevor was my boyfriend or husband and tell me what she wouldn't have shared with his best friend, family or not.

She sighed before starting to check all the wires and tubes he was connected to. "I wish I had an answer for you. But any timeline we gave would probably be wrong. We'll be here for him, monitoring his vitals, and doing all we can, but unfortunately, Mr. Finley has to do all the real work. He has a severe concussion, and his body is dealing with a lot right now. Plus, as I'm sure you know, a lot of damage was done well before last night." She went to her mobile computer station and looked up something on the screen. "He's a tough guy, though—I'll give him that. Although, maybe you'll be able to answer a question for us. The friend who came in with him didn't know about it, and the hospital's records don't show any follow-up care he's received after he came in for the initial diagnosis. So, what has he been doing for his pain?"

"What pain?"

"For his pancreatitis."

Pancreatitis? "Is that like appendicitis?" Painful but no big deal. He goes into surgery, they slice him open, cut out the bad bit, staple him back up, and he's one hundred percent again a week later. Unless I asked the surgeon to cut off his balls while they were there. His punishment for putting me through this shit again.

The nurse shook her head, pausing as if she were wondering how much she could tell me. "Trevor's pancreatitis is chronic. For men his age, the most common cause is long-term alcohol abuse. Do you know how long he's been an alcoholic?"

It would've been easier to answer how long he *wasn't* an alcoholic. "A while, I guess. He started drinking when we were fourteen or fifteen, but it wasn't too bad until he was around twenty." When she raised an eyebrow, I nodded. "It could've been worse than I thought, I guess. He's always been good at holding his liquor." As teenagers, I could keep up with him. Except that while he could still function well enough to fool my parents, all I could manage was aiming for the toilet.

"We'll keep watching his vitals and giving him fluids to rehydrate him, and there are some more tests we'll need to run. But he's going to have to wake up before we can find out how much neurological damage he suffered. And then we go from there. Thankfully, he's young."

"And as stubborn as hell."

She smiled. "In this case, that will probably help. I'll ask the doctor to come in to answer any more questions you have. But it's been a busy night, so I can't guarantee how soon it will be."

Once she'd left, I sat back down. It felt even quieter now. Colder, too. I thought about what she'd said. Pancreatitis, a chronic disease that Trevor apparently had but hadn't mentioned, caused severe pain that he hadn't mentioned. Why would he have kept something like that from me?

"Wake up, you bastard." Even my whisper had an edge to it, hinting at the betrayal I felt. "You're not allowed to die. You understand me? Not after all the shit you put me through. Not after everything we've been through together." I rubbed my hands over my face. "If you make me go through all of this and then die, I will hate you forever. You hear me? Forever. And I won't feel bad about it." On a scale of one to a thousand, how bad was it to lie to someone who might be lying on their deathbed? At twenty-fucking-four years old.

Jackass.

I laid my head down on the bed, my arms resting between it and Trevor's hand, hoping I'd feel him twitch or touch me. Hell,

I'd even be happy if he smacked me. Because that would mean he hadn't given up.

I was a mess, reliving something I'd sworn to myself I'd never have to go through again. Unfortunately, I wasn't the one who could keep that promise. The only way I could've was to have pushed Trevor out of my life, something I refused to do. Because I'd been so worried it would shove him into a depression so deep that it made him think this exact situation was the only way to deal with it.

Losing someone is hard, whether they are ill or in an accident. But when someone is mentally ill and the loss is no accident, being left behind feels like the universe just wants to be cruel.

But the truth was that I hadn't lost my best friend. Not yet. And there was a chance I wouldn't.

"Don't die, you shithead. Because..." Why? The only thing Trevor had ever really cared about was Self Defense. And I'd taken that away from him. I should've trusted my gut, known he was full of shit when he'd said he was okay with the band breaking up. If I hadn't said anything, he wouldn't have spent the night partying as if it were his last.

It couldn't be his last. It just couldn't.

Maybe if he knew things would go back to the way they were, he'd wake up. "Because I changed my mind. I don't want the band to split up. Yep, I want to give it one more shot."

I'd never bought into the idea unconscious people could hear the outside world before now. Now, I understood why people did—they *needed* to. *I* needed to. Talking to him was the only thing I could do to stop feeling so fucking useless.

"Let's do it, man. Do it right this time. I'm all in. I'll fucking post on Instagram, talk to fans, wear as much leather as Doug wants me to. We can do it. Together." I took a quick breath. "Plus, Sara and I got back together. I want to show her what it's

like to be on tour. I can't wait to bang her on the bus, actually."
My laugh sounded ill. "But you're not allowed to watch or listen.
In fact, I regret mentioning it to you right now. Thank God
you're in a coma and can't hear me."

I flipped from watching his eyes and his hands, looking for
any sign he could hear me. "Unless you're awake now. Are you,
man? Are you awake?"

38

SARA

*A*fter Declan had left, I couldn't go back to sleep. I was flattered that he trusted me enough to leave me alone at his place without warning—I'd be too worried someone would go through my drawers and find my vibrator or the stash of kinky erotica on my e-reader. Shockingly, I was completely comfortable here, even without him. Kitty was actually great company. She snored a little, but she was almost as good a snuggler as her dad. The more time I spent with her, the more I liked the idea of living like this. Just the three of us.

Although, it was a little early to start daydreaming—Declan and I hadn't even broached the subject of what would happen next. If he was serious about leaving the band and didn't feel the need to babysit Trevor, he wouldn't have to tour. And I wouldn't have to either live on a bus if I went with them or worry about all the groupies that hit on him if I didn't go.

Around three thirty, I decided to go to my parents' house, shower, and put on some makeup so no one would be able to tell how much crying I'd done over the last few days. If I waited until normal morning hours, my mom or stepdad would be awake, and I might have to talk to them. Or, knowing my luck, Cal would be there, asking Beatrice to make him something for breakfast.

So, if I wanted to grab some stuff to bring back to Declan's, or go stay with Andi and Hayden, now was the time to do it. Hopefully, I could get in, toss the necessities into a bag, and get out without having to explain why I was leaving and where I was going.

On the way to my parent's house, I considered calling Declan. Then I remembered that annoying hospital policy about not allowing cell phone use inside the rooms. So, I decided to wait a little while before calling him. Hopefully, he'd save me the trouble and call me as soon as he could, anyway.

I asked the ride-share driver to let me off on the sidewalk to avoid waking up anyone in the house. Besides the sound of my key slipping into the deadbolt of the front door, everything was silent as I tiptoed inside.

I took a quick shower, got dressed, and had just about finished packing when I heard a quiet tapping on my door.

Shit. Please let it be Beatrice. Please let it be Beatrice. She didn't live with us but started working sometime between when I got home from my longest nights of partying and when I woke up on my earliest mornings.

Unfortunately, it wasn't Beatrice. It had been so long since I'd seen my mom without her hair and makeup done I almost didn't recognize her. Her medium-length, fake blond hair was heading off in twelve different directions, and her pale skin made the half-circles under her eyes look like dark sides of the moon. She used the sleeve of her silk pajamas to brush the hair off her face.

"Geez, Mom. Go back to bed." Since my time was now up, I slung my bag over my shoulder and pushed past her, heading straight for the stairs.

Unbelievably, she followed. "Where are you going?"

"Out."

"Sara Elizabeth Antonopoulos, you stop right there and tell me where you're going." She hadn't used my full name in years. Especially considering how much she hated that I'd chosen to keep my father's name instead of switching to Timothy's when they got married.

I spun around to face her. "I'm meeting a friend. Is that alright with you?"

"This isn't a hotel, young lady. You can't just come and go as you please without sharing anything about what's going on in your life. Where are you going in the middle of the night?" As if she'd ever cared before.

"I know you don't see many of them, but it's morning, Mom." I clenched my teeth together to stop myself from saying anything else. But I guess being treated like a child made me want to act like one, so I opened my big mouth. "Maybe the reason I don't tell you anything is because I know you won't listen."

"What is that supposed to mean?"

I sighed. "Nothing." I didn't want to fight. I wanted to leave. And the easiest way to make that happen was to humor her. "I'm going to Declan's place. Okay? I'll be back later. I don't know when exactly, but I'll text you this afternoon."

"We need to talk about Cal."

"Later." Because nothing could've made me want to leave more than the thought of talking about Cal.

"No, Sara. Now. God only knows what *later* means to you these days."

"Wow. Great way to make me want to stay and chat, Mom."

Either it was too early for her to pick up on sarcasm or too early for her to care. "Your father and I sat down to talk with Cal last night."

"Stepfather," I said without thinking. Then the rest of the comment sank in. "What about?"

"He told us some unpleasant things about you, things a mother never wants to hear about her child. Have you been spreading lies about him?"

My bag slipped off my shoulder and hit the hardwood floor. She jolted at the sound. I didn't move.

"What did he tell you?" I felt ill. Since our confrontation had gone so miraculously badly, I knew he hadn't suddenly grown a conscience and told them the truth. Cal didn't know what truth was. But telling them that *I* was the liar? How would stirring up trouble for *me* benefit him? I would've assumed he'd just keep his mouth shut.

"Cal told us about the drugs, Sara." Bits of anger, pity, frustration, and sleepiness all made it into her expression, leaving it unreadable. "If Declan has gotten you involved with something illegal, you have to stop seeing him immediately, Sara. Don't let him take you down with him. Timothy and I are committed to getting you whatever help you need. Timothy has a good lawyer, and there's rehab—"

"Wait. What?" I backed up a second, unsure of what I just heard. "I don't need help. Declan has been nothing but good to me. And he *definitely* isn't involved in anything illegal." Halfway through speaking, I got it. Cal was on the offense now. After I'd confronted him, he must have decided I finally had the courage to start telling *other* people. And if I were brave enough to tell them about the rape, what would keep me from telling them he dealt drugs, too? So, before the truth came out, he preemptively started covering his ass.

"I don't do drugs, Mom. Neither does Declan. And neither of us would ever sell them. I swear to you."

This time, it was easy to read her expression. She didn't believe me. Again.

Damn, my stepbrother was an amazing liar. He'd even thrown Declan in there to make me seem completely unreliable and untrustworthy. He used Timothy and my moms' fears to guarantee they'd believe the worst about Declan and, by association, me. The wild, troubled daughter who was dating a member of a rock band would say anything to get out of trouble. Never leave a stereotype unturned.

"No!" I shouted. No, he didn't get to do that. "Everything Cal told you is a lie, Mom."

She stepped toward me with her arms out but not with any trust. "Honey, please—"

"Why do you always believe him over me?" My eyes stung, and I felt the heat of tears running down my face. "You've known me my entire life. Do you really think that all this time I've been hiding how evil he told you I was? I know I've screwed up and haven't been the greatest daughter in the world, but I've never lied to you. I've made mistakes—stupid mistakes—but I've never deliberately hurt anyone. I wouldn't do that."

"Sweetie—"

"No." I cut her off again, knowing I still hadn't convinced her. So, anything she said right now would just be hurtful, and I didn't want to hear it. But I also didn't know what else to say.

"I wasn't lying when I told you he raped me," I said more softly. "I wasn't lying then, and I'm not lying now. If you still don't believe me, well...I guess I have to accept that. But maybe you should think about why you believe him instead of your daughter. Does who he tells you I am really sound like the person you know? Don't you ever get the feeling that something isn't right about him? That he's just saying what he knows you want to hear? And have you ever thought that maybe when I *don't*, it's not because I'm an idiot? It's because I don't want to lie to you, Mom. Because I love you too much to lie to you."

She stared at me silently. For long enough to make me hope

she'd actually start thinking about what Cal got out of telling her that crap, or how he would even know if I were doing something illegal.

Boy, did I hope.

"I need to go." I'd give her time to wake up and decide who really deserved her trust. I left her standing on the landing, watching me pick up my bag and walk to the stairs. "I'll be back this afternoon. Promise. And I'll listen to whatever you have to say to me then."

39

SARA

On my way downstairs, I reached into my bag, tired of waiting for Declan to call. Hopefully, I'd catch him while he was somewhere he could talk.

That's when I saw all the missed calls and texts. I had to scroll down through my notices to see them all. The first call had probably come in while I was in the shower. The others while I was arguing with my mom.

Five missed calls. Four texts that were all variations of '*I really need to talk to you.*'

"Shit." I called him back, the apology already forming on my lips.

"Where the fuck are you?" Declan shouted as soon as he picked up.

"Where do I even start?" I asked, glaring at my mom who was still staring at me from the top of the stairs.

"You know what? Don't bother," he spat, completely misunderstanding the direction my flippancy was aimed in. "I can't take any more of this shit, Sara. I just can't deal with it. Not now. Not...now. You promised you'd stay here until I got back. You promised you'd pick up your phone. Damn it, Sara, I needed you. I needed someone who understood, who knows me. But you weren't fucking here."

"I'm here now. I'm—" I wished I could've reached for him to prove it. To prove that I was real and with him.

"I gotta go."

"Wait, Declan! I missed your call because I told my mo—"

I'm not sure he heard it before he hung up on me. It had been an accident, but in his current state of mind I wasn't sure he would've cared. Since I'd been the first to break our promise to one another—good reason or not—why would he care about breaking it now?

It wasn't about me, or even us. I couldn't take his reaction personally. I should go to him, explain it to him in person, face-to-face. Even if he walked away or screamed at me again, I should go. He deserved that, especially now when he was hurting so badly.

Of course, I couldn't do that without knowing where he was. I wished Andi were here—she'd have been able to triangulate his cell phone location or whatever computer geniuses did.

I tried calling him back even though I knew he wouldn't answer. As soon as his voice mail message picked up, I hung up and then called him right back, hoping he'd be annoyed enough with the incessant ringing that he'd answer just to tell me off again. No such luck.

So I texted. No idea how many times. Then I gave up and called Trevor. I didn't know what was going on, but if anyone other than Declan did, it would be his best friend. Before he left, Declan had said something about Trevor knocked out. I hoped it wasn't bad enough to keep him off his cell phone.

Trevor didn't answer my call...but someone else did.

"Trevor's phone," a slow, groggy-sounding voice said.

"Who is this?"

"Sam. Who are you?"

Thank goodness. "Sam, it's Sara. Declan's...girl...friend." Why did that word suddenly make me feel like a liar? "I'm looking for Declan. Do you know where he is? And do you know what's happening with Trevor?"

"I think they're still at the hospital. Well..." Fatigue and sadness slurred his words in a way alcohol could never do. "Obviously, Trevor is still there, and Dec probably is, too, but I'm not a hundred percent on that. Or much of anything right now, actually."

"You sound exhausted. I don't want to keep you from sleeping. But I wanted to find out if everyone's okay." I held it together while he explained. I think I understood about half of it because his story kept bouncing around from the bar, to Trevor, to the past, to Declan until I was so confused I had to stop him. "Trevor's going to be alright, though, won't he?" In the short time I'd known him, I'd come to believe that Trevor had a superhero's liver and a toddler's *joie du vive*. Nothing was strong enough to keep him down.

"Fuck, I hope so. I'm going back to see him in a few hours. Just came home to shower and grab a few z's."

"I'm sorry for keeping you from it. One more quick question?"

"Anything for you, Sara." His sincerity caught my breath and held it for a second. From the moment I'd met them, each member of Self Defense had shown me nothing but respect and friendship. It was fairly obvious that they all were as screwed up in the head as I was, but that had never affected how well they treated me, or each other.

"What did I ever do to deserve you guys?" Then, realizing I'd just said 'one more question,' I added, "Don't answer that. Because then you might realize I don't deserve you."

"Never. But I'm..."

"Right. You don't think he'd want me to be there?"

"Declan? Nah. I think he *needs* you to be there." Sam would've been right an hour ago, but now?

I wanted to scream. But with so much crashing down on top of me, I couldn't even manage a whisper. Somehow, everything had gone wrong, and I'd ended up in the middle of it. How did this happen? Had I been avoiding what was really going on around me for so long I hadn't seen the inevitable?

"Where is he, Sam?"

After he'd told me which hospital to go to, I thanked him, told him to call me if he needed anything, and then hung up.

Okay. It was time to prove I could be there for Declan like he'd been for me. He needed me now.

"Sara, what's going on?" my mom called from upstairs.

"Nothing," I yelled as I yanked the door open and ran down the driveway.

Cal's lies would take time to unwind and prove wrong. I couldn't fix Trevor, but I could help Declan. I could stand by someone who'd never once hurt me and who'd proven over and over that I could trust him.

Declan had listened and believed in me when no one else did—when I'd been too afraid to even tell my best friends. He'd heard me when I wasn't even speaking. He'd *known* me even though I hadn't deliberately let him in.

I heard my mom still calling me, but I didn't stop. I stood on the sidewalk in front of the house, willing a cab to drive by. But they didn't come to residential areas without reason, and they couldn't read the desperation in my mind.

Fuck! I took out my phone to check my ride-share app. Hopefully, a car was dropping someone off nearby, and I could reserve it before anyone else did. I was too upset to get my thumbs to function correctly, so before I'd even been able to enlarge the map's screen view, my mom was next to me, out of breath.

When she grabbed my arm, I realized how she could help. "Mom, I need your car."

"What's going on, Sara? What happened?"

It would take three days and more energy than I had to tell her everything. "I'll explain it to you later, but right now, I really need you to let me use your car."

Growing up in the city had given me very little experience behind the wheel, and I didn't even know where the hospital was. Hell, the only reason I even *had* a license was to prove I was over twenty-one. But there was no other way, so I had to risk it.

"No way."

"Goddamn it, Mom! I can't deal with your bullshit right now."

"I'll drive you," she said. "You're too upset to drive yourself. It's not safe."

True, but was it any safer if she was drunk? I leaned closer to her, smelling her breath.

She knew exactly what I was checking. "I haven't had anything tonight. I...I've been trying to slow down."

How many times had I heard her say that?

"I swear to you, Sara. I'm sober. Tell me where you want to go, and I'll take you. No questions. No bullshit. Please, let me do this for you."

After another moment, I nodded. "Fine. Saint Francis Memorial Hospital." It was the only place he'd go—to be with his friend, to be there for his best friend, even if Trevor were still unconscious. Or...worse.

No matter what, Declan would be there. And so would I. No matter what.

I hurried back up the driveway and into the garage, my mom a few steps behind me.

I held on to the door handle and my seat as Mom drove, bracing myself as we came to each corner. She was driving faster than I'd ever seen, her eyes stuck on the road, never speaking. Thank goodness.

A few minutes later, she pulled the car into the emergency drop-off area and skidded to a stop.

"I'll go park and—" She sighed, looking at me with wet eyes. "Can I come in after I park, or would you rather I—?" I was fairly certain that this was the first time she'd ever stepped foot out of the house without her makeup and hair done, not to mention that she was still in her pajamas.

"I'll be okay. I can get a cab back to the house when I'm ready. Just don't freak out if I don't come back for a while." I walked away before she tried to change my mind.

40

DECLAN

I couldn't believe I'd had to leave my friend and come back to our building to search through Trev's pigsty of an apartment for his insurance card and ID.

My fists hadn't relaxed from the second that fucking hospital bureaucrat came in to bitch about needing the damn cards. They'd still have been tight and ready to punch something if I hadn't had to use both hands to search through all the shit Trevor had been hoarding since he moved in.

"Seriously, Trev?" I'd mumbled. "You've only been living here for a month and a half." Where did all that crap come from? Takeout menus, crumpled-up receipts from close to everything he'd bought in the last few years, four pairs of sunglasses —three of them broken—a crushed pack of gum, and four thousand other things. But no ID or insurance card.

"Fuck. Fuck the world and everyone in it." And yeah, I meant everyone.

It shouldn't have been possible to be more pissed off than I was about having to leave my comatose friend just so the hospital could fill out their stupid paperwork.

I'd really underestimated the limits of my anger.

When I'd called Sara to ask if she could grab Trev's cards and bring them to me, I'd only been pissed at the hospital. After she missed the second call, I figured she might've been in the bathroom or in a deep sleep. I was disappointed, but not upset about it...yet.

At the bottom of one of his many junk drawers, I'd finally found his insurance card. I'd slipped the card into my wallet and gone up to my place to quickly vent about the hospital administrators to Sara before I headed back, to hold her in my arms and gain the strength I'd need to go fight with them over Trevor's care. I couldn't wait to see her, even if she were asleep. After all, she'd be there because she'd promised she would be, right?

Wrong.

At least Kitty was still there. She followed me as I stomped from room to room, calling Sara's name. The sheets were still a rumpled mess, but Sara wasn't wrapped in them or even hiding under them—yes, I checked. Fuck, I even checked the pantry, where I'd found Kitty once after she'd somehow gotten herself locked in. No one was there. No one was in the bathroom or kitchen or even on the microscopic balcony.

No ransom note. Not even a fucking *Be right back* note.

I knew she'd been through a lot recently with that asshole Cal. So, I should've been more understanding and less angry. But knowing that and feeling that were two very different things.

So, when Sara hadn't picked up her phone when I needed her and wasn't where she'd said she would *stay* when I needed her, I was all out of empathy. The only thing I could think about was how fucking alone I felt.

The first and second promises she'd made me, she'd broken less than two hours later. And what capped it all off was what she'd said when she finally *did* pick up her phone.

Know what the world's shittiest response is when someone

asks you why you aren't where you said you'd be or answering the calls you said you'd answer?

"Where do I start?"

Was she serious? How about she start by thinking about the guy lying in a coma right now. Or maybe the guy she claimed to care about, who was an inch away from losing it because he'd had to leave his friend in the hospital to get a fucking plastic card that she should've been around to get for him.

At that point, I didn't even care if I was being irrational or not. Because *she* didn't care enough to keep her promises. At least not the ones she'd made to me.

*D*eclan wasn't in the waiting room, and I didn't know how to get past security to get to Trevor's room. So, I stood there and tried to think of the right thing to do, my arms wrapped tightly around myself to stave off the cold.

When I felt a hand touch my shoulder, I flinched and spun around, hoping the warmth was Declan's.

I let out a sigh when I saw my mom's face instead of his. "I told you I'd be fine."

"And I knew you would be. But I still want to be here." She glanced around the room and quickly seemed to understand why I hadn't made it any farther. With her arm tucked around my waist and with me too confused to shove her away, she walked us both up to the reception desk.

"Excuse me," she called to the woman behind the security glass. "My stepson is here. I need to see him."

"What's your stepson's name?" the woman asked.

My mom's eyes hinted that I should play along before covering her mouth and pretending to be overcome with emotion.

"His name is Trevor," I said quickly. "Trevor Finley. They said he came in a couple hours ago."

My mom winked at me as the woman typed Trevor's name into her computer. The first time we worked together on anything, and it was probably some kind of crime.

The woman told us where to go and buzzed us through.

As soon as we were out of earshot, I asked her why she'd lied.

"They would never have let us back if we weren't family," she explained. "And since I'm his 'stepmom,' I won't be expected to know his medical history or insurance information if they ask."

"Should I ask why all of that occurred to you thirty seconds after you walked into the waiting room?"

"I was triple the wild child you've ever been, hon." She grinned. "It never goes away completely."

She stepped back when we got to Trevor's room, giving me space as I knocked on the wall just outside of it.

"Trevor? Can I come in?" When no one answered, I slid back the curtain nervously and took a few steps toward him.

Trevor was lying there alone with the machines tracking his vitals and whatever else they did. His eyes were closed, and without his normal bluster, smile, and *joie du vive*, I barely recognized him.

"Oh, the poor boy," my mom said from behind me. I'd almost forgotten she was here. "Is there anything I can do, Sara?"

"I don't know." I wasn't sure what *I* could do. Other than stand there and stare at him, frozen both in action and in temperature and wishing Declan's incredible warmth were here.

She brushed by me and went to Trevor's bedside, wiping a lock of hair off his forehead. "What did you get yourself into, kid?" She gently adjusted a pillow behind his head and pulled the blanket up higher on his chest. When she looked up at me, her eyes were shining.

Why did she care so much about someone she'd never met before? Just because he was important to *me*?

"Do you know if they've contacted his parents?" she asked.

I shook my head. "I don't think they get along very well."

"Even so, I'm sure they'd want to be here for him." She nodded resolutely and patted his arm. "I'm going to go find out what I can, Trevor. Try not to upset my daughter too much if you can help it, would you?"

I stepped out of her way when she started to leave.

As soon as she passed me, she stopped, put her hand on my shoulder, and squeezed gently. "Sara?" She paused a moment. "I think you should press charges on your stepbrother." As shocking as the comment was, it was too little, too late. For a lot of reasons.

I shook my head. "I can't. I don't have any proof. No one would believe me." Thankfully, I hadn't turned to look at her before I finished my thought, part of me afraid to see her reaction, and part of me afraid she *wouldn't* react.

"Because *I* didn't?"

I didn't need to look at her to hear the tears in her voice.

"Cal, he... He was never in a bar fight, was he?"

I shook my head slowly, remembering with very little satisfaction the only thing I'd done to help myself that night, something I hadn't even realized I'd done until the next day. Until my mom asked me if I'd been at the same club Cal had and if I'd seen the brawl that had left him with a split lip and a couple of deep scratches near his left eye.

When all I'd managed to answer with was a shrug, she'd flipped out, shouting something about how I could be so uncaring when my stepbrother could've really been hurt, and somehow *I* was lucky that he'd only gotten a split lip. I didn't even have the energy to laugh at the irony.

Even if he hadn't made up the whole bar fight lie to cover up what he'd done to me, how could it be my fault for not caring enough about his safety? I'd never wanted a brother or a step-dad. I'd never wanted any of it. My mom was the one who'd needed it. Someone to take care of her, be living proof she was still attractive and could land a quality man. And she was the one who couldn't let go of it when I told her the truth.

The bloody lip and scratches I'd given Cal had taken over a week to heal. I did everything I could not to see him after that night, but about a week afterwards, he'd come over to pick up something from his father. He'd acted as if nothing had happened.

When my mom had held his face in her hands and examined the injury from that awful *bar fight*, he'd glanced at me, looking to see how I'd react, I guess. Then she'd touched his lip.

Cal had howled in pain, and I'd felt a moment of pride. Although, it might have been more than a moment, because that night I'd tried to tell my mom what he'd done to me. Of course, any pride I had left disappeared as soon as she asked me why I would say something so hateful about my stepbrother when he'd never done anything to deserve it.

"'He's never done anything to deserve it,'" I mumbled. "That's what you said to me."

"Oh, Sara."

When I looked at her, I saw the tears welled up in her eyes, and I almost felt sorry for her. I didn't want to see her cry. I didn't want anyone to cry. But I was done pretending not to hurt or thinking that it was easier to protect myself if I were invisible. My silence hadn't made anything easier. It had just taken away the trust I'd had in the people I loved.

"The only reason I would say something so hateful about

him was because I was jealous. Right? I would tell my mother I'd been raped with tears running down my face"—like hers were doing now—"because I was jealous. Because I wanted attention. You believed him then, and you believe him now. You think that Declan and I are the ones dealing drugs, even though Cal is constantly sniffling and carrying around big rolls of cash."

"You're right. I'm so sorry for not believing you, honey. I can't... I'm so, so sorry."

I hadn't thought about this moment—what I would say if she ever asked me for forgiveness. I'd never really imagined it would happen. I'd thought I had healed and moved on, a little wiser and a lot less trusting.

I'd spent the last year thinking that to feel whole again I needed to confront Cal. I was wrong. There was no way for me to really move on and start trusting people again until I knew my mom believed me.

And while I'd been so busy coping badly, I'd almost missed out on something amazing with *someone* amazing. If Declan hadn't been so patient, so stubborn, I would've kept thinking I could go on like I had been indefinitely. Being invisible, sharing only the pieces of myself that couldn't be hurt, that didn't feel pain, disappointment, or shame. *Those* parts I'd kept for myself and no one else, not even the people who loved me. *Especially* not anyone who loved me. Because they were the most dangerous.

The cruelty of a stranger meant nothing. The betrayal of a loved one had *left me* with nothing.

"What can I do, Sara? What can I say?"

I took a box of cheap tissues from an equipment cart and handed it to her. "Honestly, I don't know."

I glanced at Trevor, feeling guilty this was all happening in front of him, even while he was unconscious. If he could still hear, he probably didn't *want* to wake up. At least not until we'd left the room.

"All I know is that I'm not ready to forgive you right now," I said. "I need to focus on helping someone I care about. *Two* people I care about. Because while I may not be able to do anything for them, I need to try. And in order to do that, I can't think about myself right now."

She nodded, most of her face hidden by a tissue.

"But once I know they're okay, I'd like for us to talk."

"I'd like that." The corners of her eyes wrinkled as if she were smiling, but her tears flowed double time. "I'd like that very much."

42

DECLAN

*J*ust in case the hospital called me about Trevor, I couldn't turn off the ringer to my cell phone. Luckily, at some point, I'd set Sara's ringtone to something cheesy and lovesick, so I knew when not to pick it up. When the swish sounds of new text alerts started, I hadn't even taken it out of my pocket. The hospital wouldn't text me, and I wasn't interested in reading Sara's excuses. Maybe later, after this shit with Trevor was over, when I was ready to have my heart busted open again, I'd find somewhere quiet to drown my sorry self in whiskey and read through them all. Or maybe I'd just get a new phone with a new number.

I flinched when I heard my generic ringtone, yanking the phone out of my pocket, praying it wasn't more bad news from the hospital.

I didn't even look at the caller ID before accepting the call and shoving the phone against my ear.

"Hello?"

"Declan, hey."

It took me a second to recognize the voice—slow, non-caring, irritating as hell. "Hey, Doug. What's up?" Why was our manager calling me this early on a Sunday? I'd have thought Satan's minions slept in.

"The owner of Tunnel Vision called to ask how Trevor is doing. Wanna tell me what the fuck is going on?"

Nope, not at all. Doug couldn't give a single shit how Trevor was doing, and this call was only so he could decide how to spin my best friend's disaster into a media-friendly dramatic event that would help the band's popularity.

"He's gonna be okay," I said, hoping it was fact and not just wishful thinking. "You know Trevor—he had a bit too much fun and will need a little time to get back on his feet."

"Yeah, I know Trevor. I also know an entire club's worth of people watched his drunk ass get taken out by paramedics."

"He went a little overboard, but—"

"I'm still not quite sure when the boys started slinging beer bottles at each other in a fucking crowd of people. But I followed along really well when Sam told me Trevor drank his ass into a coma surrounded by fans who all had cell phones to record the fucking mess and put it up on YouTube, though."

"Well…" My voice was flat, emotionless, while I silently fumed. "If you've already spoken to Sam, why'd you call me?"

"Because, since you're the only halfway intelligent one in this godforsaken, piece of shit band, I'd hoped you'd have figured out what I'm going to say next."

My jaw clenched even tighter, my fingers practically crushing the phone. "Why don't you keep treating me like an idiot and just tell me?"

"I'm so fucking done with this shit. It never stops with them. I could go out onto the street right now and pick three equally skilled idiots who are willing to do whatever it takes without giving me so many damn headaches. It'd take me five minutes to find them."

My gut was screaming for me to tell the prick off, to tell him that was still three days less than it would take him to find someone who'd fuck him. Even if he paid her.

But I couldn't. I couldn't ruin it for Trevor. Not now that I'd promised him I'd give it another shot. Whether he'd heard me say it or not, the promise had been made. And if there was even a chance in hell that those words had made their way into his subconscious, if they helped him recover, I'd stand by them.

So, as much as I wanted to tell Doug to go fuck himself with all his bullshit promises and threats, I had to keep my mouth shut. No, I couldn't even do that. I had to talk this asshole out of dropping the band.

Once things were back to semi-normal, I'd try to get out of it again. Maybe that had been my biggest mistake—everything had happened too fast. Too fast for Trevor to deal with. Not enough time to make sure the band could go on without me.

"This is the last time, Doug. I promise. Trevor will need a break, go to rehab for a bit, but we can spin that, right? Turn it into a public service message about alcoholism or something." I fucking hated the desperation in my voice. Not to mention the absolute void of pride or integrity. "Tons of bands go through shit worse than this, and they don't even have you in their corner."

I guess he'd been right, after all—I was coming back, begging him for something. Of course, he'd been wrong about why or what I'd be begging for.

"I'm going to speak slowly, so there's no way you'll misunderstand me," he said. "There *is* no more band. Say goodbye to Self Defense, Declan. And if you ever pull any of the shit Trevor has, you're off my books, too."

"Wait. What are you talking about?"

"I'm dumping those tragedies you call bandmates. There's a reason all my most successful clients are solo acts. Because I'm fucking good with the *mano a mano*!"

I hoped his one-on-one skills were better than his Spanish. But I didn't say anything about the mistake because it would probably only get him more fired up.

"I knew I should've gone with my original plan, but I was nice. I saw how tight you and Trevor were and figured I'd be nice."

In what world had Doug ever been nice to me or to anyone else? Ass-kissing wasn't the same thing. Neither was patronizing people who saw you as the gatekeeper to their version of Heaven. It had made me sick the way Doug talked to my bandmates, as if he were the only one who could make their dreams come true. Maybe the only reason I'd seen through his bullshit was because fame had never been my dream. I'd *always* known he couldn't get me what I wanted.

"I'm not going to keep playing babysitter to a bunch of brats, Declan. Not when I can take you a lot further with a lot less trouble. And a lot more dollar bills for both of us."

"You're serious?"

"You bet your ass I am. We get you the right songwriter, and you're golden. And look, if you want, we can even buy the rights for some of Self Defense's songs from the guys. That way, they'll walk away with a little cash in their pockets."

"Buy the songs from the guys?" I asked stupidly. On top of everything else wrong with what he was saying, he didn't even know that I wrote our fucking music. Someone else must have filed the legal forms, written the contracts, and looked over every other piece of paper where my name was listed. Doug had seen me as a pretty face with a pretty voice and no actual talent.

I almost laughed. Almost. Because I think I finally understood him. He thought he and I were the same—the guys who stood out front looking good while other, expendable people did all the actual work.

"I know you care about him, Declan. But you can't get to

317

where we're going if you're carrying a sack of shit on your back the whole way."

"You're right, Doug. I don't want to carry a sack of shit anymore." I saw it all flash in front of my eyes—telling the sack of shit where he and his fucking contract could go. Imagining the look on his face when he realized there were people he couldn't control, couldn't make or break.

But that couldn't happen. Not today. Not with everything I had to lose. So, I swallowed my pride and let him win.

"Okay. I'll do it."

"Hallelujah," he said dryly. "I'm glad you're finally getting it. And, Declan, you're doing the right thing."

Was I? Sure didn't feel like it. "Look, I'll do whatever you say, sign whatever you want me to sign, be whoever you want me to be. On one condition."

"Oh, for fuck's sake." He sighed, long and hard. "What do you want?"

"Six more months. You give Self Defense six more months to pull it together and see what happens. If we don't have a contract by then, I'll sign whatever you put in front of me."

His pause gave me a chance to regret the offer and every choice I'd made that got me here. It also gave me time to accept I had no other option now.

"Three months," he said finally. "Starting today."

I still didn't know how long it would take Trevor to regain consciousness. But three months would barely cover his time in rehab, let alone any recovery he'd need.

"Come on, Doug. The guy's in a fucking coma. Give him a break."

"I'm done giving Trevor anything. I'm giving this break to *you*. If you want to include anybody else, that's your problem. Three months, Declan."

"Without Trevor, I have to find another bassist and teach him all our songs." And I'd have to pay him with money I didn't have. Plus, who'd want to put in the effort, knowing he was just a placeholder until Trevor could come back?

"No one is irreplaceable, Declan," he said. "Come on. Tick, tock. Take it or leave it."

"I'll... I'll take it." With each word, it felt like a hundred pounds dropped onto my shoulders.

"Good. So, as of this moment, we have a deal—a verbal contract. By the time you get here, I'll have the specifics written up, so there's no confusion and nobody accidentally *forgets* our agreement three months from now."

"You want me to sign something *now*? I have to get back to the hospital, Doug. Trevor might wake up any minute."

"Then he'll be awake when you get there." He muttered, "Shit," before returning to his normally abusive tone. "It's Sunday, so I'm on my own today."

"Then let's wait until tomorrow." I'd be just as desperate then.

"No, I can write it up myself. I want this done today—signed, stamped, and delivered. My office is barely out of your way, and it'll take you a whopping thirty seconds to sign. I'll even meet you in the lobby."

Wow, what a saint. "Fine." I wanted this over with as much as he did. "I'll get a cab and be there in ten minutes."

"Great. And, Declan? If you tell the guys about the deal and they decide to spend the next few months fucking me over, you'll be the one paying for that mistake. Understood?"

"Yes, boss. I understand." Getting screwed isn't something that's easy to miss.

43

DECLAN

*W*ith Sunday morning traffic, it had taken me eons to get from my place to Doug's, then from there to the hospital.

But I was here. Finally. I wasn't sure if I was more motivated to be here in case Trevor woke up or to be anywhere Doug wasn't. But I'd signed the paper, tossed the pen at him, and was out the door in three minutes. I hadn't even waited for him to make a copy for me. Doug had so helpfully offered to send my copy to the hospital by bike messenger, so it was probably already on its way over.

I had three months to make sure Self Defense got a recording deal, or I would be forced to hand over my soul and let him do whatever he wanted with me. I'd had some choice words for him when he slipped in the fact that for those three months, Self Defense would be on tour again. But I'd already agreed to it, and I knew Doug would never change it out of the kindness of his heart.

I didn't know what I was going to tell Trevor. Part of me hoped he wouldn't come out of his coma until I could figure it out. And that might take a while, considering I hadn't slept at all last night. Honestly, I couldn't even remember a night I'd slept *well.*

That worry morphed into a whole new one when I saw Sara's mother sitting on a chair in the hospital waiting room. She was looking down, typing something on her phone.

Fuck. "Is she okay?" I asked loudly enough so that everyone turned to look at me, including Elaine. "Is she...is Sara okay?"

Please, don't do this to me. I couldn't take any more.

Her eyes widened in recognition and concern. "Sara? Yes, she's fine. I drove her here to see your friend."

I'd barely finished my sigh of relief when the last part of her comment sank in. "She's here to see Trevor?" I shouldn't have been angry, but my brain was running on anxiety and sleep deprivation. So, somehow, that turned the fact that Sara was here to support *him* instead of being there to support me into one more blow—and this one stung.

"Well, she was looking for you, but she's back there, waiting with him now." She flicked her head toward the heavy door that led back to where I'd left Trevor.

"So, she's okay? Promise?" I wasn't sure why it seemed so impossible to understand. Maybe because over the last eight hours, I'd gone through every terrible emotion, one after the other, with no sleep. My mind couldn't keep track anymore. It had forgotten what an appropriate reaction to anything was. Any second, I'd start laughing hysterically, or crying, or breaking out into song. I just didn't know.

"Declan?" She stood quickly, dropping her phone and purse onto the floor and rushing toward me. "Are you alright?"

No. But I hated to think my emotional state was so obvious that anyone could tell just by looking at me.

"Sit down. You look like you're going to faint." She took me by the arm and tried to lead me to a chair. I didn't move. I barely knew her, and what little I *did* know about her hadn't made me her biggest fan.

"I can't. I need to go check on Trevor. He's not doing well."

"Neither are you, honey."

I pulled away from her. "I gotta check on…" Why couldn't I remember who needed me? *Did* anyone need me? Yes. I shook the fog out of my mind and body. "Trevor. Trevor needs me."

She might have followed me through the door and down the hallway toward Trevor's room, but I couldn't be sure. And I didn't look. Because I couldn't care about anything other than my best friend right now. Anything else would be too much.

As if the universe wanted to prove me right, as soon as I opened the curtain to Trev's room, I saw Sara. She'd pulled the chair closer and had fallen asleep with her head on Trevor's bed.

"You're in my seat." I didn't even try to hide the shitty attitude in my tone, didn't care that I'd woken her up. Or maybe I did. Maybe I just couldn't stand the thought of her sleeping peacefully while my world collapsed around me. While the life of the jerk who'd stuck with me since we were kids was still controlled by machines, only a series of beeps and lines proving that he was alive.

She straightened and looked at me but didn't say anything.

"It's good you're here." When she smiled, I added, "A beautiful woman is probably the only thing he'd wake up for."

"You should sit down. You look—"

"Like shit. Yeah, your mom told me."

"She's still here?" She blew out her breath and then shoved the chair toward me. "Sit down before you fall down."

I did both—collapsing into the chair, leaving her nowhere to sit down. Hopefully, chivalry would be the only thing to die tonight.

Fuck it. I might look like shit, but I didn't want to act like it. I got back up and dragged my ass down the hallway to the nurse's station, ignoring Sara's calls.

"Can I take one of these chairs to 13B?" I asked.

"I'll take it for you. 13B?" A male nurse or orderly or whatever the fuck he was stood up, looking at me with concern. I stared right back, wondering how he managed being here, smothered by tears and antiseptic every day.

I followed him back down the hall and stood outside Trev's room while the nurse and Sara rearranged the equipment carts to fit both chairs next to each other. After thanking him, I slumped into the seat, only realizing just how small the space was when my thigh pressed against Sara's.

After a couple of minutes, she inched her hand closer to mine. I grabbed it and used it to pull her into me, wrapping both arms around her tightly.

"I'm so sorry I wasn't there," she whimpered, her voice muffled by my shirt.

"It doesn't matter."

"Yes, it does. I wanted to be there. I was on my way back, but—"

"It doesn't matter." I didn't want to talk about it, didn't want to be disappointed or wonder what would happen to us. I was too tired to argue, too tired to speak. So, I closed my eyes and breathed her in. The sweet scent of her hair helping me forget where we really were, how we'd all gotten there, and where we would end up next.

44

DECLAN

*I*t took hours of waiting for a room to open up for Trev in another part of the hospital. No idea why it took so long, unless they were waiting for someone to croak so they could haul out his body and give his room to my friend. Honestly, I tried not to think about it too much. Because no one would tell me why Trev was being moved to begin with, and the more I thought about the staff waiting for someone to croak, the closer I felt to a breakdown.

By the time we got settled into the room and the new round of nurses had dragged me through his entire medical history *again*—as if I knew, as if he'd told me anything about it lately—it was noon.

"I'm going to go get you some food," Sara said from the vinyl-covered couch across the room. I was still hovering at Trevor's bedside, keeping a close eye on his chest to make sure it was still moving up and down in the same rhythm as the lines on one of the machines.

"I'm not hungry."

"Well, I am. And you should eat something. I'll be back as soon as I—" She stopped as soon as our eyes met. They hadn't been doing much of that because I couldn't deal with our shit right now. And looking at her would force me to remember.

"You don't have to stay here, Sara."

She took a few steps toward me. "You can ignore me completely." There was no antagonism in her voice, no drama. She must have known I couldn't take it. "But if it's okay with you, I'd like to stay, just in case. So that if you need anything—anything at all—I'm here."

I sighed and nodded, breaking eye contact and looking at the tile on the floor. "I could use some coffee."

"I'll get some. Anything else?"

To hold her. For a minute or a month. To feel as if I weren't dealing with this on my own. But I didn't say any of that. Instead, I shook my head and turned back to Trevor and his machines, listening to the soft click of Sara's shoes on the tile, the opening of the door behind me, and the lurch of the hinge when she let it go.

A few minutes later, I heard a knock. Since the hospital staff didn't bother with that kind of thing, I turned around to see who it was.

Ed stood outside, waving at me wildly as if we were across a football field from each other. I didn't know how he'd heard the news but was happy he'd come.

It seemed like I hadn't seen him in forever. Although, *everything* seemed like forever ago to me now. I knew he and Trevor still spoke a lot. Trev was helping him put some demos together or something.

Once I'd motioned Ed into the room, he pushed the door open. He was my height but maybe half my weight, so when his gigantic black messenger bag caught on the latch, it pulled him off balance for a second. He figured it out pretty quickly and swung the heavy bag away from the door and into a rolling tray the nurse had left there earlier.

"Hey, man," he said quietly, as if the guy lying on the bed in front of us was just sleeping and not unconscious.

"Good to see you, Ed. Thanks for coming."

Ed shook my hand and looked down at him. "How's the fucker doing?"

I shrugged. "Did he ever tell you about any pain he was having?"

"You mean from his pancreas or whatever?"

I nodded unhappily. "Fuck, really? You knew about that?"

He grimaced. "Sorry, man. Yeah. I forgot he didn't want you to know."

"Why the fuck not?" Luckily, I was so exhausted, the question didn't sound angry. I didn't want to scare the kid—he looked guilty enough already. I just wanted to know why my best friend had kept something so important from me.

"He didn't want to fuck things up for the band," Ed said. "He figured that once you guys had a solid contract with a label, he could quit without it being a big deal."

"He was planning to—" Nope. I couldn't say shit. I'd done the exact same thing to him—kept something serious from him because I didn't want to hurt my bandmates. No wonder he'd taken my big confession so well. He had the same fucking exit plan. Although considering how long he must have known he couldn't keep up with the rest of us, he'd probably been planning it for a lot longer than I had.

Ed and I stood there without speaking—me in stunned silence, and Ed fighting with whatever was in his bag, a needle in the haystack maybe.

When he found whatever he'd been searching for, he held it up above his head and yelled, "Got it, Trev!"

I turned toward him to see what he was talking about. He held out a red thumb drive with something written in sharpie on one side. I couldn't read what it said until he put it into my hand.

"What's this?" I turned it over and read: *Declan Rocks*. "Cute title."

"My idea. Trevor didn't even think I could put it together so fast." Ed stood there smiling, glancing at Trevor every once in a while, with the same shit-eating grin, while I tried to figure out what was going on. "Told you I'd have it for you tonight, jackass. Wake the fuck up and listen to it, so I can see your expression while you fall in love with my superb and speedy work."

"What is this?" I asked.

His brow came together. "It's your demo. Didn't Trev—" His mouth dropped open a couple of inches. "Oh shit. You knew about it, right?"

"I'm not having the best of days here, so could you just fill me in on..."—my volume lowered to barely a grumble—"everything?" All the shit that my best friend had neglected to share with me.

"About a week ago, he gave me the original, acoustic versions of all the Self Defense songs. You know, the ones with only you or only you and him, before they were remixed."

I knew Trevor had my originals. I'd been the one to give them to him. But I didn't know why he would've shared them with Ed.

"Then yesterday, he sent me two new ones. Said they were a rush order. One was a ballad with just you and an acoustic guitar—that's a good fucking song, by the way—and the other was you, your guitar, and some chick giggling in the background. That one was good, too, but you should fire whoever recorded them. Aside from the dual track screw-up, the mix and background was shit."

I nodded as if I had followed that well enough to agree with him, but inside, the information kept spinning on repeat, and I couldn't catch a single fucking thing.

Why would Trevor have given all of my songs to Ed? If I

stretched my limited imagination, giving him the original versions of the Self Defense songs made sense—maybe Trevor wanted to experiment with something new and decided to go all the way back to the beginning for some reason.

And sure, Trevor sending Ed my brand-new, pity-me ballad made sense if I accepted that Trevor was a big fucking liar who'd gone back on his promise not to share it with anyone.

But the last song he'd mentioned had to have been the one I'd written for, and with, Sara. How'd Trevor even know it existed?

Oh shit. I was an idiot. "When Trevor sent you the last two, they were overlapping, weren't they?"

Ed nodded. "Yep. Recorded as two separate tracks instead of two individual files. The one with the girl laughing was hidden, but all I had to do was extract it and move it into its own file."

I wasn't sure if Ed had figured there was a reason I'd done it like that, or if he'd just decided I was an idiot who'd done it accidentally. If he'd guessed the latter, he'd have been right. When I recorded the new song yesterday, I must have accidentally connected the tracks together on my laptop, stacking them on top of each other without realizing it.

So, when I'd given the new song to Trevor, Sara's song had been hiding underneath it.

I had a flashback to the day I made that recording with Sara. I hadn't pressed the record button to have a track of the song, or even to be able to listen to her laugh whenever I wanted to. Why would I need a recording of something I heard every day?

I'd recorded it because, in twenty years, I wanted to be able to hear the way we talked to each other while we were falling in love. So that whenever I annoyed her, I would be able to pull it out as proof that she used to love my voice.

I'd recorded it when I was one hundred percent sure we

would have a forever. Back before I realized that *nothing* was forever.

"I worked on them all yesterday and last night," Ed said. "Didn't even hear what happened to him until an hour ago."

He'd worked on them?

"Explain what that means, Ed."

"Um..." He rubbed his cheek and glanced at Trevor.

"I'm not mad at him." I chuckled. "Not for this, anyway. I know he wouldn't have given you something he promised he wouldn't show anyone unless he had a good reason." I gestured to the guy who might never be able to explain it to me. "He can't tell me that reason, Ed. But I really need to understand *something* right now."

"You really didn't know anything about it?" He looked at me oddly. "I figured you guys had decided to do it together, since you were the one who wrote them."

"If we'd done this together, I doubt my head would be this close to exploding." I rubbed my eyes with both hands and then brushed my hair back.

"Okay. So, uh..." Ed rummaged around in his satchel again, pulled out a bottle of Advil, and handed it to me. "Basically, Trevor asked me to remix all your songs, so I could start playing them in the clubs and on my social media pages. I tested a couple of your early ones at a gig last weekend, and people went ballistic over them." He smiled at the memory. "I posted the newest one with just you and the guitar on YouTube around four o'clock this morning—just the music with a black background, not the kind of thing that goes viral, you know? When I left my place, it already had over 25k hits, and aside from a few fuckhead trolls, people are loving it, man. Congrats. No idea what it's up to now, but we need to figure out the financials before I put out any more. I don't want anyone to feel like they're getting screwed."

"Financials?" I scrubbed my hands over my face a few more times. Might've helped more if someone slapped me a few times.

"Yeah. For the site hits, royalties, and what we sell at the online retailers once we put them up."

"You and Trevor figured all this out?"

He shook his head. "It was all him. Remember? I thought you two were doing it together." After he set down his laptop on the rolling table next to Trevor's head, he clicked open his Internet browser. "Sound quality won't be the best through the speakers, and I bet the hospital Wi-Fi is crappier than dirt, but it'll have to do."

I slumped down on the arm of the couch and waited for the page to load.

"Completely unbiased here, but they came out amazing. Except the ballad. I mean, it still sounds great sped up and with REC'Ed's signature old-school techno sound behind it. But I think Trev was right—you should release that one mainstream alternative, at least initially. Then, after it's really hot and before everybody starts begging to remix it for you, we release my version. And boom, we both need to start storing our cash in the Caymans, know what I mean?"

No. Kind of. Maybe a few parts, but definitely not the majority of it. "I'm going to need you to explain all of that again. Because I'm still lost. Trevor gave you my songs and told you to release them as dance music? All of them?"

He nodded. "Aside from the ballad. You'll make a fortune if you leave it more mainstream. Listen to this."

I leaned closer when the music started and closed my eyes to block my other senses out. He'd obviously sped up the chorus a little, but I recognized the notes and the lyrics. "That doesn't even sound like me."

"It actually sounds exactly like you. Just not the way you sound when you're singing Self Defense songs, and that's kind of the point, right? Trevor told me you didn't want anyone to know you were still writing."

"He really said that?"

"That's what *he told me* means, Dec. Yeah."

I wanted to listen to more, but before I could stop him, he clicked away from that window and opened up another.

"This is the other. I like it, but I'm not crazy about the chick giggling in the background. Does it symbolize something too deep for me to get?"

45

SARA

"The laughing symbolizes Declan's incredible patience with a girl who knows nothing about music," I said from the doorway.

Luckily, Declan had been too confused, and the other guy too excited about the deal to hear me come in. I'd been standing just inside the door for the last few minutes, eavesdropping. Not proud of it, but I definitely didn't want to interrupt what sounded like great news for Declan. Because he so desperately needed some good news right now.

I held out the tray when they turned around and finally noticed me. "But he'll definitely take her out."

"Hey," Declan said.

"Hey," I said back. "Yours is the one on the right." It was decaf. I knew it was dishonest, but seriously, the last thing he needed was caffeine. The first thing he needed was sleep. So, I'd made an executive decision he was better off not knowing about.

"Thanks." Declan's face was so pale, the circles under his eyes so dark. He walked over to me and took the coffees off the tray, so I could unpack the bag I'd been holding tucked between one arm and my side.

"I'm wrecked," the other guy said.

Until he pulled the bottom of his T-shirt out to show off "REC'Ed" written in airbrushed graffiti, I thought he was referring to how he felt. And was about to tell him we all feel that way.

"But during daylight hours, you can just call me Ed."

"Sara," I said, shaking his hand. "You can call me that twenty-four seven. If I'd known you were here, I would've gotten you a cup of coffee, too." I could've given him mine, but I needed it too badly to let it go.

"Thanks, but I don't drink coffee—it messes with my temple." After slapping his hand on his chest, he helped himself to one of the many cafeteria pastries I'd dumped onto the tray.

"I can see that," I said as I watched Ed finish his first in two bites and reach for another. Then I held them out to Declan, hoping one of them would be so appealing he wouldn't be able to refuse it. Unfortunately, it seemed he was the only one in the room—besides Trevor—who *could* refuse it. Hell, I'd planned on eating at least half the tray by myself. Carbs, especially sugar, help refuel the emotional well in times of stress.

"So, you're the giggler?" Ed asked.

"Not something I imagined would be part of my legacy, but, yeah, I guess I'm the giggler. Sounds like a rejected comic book villain."

"Ed," Declan said, "if I agree to this plan, I don't want to show my face."

Ed laughed. "Because you're so ugly?"

"I'm serious, man. Not on posters, albums, promotion, or onstage. You can do all of that shit, but no one ever knows it's me who's writing or singing."

A nurse opened the door and peeked into the room. "I'm sorry, but a bike messenger dropped this off a bit ago. It's for Declan Hollis? She said it was a legal document and was"—she rolled her eyes—"very insistent that the sender wanted someone give it to you right away."

"Oh, fuck." Without explaining his response, Declan took the envelope from the woman and cursed at least a half dozen more times before she made it all the way out of the room. "Fuck. Fuck. Fuck."

"Wanna tell us what that envelope did to you to make you hate it so much, dude?" Ed asked.

Declan looked at me, terrified. "I already gave up." Then he looked at Ed. "I can't do it—what you and Trevor set up for me. I can't do it because I already gave up."

I took the envelope from him and pulled out a four or five-page document. As soon as I saw the letterhead, I understood why he was so freaked out. *Another* reason he was so freaked out.

I sat down and started skimming. "Let me read it before you panic."

"Too late for that," Ed mumbled.

I wasn't an attorney, but I'd seen enough contracts to know this one had been slapped together. There were a bunch of typos and a few sentences that started but never went anywhere, as if someone had been a lot too hurried with their cutting and pasting. Evidently, Declan's manager had done the same thing Emilia had—instead of using a master template, he'd written it up from scratch, copying legal-sounding bits from one and trying to force them into coherency for another.

After about five minutes, I understood enough to give Declan some good news. And some not-so-good news. "This gives Self Defense three months to be offered a recording contract." And they would be on tour the whole time. "If the band hasn't been signed by the end of that period, you agree to have Doug manage your solo career for a period of one year."

"Fuck." Declan leaned against Trevor's bed and covered his face with his hand. "I'm sorry, man."

"The good news is there are no mentions of your music, so you can do whatever you want with it. And Doug doesn't get anything from any deal he doesn't negotiate."

He dropped his hands to look at me. "Really?"

"That's great," Ed said. "So, you can release it however you want to."

I nodded. "Whatever money you earn from it is one hundred percent yours. He doesn't get a dime."

"Yeah, but if Self Defense doesn't get signed..."

"If Self Defense doesn't get signed, you're screwed."

"Fuck."

"But— Now, remember, I'm not a pro, so you should get someone who *is* to look at it again." God, I hoped I was right, though. "But the way it reads to me, Self Defense is an entity in and of itself. Nowhere in here does it say Self Defense is Declan, Pete, Sam, and Trevor."

Declan nodded. "Probably because I told him we'd have to find another bassist. Three months isn't enough time for Trevor to get better and rejoin the band."

"Well, then, Trevor gave you a giant loophole to get out of the contract." After reminding them not to get their hopes up too much because there was a distinct possibility I was wrong, I explained. "By not mentioning the band members by name, Doug unintentionally determined that, as long as a band called 'Self Defense' signs with a recording label, it doesn't matter who the band members are."

Ed came closer and looked at the contract over my shoulder. "So, Self Defense could be made up of the four Ninja Turtles, and it would work?"

"If they were good enough to be signed by a label."

"You'd be off the hook, Declan."

Declan didn't look nearly as pleased as Ed did. "What are

the chances I can pull off something in three months that we haven't been able to make happen in three years?"

I cocked my head and looked at him. "I know you're exhausted and overwhelmed right now, and that's clouding your thinking. But after a good night's sleep, I hope you remember telling me that the only way to turn *yet* into *never* is by giving up."

He bent down in front of me and took the contract out of my hand. "My mind is clear enough to know what those three months are going to look like." Instead of looking at it, or even ripping it up, he set it down on a side table, never letting his gaze leave mine.

"I'm going to be gone for three months, Sara. Minimum." He pushed his hair off his forehead. "Any free time I have will be taken up by finding my replacement and trying to get Defense signed. And if I can't, who knows what Doug has planned or how long I'll be gone."

My throat went dry. I had a few more months of school to finish before graduation, so going with him was impossible.

"Maybe after I finish school—"

"Do you really want to put your life on hold for a whole year? Follow me around while I'm miserable and being forced to do everything I hate about this business?" He shook his head. "I don't want that *for* you."

When the first tear slid down my cheek, Ed coughed and said he needed to use the bathroom. The door clicked closed ten seconds later.

"We don't have to make any decisions right now," he said softly. "We'll both be swamped, so three months will probably feel like nothing. But whether or not I pull this off, you need to live your life. Don't wait to see what happens to me. Okay?"

I couldn't bring myself to nod, but I understood. Neither of us knew if he'd be free in three months or fifteen. I'd been ignoring life for too long already. If I didn't start moving, I might wake up one morning and realize I'd wasted most of it.

"I'm going to use every minute of every day to make this happen." He lifted my chin and kissed me lightly. My lips trembled until he pressed his lips against mine. I threw my arms around his neck and squeezed, breaking the kiss to cry into his chest.

"I won't give up. On it or on us. You hear me?"

"Yeah," a low, scratchy voice behind us said. "I hear you, man."

We both turned to see Trevor. He still looked like shit, but at least his eyes were open.

"Trevor!"

I let go of Declan, so he could go to his friend. He didn't let go of me, though. Instead, he pulled me along as if letting me go now would be letting me go forever.

"You're awake," Declan said in wonder.

"Yeah," Trevor grumbled. "Now, shut the hell up so I can go back to sleep."

46

DECLAN

Three excruciatingly long months later...

"Get over here, my brother!" Trevor yelled from the front door of his parents' house. He'd been staying with them for the last few months while I'd been on tour with Pete, Sam, and "Trevor #2," as the guys kept calling Steve, the bassist we'd hired to replace our friend.

With three months of sobriety, counseling a couple of times a week, less stress, and proper medical care, Trevor had pulled through. Even with a chronic disease, he was probably the healthiest he'd been in years.

Kitty got to him before I did, jumping up and licking him on the face.

"Eww." He pushed her away, laughing. "I hope you're not planning to do that to me too, Dec."

"I'll try to control myself." I pulled her back and told her to sit, so I could say hello. "You're looking good." I'd barely gotten the words out when he wrapped his arms around me and squeezed me so hard, I could've sworn I heard a few bones crack.

He let me go and stepped back to survey the damage he'd just caused. "Wish I could say the same thing about you."

"Shut the fuck up. I just spent three months on the road, busting my ass to keep the guys in line, begging a label to sign the band, and then finding a new Declan to sing lead."

"How's he working out?"

"My replacement? He's good. Talented. Smart." I cocked my head to the side. "Mormon." Finding a guy who could not only perform well, but who I knew wouldn't fall into any of the traps that could so easily break up a band had been the part that let me sleep at night.

"You lucky son of a bitch." He led Kitty and me inside, through the maze of rooms, and into the backyard. "Let her roam around. Dog piss is good for roses, right?"

As soon as I'd unclipped Kitty's leash, she was off and running across the large expanse of grass, straight for the—

"Oooh," Trevor and I groaned simultaneously as all four of her paws hit the water.

"You should really have a gate around that pool, you know?"

"Now I do." He shrugged. "Don't worry about it. She's fine. And I want to hear more about what Doug's face looked like when you fucked him."

"Over," I added quickly. "When I fucked him *over*, you pervert. And I didn't fuck him over. He made the rules, wrote the contract. He just didn't know I would have someone smarter than him on my side."

He nodded. "Speaking of Sara..."

"I should get Kitty out of your mom's pool before she comes home and kills me." I gripped the arms of the patio chair and started to stand.

"Sit back down, you coward. The woman saved your ass. So,

why haven't you contacted her? At least to tell her the good news?"

I let out a deep breath. "It's been months. What am I supposed to say?"

"Maybe start with 'Thanks for saving my ass.'"

She really had. But our calls had gone from multiple times per day, to every couple of days, to almost never in the first month. For the last two months, they'd stayed at *never*. Voice mail messages and texts weren't the same, especially with us having opposite schedules and barely any free time.

Eventually, I couldn't even fake happiness or hope. So, I'd deliberately avoided calling her, thinking that, instead of spending that time depressing the fuck out of her, I could be using it to make sure three months apart didn't turn into fifteen.

But I'd been wrong about the time passing quickly. Even with every waking hour being spoken for, months of constantly missing someone felt like an eternity.

"Then following it up with something sappy," Trevor said. "Actually, maybe you should apologize for being such a dumb shit and *then* say something sappy. But you'd better hurry the fuck up. Like you said—it's been months—and women like her won't stick around forever, even for a face as pretty as yours."

"All the more reason to leave her alone. If she's already with someone else, I don't want to screw it up for her." The thought was on two-hour loop in my head. If she really were dating someone, I wouldn't be able to handle it. Every time I passed the end of my driveway, the fear of accidentally running into her and seeing her hand in some other guy's set in. It was crippling.

"Declan, I love you, but you're clueless." Trevor sighed dramatically. "Before you met her, I doubt I would've needed both hands to count the times I saw you truly happy—the light-up-your-face kind of happy. I mean, you weren't walking around all depressed or anything, but we both just kind of pretended not to know that your smile was only skin-deep."

I nodded slowly. "I can't just call her up after all this time and pretend I haven't been thinking of her every day for the last three months."

"That's so fucking pathetic." He chuckled. "You're a writer. Go write a song for her and snail mail it to her. Fuck, worst case scenario, she never speaks to you again, but you still end up with a song to release that could potentially sell as well as the first one does."

I sat back and thought about that song. With Ed and Trevor's help, it had gone viral. Of course, a big part of that was the mystery surrounding who'd written and sung it. There were actual forums where people argued about whose voice it was. I looked at them occasionally to check, but luckily, my name almost never came up. Probably because the old lead singer of Self Defense wasn't nearly as well known as the anonymous voice was.

We'd opted not to use any of the songs the band had ever recorded, knowing that could lead fans back to me. But I'd had a stack of stuff I'd written for myself that no one had ever heard before, and now they were selling almost as well as the song I'd written for Sara.

Even after giving a cut of the royalties to Ed and Trevor, I was making way more money than Doug had promised me. And I was writing the kind of music I wanted to without having to do any of the shit I hated. My life was almost exactly what I wanted it to be. Almost.

"I have something for her, actually," I said. "I've been holding on to it for a while, waiting until I could figure out how to explain it to her."

"If it's a dick pic, don't send it. No explanation is good

enough for sending a dick pic to a woman who doesn't ask for it."

Trevor's incredible wisdom was interrupted by the fine mist of chlorinated water that rained down on us and the horror of seeing a freshly-shaken but still dripping wet Goldendoodle running straight for us.

"Oh shit!" We sprinted for the house, jumping over patio furniture and shoving each other out of the way. As soon as he slammed the door behind us, we both burst out laughing. Kitty stared at us through the glass, probably confused about why we didn't want to play. After a few minutes, she wandered away, trotting back into the garden to go explore, and hopefully not to go swimming again.

Trevor handed me a bottle of water out of the fridge and leaned against the counter. "I've been thinking about my future lately." He paused. "Kind of started seeing someone."

"Holy shit. That's great. When do I get to meet her?"

"Once she's so enamored with me, a pretty boy like you won't distract her."

I rolled my eyes. "Tonight sounds perfect. Just let me know when and where." I waited for him to agree before continuing. "So, you see a future with her?"

"Yeah, I think so. Her name is April, and she's amazing. She has a real job that she has to wake up early in the morning to get to. She's shy, and stable, and listens to the worst fucking music I've ever heard. But I kind of love that about her."

Nothing he'd ever done or said had made me happier than hearing that. Being with someone like April would help keep him from backsliding.

"And I've also been thinking a lot about Doug."

I grimaced. "You poor thing."

"I want to do what he does, Dec. But better. I want to help

little shitheads like we used to be get what they've always dreamed of."

"You mean become a manager? That's fucking brilliant." I smacked him on the arm. "Why didn't you think of that sooner? It's perfect for you." He could use his firsthand knowledge of the industry to help musicians do it the right way. "Those little shitheads better appreciate how lucky they are. On day one, the first thing you should tell them is what you said to me once." I cleared my throat. "And I quote, badly, 'Until you quit trying, every moment you have is a moment you can get the thing you want most.'"

"I said that?" He rubbed his chin. "I'm so damn smart. There's just one problem with it."

"What?"

"How sad it is that you remember me saying it, but you haven't been living it."

"What do you mean?"

"Stop being such an idiot and go get the woman you love."

47

SARA

$\mathcal{I}$ hadn't gotten anything in the mail other than bills and junk since I'd had a Peruvian pen pal in the fifth grade. So, when the two most important letters I'd probably ever get in my entire life arrived in the same month, I considered looking up the Vatican's official rules about declaring something a miracle. Because this had to be close.

Since I'd already told all my friends about my acceptance letter to law school this fall, only one of the over-read letters was shoved into the absolute bottom of my bag when I rang the doorbell.

Emilia and Rob's new house was the kind of place that people from the other side of the world come to San Francisco to see. The blue and white Victorian had bay windows, brick stairs, and ribbon-like detailing around each window and the roof.

Emilia looked flushed but happy when she answered the door. "Thank God you're here. I spent the last three days unpacking and cleaning to get ready for this damn party. Now, my body hurts so badly I think I should start saying my final goodbyes."

"You can't die! You just signed a thirty-year loan on this sucker. Just be glad someone was smart enough to come up with the idea of housewarming gifts."

"As always, you're right. I give thanks for that and for my wine rack, which has never been so beautifully filled as it is right now." She gave me a quick hug and led me inside. "But please tell me you didn't bring Chardonnay. I swear, every single one of Rob's friends brought us a bottle, and I can't stand the stuff."

"Good thing *your* friends know that about you." When I took out the bottle of pinot noir I'd brought, I pushed all my other crap deeper into my bag to make sure the envelope didn't fall out. "Although, truth be told, I'm fairly sure there are only about ten bottles of Chardonnay in existence, and since no one actually likes it, they just keep getting shuffled from housewarming party to housewarming party."

I'd been to the house only a couple days ago to help Emilia get settled, so the downstairs tour she gave me was really just an excuse to step away from playing hostess to Rob's work friends. After I said hello to Andi and Hayden, I gave Rob an especially tight squeeze with his hello hug. His firm's recommendation, along with whatever strings he'd had to pull, were the reasons I'd gotten into Berkeley's law school with such short notice.

The bright silver lining of everything that had gone wrong three months ago was that Emilia, Andi, and I were closer than ever. After I started virtual assisting again, I finally had enough money to afford my own teensy, tiny apartment and the time to meet my friends regularly. And even though Carissa had gone back to Texas right after graduation, we talked on the phone about once a week. She'd been almost as excited as I was when I told her about Berkeley Law.

"Enough people-ing. I'm dying to share my wisdom about whatever you need help with." Emilia was obviously as anxious as I was to discuss what I'd texted her and Andi about earlier—something important I needed their advice for.

She grabbed Andi before we went upstairs and into her home office. "You get the hot seat." She spun the leather chair away from the view out the window to face the chaise lounge that she and Andi sat down on.

"Go!" she said, looking at me expectantly.

"I got this today." I put the padded manila envelope onto the coffee table between us after I'd pulled out the letter-sized envelope that was causing me so much confusion.

"You really know how to build up anticipation," Andi said. "Should we try to guess what it says?"

I shook my head and held it out to her. "Read it."

Emilia shook her head. "You read it to us. It's more exciting that way."

"I hate you both," I lied, straightening the letter out and setting it and the check that had come with it on the table. "It's from Declan."

I knew the second they saw how much money the check was written out for because Emilia cursed and Andi snatched the letter off the table.

I picked up the check to make sure I'd read it right as Andi started reading aloud.

Sara,

This is your cut of the royalties I made from your song. If you're thinking to yourself that you don't deserve the money, you're wrong. The fact is that being with you was the only reason I could write it, and if you read any of the comments or mentions online, you'd know how true that is. A lot of people have called For You *this year's sappiest love song or something. So, if I'd never met you, had never* fallen in love with you, that song wouldn't exist, and I wouldn't have made any money from it.

Since I didn't think you'd take it, I put the money to the side until I knew what to do with it. I swear I haven't been stalking you. But guess who just happened to be at the band's show in Houston a couple of weeks ago. Yep, Carissa. It was good and bad to see her again. Bad, because she was a big reminder of something I can't go a day without remembering. And good because, as soon as she told me you'd been accepted to law school, I knew where the money needed to go.

The deal I made with Doug ended last week, so no more band or shows or unpleasant attention. I'm happy being known as the guy who used to be the lead singer of Self Defense. I'm going to love being invisible.

So, I don't want credit for it, and I'd prefer if no one knew I was involved. Your school doesn't share financial information with the public, but they refused to keep it a secret from you. Since I know how grumpy you'd be if you thought I was paying your tuition, and I wasn't sure you'd accept the royalty money to begin with, I figured it would be best if you heard the explanation directly from me.

Maybe you noticed that the check is written out to the university and not you. From what I've been told, that means it doesn't actually belong to you, and you're not allowed to rip it up. Other checks will be coming. They might not be for as much, but they should be enough to cover your tuition, books, and most of your living expenses for a while. Helping you reach for your dream is the least I can do to repay you for helping me reach for mine.

Believe what you want, but if we'd never met, I wouldn't be here right now, doing what I love and not doing what I don't. Trevor might not be three months sober, and Kitty would still be worried about her dad. Actually, I think she is still worried about me. Because as good as things are going for me right now, something is still missing. Something about your size and shape.

God, I miss you, babe. I miss you. And I can't imagine a day when *it will ever stop. That's probably a shitty thing to say after all this time, but I don't care. It's not about making you feel bad. I just want you to know that somewhere out there is a man whose entire life changed for the better because of you. He found out what love feels like, and he finally understands that he can love someone who isn't there anymore. And know that he always will.*

Whatever your future brings, I hope it makes you happy. I hope whoever you're with now, or will be in the future, can see what's in front of him. I hope he sees as much beauty in you as I do.

Take care of yourself, would you? Study hard or hardly study— whichever brings you joy. And who knows, maybe someday, I'll get in the kind of trouble that only a great attorney can get me out of, so I'll be able to see you again.

Always for you,

D.

"Wow," both Andi and Emilia said at exactly the same time, Emilia drawing hers out a little longer. She always was the more dramatic of my two best friends.

"I'm going to need more than that, guys." I'd come to them for advice, not to have the damn letter punctuated with a sigh at the end of every sentence. "What should I do?"

They glanced at each other, turned back to me, and then answered at the same time again.

Andi replied with, "Use the check." Emilia's response was more complicated: "Track him down and propose before anyone else does." I didn't think she was joking.

"I want to change my answer. Do what she said." Andi flicked her head toward Emilia. "And *then* use the check."

"Definitely. Get the guy and use the check. In that order." Emilia held out her hand. "Can I see it again? I don't think I've ever seen that many zeros on anything before."

"Please, take it." I handed it over gladly. The less time I spent staring at it, the better. "It's too much temptation to hold on to when I'm trying to make a decision based on logic."

"Wait a sec," Andi said seriously. "We're talking about enough money to let you finish law school with no student debt. Money you earned—" She shut me up with a look. "Regardless of whether you think you earned it or not, Declan was pretty clear on that front. And if you can't take his word for it, remember that people hire consultants, life coaches, and inspirational gurus all the time. You were his muse, and he thinks your help was worth compensating. So, please, *please* tell me you're not stupid enough to refuse the money."

Emilia was still staring at the check, nodding along with every word Andi said.

"Fine. I'm not that stupid. But you guys are missing one large detail about it." I can't believe Emilia hadn't spotted it yet, considering how close her face was. "One large detail that's *missing* from the check, actually."

"Oh shit." Emilia popped her head up and stared wide-eyed at me. "He didn't sign it!"

Neither of them saw my shoulders slump because they were too busy triple-checking the signature line.

"Now you see the reason"—another reason—"I don't know what to do."

Andi, ever the realist, shocked me by saying, "He left it blank on purpose. Anyone who spends however long it took to write such an amazing letter pays attention to every detail. I bet he obsessed over that check more than you are."

"Why wouldn't he have signed it, then?"

"Because he's still in love with you, dumbass. He knows the school won't take it without a signature. So, if you took it in, what would they tell you to do?"

"Um...get it signed?"

349

"Right!" Emilia took over from there. "They'd tell you to go back to the person who wrote it and get him to sign it." She looked at me for a minute and then smiled. "Oh man, you really are a dumbass. Don't you get it? Declan set it up so you'd have to see each other again."

Andi nodded. "One more chance to see you, whether you end up taking the check or not."

"I could send it back the same way he sent it to me."

"By mail? Would you really? That's like breaking up with someone by text. Okay, so, if you sent it back in the mail, at least he'd know that you're a wussy jerk and that he's better off without you."

Emilia pulled out the other gift he'd sent along with the check.

"Don't read that." I snatched it back from her before she could see what Declan had written on it.

"What is it?"

"It's a slate—a writing board that can get wet. For when you think of something while you're in the shower and want to write it down. I used his once, but he said I had to get my own. So, I joked about it being magic—that everything you write on it comes true."

"Wow," Andi said concerned. "Since when did you become so Disney Princess?"

I grimaced. "Believe me, no Disney Princess would've written what I did."

"That's because Disney refuses to consistently write the kind of princess little girls need as role models."

"No," I said slowly. "What I wrote really isn't the kind of thing little girls should be exposed to."

Both of them let out a long, "Oooooh."

"Now we get it," Emilia said. "Right, Andi?"

Andi nodded. "So, did whatever you wrote on his happen?"

"Yep. Every single, blissfully sinful word."

She folded up the letter and slid it across the table to me. "I really like this guy."

Emilia slid the check over. "Me, too."

"Me, too," I said softly.

Emilia's eyes widened when she turned over the envelope she was still holding. "He said his tour ended last week, right?"

"Yeah. His old manager doesn't know about Declan's other persona, and there was nothing about it in their contract, so Declan gets all the money from online clicks and sales."

"Declan and *you*," Andi corrected.

"Actually, that's not why I was asking." Emilia set the envelope on the table with the address label facing up. "I meant that if his tour ended last week, maybe you should look at the return address."

As soon as I did, I wanted to cry. It was local. A small town just outside the city in the East Bay. I could be there in thirty minutes. I hadn't really thought about where he'd go after his tour ended. I figured that since he could write music anywhere, he'd go anywhere he wanted. I guess he wanted to be here.

"Sara," Emilia said. "If you don't go see him, I'm going to disown you."

Once Andi agreed, a weight came off my chest. It had never been a choice to begin with—they'd known that before I did.

"I guess I have to go see him, then," I said finally. "I can't do something that would get me disowned from the two best advice givers ever."

"I told you she was smart, Andi." Emilia laughed. "As long as you go tomorrow. Putting it off any longer would make us very unhappy. And you wouldn't like us when we're unhappy."

"Hang on a sec." Andi looked confused. "Let me get this straight. Along with a big, fat check and a totally sweet letter, Declan sent you a little magical whiteboard that makes everything you write on it come true." Andi pointed to the slate I was currently clutching to my belly. "And you're not going to show it to us? Not even if we beg."

"Nope." I slipped it back into the envelope, making sure my friends couldn't see what he'd written.

Because while *my* wish had been for a gorgeous, sexy-as-fuck man to take me to bed and torture me with his tongue, Declan's was just a single word:

You

I answered the door, expecting a package or maybe someone trying to sell me on a new religion. I hadn't expected *her*. I'd caught her off-guard, her arms still up adjusting her ponytail.

"Hi," Sara said, looking every bit as beautiful as I remembered. Maybe even more.

"Hi." It took every ounce of willpower I possessed not to just grab her, haul her inside, and kiss her until tomorrow.

I'd known the chance I was taking when I sent her that unsigned check. She could've sent someone else, but she'd come herself. She was here. Standing on my doorstep. A moment I'd been simultaneously dying for and dreading had come, and I didn't know what to say.

"Are you going to invite me in?" she asked after a moment. "It's really hot out here."

"Yeah." I jerked into action. "Yeah, of course. Come in."

She stepped inside, looking around. I led her into the kitchen and offered her some ice tea.

"So, how are you doing?" Dumb question but better than all

the others I could think of. Like, *When can you move in?* or *Can we pretend the last few months never happened?*

"Really good," she said, taking a sip. "Not sure if you heard, but Cal was arrested."

"Oh shit." I spun around to face her. "That's great news. What for?"

"Dealing." She leaned back against the counter. "No one is exactly sure how the police found out, but my guess is that it had something to do with my mom calling in an anonymous tip."

"Good for Elaine. I wish I'd been there to see the bastard's face."

"Me, too. My mom said she wished there had been a way to have him arrested for what he did to me. But as long as he ends up miserable, in prison, and with her and Timothy knowing what kind of man he is, that's enough for me."

"I think I'd wait for him to get a good, solid beating in there before letting it go."

"Me, too." She shrugged. "I just thought that was so obvious, it wasn't worth mentioning."

I'd never been in a stranger situation—knowing her well enough to feel naturally comfortable with her whether we were talking or not, yet struggling under the weight of all the things I wanted to say that might scare her off.

"I really like your house."

"Thanks. We lucked out—finding a place with a Kitty-sized yard and a pool sweep that's strong enough to filter out all the dirt she drags into it. It's a lot bigger than I need, but it's okay."

"Oh," Sara said on an exhale. "It seems perfect."

"Almost. It's a little lonely, honestly." I kept my hands deep in my pockets, wishing I could just tell her how I felt about her without holding anything back. "Kitty misses you."

She smiled, taking a small sip of ice tea. "I miss her, too. How is she?"

"Things were hard for a while, but she's better now."

"What happened? Did you finally tell her that she was adopted?"

"Actually, I was going to wait until she's a little older," I said, laughing. "But she hates being on the road. So, now that we have a home and aren't planning to go anywhere for a while, she's a lot happier."

Her eyes grew. "Does that mean Self Defense...?"

"Finally signed a contract, yeah." I nodded. "Sam and Pete are happier than I've ever seen them, and the new guys are still in shock—going from auditioning for a spot they thought would only be temporary to signing a contract with a label in less than three months has got to be some kind of record. Plus, of course, I'm off the hook and free to do whatever the hell I want. Thanks in large part to you."

She brushed my compliment away. "And Trevor?"

"He's doing great." I filled her in on Trevor's new girlfriend and career goal.

"That's so great."

I loved seeing her smile. I wish I didn't ever have to see it go away.

"Is Kitty around? I'd like to say hi."

"She's out back." I pointed toward the back patio. "That way." I stayed a few feet behind her until we reached the glass French doors.

What was I doing? I'd never treated her more like a stranger than I was right now. After everything we'd been. Everything I prayed we'd be again.

"Wait." I let out a deep breath. "Can we stop this now?"

"What?" She jerked when she spun around, not knowing I'd be so close to her. And had no intention of moving away.

"I need to know how you really are."

Her entire body tensed. "What do you mean?"

"Look, I'm glad you're working, and are excited to start school, and have good friends. I am. But when you're done with that and you go home to your place, are you okay? Are you happy?"

"Well, I mean..."

"Because *I'm* not." Once the words started, I couldn't turn them off. It was as if admitting how messed up I'd been popped a cork and let my entire pathetic story shoot out. "If I didn't have my dog, I'd be crying myself to sleep every night. And even then... When I wake up at night and can't get back to sleep, all I think about is *you*. I can't stop thinking about you. Remembering you. Wishing you were next to me or that I could at least talk to you. No matter what, I want you to be happy, but— Fuck!"

I took a step backwards and ran my hand through my hair. "I want you to be happy with me. With us. I'm sorry I didn't tell you I love you before I left. I should've. I thought it would just make things harder. But nothing could've possibly made those months any harder than they were, because you weren't with me. So, even though you might break my fucking heart again right now, I can't handle another minute without being absolutely sure there's not a single shred of a chance for us to be together."

Tears filled her eyes, one of them cresting her bottom lid and running down her cheek until it touched her lip. "I love my job and my friends, but..."

But—the fucking worst word in the English language. Because you never knew what would follow it. It could be exactly what you wanted to hear, or it could break you.

"But I need you, too. And I wish it hadn't taken three months without you to make me realize how crazy in love with you I am."

"Wait, what did you just say?"

"I love you, Declan Hollis."

If I hadn't been so busy trying to prepare for my own destruction that I hadn't actually been listening to what she'd said, it would've sunk in faster. And I'd have been ready for her when she jumped up and kissed me.

I lifted her into my arms, holding on to her for dear life.

For *my* life.

For *our* lives.

Once Upon a Time…

There was a woman who, though everyone believed her to be blessed from birth, wasn't. Because those blessings were only material, beautiful only to others who were blinded into seeing only what they chose to see, regardless of the truth. With time, the woman grew to believe it would always be such, that nothing good would come from looking in the mirror because she would see no reflection at all.

Until one day her life actually did become blessed. The day she met a man who looked beyond the material, under the trappings, and helped her become visible again. For he could see her beauty even when his eyes were closed, even when things were so dark and awful that she dared not hope she would ever see the light again. But the man saw her, and he believed her, and he healed her. Simply by showing her how to see herself as he saw her—strong and important and beautiful and true and real and…

His.

The End

THANK YOU FOR READING!

I hope you enjoyed Declan and Sara's story.

If you did, *please* consider leaving a review on your preferred retailer's website. No matter how long it is or how non-poetic you think it is, each review you leave is like a little chunk of gold for authors like me.

Your support and help spreading the word about this book and all my others means the world to me - and no, I'm not just saying that.